Wordclay
1663 Liberty Drive, Suite 200
Bloomington, IN 47403
www.wordclay.com

First published by Wordclay on 4/20/2010.
ISBN: 978-1-6048-1726-3 (sc)

Cover Photo by Richard McGuire www.richardmcguire.com

Printed in the United States of America.

This book is printed on acid-free paper.

The Key

by

Janet Rosenstock
and Dennis Adair

June 25/ 2012

Teresa

Best Wishes Happy Reading and Regards

Dennis Adair

CHAPTER ONE

1996

Corrie Henley paused to catch her breath. They had reached the first ruins of the outskirts of the deserted village. "Quite a climb."

"It's worth it."

Willie O'Donnell spoke in a distinctive Australian accent. He was tall and lean, wore a turned up outback style hat and sported shorts in spite of the brisk winds and cool temperature. He was a virtual Aussie movie stereotype. Corrie half expected him to burst into a chorus of *Waltzing Matilda* at any moment.

For over an hour they had followed a winding upward path toward Easter Island's volcano, Rano Kau, heading toward Orongo. Once, it had been the center of an ancient *Birdman Cult* and like a nest, it was perched atop a cliff overlooking the ocean nearly four hundred meters below. It was a rough hike made more difficult by the strong unceasing wind.

Hours ago they had left behind the famous *Moai,* the mute stone sentinels that guarded the beach and were considered one of the world's wonders. It was the *Moai* and the mystery of their creation that made Easter Island famous. On their climb, they had passed the ancient work sites where the *Moai* were built and where many of the uncompleted monoliths lay tossed about like the discarded toys of a giant's child. Then they had scrambled up to a hazardous, dizzying perch on the rim of Rano Kau's crater. Above them falcons soared, dipping and floating crazily on the wind drafts. From their vantage point Corrie could see the largest of the uncompleted *Moai.* It was prone, a stone stillbirth, aborted at twenty-one meters in length. Below, the crater was filled with water and tall brown reeds grew in it. The reeds hummed in the wind where once the great quarry had existed.

As they now stumbled into the ruins of the village, Corrie paused to take in the full panorama of the ruins. She was not a casual observer, not a simple tourist. She was a trained academic with a vivid imagination. At least that was how she explained to herself what she saw when she looked at ancient sites.

Sometimes she wondered if others noticed her flights of fancy, if they saw in her expression any evidence of what was happening inside her head. Long ago she decided the things she saw and felt were doubtless the result of reading too much, of always having had an overactive imagination, and of being alone too much as a child. When she looked at ruins she saw in her head how they had once looked, how the people appeared, how they dressed, sometimes she felt she even knew what they talked about. It was as if the ruins came alive, as if she were transported back in time. It had happened to her in Pompeii, Delphi, Thebes and when she visited the Gila cliff dwellings of New Mexico. At first the vividness of her visions had disturbed her but now she embraced them. She felt certain many writers felt as she did. Lawrence Durrell, the great travel writer had written about, "the spirit of the place." She felt the spirit of places vividly, and in her imagination she actually experienced them.

Corrie was transfixed, and only vaguely aware that Willie O'Donnell was behind her as she began walking about the village, her hands caressing the ancient walls. She walked inside the ruin of what appeared to be the most solid of the dwellings. She paused and picked up a fragment of a wooden tablet that was on display. It was completely covered with symbols in what was known as boustrophedon style.

"Is this an example of *rongo-rongo hieroglyphs*?" She asked, turning to O'Donnell who had caught up with her.

"Just a fragment. There are more in the museum; they found a lot of them."

"Do you know much about them?"

"Sorry, I'm no real expert."

"They're in boustrophedon script. It's from the Greek and means – like oxen plowing -. See, the lines are continuous, right to left and left to right." She ran her fingers along the marks.

"Oh, yes. I see what you mean," he said.

"Was this fragment found here?"

"As far as I know."

"I've heard of them but I hadn't seen one till now. I suppose they tried to piece them together." Corrie turned the piece slowly in her hand.

"None of them fit together. In fact, they all seem alike, as if the same marks were copied over and over. There were attempts to translate them, but no one has succeeded."

Again, Corrie turned the piece. It was like fire, she felt a chill run along the back of her neck and down her spinal cord. The fragment was important, that much she knew. She vowed that when she got back to Hanga Roa, she would ask the resident director of the museum about the fragments. She knew full well that Easter Island had been discovered and settled by two distinct groups of people. One group had come from Polynesia, the other from one of the cultures of South America. This village was thought to have been built and inhabited by the latter group. The bird was a common symbol among Andean cultures; the inhabitants of this village were known to have belonged to the cult of the birdman.

She continued to hold the fragment almost as if it were her guide rather than the Australian who accompanied her. She wandered about and after a moment, approached a crumbling stone throne; at least it looked like it might once have been a throne. It was then that her imagination conjured up the past. The throne was suddenly covered by rich cloth and a broad shouldered man sat, staring at her. She noted his sculptured features. They were Andean features, not Polynesian. A great beaked mask partially covered his head and forehead and he was adorned in fuchsia plumage. In his hands he held a wooden tablet. It was like the fragment in her hand but it was whole. It was covered with the continuous script.

For a second, Corrie felt almost faint with the vividness of what she saw. She sat down, slumping on a nearby rock.

"Tired? We've hiked a long way and the air is thin."

Willie's voice cut through her vision like a knife. The aberration faded. "A little," she answered.

"I've got some fruit in my pack. I think you need a pick-up."

"Yes."

She watched as he fished in his pack, but her mind was still on the tall man in the fuchsia plumage, and on the mysterious tablet he held. She felt puzzled. It was almost certain that this village had been inhabited by those thought to come from what was now Peru. But they would not have had such tablets – they had no written language. She silently laughed at herself. Having visions, or hallucinations, or whatever they were was bad enough, but now they were academically impossible.

"Have an apple," Willie urged.

She took the green apple and thought of its flight from Washington State. It was almost as well traveled as she. Easter Island was two thousand miles from the nearest habitation and even further from where Granny Smiths were grown - from the sublime to the mundane, in a single second. Her mind was flitting through centuries and apple orchards.

"Ready to get on with it?"

Corrie stood up and stretched. "Sure." She turned quickly and glanced behind her. Her vision did not return. The stone throne was empty; it was simply a fashioned piece of volcanic rock.

#

The curator's office was completely cluttered save for a small square on his desk that he obviously reserved for writing. "Excuse

4

my office, it's far too small but the view is good." He motioned toward a window that looked out on the beach. One of the great stone statues was clearly visible.

"It's quite all right. My own office is the same."

The coastal winds, the sun, and fluctuating temperatures had sculptured Dr. Lopez's skin. Like the land on this rugged volcanic island, he suffered from erosion; valleys and crevices covered his face while his pale blue eyes were like lakes parted by the great mountain that was his nose.

"Please sit down, Miss Henley. Tell me, aren't you an archeologist like your father?"

"Yes. But we're in different fields. I specialize in the classification of pottery, primarily pottery of the Americas."

"So, this trip is mainly for pleasure?"

"Yes. I do appreciate your seeing me."

"It's not busy here. What does not get done today gets done tomorrow."

His English was precise and he spoke slowly. She could have easily spoken Spanish to him but he had begun in English and she had said nothing.

"So you have some questions about our fragments of rongo-rongo."

"I find them fascinating. I wonder what you can tell me."

"As you no doubt know the statues for which this island is famous were made during different periods. The fragments of the wooden tablets appear to have been made during a single period. They were no doubt copied from an earlier specimen and may have been used for ritual purposes of some sort."

"And there is no clue as to their meaning?"

"Much work has been done and some false claims made, but, no."

"Such a pity none were found intact."

"There was a great deal of destruction. We believe the destruction began after a long period of troubled coexistence between two peoples. Each of them had a distinct culture and language." His tone was professorial as he warmed to his mini lecture.

"These two groups were called the *long ears and the short ears.* It seems that for a long time the *short ears* were subservient to the long ears and then the *short ears* rose in rebellion. In any case the long ears seem to have been exterminated and buried in a pyre along an ancient ditch in Poike on the northeastern coast."

"And the fragments of the tablets?"

"Were found in many island areas. It is uncertain as to which period they originally belonged because they are copies. Certainly, there is no doubt that the early settlers came with highly developed architectural concepts, and amazing masonry skills. Many artifacts, and of course the existence of the *Birdman Cult*, suggests they came from South America and that they arrived as an organized party of emigrants."

"I knew that one of the two groups on Easter Island was thought to have come from South America. I find this all really interesting, and a little puzzling."

"I hope I've at least cleared up a few of your questions."

"Yes. Do you know if the tablet fragments were originally found in the village of the *Birdman Cult*?"

"There were some fragments found there."

"I wonder how they would have been used. If the people of the *Birdman Cult* came from South America, they would have had no written language."

"A great mystery, I agree. I'm afraid it's one I can't solve. We are not sure if some of the fragments found their way to the village or if they originated there. But as you say, the Andean cultures had no written language, so we must assume the tablets originated with those of Polynesian origin. I hope this helps a bit."

It didn't really help that much, but he was kind to have seen her. "Yes, thank you."

"Will you be joining your father?"

"No, at least not right away."

"How long will you be here?"

"Just a few more days. Then I'll be going back to Boston."

"Well, enjoy yourself and don't hesitate to come back if you have more questions."

"Thank you so much."

Corrie shook hands with Dr. Lopez and wandered back to the guest house where she was staying.

She certainly could not tell him what she had imagined and felt in the village. To talk about that sort of thing when it was nothing more than the product of an overactive imagination, seemed unwise. People would think she was crazy. The truth was, as vividly as she saw things; she had come to regard it as a sort of insight. On more than one occasion something she had seen or sensed, had turned out to be correct and then she felt as if she had some sort of sixth sense. Was it possible that the tablet did belong to the *Birdman Cult*? Perhaps some form of written language had been developed after they came to the island. She opened the door to her room and immediately flung herself on the narrow bed. It was already six o'clock; she had less than an hour before dinner would be served. "No rest for the wicked," she murmured.

#

They scrambled over the wrought iron rail, for a split second they clung to the balcony's cement overhang, then they dropped in unison to the ground. "Run!" Katsura hissed as she hit the grass. She looked around and finding a path, headed down it without looking back to see if he followed.

7

From the front of the Japanese Embassy, the sound of rapid, unceasing gunfire and random screams of terror rendered her order totally unnecessary. Jeff had no intention of stopping, even though he knew full well there was a high wall around the garden.

They reached the wall and as if she knew exactly where it was, she led him to a vine covered trellis. It struck him that the vine was tangled rather than trimmed, that indeed, unlike most Japanese gardens, this one, at least this part of it, was totally unkempt.

Katsura climbed the trellis with cat like agility and then straddled the wall looking down on him. He couldn't read her expression in the semi darkness but her posture was confident, somehow challenging.

Jeff shook the trellis. It was rickety and he was heavier than Katsura. He put one foot on it and as he stepped up, he heard it crack under his weight. He swung his other foot toward the wall and found a foothold in the stone. He managed to get his arms over the top. He pulled himself up just as Katsura was lowering herself down the other side. He dropped down to join her. Once again she led the way.

The back streets behind the embassy were dark, illuminated only by dim streetlights at the end of each long block. There was no light from the night sky because of the thick cloud cover so common in Lima during the month of December. It was uncomfortably hot and humid and Jeff felt sticky all over from the exertion of their sprint from the second floor of the embassy to this dim back street. But they kept moving. The streets in this part of town were not really safe, especially at night.

"You must never tell anyone you were inside the embassy."

He could hear the urgency in her voice - not just urgency, a desperate urgency. "I'm a reporter," he protested. "This is a big story - at least it will be by morning."

"You wouldn't even have been in the embassy if I hadn't taken you there. You can't tell anyone you were inside when it happened. Promise me."

"You'll have to give me a reason. I was there; I was a witness to what happened."

"You were not a witness!" She sounded angry. He wondered why.

"You were upstairs with me. You didn't actually see anything. You don't really know what happened."

She could not know what happened either but she acted as though she did.   Nor did 'not knowing' explain why he had to keep secret the fact that he had been there. He decided to argue about it later.

"We're going in the opposite direction of the car."

"We can't go back that way," she snapped.

Again he did not argue. He could hear the sirens. The road would be blocked off in any case. "Come on, we can catch a cab on Avenue Alphonso Aguarte."

The cab smelled of diesel fuel and something else – urine? The seat beneath him was worn and he could feel every bump. The springs were shot.

They had been in heavy traffic for over an hour. But it was an instructive hour in that he certainly had not underestimated the events at the Japanese embassy. All traffic was being re-routed and there were police and army everywhere. Long ago, he had concluded that the various police forces, federal, provincial, and local were, together with the army, the main source of employment for young men. Sometimes it seemed as if almost everyone had a uniform and a gun. Mexico, he thought, was much the same.

He leaned back against the seat and tried to concentrate on the cab radio as events were reported in rapid, almost hysterical Spanish. The broadcaster was so excited his words spewed forth like machine gun fire.

The driver cursed at each announcement of another street closing.

Jeff glanced in the rear view mirror. Katsura sat in the back, her eyes closed. She was wearing a bright red satin dress that looked as if it had been sewn onto her slim body. Having torn it, the slit on the right side was higher than it was before she climbed the wall to escape the garden. Apart from her slightly torn dress, no one would guess she had so recently been running, climbing and jumping. Her hair was still in a tight bun, her fringe of black bangs looked as if they had just been combed.

He had chosen to sit up front with the driver in order to hear the radio above the noise of the engine. The police and army had surrounded the Japanese Embassy. Inside, a terrorist group had apparently taken more than a hundred hostages. There were wounded and there were dead. It was a stringer's dream.

His head was full of questions. How many terrorists were there? How had they got past the security guards? Which terrorist group was it? Peru had more than one political group dedicated to violence.

He and Katsura had been on the second floor of the embassy when it began. She had led him through a maze of corridors in search of a series of block prints she wanted to show him. "They're hanging in the hall on the second floor. There are four Hiroshigi's. They're quite rare, you really must see them."

The shooting and screaming started all at once and looking back on it, he was certain he had smelled the faint odor of some sort of gas. He had heard a man shouting in Spanish through what he assumed was a megaphone. The voice ordered everyone to lie down.

Katsura had led him into one of many guestrooms and then, out onto the balcony. She seemed to know her way around, and that too puzzled him because she had told him she had only been in Lima for a week. But in that moment of the attack, he had been anxious to get out too; he hadn't stopped to ask any questions. As they ran, they heard the sirens in the distance. "We should go back. We should talk to the police."

"Grow up. Where the hell do you think we are?" There was cutting anger in her voice. "They'll ask why we were upstairs, how we got out; they'll assume we were part of it. The police here don't ask questions politely, you know. They'll throw us in some stinking cell because we'll be guilty until proven innocent."

She was right. What surprised him was not her desire to avoid the police, but her demeanor. She didn't seem at all shaken by the attack. In fact she didn't even seem surprised. It wasn't he who had led her away protectively, but she who had led him. Something wasn't right. Did she know the embassy was going to be attacked? He didn't ask her the question, yet. But he still couldn't put the thought out of his mind.

The rattletrap cab pulled up in front of the house where he had an apartment. He paid the driver and they walked in silence around the back to his private entrance.

He unlocked the door and switched on the light. Katsura followed him inside and immediately curled herself onto the sofa.

He went to the fridge and took out a cold beer. He took another to Katsura. "Now tell me why I can't tell anyone I was in the embassy."

"It's personal. Besides, you don't know anything that would help the authorities to end it - to get all those people out. Of course I expect you to report the story, but you don't have to tell anyone you were there when it started - that we escaped."

"What were we doing upstairs? Why did you take me up there?" He tried not to sound suspicious but he *was* suspicious.

"I told you, I wanted to show you the block prints in the upstairs hall."

The building was rectangular and they had walked half way around the square when the shooting downstairs started. "You're sense of timing is extraordinary."

Her eyes were dark pools, her lips were pressed together. "What are you suggesting?"

He knew he was acting as if he were in the middle of a spy drama. "I don't know, just that your timing was lucky for us."

"Yes. That was just what it was, luck.

"So the reasons I can't tell anyone I was inside the embassy is because you're lucky and I didn't see anything?" He hoped he sounded as sarcastic as he felt.

"No, it's because we'll be accused – and as I said, I have a personal reason as well."

"One you can't explain?"

"Please trust me."

Trust was quite the opposite of what he felt. "I do have to call the wire service."

"Yes, I understand that. Can't you call from here?"

"Yes, but I'll have to go back to the embassy."

"I'd go directly to the police if I were you. That way you can get all the details."

He had heard plenty of gunfire and a lot of screaming. He knew from the radio that there were dead and wounded, he knew it had been a terrorist attack and that the evening was an important one. It was the Emperor's birthday and the Japanese embassy was filled with Peru's industrial elite as well as the entire diplomatic corps.

"You've forgotten. My car is still there."

"They're going to ask about your car, you know. They'll find it parked on the side street and they'll trace the plate."

"I'll tell them I drove down to see what was happening and couldn't get out."

She shrugged, "I suppose that might do. It's certainly another reason to go to the police station first. You can complain that you can't get to your car. That will give your story an air of truth."

He hated even this minor subterfuge but he knew she was right about the police. This was big and the police were going to be under a lot of pressure. They would arrest anyone who seemed remotely suspicious.

"I've got to make a few calls. Make yourself at home."

He headed for the other room. He had to call around, see if he could get an assignment. The American news media did not keep correspondents in Latin America. They sent them if necessary - usually for international conferences. Sometimes they utilized local reporters, and some publications would use a stringer – a freelance journalist who was resident or traveling in the country. He was a stringer. He had lamented the fact that for the most part the U.S. media ignored everything south of Mexico. As a matter of fact, they didn't report on events in Mexico very extensively. Long ago he had concluded that it was a "class thing." Americans, on the whole, still regarded Spanish as a language spoken only by poor illegal immigrants. What of any import could be happening on a continent where the vast majority spoke Spanish? America looked to Europe and Asia; she had steadfastly ignored the sleeping giant south of the Panama Canal. News stories about Hispanic America from the Mexican border to the tip of Tierra del Fuego were sparse and usually on one of three subjects: a petty dictator who became too strident; an earthquake that caused grave destruction; or a drug story. Needless to say, Colombia got the most press.

The only Americans who cared about South America were either academics or like himself, young graduates filled with curiosity. When he had first come to Latin America he had intended to stay for three months in each of five countries, Peru, Chili, Argentina, Brazil, and Ecuador. He had been in Peru for four months now and worked as a stringer for International News Service. He had managed to eke out a living with INS, and by writing short articles for a variety of magazines. Peru was almost interesting to Americans because the President was Japanese and it had a large Japanese population.

Katsura was Japanese, but she was not from Peru. She was a Japanese-American, or so she had told him. He had met her in his Aikido class. She told him she was visiting from Los Angeles, a

13

story he now doubted. They had gone out for coffee after class and then she had confided that she had an invitation to the Emperor's birthday party at the Japanese Embassy. She asked him to accompany her and he had agreed for two reasons. First, he thought her extremely attractive and second he hoped to come across some story of interest. It was a coveted invitation because the entire power structure of the country had been invited. He shook his head. He'd come across a story all right.

He dialed the International News Service number and not surprisingly found the long distance lines were all busy. He called the operator and talked her into putting him on hold till a long distance line was open.

He stared into space and thought about Katsura. She was a sinuous female with a lithe smooth body, straight black hair and full lips. But as attractive as he found her, he already knew they wouldn't have anything but the most casual relationship. During their short acquaintance, even before tonight's startling events, he had observed that she was guarded. Some might have said she was mysterious and found the mystery intriguing. He did not. He felt she was hard to talk with, and he had almost immediately felt he could not completely trust her. Tonight, his 'feeling' had deepened. Her every action seemed to confirm his suspicions that Katsura had something to hide.

Katsura was Corrie's opposite. Corrie was open and honest, though he conceded she too had a mysterious quality. As soon as he thought about Corrie Henley he wondered, not for the first time, why he compared her to every woman he met.

"I don't think you're capable of making a commitment," Corrie had once told him. She hadn't said it meanly; it was simply an honest observation.

"Not now," he had wanted to say. But then, he wasn't sure if he should have said, 'not ever.' Thus far, his relationship with Corrie had proved the most important in his life. Or, maybe he was just romanticizing a past he couldn't change. He hadn't seen nor heard from her for nearly five years, but he hadn't forgotten the time they spent together. Maybe he could have made a commitment to her, maybe he should have tried. Corrie was the reason he had chosen to come to Peru first. She had spent time in Peru as a child when her father, a well-known archeologist, was working in the South of the country, studying the Nasca.

He looked at the phone. He hated waiting. The story would already be on the wires. Still, if he were lucky, his editor would realize that a Spanish-speaking reporter familiar with the terrain would be a terrific asset - more so because he was an Aikidoist and had contacts in Lima's Japanese community.

"Whatever took you so long?" Katsura asked.

She had washed her face, reapplied her make-up and looked almost cool.

"The long distance lines were jammed."

"Did you get an assignment?"

"Yeah, I'll have to go back down there." He didn't bother telling her, but he had learned that there were apparently over a hundred and twenty hostages – important hostages.

"Are you going now?" she asked.

"Yes."

"You could stay awhile. We've hardly spent anytime at all getting acquainted.

He knew what she meant, it was an invitation but he had already decided not to get involved with her. She was too complicated. Now she was apparently offering a sexual encounter to compensate for her lack of honesty. He felt ill at ease with her but he was still curious about her. He decided to give it one more try.

"I might stay if you told me why I can't tell anyone we were in the embassy – that you were in the embassy."

Her expression immediately hardened. "I told you. It's personal."

Three times he had asked, three times she had given him the same answer. He wasn't going to ask again. "Are you staying here?"

"May I?"

"Sure. Give me a couple of hours."

She nodded.

He headed for the door. Most women were full of secrets, Katsura had more than most and even as he closed the door, he was certain she would be gone when he returned.

#

April, 1997

A Warm polluted rain fell steadily from dense gray clouds. It was the kind of rain that made him feel dirty all over. Who would have thought that the hostage taking at the Japanese Embassy would have lasted for so many months? It was inconceivable. Day after day the street in front of the embassy was filled with representatives of the world media. Each, as one might guess, was primarily interested in the fate of those hostages who were of their own nationality. Vaguely, he remembered a satire of a newscast. "Today, Bombay was destroyed by an earthquake. There are no known American casualties." In his opinion, reportage was all too often reduced to navel gazing. In this case, no one seemed to care why the hostages had been taken. He wanted to write about those responsible, but he knew his chances of selling such a story to any widely read publication were low indeed. Still, when this was over he intended to go hunting for the *Tupac Amaru* who claimed responsibility. He wanted to make contact with them. Until a resolution came about, however, he had decided to remain in Lima.

Unlike television reporters, he was not made to camp out in front of the embassy. CNN and the networks would have the story first because they were always there. Those in the print media didn't have to be there every second of the day and night, and considering how many weeks it had been, he was supremely grateful to be a less glamorous, if badly paid, freelancer in the world of print.

He stuffed his notes in his pocket and looked around; waving to the camera crew from CNN with whom he'd had a few beers the night before. Then he turned and headed home, once again reminded of the puzzling events the night the embassy had been taken over by the terrorists. He still had unanswered questions.

Katsura had never explained her personal reasons for not wanting anyone to know they had been in the embassy. And as he knew she would be, when he returned to his apartment the next morning, she was gone. He had phoned her hotel but no one answered. He went off to his Aikido class, expecting to see her but she wasn't there. After two days he went round to her hotel only to discover she had checked out and left. There was no forwarding address, no message, and no clue as to what had become of her. Even Kenji, the young Japanese in his class who had introduced them had no idea where she had gone.

"Not the first woman to walk out on me," he said under his breath. But knew he was not the reason for her sudden departure. There was something else, something he didn't understand, and something he felt was connected to the events in the embassy. Did it have to do with the block prints on the second floor of the embassy – the ones she had wanted to show him? Was there even a collection of Hiroshigi block prints in the embassy? Maybe she was involved in a conspiracy of some sort – perhaps she had guided him upstairs to get them out of the line of fire because she had known what was going to happen that night. He shook his head. It was probably not that interesting or intriguing. After all, why go to the embassy in the first place if she had known? Maybe she wanted to steal the block prints – after this was over he intended to go to the embassy and make inquiries about their artwork. For now there were no answers to any of his questions.

Jeff reached his car and climbed in. On the front passenger seat the local daily paper lay folded. For the 100th day it carried a picture of the Japanese Embassy and headshots of some of the hostages.

He turned the paper slightly and a name in the left-hand column jumped out at him. He picked up the paper and turned it so he could see the whole article. It was the only story on the front page totally unrelated to the hostage taking. It revealed that Dr. Jonathan Henley had left Palpa and gone to oversee some work on the Moche archaeological site, several hundred miles north of Lima. "Dr. Jonathan Henley," he said aloud. He was Corrie's father. Did that mean she might come to Peru? He closed his eyes and pursed his lips together. Might their paths cross again? He was pretty sure he wanted them too. But what if she was married? He shook his head. He was really getting ahead of himself. And even if their paths did cross, it wouldn't be for quite awhile. He knew he would get another assignment, he knew he would be leaving Peru for a while.

#

May 1997

Karim lifted up his head and wiped his brow. It was humid and hot. He noted that the meandering line of tourists was getting ahead of him. They were not part of an organized group from a single country, nor were they part of some international tour. They were a hodgepodge of visitors from Europe, Asia and the Americas. All had come here, to the Angkor Valley of Cambodia, to view the incredible temples built in honor of the God-Kings who worshipped here hundreds of years ago. The Cambodian government had gathered the tourists together from assorted hotels, and insisted they

18

visit Angkor together, submitting themselves to a chattering guide
with hair that stood up straight, as if he had been electrocuted.
Almost no one seemed to be listening to him. Karim doubted most
could even understand his particular brand of singsong English
mixed with foreign words and phrases.

He hated tour groups, it was not his way to travel, and in
rebellion, he loitered behind. The road was shaded by rows of huge
graceful trees, and bordered with lush growth. Tall reeds grew
nearby, and there were wild flowers of amazing color and beauty. It
seemed to Karim as if there was water everywhere; it was quite the
opposite of his desert. Yet he felt a familiarity with this place. It was
as if he had walked this path before, as if, for all its strangeness, it
was a place he knew.

Currently, Karim traveled with a Mexican passport issued
under the name of Ramon Garcia. When he created his Mexican
identity he carefully selected a background. He visited each and
every locale, bought a home in Monterey, and operated several
businesses there.

His Spanish was excellent, his knowledge of Mexico splendid.
He could talk about his years at the university in Mexico City, or
about the year he spent at the language school in Cuernavaca. He
could discuss environmental problems in the Gulf of Baja California
and the dismal effect of the drug trade on border towns. For all intent
and purpose he *was* Ramon Garcia, an upper class Mexican male
with a good education and a yen to travel. Becoming the identity he
chose was his special gift; it made his life easier.

For a short time, his mind wandered as he contemplated the
matter of identities and the importance of choosing one that was
believable. An American identity precluded his moving about
comfortably in the Middle East, and a Libyan, Iraqi, Iranian or
Syrian identity ruled out moving about Western Europe and the
United States with ease. His adored and adopted home, the Sudan,
was considered an 'outlaw' nation so he could not 'be' Sudanese

either. Syria was now undergoing a process of what he rather
sarcastically thought of as, 'international rehabilitation.' Still, a
Syrian identity would have involved far more red tape than he
desired.

In the end, it was simply easier to be from a neutral country.
Security measures tended to be less stringent; people did not stare at
you fearfully. Canada was a neutral, if not innocuous country. Like
Mexico, it lived in the shadow of the American elephant and
somehow managed to be acceptable to all – largely because no one
knew much about it. But he had not chosen a Canadian identity
because of his appearance. He had chosen to be from Mexico
simply because its people were Mestizo, and with his swarthy
complexion he was easily accepted as Mexican. Thus, the identities
he chose were usually Mexican, Central American or even Brazilian.

All that aside, he truly considered Sudan his home. It was one
of the first countries, he thought with a wry smile, to battle
westerners. For nearly two hundred years now its people had fought
against the infidels and against colonialism, and for the most part
they had won. In his mind's eye he returned to the film, Khartoum
and to the shouts of *Mahdi! Mahdi! Mahdi!* He could see the dark
clad figure with the compelling eyes; eyes like my own he thought.
The Mahdi had led his hordes and massacred Chinese Gordon and
the defenders of the besieged city of Khartoum. He knew that in that
lifetime, he had been the Mahdi, Muhammad Ahmad ibn'Abd Allah.
He was soon to be the Mahdi in this lifetime.

The road narrowed slightly, and Karim found himself on a
bridge as the road crossed a wide, deep moat. Ahead, he could see
two massive gates. Beyond the gates, a great temple, a mountain of
stone, built on a stone platform. It dominated the center of the
courtyard while smaller, surrounding stone towers, were decorated
with nymphs, divinities, and the story of the *God Kings*.

He was enthralled with the structures. They were not like the
pyramids of Egypt but they were, nonetheless, man made mountains

that reached for the sky. As he understood it, the *God Kings* who once ruled here on the flat plain, demanded mountains and thus faithful adherents made these artificial temple mountains. Within the temples there were exotic carvings and paintings.

Again he thought of the pyramids. In the Americas, as in Egypt, the pyramids were defined. They were step pyramids built around a ceremonial plaza on the Olmec plan. In Egypt, the famous pyramids had a mathematical perfection.

It was essential that he understand these matters, that he visit all the great religious monuments of the world. It was a command given by in inner voices and it had brought him here to the religious monuments of Angkor. He opened his guidebook and began reading about this remarkable place. He would remember everything because he had a photographic memory. "Here, between 900 and 1150 AD the people of the area combined elements of the Hindu and Buddhist religion with king-worship. It is said that the great temple at Angkor was the home of the *God King* during his life. Priests performed rituals and pilgrims came to worship. According to legend, after the *God King's* death, the temple became his eternal home."

Yes, these temples served a purpose similar to those of the pyramids. As he had before, Karim suddenly felt a surge of power. Such a feeling often filled him when he was in a home of the Gods. His voices directed him, he was a man possessed.

Again he thought of the Mahdi. For a long while the Mahdi thought of himself as a *mujaddid*, a re-newer of the faith. *Of course he became much more and so will I.*

Many Moslems claimed descent from the Prophet Mohammad, Blessed be His Name, but they attempted to trace their ancestry by piecing together complicated blood lines most of which were lost forever in the desert sands. Who could truly say he was the progeny of the prophet? The Mahdi had taken another path, the path of the mystic.

Karim smiled to himself. He had emulated the Mahdi since he was sixteen, since the day his voices directed him to murder that pathetic Jewish boy, Sheldon Rabinowitz. He had followed the path.

First, he studied with one of the Sufi orders, the Sammaniyah. Then, like Mohammad Ahmad ibn'Abd Allah, he secluded himself on Aba Island in the White Nile, there to learn the discipline of religious asceticism. The voice of the Gods, who directed him, bade him travel and learn many languages, and study all religions. When money ran short he became a spiritual advisor to a wealthy Sheik. He married the sheik's daughter, Fatima and when the sheik died, he inherited great wealth. At that point he turned his boundless energy back to his original talent, math and computer technology. By the mid 1980s he had mastered all there was to know about computers. He had a golden touch, and together with an astute Wall Street broker, he turned his inheritance into a great fortune.

Allah and all the Gods who spoke to him had given him the means by which to achieve greatness. He considered himself a fortunate man, a leader, a man who communicated with the makers, and a man to whom the creators spoke. He had a vision, a wonderful vision! He was to be not simply a new Mahdi, but a great Jewish Islamic Savior who would re-unite two ancient peoples and subdue the infidels in a Holy War that he would win with the leadership of the divine!

He felt almost dizzy as his voices filled his head. He sought silence and refuge under a tall tree, where he slumped to the ground and sat for nearly half an hour, allowing a trance to settle over him, allowing his soul to fly free. Then, he slowly stood, stretched, and continued his journey alone, the others were long gone.

He entered the temple, grateful that he was by himself. He looked about and thought that it was a wonder that any of this had survived the war in Indo China. But the restoration was remarkable; the glories of the past were now as they once had been.

Two years ago, he would have stopped to curse the Americans for causing the war that nearly destroyed this shrine, but his hatred of America had changed from surging emotional outbursts to calculated planning. His voices called to him and told him he would be the avenger. A true avenger could afford patience.

After many hours he left the temple compound and began to walk. Not far from the temple Karim found a rambling open-air market. He strolled through it in leisurely fashion, taking in the color and relishing in the sights and smells. He wandered aimlessly, allowing fate to guide him forward through the maze. The sounds of the Asian market filled his ears while the pungent aroma of spices filled his nostrils. Even though much was different, he was, nonetheless, reminded of the markets of North Africa and even the great souk in Istanbul. It seemed as if everything was for sale here.

Karim came to a sudden halt before the stall of a trader, a small man whose wares all appeared to be replicas of historic artifacts. There were statues of the various gods, images of Buddha, and calendars made from metal. Swaths of cloth hung side by side with finely woven prayer rugs. He was looking at the wares the trader offered, and generally ignoring the man's ceaseless chatter, when he saw the tablet. He was so stunned he felt as if he had been momentarily turned into wood himself.

The rectangular tablet was roughly fourteen inches high and twelve inches wide and covered with strange symbols. It was an artifact he recognized instantly.

What miracle had led him to this place? Surely it was divine guidance.

Again, he felt the thrill of having been selected. He was truly not just a *mujaddid* but a Mahdi! A Savior! It was all quite clear. He was the eschatological figure, born to foreshadow the end of the age of darkness and herald the new era of light and righteousness! As surely as he saw this tablet, he knew the truth.

"That," he muttered, pointing to the tablet.

"It is something unusual," the shopkeeper said, sensing a sale. "Tell me about it."

"There isn't much to tell. It was found near here during the restoration, brought to me by a small boy."

"What is it?" Karim asked cagily.

"Probably something left by a visitor. It is obviously not of this place. No one understands it."

"I'll give you ten dollars for it."

The man's bright eyes flickered. "American dollars?"

"Yes."

"Twenty and it is yours."

Karim might have bargained longer and harder, but he could not be bothered. In any case, twenty dollars for something priceless was quite a bargain.

He watched while the stupid little tradesman wrapped his purchase in layers of old newspapers and tied it with string. A new heated energy filled him. There was suddenly much to do.

CHAPTER TWO

Sipán, Peru 2001

Jonathan Henley tossed in his bed, then propping himself up on one elbow; he stared out the window, and looked across the undulating landscape that led to the distant mountains.

A pre-dawn chill passed over the silent earth, the cold breath that heralds the rising sun. Here, just below the Andean foothills, the early morning stirring was particularly cool; passing as it did over the distant snow capped peaks of some of the world's highest mountains. On this unusually clear night, those peaks were starkly silhouetted against the star-studded black velvet sky. As chilly as it was now, it would be sweltering by noon. It was summer in the Southern hemisphere.

In his mind he could see the whole valley as if he were flying above it. Beyond the lush bushes that grew along the riverbank there were great mounds of soil caused by an alien invasion. It appeared as if they were vomited up from the earth, or as if an army of giant moles had stalked the netherworld beneath. But the untidy mounds were not the work of other worldly creatures, or strange mutant burrowing insectivores. They were, in reality, the dried man-made mountains caused by hundreds of excavations made over a period of three hundred years. These were the unearthed graves of the *Moche* and in the silent night, he knew that even now grave robbers moved with stealth among the skeletons, searching for yet still undiscovered treasures.

Once again Jonathan Henley tossed as he reached for the blanket he had discarded earlier when the heat of the day still filled the house. Beside him, oblivious to the temperature or to his stirrings, Myra stretched out naked beneath a white sheet. The stream of moonlight that came in the window fell on her, and

Jonathan stole a look at the hidden curves of her mature, yet still lithe body.

He succeeded in pulling the blanket up, but his hand crept out from beneath it to cover the tempting swell of Myra's half-exposed breast. Sleepily he thought that her breasts were the only soft part of her. The rest of her body, her incredibly long shapely legs, her firm buttocks, her arms, was hard and toned from daily workouts. Myra Rojas was a part-time model. She cared about herself; she cared with a passion and she worked for hours every morning to keep herself in shape.

Her breast beneath his hand moved slightly with the rhythm of her breathing. Now, more awake, a strong feeling of sadness swept over him as he thought of his wife, Inge. She had died seven years ago, succumbing to ovarian cancer, the 'silent killer'. He felt guilty, though he knew he had no reason to feel guilt. Inge would not have wanted him to be lonely, to remain celibate. *What's wrong with me?* Seven years, yet his guilt and lustful desires still warred within him. A world of wonderful memories still challenged his fleeting needs.

Tonight, it seemed as if his mind was a stage. One thought was front and center, then a new memory crowded in and chased the first away. He was glad. He could not think of Inge for too long, her death had affected him profoundly. His thoughts of Inge brought a vision of his daughter, Corrie to mind.

Corrie was following in the family profession. To have your daughter choose the same career is flattering, though he admitted, hardly surprising. Corrie had not been sent away to school until she was twelve. Her early years and all her summers had been spent with her parents on various archaeological digs in Columbia, Bolivia, and Peru. Last year she had graduated from Harvard, this year she was interning at the Conway Museum in Boston. Next year she would spend a year in the field.

Got to call her this weekend, he vowed. Then he turned his eyes back to Myra.

Myra was sexually exciting; she was an interesting diversion. She was, he admitted, typical of the kind of woman he now sought out though as he thought about it, he realized that Myra had pursued him.

Well, which one of them initiated the relationship was unimportant. Corrie disapproved of all his women, "You're running from a memory," she would insist. They would argue. Corrie would be angry, he would become sullen. Corrie was too young to understand that he purposefully chose women who were Inge's complete opposite. He wanted no one to challenge Inge's supremacy in his thoughts.

How can I make you understand that I truly loved your mother? He loved Inge as he hadn't been able to love anyone since she had died. He let out his breath and fixed his eyes on the full moon outside his window. His wife was gone, lost to him forever. For four years he had remained faithful to her but then he stopped punishing himself, stopped blaming himself for her untimely death and the fact that she had not been diagnosed in time.

Myra was a dark beauty, a mythic temptress, an earthy woman, and a woman in whom he could lose both himself and years of painful memories.

He sighed, she was so enticing, he wondered if he should waken her; lose himself in her now, at this moment.

"*¡Profesor! ¡ Profesor!*" The voices and sound of half a dozen booted feet on the flimsy wooden steps of his caseta caused Jonathan Henley to sit upright. He moved his hand quickly off Myra's breast like a guilty teenager caught in the act of feeling up his first date. Then he shook his head, to dispel both his lecherous thoughts and his lingering sleepiness.

"*¡Profesor!*" the shouting continued and Jonathan Henley struggled from his bed and groped for his robe, responding with, "*¡Un momento!¡Un momento!*" in obvious irritation. His *caseta* was

27

less than a kilometer away from the excavations in the ancient
Moche City of Sipán. Sipán was more than twenty kilometers from
Chiclayo a town of half a million, and the capital of Peru's
department of Lambayeque. The town of Lambayeque itself was
some twenty kilometers further north. His was one of five *casetas*
built for archeologists and support staff, but at the moment the others
were unoccupied. He chose to live here because it was close to his
work and because it was reasonably isolated. He seldom had visitors
in the daytime, so visitors at this hour could only mean some sort of
trouble.

"Un momento!" He shouted again.

At the sound of his voice, Myra stretched languorously and the
top of the sheet caressed her dark taunt nipple. "What is it at this
hour?" she murmured sleepily.

Fully awake now, Jonathan Henley glanced at her body and felt
a sudden surge of real desire, but more shouting at the front door
chased it instantly away. "Who the hell knows," he muttered. "Stay
here, Myra, I'll find out."

Not, that she would have gotten out of bed. No, Myra was quite
content that he should find out what the trouble was and the chances
were she would be asleep when he came back to bed. That meant
that in order to fulfill his desires, he'd have to wake her up. He
stumbled toward the front hall.

He reached the front door, unbolted it, and flung it open. He
squinted at the three men on his porch. They were tall, lanky men
and all three wore the familiar broad brimmed hats and large
glittering silver badges of the Peruvian Federal Police. *"¿Que
pasa?"* he asked.

"¿Profesor Henley?"

"Si, soy Profesor Henley."

"¡Viene usted, por favor!

It was not a request, it was an order. Why did they want him to
come with them? Good God, was he being arrested? Aware of his

increased heartbeat, he struggled to look absolutely calm. His mind
flew over a number of possibilities, all of them were unpleasant.
Perhaps there were some sort of charges - God, hadn't he been
careful? The Peruvians were hell bent on prosecuting anyone who
breached the law that forbade precious artifacts being taken out of
the country. He knew exactly how intent they were, and how careful
he was. No, he had done nothing. Both he and the museum he
worked for acted 100% within the law - he had always worked
within the law. But these men might not be police at all - perhaps
they were dreaded *Shining Path* rebels disguised as police. There
had been kidnappings and murders, but the rebels didn't usually
work this part of the country. Or maybe they were from the *Tupac
Amaru*, the group that had held almost the entire diplomatic corps
hostage in the Japanese Embassy for months. No, he felt certain that
the *Tupac Amaru* was pretty well broken up and that these were not
Shining Path rebels. He looked at the men hard. "Identification?" he
demanded, and then reminded himself that this was not America and
even if they were police officers they were under no obligation to
show him anything.

Nonetheless, he felt relieved that they actually looked
bewildered. Almost in unison, all three pointed to their badges. "I
have to get dressed," he told them in Spanish. Without invitation,
they pushed into the small dark living room and still mystified, he
went back to the bedroom to find his clothes.

Myra wasn't asleep. She was sitting up, the sheet curled around
her waist, the top half of her body naked in the bright moonlight.
Her brown nipples were hard in the cool air. Her long dark thick hair
fell to her shoulders in a tangled mass, her huge velvet brown eyes
were questioning.

"It's the police, they want me to come with them," he said
flatly.

"Are you under arrest?" she asked, verbalizing his own initial
fear.

29

He shook his head and shrugged, "I don't think so. I don't know what they want."

"It's four fifteen," she complained. "God, can't it wait till the sun comes up?"

"I guess not." He pulled up his pants and then grabbed his white shirt off the chair.

"I suppose if you must go, you must go," she held out her long arms, "Give me a kiss, darling."

He leaned over and kissed her full lips and she nibbled at him as her hand slid between his legs. She grabbed him, "Hmm, ready for love," she breathed lustily into his ear.

He fondled her nipple in response, then seized her wrist. "Shit, stop that," he pulled away from her. She looked at him from the bed and smiled slyly, "Hurry back, I'll be waiting."

"Damn." Good thing it was dark out front, at least the *Federales* wouldn't see his erection.

When he reached the front room, he grabbed his jacket off the back of the chair, "Let's go!"

The old World War II Jeep into which they climbed was a tribute to the ingenuity of local mechanics. He was calmed slightly to discover it did, in fact, bear the emblem of the National Police. It jolted to a start and like something out of an old-time *Keystone Cops* flick they bounced down the rutted dirt road, two in the front seat, and two in the back. They were racing into nowhere without explanation.

They sped for ten minutes through the night and then turned, leaving the pavement. As nearly as he could make out, they were headed in the direction of *Pampa Grande.* It was some fifteen kilometers east of Sipán. Once it had been the primary settlement for the *Moche*, having housed as many as ten thousand people. Then the Jeep turned again and for another fifteen minutes they drove down an unpaved, unmarked road, leaving a trail of dust in their wake.

"Where are we going?" Jonathan demanded in Spanish as they got further and further into the barren foothills where he knew dangers ranging from *bandidos* to packs of wild dogs lurked. He felt his initial alarm returning.

"*Paciente!*" one of them commanded.

He didn't usually smoke, but he carried cigarettes in case the need arose. Right now, he felt the need. He fumbled in his jacket pocket and finally found his crumpled pack of Camels. At least he didn't have to ask if he could smoke. The Surgeon General's warning hadn't reached Peru, and it seemed all Peruvians smoked - if not one thing, then another.

In his other pocket he found his Zippo lighter. This souvenir of the Vietnam War was probably only slightly younger than the Jeep. He flicked it and the flame shot up causing the *Federale* next to him to jump in alarm and curse in Spanish under his breath.

"*Madre de Dios! Es una inferno!*"

Jonathan smiled at him and with satisfaction, lit his cigarette. The lighter was twenty-six years old and he was fifty-five and they were both in great shape. He drew on his cigarette and looked around. They were climbing up yet another hillside and were well off the main road. He squinted into the distance. There were bright lights- lanterns. They surrounded a dilapidated shack. In moments the Jeep rumbled up to the hovel and was brought to a clattering halt.

As they climbed the crumbling steps a swarthy, a *Federale* sporting a Pancho Villa style moustache and clearly wearing a captain's uniform stepped through the doorway to greet them.

"*Buenas tardes, Profesor.*"

Henley glanced up at the thin line of dawn in the eastern sky, "More like good morning," he said with undisguised sarcasm.

"*Capitan Raoul Toro, para servir, Profesor.*" The captain bowed from the waist.

Henley wondered if the captain really was at his service. He decided not to test the comment right away.

31

"Viene usted," the captain ordered, motioning him into the shack.

Wearily, Henley followed. The captain swung open the front door and Henley gasped, fighting off nausea as the smell of rotting flesh assaulted him. His guide, the svelte captain, had withdrawn his handkerchief and held it to his nose. He offered a second handkerchief to Henley.

"Shit," Henley muttered even as he still fought the desire to retch. The odor was made worse because the air outside had been so clean and fresh.

A decomposing, decapitated body lay stomach down on the rough wood floor in the middle of the room. It lay in a pool of dark dried blood. A few feet away the severed head stared at its body while maggots swarmed in the nose and mouth, devouring the rotting flesh. The room buzzed with flies. As far as Henley could tell, the naked man was an Indian.

"Do you know this man?" the captain demanded in Spanish.

Henley felt the vomit rising in his throat. He shook his head rapidly and partially shrugged. Then he pushed past the captain and stumbled out onto the porch where, leaning over the side, he threw up while the three other *Federales* stared at him.

He was aware that the three had faint smiles on their faces. It no doubt pleased them to see him ill, or made them feel superior at the very least. Machismo was a big part of the culture. No sooner had he finished being ill then he felt the captain's hand on his arm. He was pulled back into the stench filled shack.

As if the dead man were an insect, the captain gingerly touched him with the toe of his highly polished leather boot, then with a swift upward kick, like that of a practiced soccer player lifting the ball, he rolled the body over.

Henley winced. Like all Indians this one was small. His body looked as boyish as his decapitated head - though he was probably in his thirties. He looked again at the head. What was left of the face had a kind of innocence, which, in death, was frozen in a mask of fear.

"Do you know him?" the captain repeated.

Henley forced himself to lean over and look into the face. It was true that he employed hundreds of Indians, but how could he possibly remember all their faces? They all seemed to look so much alike to him. "I don't know," he admitted. "I can't remember."

"Viene," the captain motioned him away from the body.

Grateful to see they were leaving the central room of the shack, Henley followed. They went into a second room where a trap door in the floor had been propped open. Curiously, Henley peered down into the darkness. It appeared to be some sort of cellar. A crude ladder descended into the black pit.

The captain lit a lantern and leading the way, moved onto the ladder. "You come down too," he ordered in Spanish.

Reluctantly, Henley followed the captain into the dark dampness of the cellar. When he reached the bottom, he turned to examine his surroundings in the light provided by the lantern. The captain obligingly moved it around slowly, illuminating all of a reasonably large underground chamber apparently leading to another. Henley gripped the ladder as his eyes scanned the room and its shocking contents. "Holy shit!" he mumbled. "Sweet Jesus!"

#

It was twilight, and the rays of the dying sun combined with the dust of the desert to paint an outrageous sunset of blazing orange and gold. To the east, the jagged mountains were black against the royal blue sky of impending night. Jonathan Henley stumbled up the front steps of his *caseta* and for a moment before opening the door, he looked at the sky. Here, at the foot of the Andes the colors of the rising and setting sun were incredibly vivid. He imagined it was like being at the center of a prism.

33

He wiped his brow, aware that he did not look as he had when he left three days ago. Then he'd worn clean trousers and a clean shirt. Now his trousers were filthy and his shirt was grubby and torn. He had tied his bandana around his head for use as a sweatband, and he had forgotten to remove it, so it remained, stained and dirty like the rest of his clothes.

His hand was on the door handle, but Myra flung it open from the inside, surprising him. "Where have you been?"

He looked at her and blinked. The sight of her was startling to say the least. Her hair was built into a magnificent beehive decorated with a jeweled Spanish comb. Her body was covered with an elasticized bodysuit made of a snakeskin like fabric. It had a deeply cut halter-top so her back was an expanse of bare flawless human flesh and from the front fully half of her full breasts were exposed. She wore black spike heels that made her appear taller. The whole effect was a science fiction sex fantasy. But if she appeared as a sinuous snake woman from another planet, her question was 100% earthly, asked in a voice filled with an emotion somewhere between panic and sheer exasperation.

He pushed into the house and she followed, allowing the door to slam behind them.

"I'm surprised you're still here."

"Where was I supposed to go? There's been a police car across the street since you left. Were you in jail? God, should I have called the embassy?"

He shook his head, "I'm relieved you didn't. I was afraid you might." He collapsed into a chair, "Get me a drink, will you? A gin and tonic."

She didn't usually do things for him but this time she went about the business of fixing his drink without complaint. He leaned back, stretching his aching muscles, his eyes closed. He asked himself how much he should tell her, he wondered if it mattered. After all, he reasoned, too many people knew already. Neither the murder, nor the incredible find in the chamber below the shack, could be kept a secret for very long.

She brought in two drinks, one for each of them.

"You look as if you've been excavating," she ventured. "I really thought you'd been arrested."

"No, I wasn't arrested. I haven't been excavating either, at least not in the traditional sense. He was very much aware of her musk perfume. Its pungent aroma filled his nostrils.

"Well, are you going to tell me?" she leaned over, her eyes flickering. She smelled money, big money. Myra was the kind of woman who sensed money. She sensed it and it excited her. It was no doubt the hope of being wealthy that had convinced her to join him in Sipán, leaving her worldly possessions in Lima. Not that he had ever promised her anything. Indeed, he had been careful not to. He sipped his drink and carefully weighed just how much to reveal and how much to censor.

There was no need for preamble. Myra knew full well that the entire area between here and the sea was honeycombed with the excavated or partially excavated graves of the ancient *Moche*, who had lived in this area of Peru from the first to the seventh century AD. Along with their dead, the *Moche* buried fine gold and pottery in huge sun baked mounds now called, *huacas*. In reality, they were flat-topped pyramids. The Spanish conquistadors had plundered the living Inca and then robbed the dead in their graves, but they somehow missed the treasure trove of the *Moche*. These graves were on a site called *Huaca Rajada*. They had been unearthed in 1987 and yielded a wealth of precious artifacts equal to those found in the pyramid of Tutankhamen. The first *Moche* pyramid had been discovered by grave robbers who took a valuable haul out of Peru and into the United States where they intended selling it on the black market. One of the robbers, feeling his unsavory brethren had cheated him, went to the authorities. Thanks to his anger, the contraband treasure was recovered after a bizarre police chase on the

New Jersey Turnpike. The director of the archaeological museum in Lambayeque saw to it that the tomb was secured immediately. But there were new sites and undiscovered tombs, so the robbing went on, and it continued even today, albeit on a far lessor scale. The locals often ran short of cash between sugarcane harvests and when they needed money, they eyed the many flat-topped pyramids. In spite of all the laws and the heavy penalties, they stole off in the night to loot the once lucrative graves of any article, however small, that might have been overlooked. Almost any bit of gold jewelry or artifact in reasonable condition, mysteriously found its way overnight into the insatiable international black market of stolen pre-Columbian treasures. For the last five years it had been assumed that there was nothing left of great value and that made the discovery in the dead *huaqueros* cellar even more fantastic.

"One of the *huaqueros* was murdered," he said, sipping his drink. *Huaquero* was the term used for local grave robbers.

"You weren't gone three days because of some dead *huaquero,* Myra retorted.

He heard the sharpness in her voice. He looked into her face and felt she was straining to control herself. "No. I was gone three days because of what was found under his house."

"Valuable things –"her golden eyes flashed like one of the golden cats he had just found beneath the shack. The cats had round lapis eyes that caught the light.

"Hundreds of antiquities - all gold and semi precious stones."

She leaned over, her interest so intense it was palpable.

"There must be a grave somewhere that has not been looted, she whispered, then, "Why didn't the killer take the valuables with him?"

In a second she had grasped the two essential elements of the mystery that had consumed him for three days; the probable existence of another rich find and the fact that so much of value had been left following the murder.

"That's where I've been these last three days. I was looking for an unexplored grave. There, beneath the shack, there are three chambers, each one smaller than one before it. I worked all around the site but so far I haven't found anything more. I don't know where this stuff came from or how it got into the chambers beneath the shack."

She let out her breath and he knew her imagination had taken over. She was envisioning the possible treasures that might be found. Then, she frowned. "The killer must have taken something far more valuable than what he left behind. That's why he didn't take what was there... it was probably – how do you say? *¿Comido por los pollos?"*

"Chicken feed. Perhaps the killer was discovered and had to run. Perhaps he couldn't carry everything."

"No." Myra shook her head vigorously, "No. He was seeking something more valuable than all that was left."

"Do you think he found what he was looking for?"

"Maybe yes, maybe no," she replied. "Are you sure you're telling me everything?"

"Sure, why would I hold back? The police think the body was there some time before they found it. God knows it certainly smelled that way."

"So they are not the ones who frightened away the killer," she said with a shrug. Then she smiled, "I know there is something of great value – it might still be there. I feel it."

He looked at her long and hard. Perhaps, he decided, she did feel it. Perhaps she was right. After all, that was why he had spent three days looking.

"Where are the artifacts you found?" she suddenly asked.

"Under lock and key," he answered. "In the museum vault in *Lambayeque.'*

"And I suppose you will send every one of them to the museum in Lima."

37

"That's the law. You know that, I've told you a hundred times. Since 1967 it's been illegal to take any artifacts out of the country, and it's illegal to sell them."

A devious smile crept across her lips as she slithered closer to him, "And you would never break the law, would you?"

He was tired but she had a rejuvenating affect on him. Her perfume was intoxicating. She always seemed to hold some exotic promise; she was truly the mistress of sexual invention. He smiled back at her and ran his finger round her lips, "I won't break the law," he said, kissing her. "Not even for you."

#

Corrie Henley paused and wiped the snow off her face with the back of her arm. For a moment the forty steps to the entrance of the museum looked insurmountable, the last obstacle on her way to warmth and serenity. She glanced at her watch. It was nine a.m. and the temperature could not have reached even 0 degrees. She wore her warmest coat, high boots, tights, thick gloves, a scarf and a headband. Beneath her coat she had on a wool skirt and sweater. Her thick blond hair was in a French braid that dangled down her back and her cheeks were rose pink from the cold.

The trip to work was a journey through assorted stages of discomfort. She was dressed for the unmerciful Boston winter but the subway was hot and stuffy, causing her to perspire. The result was that seconds into the above ground world she felt cold and clammy. The four-block walk from the subway to the museum left her exposed skin numb. By the time she reached the museum, she felt as if she had been breathing ice crystals. She trudged up the stairs and hurried inside, pausing for a moment just inside the entrance. "Nirvana," she whispered. It wasn't that it was so much warmer; it was the absence of the wind. It was like another world.

She knew as soon as she took off her winter clothes she would feel like a new person.

"Corrie! It's a freezer!"

She looked up at Jack Marsden and forced a smile. She had hoped not to see or talk to anyone till after she had washed her face and more or less repaired herself. And of all the people she hadn't wanted to run into, Jack Marsden topped her list.

As everyone acknowledged, Jack was a rarity within these hallowed walls. He was young, good looking, well built, and well educated. Some fifty-two men worked in the museum, and Jack was the only one who was not already on his way to becoming a fossil. Unhappily, Jack realized all of his assets, and Corrie thought him arrogant.

"You didn't take the subway in, did you?"

He raised one brow with his question and she felt annoyed. As if a bus would have been better in this weather, or perhaps he thought she had a chauffeur driven limousine at her disposal. "Yes," she answered. "I always take the subway."

He ignored her tone and his ingenuous smile remained frozen on his face.

She decided that Jack had too many teeth and that his dark hair was too slicked down. He was too well dressed, too well groomed and manicured. He wasn't effeminate but his appearance did not exude that slightly unkempt masculine quality she found so attractive in a man. She supposed she just preferred L.L. Bean to G.Q.

"Could I see you in my office? I've some good news for you."

The best news he could give her was that he was resigning, but if that were the case he would have made a public announcement. She felt mildly irritated that he had accosted her before she had even had a chance to catch her breath.

"I was just on my way to the ladies room. Can it wait a minute?"

"Sure, no hurry."

He winked at her and turned toward the hall that led to his office. Vaguely she wondered if he was going to ask her out, and that led to a feeling of even greater irritation. Jack was in love with himself and he assumed everyone else loved him too. He knew he was the museum stud; she disliked the fact that he enjoyed the role. And even if he had not been conceited and arrogant, she still would not go out with him because he was not just a colleague but her superior in the hierarchy.

Not that he was her direct superior. He worked in the Latin American Section and she was currently interning in the North American Section headed up by Eugene Anderson, one of the museum's most loveable and meticulous fossils. Naturally her own interest was in South American Archeology, as was her father's. But one took what they could get. When she had applied, the only internship available had been in the North American Section. Still the two areas blended in antiquity as they did not blend in the modern world. The Aztec and Mayan cultures of Mexico shared commonalties with the Mimbres and other southwestern tribes just as they did with the Inca and the *Moche* of Peru. The Tsimshian, native to the north Pacific coast spoke a language that was classified as being in the Penutian language phylum, the same as South American Native Languages in Peru and Ecuador, such as *Quechua*. In her work, Corrie looked for the relationships among the pre-Columbian native peoples of both North and South America, thus she did not feel frustrated by her internship in the North American section. If she felt frustrated at all, it was because she was not working out in the field. The museum was too enclosed, too rarified, and too purely academic.

She hurried into the restroom. She took off her coat, headband, scarf and gloves. She smoothed out her hair and looked into the mirror. She was beginning to warm up and feel human again. *He must want to go out. What else could he want? I won't go. But what excuse will I use?* Again she felt angry. She should not need an excuse but in the working environment one had to keep things civil and blurting out, 'No thanks, I don't like you because you're a phony,' would hardly be civil. *Maybe there's something wrong with me. I haven't had a satisfactory relationship with a man since the summer before grad school. I'm sure I'm the only woman in this whole place who isn't pining for Jack Marsden to ask her out.* Corrie shook her head to dispel her conversation with herself. She went to the locker room and hung up her coat, took off her boots, and put on her shoes.

In less than five minutes she was outside Jack Marsden's door. She knocked and he called out for her to come in.

"Corrie, welcome to my den of iniquity. Have a seat."

In fact, she found his office alarmingly uncluttered. He was too neat for his profession. Her father's office had always been cluttered. Her office was cluttered. She had decided long ago that archeologists were not neat people. They could painstakingly label, sort and classify endless artifacts, but when it came to their offices they were hopeless. Their offices always looked like a sorting area for waste paper.

"Coffee?"

"Thanks. Cream and sugar."

He turned aside to a coffee butler and poured her a cup, adding sugar and some whitener. "Heard from your father, lately?"

His question was unexpected. "Not for a couple of weeks."

Jack nodded. "He's made a new find. Some really valuable pieces."

"Oh, my." In truth she didn't know what to say. She was honestly surprised her father hadn't called her. She was usually the first person he told when he found something. Archeology – their mutual work – was one topic they could discuss without arguing.

41

"I'm going down there myself, probably for a month. Since we fund the project, I'm going to negotiate for some pieces for the museum."

"That seems fair."

"I need someone to help me. I'd very much like you to come."

Corrie stared at him in surprise. "What about Katherine?"

Katherine Langley had been Jack's assistant for at least a year. She was attractive, bright, and had considerable expertise.

Jack grinned, "She gave notice a week ago and left yesterday. She had some vacation time. She's getting married. Listen, I know I should have spoken to you first, but I already asked for you to be transferred over to my section. I know you want this area eventually and it's a chance to see your father."

Corrie felt stunned. It was really too good to be true. She wondered if he would want a *quid pro quo*. But that wasn't what this was about, and if Jack thought otherwise she would put him straight very quickly. No, this was about opportunity. She felt more than certain that being her father's daughter was a bonus, but not the real reason why Jack wanted her. She was known to be well versed in this area, it was her first interest, and she had spent two summers in Peru. Regardless of Katherine's expertise, Corrie knew she would be far more valuable to Jack than Katherine would have been.

"Yes, of course I want to come with you, and I want to transfer into this section too."

"Done," he said with a grin. "I've got a load of reading for you to do and we're leaving on Monday so you'll only have the weekend to tie things up."

"I'll manage."

"Do you need a list of things to bring?"

Corrie shook her head, "I was raised in the business."

Jack laughed. "Okay. Good. Dr. Tandy can fit you in this afternoon. He's been briefed so he knows what shots you'll need."

"I hate that part."

"We all do. Now, if you can have lunch with me – say at one o'clock, I have some things to go over. Your passport is in order, isn't it?"

"Yes, I always keep it current."

"That's what I like, a woman who's prepared."

Again he winked but she ignored it. She pushed Jack's flirtatious manner out of her mind and tried to concentrate on how very good it would be to see her father. It had been almost a year; they had a lot of catching up to do. She bit her lip and reminded herself not to argue with him. *He's an adult, he has a life.* It was something she told herself again and again.

#

"Myra!" Jonathan Henley strode through the door of his *caseta,* letting the screen slam shut behind him. The house was silent. He called her name again and then walked through the rooms. She was definitely not there and it perplexed him. There was no public transportation between here and Chiclayo. The only conceivable place to go was the local Indian market, but it was totally out of character for Myra to go to market like a common house frau.

He walked into the bedroom and looked in the closet. Her clothes were all here, she obviously had not left him, though if she had he would not have been surprised. She had been plainly miffed when he wouldn't give her details or agree to smuggle out pieces of his surprising find. *Maybe she went for a walk,* he hypothesized. But then, even going for a walk was out of character. When she exercised, it was a methodical routine performed early in the morning to a tape she had brought. Myra was not one for walking in the sun.

He went outside and circled the *caseta,* but Myra was nowhere to be seen. Still perplexed, he returned to the house.

It wasn't a large house nor was it well furnished. The living room had two comfortable chairs and a worn blue sofa bed. He had a large desk against the far wall and the other walls were lined with overflowing bookcases. The living room led into a kitchen and dinette. The bedroom was off the kitchen and the bathroom off the bedroom. It wasn't a convenient layout since if he had company they slept on the sofa in the living room but had to come through the bedroom to use the bathroom. Myra slept with him but if Corrie came for a visit it would be awkward. Naturally, it was not just the location of the bathroom that would be awkward.

It was the cook's day off and he decided he would scramble some eggs with peppers and onions. It was as good a meal as any, though Myra wouldn't be pleased that he had eaten without her. *You could have at least left a note,* he thought with annoyance. But it was like her to be thoughtless.

Still between bewilderment and mild irritation, he went about the task of fixing his dinner. He shouldn't after all have to starve just because Myra had gone off somewhere on a whim.

#

Las Floras Blancas was ill placed, ill named, and unclean. It was a small, usually crowded little bar on the edge of the outdoor market in *Chiclayo*. It belied its name; there wasn't a white flower in sight. The umbrellas over the five rusted metal tables were a dirty faded blue and advertised *Trujillo* the name of a locally produced beer.

"I don't like this place," Myra complained. "It's filthy, it's hardly private, and the chairs are uncomfortable."

"You're spoiled, the man across from her replied. There was an open pop bottle in front of him. Myra held a gin and tonic in a foggy glass.

44

"I would really prefer meeting somewhere private," she again complained.

"Have you any news for me?"

He was wearing sunglasses that mirrored a distorted version of her face. Myra shook her head. "He has told me nothing yet, absolutely nothing."

"I can hardly believe that. Have you exhausted all your feminine wiles?"

Her facial expression did not change. "I'm working on him."

"We require details."

"I'm doing the best I can. I need more money."

"You have not yet delivered any information worth paying for."

Myra arched her brow. He was an insect. Even here in an outdoor café she could smell his effeminate perfume. "And I won't unless I get more money. I'll probably have to steal some of his papers to find out what's going on."

"You'll have to come with me. As you want more money, we'll have to speak to our patron."

Yes, this was much better. She hated dealing with underlings. She very much wanted to speak with their 'patron' who was certainly no stranger to her. She thought for a moment of their previous relationship. He was a man of uncertain temperament and she suspected him of having dark desires, but he was exciting and he knew her well. Surely he realized she could not exist in this place without greater compensation.

"I'm ready," she said, standing.

"Very well, come along. My car is just down the street."

Myra felt a jolt of surprise and then a feeling of apprehension filled her. She had thought he meant to telephone but it seemed their patron was actually here in Chiclayo. She wondered why he had not come personally to this meeting.

#

The moon was a lopsided sphere, yet it was bright. Jonathan stood on his front porch and once again stared out across the expanse of the Lambayeque valley. Beyond the hills he could see the pinkish glow in the sky from the lights of Chiclayo.

Tonight was a night like that night over a week ago when he had been aroused from his sleep to go off to the hut of the murdered grave robber. In spite of the fact that the moon was not full, it was a bright night. *Where the hell are you?* He asked himself once again. Damn! Myra hadn't returned, and hadn't sent a message. His emotions churned. He was angry at her lack of consideration and yet he worried at the same time. Should he call the police? What would he tell them? That his mistress had run away? No, it would be better to say she disappeared. For the hundredth time he looked at his watch. It was eleven-fifteen. He shook his head and turned to walk inside. He would have to call the police and report her missing. This was unseemly; it was out of character – even for Myra. He had an ill feeling and he couldn't shake it. He reached for the phone and it rang, causing him to jump.

"Myra?" he said anxiously, into the mouthpiece.

"Who's Myra?" The familiar female voice asked.

The phone line crackled. Modern technology had not yet reached the ancient village of Sipán in the Lambayeque Valley of Peru. The phone itself was an artifact of the 1920s, tall and black. "Corrie? Is that you?"

"One in the same. Obviously you were expecting someone else."

He could hear the coolness in her tone but he had no intention of lying. "Just a woman I've been seeing."

"Ah, yes. I should have guessed."

There was more than a little sarcasm in her tone. "I've been going to call you."

"Promises, promises –"

"Really, I was going to call you."

"It's all right. I hear you've been busy."

"Ah, Jack told you."

"Not everything. But I suspect he will."

He wasn't happy to think of Corrie sharing secrets with Jack Marsden. Then he reminded himself that he could not expect her to accept his relationships if he did not accept hers. There was a moment of silence. The truth was, he wasn't as fond of Jack Marsden as he knew most women were. Moreover, he was jumping to conclusions. He didn't know how Corrie felt about Jack.

"Are you seeing Jack? He asked, knowing he sounded casual.

"Not like you mean. No. But something wonderful has happened. Dad, I've been transferred over to Jack's section for the balance of my internship. We're flying down to Peru on Monday."

"You're coming here! That's great."

"I won't talk now. We should be in Chiclayo by Wednesday at the latest."

"Shall I drive out to the airport and meet you?"

"No. We're picking up a car. I'll meet you at the hotel."

"Great!" He was still smiling when he replaced the phone in its cradle. Then he quickly picked it up again and dialed the police station. "*Capitán Toro, por favor.*"

Now he had to find Myra in order to send her away. Corrie would want to stay at the *caseta,* and there was no way to have them under one roof.

"Toro," the male voice answered.

"Dr. Henley."

"Have you information for me?"

"Afraid not. This is personal."

He thought for a moment and then quickly explained in Spanish about Myra's disappearance. Captain Toro said he would send someone to ask questions in the morning. He sounded anything but alarmed. "She's probably gone back to Lima," he suggested.

"Perhaps," Jonathan allowed. He didn't tell Toro that she had left her clothes, wrote no note, nor even hinted she was leaving. She had been with him for two months but her disappearance was going to be hard to make the police understand – especially as Myra had a certain reputation, even locally. He muttered his thanks and hung up.

He sank into his favorite chair and took a sip of his now warm drink. The phone rang again. It was Captain Toro and he sounded totally pleased with himself as he explained that one of his underlings had, that very morning, seen Myra board the bus for Lima.

"She must have had a better offer, a lot better offer to leave her clothes."

There was silence for a moment. Then, soberly, Toro said, "I shall look into this further."

Before he could say anything, Toro hung up. Jonathan replaced the receiver in its cradle. He was only slightly relieved.

CHAPTER THREE

Jeff Richards closed his eyes, lifted his head, and let the lukewarm water from the shower spray into his face. After a second, he reached for the soap and scrubbed down. Two hours of Aikido practice and he was wiped. Getting soft, he thought to himself. But he knew it was more that he was out of shape. He had been away from Lima for almost a year and during that time he had not been able to practice except for sporadic visits to the dojo in Buenos Aires. Moreover, this Dojo, unlike the one back home in Las Cruces or the one in Buenos Aires, was run by a Japanese sensei from Kyoto. Of the twenty or so people on the mat he was usually the only non-Japanese or, as the Japanese called him, the *gaijen*. Having a Japanese sensei meant that the practice sessions were extremely vigorous and lasted longer. The style of the art was also slightly different from that which he had been taught in New Mexico, and different still from Buenos Aires. He was still re-learning how to move with precision and blend with his opponent's energy; nonetheless, these nightly classes were a lifesaver.

Some years ago he had first come to Peru, his fellow Aikidoists had helped him find decent and reasonable housing as well as guide him to fine Japanese restaurants.

When the hostage taking at the Japanese embassy occurred in 96 he had been freelancing, but was quickly assigned to cover the story.

What had happened in December of 1996 had been big. It was big enough that for a time Lima was transformed into a minor international media circus. When it was over, he picked up another assignment in Bolivia and then another in Argentina. Now he was submitting a weekly Latin American Report, and he judged Lima as good a place as any for a base and so he had returned.

He finished showering and stepped out of the cubicle onto the black and white tile floor. The room was steamy and smelled of an odd combination of sandalwood soap and medicated talcum powder. He grabbed his towel off the hook and dried himself. Kenji, a small bear of a man was there too. Kenji had finished drying, and was half dressed and sitting on the bench. Jeff knew that all the Japanese regarded him as a giant, and he supposed that at slightly over six feet two, he was just that to his Japanese compatriots. Not one of them was over five feet five and most were shorter. He knew full well that the Japanese from the northern islands were tall but there were none from that area in this dojo. Indeed, most had been born in Peru or were from Tokyo proper.

"Are you still interested in leads?" Kenji looked up at him. He had one sock on and held the other red sock in one hand.

"Sure, got something?" Even as he asked, his curiosity peeked. Kenji worked in the Rafael Herrera Museum. He seemed an unlikely source for any earthshaking story.

"Do you know much about the Moche?" Kenji asked.

"I know there was a rich archaeological find of Moche art a few years back."

"In the 1980s. A great find! A spectacular find!" Kenji said enthusiastically.

"But old news," Jeff reminded him. Still, he was more interested then he revealed. Corrie's father was working with the Moche find; at least he assumed Jonathan Henley was still there. For a time he had thought about trying to contact Corrie through her father, but he had not. Events and taken him away before he had acted.

"Ah, quite so. The original find is old news," Kenji continued. "But more has been found and there has been a murder. A really horrible murder of some grave robber." Kenji had lowered his voice and spoke in a conspiratorial whisper.

"Murder? I didn't see anything about a murder in the papers."

Kenji shook his head, "No one knows, I mean no one outside a very few people. The authorities are trying to keep it quiet. It's all a mystery. I saw a fax that came from Dr. Henley the archeologist in Sipán. It was addressed to our director. Then there was another fax from a police captain in Chiclayo."

Jeff thought only for a moment. It had been months since he had gotten out of the city, and he had never been to the site of the Moche find. He had done most of his traveling south and east of Lima. He was unfamiliar with the north. He needed a trip, needed to get away. "I might go up there. Should I drive?"

Kenji shook his head. "It's almost to the border with Ecuador. There's an airport outside of Chiclayo that serves the port area. You can rent a car there."

Jeff smiled, Kenji was a veritable travel guide.

"The person you must speak with is Dr. Jonathan Henley. He lives outside Chiclayo, near the dig in the ancient city of Sipán."

Have to speak with him? He wouldn't have thought of speaking with anyone else.

Kenji leaned closer, his dark eyes intense. "Don't mention my name. In fact, don't tell anyone where you heard about this, please. I was not even supposed to see the fax."

"Of course not." It seemed to him that Kenji was being a trifle too secretive but then one never knew what kind of Byzantine politics operated inside a museum. Especially a museum that was funded by the Japanese, had more than a few Germans working in administration, and some prominent American archeologists involved in the actual digging. To top it off, the Peruvian government oversaw the place. It was a kind of international hotbox, and he imagined there were all manner of minor intrigues. But Kenji meant well. Jeff smiled again and touching Kenji on the shoulder muttered, "Thanks."

#

51

It was late afternoon as Jonathan Henley drove down the dusty road toward Chiclayo. He reflected on the way matters had apparently worked out. He was still more than a little mystified by Myra's sudden disappearance, though, all in all, her departure, for whatever reason, certainly seemed for the best. Of all the women he could think of, he was sure Myra would cause Corrie the most consternation. Reluctantly, he admitted he didn't want Corrie to meet Myra. Myra was a sex kitten, certainly not the kind of woman a man wanted to introduce to his daughter.

He turned his thoughts away from Corrie and looked at the barren landscape. It was dotted with the hovels that were primarily occupied by grave robbers. As he grew closer to the city, the hovels gave way to the shantytown that surrounded Chiclayo and climbed the hills behind it. They represented a veritable flea market of construction materials made, as they were, from discarded bits of wood and cardboard, canvas, old shingles, tarpaper and lengths of rusty corrugated steel. The houses, if one could call them that, appeared to support one another. Each time he drove by, he thought of dominoes and wondered if one fell, would they all fall into tattered bits. Still he liked the humanity that filled the shantytown. These were good people, people kept down, people deprived. They were poor in a way that made the inhabitants of a New York slum look rich. Yet they kept struggling, they worked hard, they could still smile. He admired them, he tried to help them by employing as many as he could.

He waved at the children that played by the side of the road while their skeletal, ill kept dogs slept in doorways or stood, staring into space and barked lethargically. The dogs as well as most of the livestock looked as if their skin were simply stretched over their bones. Every few houses or so, a woman had set up a stand to sell some produce or eggs. As he drew nearer to the center of town he passed street vendors cooking over open fires. As it was nearly sunset, a variety of aromas floated on the air, an invisible, silent call to the evening meal.

Jonathan cursed as he swerved to miss an errant chicken that, in its effort to elude the cooking pot, fled across the road. It nearly ran under his wheels, though mercifully the man in pursuit of the bird had seen him. If he had hit the chicken he would have felt the necessity to get out of the car and pay its owner. In this place, the loss of a chicken was no small matter.

Another half-mile further on and the structure and appearance of the houses improved. The precarious makeshift dwellings gave way to stone and mortar even as the traffic grew thicker.

He turned onto a street that paralleled the main street and drove along it till he came to the park. At least he called it a park. In actual fact it was a small square, a lone spot of greenery and cultivated flowers surrounded by buildings. He pulled up across the street from the hotel, *La Gan Vida.* Though translated into Spanish, it bore the same name as an Italian film made in the late sixties, *La Dolce Vita.* Putting the name of the hotel together with its appearance always amused him. It was a three-story white stucco building with red shutters on the windows and a red tile roof. The white wash needed a new coat, and weeds were threatening to evict the flowers from the beds around the building. What grass remained appeared as clumps of green amid brown dying turf. He knew the hotel was clean and the food was reasonable but if this was *the sweet life,* as its name indicated, he didn't want to know the sour side.

Hands in his pockets, he crossed the street. His thoughts once again turning to Corrie. Naturally, now that Myra was gone there was no reason why Corrie couldn't stay at the *caseta,* but she might not want to – more to the point, Jack might not want her to. If they were lovers he decided he didn't want to know. *Stuffy, I'm getting stuffy. I don't want them sleeping together in my house.* He knew he was being hypocritical, but he didn't feel like fighting it, at least not immediately. Anyway, Jack wasn't his favorite person.

He pushed through the front door. The lobby was just as it had been three years ago when he had first come here. True, the rug was a bit more worn and the furniture a little more faded but essentially nothing had changed. The tables and do-dads were strictly 1920s, and he imagined some of the dust catchers would fetch a pretty penny in the insatiable U.S. antique market. He had heard that a collection of far-out 'art deco' was very much 'in.'

"Ah, Herr Professor!" The elderly man behind the desk stood to greet him.

"Herr Ehrlich, how are you?"

"Fine, fine. As always."

The proprietor of *La Gan Vida* was paunchy and wore glasses, his total image was a kind of 'little old winemaker', German stereotype, though to his credit he did not wear monocle, lederhosen or long stockings.

Sometimes when he came into town, he and Ehrlich played chess together while sharing some imported German beer. Jonathan felt a little guilty because he hadn't been around for a while, not since Myra had come up from Lima. It wasn't that he and Ehrlich really had anything in common, it was just that ex-patriots usually stuck together. Besides, he knew Ehrlich was lonesome. He had lost his wife several years ago and didn't have many friends in Chiclayo.

"It's good to see you," Ehrlich said. "You haven't come lately. What brings you to town today?"

"I'm expecting my daughter."

"Ah, how wonderful for you! She's coming all the way from Boston! Will she be staying here?"

"I'm not sure. She's with someone who may be staying here; I'm not sure where she wants to stay."

Ehrlich sighed, "One can't predict the actions of young people."

"I probably should have called you."

He shrugged and his glasses slipped a little further down his nose. "There's plenty of room. In fact only seven rooms are rented. It's not as if there was a convention!" He laughed, "Not that there ever is. Who would have a convention here? Of course sometimes we're quite full during tourist season."

They both laughed.

Jonathan knew only too well what tourist season could be like, though mercifully it was not as crowded here as in Cuzco. Tourists usually came in the spring and fall when the weather was moderate. It was January now, the height of summer in the Southern Hemisphere, and thus it was hot on the desert.

Jonathan glanced at his watch, and realized how anxious he was to see Corrie. "I really thought she would be here by now."

"Patience. Come along, come into the café and have some beer." He reached down and banged on his bell till a young man in his twenties came running. "Take over the desk, Filipe. Call us in the restaurant when Professor Henley's daughter arrives."

"How will I know it is her? Filipe asked.

"Her name will be Henley too," Ehrlich replied with the patience of a saint. He turned to Henley, "Filipe works hard, but what is it you Americans say? He's short a few marbles," Ehrlich whispered.

Jonathan followed Ehrlich into the cafe. He sat down and Ehrlich went off to get the beer. Ehrlich was, Jonathan observed, a man whose age was not obvious. Jonathan believed him to be somewhere between fifty and seventy and that was honestly as close as he could come to narrowing it down. There are people who appear older than they are, and then do not seem to age at all for years and years. Ehrlich was such a person.

"Did your lady friend leave?" Ehrlich asked as he returned and sat down. He opened the two beers and skillfully poured them into ornate German steins.

"Yes, and without so much as a good-bye."

"Maybe she'll come back."

"I hope so. She left her clothes."

Ehrlich looked up and frowned, "How odd. Most women wouldn't think of doing such a thing."

"I was worried, but the police investigated. She was seen leaving town."

Ehrlich took a swig of his beer and leaned back in his chair.

"How long have we known each other?"

"Two years."

"I don't even know how old you are." Jonathan stated.

"Sixty-nine."

His answer raised a thousand more questions in Jonathan's mind. One of them was on the tip of his tongue when he heard Corrie's voice. He turned toward the entrance of the restaurant and there she was, lighting up the faded room. She was a stunning sight, a sight that sent a pain straight through him because she looked even more like her mother now than she had a year ago.

He got up and in ten strides had his arms around her. God, she even smelled like her mother. Her blond hair was pulled back in a French braid, her blue eyes were large and clear. Here, where everyone was either part Indian or leathery from the sun, she seemed especially pale. Her skin was like porcelain, just as her mother's skin had been.

He kissed her on the cheek and then led her over to Ehrlich. "This is Alex Ehrlich, the owner of the hotel."

Corrie smiled warmly and took his hand.

"Will you be staying here? Ehrlich asked.

Corrie turned toward her father. "Is there room for me in your *caseta*?"

"Sure. But it would be a bit crowded with Jack."

"Oh, he's staying here."

Jonathan nodded and was surprised at how relieved he felt to know there really didn't seem to be anything between them. If asked to explain his feeling toward Jack, he knew he would be unable to do so. It was just one of those gut feelings that said, 'this guy is a big phony.'

"Jonathan!" Jack's voice followed Jonathan's uncharitable assessment, and he looked up as Jack Marsden strode into the dining room. He was immaculate in new khaki's that had clearly not seen the outside of the museum before today. Jack was too well dressed, too charming, and just too damn full of himself.

Jonathan Henley extended his hand, "Good of you to bring my daughter to see me." It was the most sincere thing he could think of to say.

Jack shook his hand with all the firmness of a water soaked sponge.

"My pleasure, and as you know, she's more than just a pretty face. I need her on this project."

"Stop talking about me as if I weren't here."

"Sorry," Jack said. I just registered here at the hotel. I assume you're going out to your Dad's place."

"That's what I'd like to do."

"Fine, could we have an early dinner first?"

Jonathan turned to Ehrlich, "Herr Ehrlich, this is Jack Marsden, from the Conway Museum in Boston. Jack, Herr Ehrlich is the owner of the hotel."

Jack nodded at Ehrlich but did not extend his hand. *Arrogant son of a bitch, he thinks of Ehrlich as the hired help,* Jonathan thought. "Is it possible for us to get supper so early?" He asked politely, trying to make up for Jack's lack of manners. After all, he was asking a favor. Workers ate early, but most people did not even think of dinner till at least nine.

"Why not? I'll go wake up the cook. Someone will come presently. Just sit down, I'll go for more beer."

Stepping easily into his role of waiter, jovial host and owner, Ehrlich disappeared into the kitchen.

They ate bread, German sausage and hot pickled cabbage slaw for supper. It was the fare Ehrlich preferred and it was what he usually served at lunchtime. At night it was different. The evening menu offered a variety of Peruvian and German dishes but those had obviously not yet been prepared.

"A bit heavy, but good," Jack said leaning back in his chair. "I've always had a fondness for German food."

"Didn't you live in Germany for a while?" Jonathan asked.

"Yes, for a short time. But tell us about what was found. I'm anxious to hear all about it."

"When can we see the find? Is it here?" Corrie asked.

Jonathan shook his head, "In Lambayeque, under lock and key."

"We can drive up there tomorrow." Jack suggested with a wave of his hand. "Then I can see it for myself."

As if Jack could assess the pieces better than anyone else, Jonathan thought. But he held his tongue. "The drive doesn't take long now that they've fixed the road."

"¡*Profesor!*"

Captain Toro came into the dining room. He walked up to their table, and seeing Corrie, bowed from the waist, took her hand, and kissed it with a somewhat exaggerated flourish.

"My daughter, Corrie. And this is Jack Marsden from the Conway Museum. Jack and Corrie, this is Captain Toro."

Toro clicked his heels together in what Jonathan considered an annoying pseudo military fashion.

"How providential that I should find you here. I was about to drive out to your *caseta,*" Toro said, looking at Jonathan.

"Please don't tell me you found another dead grave robber."

"Dead grave robber?" Jack raised his brow.

Jonathan hadn't written about the grave robber in the report he had faxed home. He had intended on telling the whole story when, and if, there was any definitive explanation. "Yes, he was in a shack above the chambers where the treasure was found."

Toro shook his head. "No, no more dead grave robbers but something equally serious, I'm afraid."

Jonathan frowned, "Oh," he muttered, even as a strong feeling of foreboding engulfed him.

"It's that woman, the model from Lima, Myra Rojas. The one you reported missing."

"What about her?"

"We found her body. I must ask you to come along with me."

Jonathan's mouth went dry. Myra dead! "Am I under arrest?"

Toro shrugged. "I need to speak with you, alone."

The others sat like a tableau, the feeling of shocked disgust was palpable. After what seemed like an eternity, Jonathan nodded. He put his keys on the table. "Ehrlich will tell you how to get out to the house," he said, turning to Corrie. "I'm sure I'll be home in an hour or so. Make yourself at home."

Corrie looked both perplexed and concerned. "Should I call someone?"

"Not now," Jonathan replied. What he meant was, 'not yet.'

#

"Please, have a seat, Professor."

Jonathan sat down. Toro's office was a mere cubicle in the center of a larger office that apparently housed most of the local law enforcement bureaucracy. The walls were a terrible cream color with dark brown trim and the whole place smelled of stale cigarette smoke and perspiration. His desk was cluttered and there was a torn faded girly calendar on the room divider behind his desk. Jonathan looked around and fought to hold onto reality. It had been a short walk from the hotel to the police station, and he was aware of feeling 'other worldly'. One event seemed to run into another. Myra had

59

vanished and was now, apparently dead. Corrie had arrived suddenly with Jack Marsden, and he still had more work to do on the underground chambers beneath the grave robber's shack.

"I don't understand any of this," Jonathan said, looking into Toro's dark eyes.

Toro took out a cigarillo and lit it. "This woman, this Myra Rojas, what did she mean to you?"

Acrid, pungent smoke filled the cubicle.

It was a direct question and Jonathan gave it a direct answer. "We slept together. We met in Lima a couple of months ago and she came up here last month."

"Did you invite her?"

Jonathan shook his head, "She just turned up."

"And you did not find this odd?"

"No, not exactly. We'd had an affair when I was in Lima. As I told you, she was a model. She told me she had some time off."

Toro smirked, "Of course you didn't object, or ask any questions."

Jonathan shook his head. Then added, "It's lonesome here."

Again a wicked knowing smile crossed the captain's face. "Yes, there aren't any models from Lima here. The professional women here are all worn and the young girls are protected by their brothers and fathers."

Jonathan wanted to say that Myra was smart and that they enjoyed one another's company even when they weren't having sex. But Toro appeared to have a stereotypical Latin American male view of women. Women came in two types, chaste and chased. One kind you married and the other you screwed. If he tried to explain their intellectual relationship to Toro, it would have sounded both ingenuous and absurd.

"You haven't told me where you found Myra." Jonathan leaned forward. His chest felt tight. It didn't seem fair that Toro got to ask all the questions.

"By the riverbank, face down in the mud."

Jonathan frowned, "Did she drown?"

"No, she was strangled, garroted. Or at least it would appear so. The doctor is examining her body now. I won't know the actual cause of death till his autopsy is complete."

Jonathan felt ill. He should have insisted they look for her. This might not have happened if he had been more forceful, more insistent. Initially he was glad Myra was gone because Corrie was coming – now he felt guilty. "I should have done more to find her," he said under his breath, then, "I don't understand who would have done this."

"She was probably raped too, though with a woman like that it will be hard to tell."

"You think she was raped and then strangled?"

"Maybe. As I said, there aren't any women like that here – maybe someone saw her and wanted her and she didn't want them, or perhaps they wouldn't pay enough."

"She wasn't a prostitute," Jonathan insisted.

The captain pursed his lips together and scowled, "She was a loose woman."

Back home Toro's term might have been classified as *passé*, but given that this was Peru, it was not a statement with which he could disagree. "Do you suspect someone?"

The captain smiled, "You mean do I suspect you? No. You seemed far too concerned when you reported her missing. In any case, she was seen talking with another man, a man who does not fit your description at all."

He had been absent a lot and vaguely he wondered if Myra had found a local to amuse her. It didn't seem likely, but he couldn't rule out the possibility. "What can I do for you, then?"

"I need to write a report. I need to know all you know about this woman. Where she worked in Lima, what her address was, things like that."

"I'll do everything I can. I don't know if she has any family or not."

The captain opened his desk drawer and withdrew a long yellow foolscap pad and a ballpoint pen. He shoved it across the desk, "Write down everything you know about her. Then we'll go and look at the body. I need a positive identification."

Jonathan nodded. He didn't relish the idea of seeing Myra dead, but it was surely the least he could do, that and seeing that she got a decent burial.

#

"I don't know what to do," Corrie admitted as she looked at Jack. God knew she didn't want to appear to be leaning on Jack, especially now. She turned to Herr Ehrlich, "Should I be worried?"

Herr Ehrlich shook his head, "No, no. I'm sure not. Your father can take care of himself."

Jack stood up, his cheeks puffed up. "If you tell me where the jail is I think I'll drop around, just to let that Toro fellow know that Jonathan isn't alone. That he's got an important American in custody." Then he turned to Corrie, "I think you should take your father's advice and go home."

Corrie looked from one to the other. Jack's comment was so 'self-important'. She was quite certain that Captain Toro would be more aggravated by Jack than frightened by his assertion. Still, she had to accept his offer at face value. "I'd appreciate it if you would go to the jail."

"How do I get to my father's *caseta*?" she asked turning to Herr Ehrlich. She then asked, "Who was the woman whose body was found?" Obviously her father knew the woman if he had reported her missing. But did Herr Ehrlich even know the woman and did her father confide in him?

"I didn't know her," Herr Ehrlich replied and turning away he sat down and began painstakingly to explain how to get to the *caseta*. In the end, he drew a crude map on a napkin and she took the keys and left, happy to be away from Jack after so many hours on the plane with him.

Corrie started the engine and headed out of town on the Pan American Highway, which ran through Chiclayo. She turned off on the side road following the instructions on the map. The dry wind hit her face and she realized how glad she was to be here, to be near her father once again. What she would do about Jack Marsden was another matter. She inhaled and let out her breath slowly, she couldn't even discuss the problem of Jack with her father. He wouldn't understand, he would just be angry.

"Solicitous bastard!" she said aloud to the wind. She marveled how, in twelve short hours, her bad opinion of Marsden had proved so completely justified. It was a revelation, sort of, 'now I know why I never liked you.' Most women thought him to be a 'catch', a guy who was intelligent, on his way up, good looking and suave. She supposed all of those adjectives still applied but there was something missing; she struggled to try to describe it even to herself. In her mind, she conjured up a detailed cardboard cutout, perfect from one angle but totally one-dimensional. That was Jack Marsden. He was one-dimensional; he lacked depth and perhaps humanity. His opinions were pat, his views way too set for a man of his age. Maybe she was too used to her father. Maybe her first romantic relationship had spoiled her. In any case, she wasn't used to one-sided people. When she discussed something with her father, he always began with, "Let's try to look at this from all directions –." Jack certainly wasn't like that. It mystified her, he mystified her. His line of work demanded he understand other cultures, yet his understanding was superficial and however detailed, it lacked a human element. In short, he could look at the remnants of a past civilization and recite everything there was to know about it but he didn't seem to wonder about its inhabitants – their feelings, their motivations, their public and private lives. He could study time past, but could not enter it mentally as she did, as her father did. For her father, mere facts were never enough. That was why his writings were so fascinating; it was why he was so fascinating. Jack Marsden simply did not measure up.

"Prick," she muttered. And for the first time, she realized how really angry she was. He had hired her and she had really thought it was because he respected her and thought her the best candidate. Well, perhaps he had. But clearly he had a whole other agenda. He wanted her because of her father and because he wanted to sleep with her. Two for one, influence and pleasure. "I should have seen it coming," she said to herself. But the truth was she felt blindsided. When he'd hired her as his assistant, she had vowed to keep it all business.

The unpleasantness had started before they even boarded their flight. It had begun in doctor Tandy's office when she had gone for her shots. Jim Tandy was young, around Jack's age. He gave her the necessary shots and then leaned over and smiled, "Are you on the pill?"

"No," she had answered honestly and with some surprise.

"Maybe you should be," he suggested.

Somehow his advice put her on the defensive and she had answered coldly, "I doubt it's necessary. But thanks anyway."

Her suspicions started even before she got out of his office. Had Jack suggested to Jim Tandy that she might need the pill since they were going away together? Certainly Jack had been to see Tandy before her; he had made the appointment for her. On the other hand, maybe it was a normal sort of question. It just seemed odd and it bothered her. "No," she said aloud. It wasn't just his question and the advice. It was Tandy's expression. He had almost smirked. She felt certain Jack and Tandy had discussed her, 'man to man' so to speak. The whole idea made her furious.

The conversation on the flight down aced it. Jack had begun by talking about her father, about how brilliant he was and how much his peers respected him. He just kept stressing the point that being 'associated' with Jonathan Henley was a real career asset. It occurred to her that he wasn't talking about her father, he was talking about himself.

Then, he made a pass at her. When the plane was in semi darkness and the in-flight movie came on, he tried to slide his hand from her knee up under her dress. It wasn't just a pass, it was a crude pass. She objected and told him quite bluntly that she didn't want any involvement with a man for whom she worked. He had straightened up and for a long while they sat in stony silence. He apologized but she still felt ill at ease, so ill at ease that she intended telling Jack she couldn't go on being his assistant as soon as they got home. She doubled her fist and hit the steering wheel. She was mad at herself too, and wondered if she had not led him on in some way. But even if she had, she couldn't shake the idea that she was being used. She felt that she was here not because she was a good intern who knew the Moche culture but because she was her father's daughter and her father could help Jack up the ladder of international administrative success. "It's a petty little world within a petty big world," her father would say.

She hit the steering wheel with her hand again. At least thinking about how angry she was at Jack had momentarily taken her mind off her father's problem – whatever it was.

Corrie slowed down when she approached the circle of *casetas*. She knew the burial mounds were not far away and that these cottages had been built for the museum people. The last time she had been here, her father lived in town.

The *casetas were widely separated and located on a large circular road* just off the main highway. She slowed at number 3, the largest of the five houses, and pulled into the drive. It was lonely out here. The other houses did not, at the moment seem occupied.

She grabbed her backpack and climbed out of the Jeep. She opened the front door with the fourth key she tried and stepped into the house.

"Oh my stars," she breathed as she turned on the light and looked around. The house was a disaster. Some of the furniture was over-turned and had been cut open, its stuffing pulled out. Every drawer was open, and her father's desk was all but upside down.

For a long moment, she stood in the doorway. She could feel her own heart pounding. Robbers? She turned on her heel and fled outside to the car. She bolted for it, got inside and locked the door. Were they still in the house? She hadn't heard any noise but she wasn't going to stay and find out either. She leaned back. What the hell was going on? A murdered grave robber, a woman her father knew found dead, and now the house robbed – the mental image of the living room returned, the radio was there and so was the television, his books were all on the floor. What had the robbers taken? Or was it robbery? She shivered. Should she wait for her father or go back to town? The truth was, she didn't feel at all safe. She put the key back into the ignition and started the Jeep. She decided she would go back to Chiclayo and try to find her father. Maybe he was still with Captain Toro. If not, she would tell Toro what she had found and ask him to return with her to the house. Yes, that was a plan. She backed the Jeep out of the drive and headed off down the road, back the way she had come.

#

Jonathan stood up and stretched. The chair in Toro's office was uncomfortable, especially for a tall man. He felt folded up and a little stiff, moreover he wanted a drink.

"The body is at the doctor's office. It's just down the street. We can walk."

Jonathan nodded. "I need to walk."

"Where did you learn English?" Jonathan asked casually. It had occurred to him that Toro's English was quite good, too good for him to have studied here in Peru.

"I studied at the Pan American Police College in Washington," Toro replied. I was assigned here specifically because of the value of the archaeological finds."

Toro opened the door to the outer office and Jonathan saw Jack Marsden. He was sitting on a bench, tapping his foot, waiting impatiently. He stood up. "I came here because Corrie was worried," he said.

"No need. Did she go home?"

"Yes. I can drive you back."

Marsden had a rented Jeep but Jonathan decided he would rather have Toro drive him home. "It's okay," he said, putting his hands in his pockets. "We've got to go over to the doctor's office. I have to identify the body."

Jack nodded. "I'll come along if that's all right."

Jonathan looked at Toro who shrugged and muttered, "¿Como no?"

It was odd. Toro spoke English to him and Spanish to Jack. It was a sure sign he didn't like Jack. Well, that was one thing he and Toro shared.

As promised, it was a short walk to the office of Dr. Mendoza. Mendoza was hardly more than five feet tall. He was a man without a neck, a man with thick arms and legs, a round fat belly, and thin gray hair. What Jonathan noticed first, however, were the doctor's eyes. One was brown and the other blue.

"You've come to see the woman." Dr. Mendoza had a raspy grating voice. He motioned them to follow. They were ushered down a dimly lit, windowless corridor at the end of which was a door.

"Come into my cold room."

The four of them squeezed into the small, bleak room. The refrigeration unit was old and noisy. Jonathan thought it was probably an old meat locker that had been converted into Dr. Mendoza's morgue.

There was a table and the doctor lifted the white sheet and exposed the body.

It was all Jonathan could do to look at Myra, but he forced himself and not for the first time was amazed at how different one looked in death. Her neck was twisted, her facial expression frozen in terror even though her eyes were closed. He could see the mark left by the garrote. It had broken the skin and dark congealed blood formed an ugly necklace round her throat.

"It's her," he said in a low voice as he quickly turned away.

Behind him Jack Marsden stared hard at the woman on the table. *Ysabel* a voice inside him screamed. He struggled to look impassive. What the hell had happened? Why was Ysabel Ramirez going by the name of Myra Rojas? How the hell had she teamed up with Jonathan Henley? Who had killed her and why? He felt nauseated, as if everything were coming undone. God, suppose they found out who she was? Who she really was, that is. It wasn't often that he felt caught off guard, but Jack Marsden admitted he was caught off guard now.

#

Corrie turned back onto the highway. The great ball of an orange sun had already set over the graves of the Moche.

What had been found so far was of immense value. She thought about the dead grave robber mentioned by the police officer and about her father's recent discovery. Perhaps the grave robber had unearthed something even more valuable. Perhaps that was why he had been killed – perhaps someone believed her father had something from one of the graves. Could that be why the house was turned upside down? The very thought made her nervous and she began to drive faster.

She headed up the last hill that separated the valley from Chiclayo. From out of nowhere a car pulled out onto the road behind her. Uneasily she realized it must have been parked on the side of the road with its lights off. But now the headlights were on high beam as the car raced toward her. It came up fast, too fast. Her first thought was that this was like a scene from a bad film; she did not have time for a second thought. It was a truck, not a car, and it swerved around her, ramming her left fender. She gripped the wheel and fought to stay on the road. The truck stayed even with her. She glanced out the window, but she could not see the driver. The truck hit her again, and again she fought for control. The third time the truck hit her, she skidded off the road and hit something hard. The Jeep turned crazily, and Corrie was thrown forward, hitting her head on the steering wheel. Her world went black.

CHAPTER FOUR

As they walked, Jonathan noticed that Jack Marsden walked mechanically, his eyes looking into the distance but clearly seeing something else in his mind's eye. Daydreaming was not something Jonathan had ever seen the ambitious Jack Marsden do; it seemed out of character. "You okay?" he asked.

"I'm fine, just jet lag. I think I need some sleep."

Normally, curiosity would have overcome Jack's need for sleep but apparently not today. Jonathan had expected Jack to ask detailed questions about the murdered grave robber and the treasure discovered in chambers beneath his shack. So far Jack had not asked him to elaborate.

"I can get a driver to take me home," Jonathan suggested. "You look bushed. You don't have to drive."

Jack didn't look at him, "Why don't you just take my Jeep? You and Corrie can stop by and pick me up in the morning and we'll go on to Lambayeque."

"Good idea," Jonathan answered. He found himself relieved to be left alone to drive home. Corrie would be there and if she were not too tired, they could talk before bed.

They reached the hotel and Jack fished in his pocket for the keys to the rented Jeep. "Over there," Jack said indicating the red jeep parked across the street.

"Thanks. Get a good night's sleep."

"Yeah, I will," Jack replied.

Jonathan's last thought was that Jack sounded damn preoccupied, and he wasn't at all sure it had to do with lack of sleep.

#

Ramon Garcia closed the door of his hotel room and leaned against it, his eyes shut against a hundred terrifying images. *Why was this happening now?*

The first of his horrific images was Helga. He had seen her tonight – *It can't be, it can't be.* He had left her years ago, face down, garroted, her blue eyes bulging with fright, her long blond hair falling over her bare shoulders, beckoning him even though she was dead. "The girl was not Helga. She was Henley's daughter." He said it aloud in the hope that his vocalization of the facts would drown out the shrieking voices in his head. "She can't be killed yet. She is still needed." But the voices were loud, they were a chorus singing of her libidinous hair, her brazen, wild, naked hair. He wiped his brow, it was wet with perspiration.

"I killed Helga. I killed her! The girl was not Helga!" He could not remember how many times he had killed Helga. He knew it was more than once. She reappeared in other forms, she was reborn with a hideous regularity and each time the voices told him he had to kill her again because she the she-devil, the mate of Satin – Adam's first wife Lilith – oh, she had taken a thousand forms and they all visited him, taunted him and tortured him.

He shook his head again. The last twenty-four hours had been a nightmare.

Ysabel had proved useless. She was nothing but a greedy slut; she deserved to die. He had enjoyed her first, but then he had slipped the garrote around her long neck when she turned about to button her blouse. She struggled, but not for long. They never struggled for long.

Perhaps it was killing Ysabel that brought back his memories of Helga. But that was yesterday and it was only tonight that the voices had begun to harp anew, to taunt him about the girl in the Jeep, the girl he knew was Henley's daughter. She was leaning over the steering wheel, her long blond hair on her shoulders. He had stared at her, fought the voices, and fought his desires. Then he had tried to

71

open the Jeep's door so he could silence the voices. The voices would stop if he killed her. But the door was locked from the inside. He had struggled with it but realizing it was no use, he had run back to his truck and driven off into the night. He couldn't stay, someone would come along, someone would find him and there was far, far too much at stake. He was close, so close to his dream. Now, only a very few people stood in his way.

He walked across his room to the unmade bed and collapsed on it. After a moment he sat up and went to his black flight bag. It was sitting, unopened on a worn red velvet chair. He looked around the spinning room. Its drab walls seemed to be closing in on him, the massive Spanish style furniture appeared to dance in the dim light. He forced his attention back to the bag. He rummaged in the zippered compartment till he found a bottle of pills. His hand shook violently and it took all his waning control to pour some of the bottled water on the bedside table into the foggy blue glass. He swallowed two of the pills. "Let the voices stop," he rocked back and forth on the edge of the bed, his arms wrapped around himself. He had not been this way in years – it wasn't good, the voices distracted him. "I am being tested," he muttered as he collapsed back against the pillow. Long minutes passed, then slowly a drugged sleep overcame him as one by one the doors closed on his many realities.

#

Jonathan Henley drove slowly toward home. He felt unusually tired and it seemed safer to drive at a lower speed. Not that there was any traffic. The problem with night driving out here was wandering people and lack of light. Once off the Pan American Highway, the roads were unmarked by white lines and in places the pavement ended abruptly. Worse yet, people who lived out here had a bad habit of walking on the road at night. Not that most nights were pitch black. Regardless of the moon's phase, the stars were bright and the air clear, as long as there was no cloud cover. Tonight the sky was mottled, what he used to call a 'buttermilk' sky. Tonight, the light was limited and caste strange shadows over the landscape.

He forced his mind away from the memory of the dead gravedigger and from the shocking sight of Myra who had been raped and murdered. He thought instead about the Moche, about this much plundered little corner of the world.

Beyond this desert coastal plain, he could visualize the beach and imagine the white-capped waves rolling ashore. This road did not parallel the ocean shore, it turned inland.

The Moche had been extraordinary. Much of their daily life was recorded in their pottery. It revealed everyday life in every aspect right down to sexual liaisons. In fact Moche pottery illustrated a good many innovative sexual positions and some unusual activities. Rather a lot had been made of this, and one room in the museum in Lima was devoted entirely to erotic pots, most of them Moche. The pottery was, he reflected, a kind of Karma Sutra in clay.

The personal aspects of Moche civilization were fascinating enough but their real genius was evident in their engineering skills. They had channeled streams flowing down from the Andes into irrigation canals. The canals were used to water their fields of corn and beans. Their extensive agriculture supported many population centers, and these were usually located near various places of worship such as the unearthed Temple of the Sun. They were also skilled metal workers and it was known that they used a chemical means to electroplate gold and silver.

In the distance he could see the mounds that he knew to be the graves of the Moche. *A haunted land,* he thought. Jonathan shook his head. The reasons for the demise of the Moche were unknown, no one had found any pottery that told that story, or even showed the decline. It was generally assumed that the Moche succumbed to earthquakes, prolonged draught, or perhaps even to catastrophic floods. Some scientists suggested that climatic difficulties associated with El Nino might have been the cause of their disappearance, others suggested there was a plague. But disappear they had, and now where once a fruitful people had lived, there was only high desert and plundered graves. The *Moche* were buried with the valuable masterpieces they had created but they certainly did not know eternal peace. Undisturbed for 1500 years, the graves were undisturbed no more.

He turned the corner and was about to start up the hill when he saw the Jeep. It was his Jeep, and it was off to the side of the road, hard up against a huge rock and tilted at a sharp angle.

He screeched to a halt and then backed up. Corrie filled his mind and his heart began to race. And why the hell was the car facing Chiclayo?

He turned around and pulled off the road himself, then he scrambled out of the car and ran toward the Jeep. He peered inside. Corrie was slumped over the wheel. "Oh, dear God," he whispered, as he pulled on the car door. Damn! It was locked. He started to fish in his pocket and remembered that Corrie had his keys. For a second he stood motionless, then he thought of the spare key in the magnetic holder that was on the underside of the rear left fender. He hurried to the back of the car and felt for it in the darkness. His hand was shaking as with enormous relief he grasped it. He hurried back to the car door, unlocking it quickly.

He flung the door open and leaned over, "Corrie! Corrie!" he could hear the panic in his own voice.

She groaned slightly and he could see that she had fallen forward. Thank God she was wearing her seat belt. "Corrie," he said, feeling his panic dissipate slightly.

She groaned again and then lifted her hand to her temple, "Oh, my head," she murmured.

"Thank God you're all right. Can you move everything?"

She nodded and moved around a bit to show him she was not seriously injured.

"Come on, I'll unfasten the belt. Can you crawl up and out this side?"

"I think so."

He stood by to help her as she staggered out and into his arms. He half carried her to Jack's Jeep and got her inside. "We'll go right back to Chiclayo. The doctor ought to have a look at you."

She nodded and rubbed her head, then it began to come back to her through the fog of her headache. "And get the police," she managed. "Dad, your *caseta* was broken into. I left to go back to town and I was forced off the road. This wasn't an accident."

Jonathan felt his mouth go dry. First the brutal murder of the grave robber then Myra's murder. Now Corrie had nearly been killed and his house had been broken into. "Shit." He said, "I don't know what the hell is going on."

"I'm feeling a little better now." She rubbed her temples. "I think I'll just have a bad headache."

"We'll see the doctor anyway. And I think we'll both stay in the hotel, at least till morning."

"Okay. It's really too late to be driving back and forth. Anyway, I'm really bushed."

"Me too," he admitted. "God you really gave me a scare."

"I gave myself a scare."

"Did you see the car that drove you off the road?"

"Not well. But it wasn't a car, it was a pick-up truck."

"Hell, there isn't much else around here."

"I couldn't even tell you what color it was. I was too busy trying to stay on the road."

"After you've seen the doctor we'll go right to Toro. And tomorrow you're going to fly right home."

Her father was, as always, protective of her. "No I'm not," she said stubbornly. "I'm going to stay here and find out what's going on. Anyway, if anyone should fly home it's you. Whoever did this broke into your house and ran your car off the road. They were after you, not me."

He stared ahead into the night. "Or something they think I have," he said slowly. That had to be it. The grave robber was killed because someone thought he had found something of immense value and Myra had been killed because someone thought she might know where it was. Now they'd gone through the house and tried to – at that point his thoughts came to an end. Tried to do what? If they thought he had something or if he knew something they needed to know, they would want him alive. At least they would keep him alive till he told them what they wanted to hear. That was it, they had tried to kidnap him. He pressed down on the gas. He wanted to get back to Chiclayo as soon as possible. Most of all, he wanted Corrie out of danger.

#

To Jeff's left the sun was coming up over the snow capped Andes. It was a truly beautiful morning and he felt liberated. His whole mood had begun to change as soon as he had left Lima and not for the first time, he asked himself why he stayed there. "No planning," he said aloud. "You're not living your life, you're just letting it happen." He wondered if he should tell Jonathan Henley that he knew his daughter. "Corrie, Corrie," he said as he conjured up his memories. She was a wonderfully smart funny girl. And she was attractive too, a natural Nordic beauty with silky blond hair and pale flawless skin.

He and Corrie met the summer after their senior year at university. Both were headed to graduate school, albeit in different parts of the country. He had received a scholarship to the School of Journalism at Northwestern University outside Chicago. He had taken a summer job working in Deming on the local paper, *The Searchlight.*

In addition to his job on the newspaper, he also helped put together a couple of guidebooks of the area. Deming was fifty miles west of Las Cruces on I-10. It was a dusty, dry, hot little town that was partially deserted in the summer. It's inhabitants, largely easterners in trailers and mobile homes who had come to escape the winter, evacuated Deming for the northern part of the state in order to avoid the burning hot dry summer. But in spite of the heat and the dust, Deming was not without charm. It had its origins as a railroad town. In 1880 the Southern Pacific came from the West via Lordsburg to Deming. In 1881, the Atchison, Topeka, and the Santa Fe came from the Northwest arriving in Deming on March 7th. On March 8th, officials of the two railroads drove the silver spike that completed the second transcontinental railroad. In its early days Deming had been the Wild West complete with frequent gunfights. It was some thirty miles due south of Deming that Pancho Villa had invaded the United States, and today it was the red hot Chili capital of North America. Deming also had an interesting and oddly eclectic museum, as well as a number of state parks nearby.

It was while doing an article on the museum for one of the guidebooks, that he had met Corrie. She had a summer job cataloguing Mimbres Pottery that was unearthed from the ruins of nearby pueblos along the Gila River.

"Perfect for your guidebook," she told him. "It's really incredible pottery. Just look how detailed it is. You really must do a page on it."

He was immediately drawn to her energy and her enthusiasm for her work. She burst forth with an animated history of the Mimbres Valley and the Mogollan people.

"Tell me all about it over dinner," he urged.

She smiled, "Mexican?"

She was from Boston and loved Mexican food. He liked it, but it was hardly exotic fare for someone who had grown up in Las Cruces, New Mexico. Las Cruces, a truly Hispanic city in the southwestern corner of the state, was only twenty-five miles north of the twin cities of El Paso, Texas and Ciudad Juarez, Mexico. It was nestled at the foot of the mountains, just over the Texas border and in almost every way save location, belonged in Mexico.

"Mexican," he agreed quickly. He would have eaten sautéed worms to get to know her better.

One night led to another. They had dinner in his RV and in her little apartment. They ate in every Mexican restaurant in the area, which he assumed set a new record for a couple of gringos; one an exotic blond and one a tall redhead of Scots-Irish descent, both of whom spoke Spanish like natives.

Over the course of the summer their relationship blossomed. After a time it went further than dinner. Their most memorable night was spent in the *City of Rocks* State Park, under the stars. It was a strange place where natural rock formations seemed to have sprung whole from the dusty earth. It covered a fair area, and offered caves, cliffs and overhangs for the overnight camper. Its name was apt because from a short distance it looked like a city with each rock formation appearing as a separate dwelling.

That night they made love. It was perfect. The moon was full, and stars filled the heavens. The air was warm and clear and in the distance the coyotes howled. Corrie's white skin glowed in the moonlight, her silky blond hair fell on his chest, tickling him as they embraced passionately. It wasn't the kind of night you forgot, it was the kind of night you remembered for a lifetime. He imagined there were at least a million clichés about 'first love', after that night, he knew most of them were true.

He came to the sign that indicated Chiclayo was ahead 5 kilometers and he turned his rented car to follow the sign. Corrie had never talked much about her family, and now as he thought about her, that seemed odd. They had talked about everything else and she had always seemed open, uncomplicated.

He shook his head. He was mad at himself for letting her go so easily. Summer ended and they went their separate ways vowing to write. There had been a few letters but then they stopped, the distance between them made intimacy impossible. He knew better than most that good relationships were built on proximity. After a time he assumed she had met someone else and he began seeing someone himself. Time went by and he still compared every woman he met to Corrie. His memories of that summer in Deming lingered pleasantly on the fringes of his mind. Now, he was about to meet her father, Jonathan Henley.

"You're after a story," he reminded himself. She's probably married with six kids.

Where to start? Maybe he should just brave the lion, so to speak and go directly to the police. He could bluff it out, tell them he knew about the murders so there was no use hiding anything. He could promise to keep it all quiet until they were ready to go public. That kind of partnership appealed to certain law enforcement types. They would be less reluctant to share information and, in the end, he would have an exclusive. It was a plan, he decided to go with it.

#

Corrie sat in the dining room of *La Dulce Vita* and sipped her coffee. Dr. Mendoza had been very kind, considering her father had taken her to his home in the middle of the night. Still, he examined her and gave her some pills for her headache.

"Nothing serious. But you're going to have a big bump on your forehead." He was right. That was exactly what she had. Nonetheless, she had artfully combed her hair over it and applied some make-up. The bump was, she thought, hardly visible. She was just buttering a roll when her father came in.

"Oh, you look much better." He took the chair opposite her at the table. "I phoned Toro this morning. He's going to meet us here in an hour. He said he would come sooner if he could. It seems some reporter had just come into his office."

"I really slept well," Corrie said. "I don't know what was in those pills, but I went out like a light."

"Long flight, tension, and being forced off the road – I'm not surprised. You'd have probably conked right out without the pills."

"How about you, did you sleep."

He pressed his lips together and nodded, "Better than I should have."

"Here comes Jack," she said, half under her breath.

Jack sat down. "Morning."

Corrie could not help but notice that Jack did not look like the Jack of yesterday. In fact, he looked as if he had been run off the road rather than she. His face was paler than usual and there were lines under his eyes that hinted at a lack of sleep. "You look like death warmed over," she observed.

He ignored her observation. "I didn't expect you two back so early this morning."

"We spent the night here," Corrie told him. "Someone broke into the *caseta*. I was run off the road."

"What? Who? Were you hurt?"

"Just a bump," she said, parting her hair slightly.

"Have you notified the police?"

"Toro, is meeting us here." Jonathan said.

"I really don't understand what's going on," Jack muttered.

"I suspect someone wants something they think I have," Jonathan said. "I imagine they killed the grave robber for the same reason."

"You haven't filled us in on that."

Jonathan gulped down his coffee. He would have to tell Jack eventually. Now seemed as good a time as any. He began with his middle-of-the-night journey to the grave robber's shack in the hills.

#

Toro leaned back in his chair and stared hard at Jeff. He was perplexing, this lone American reporter who knew about the dead *huaca*. Moreover, the man himself was puzzling. He had red hair and blue eyes and his Spanish was flawless.

"I could deny everything," Toro said slowly. "But I'm not going to bother. I don't know how you found out about these things but if I tell you anything, you must promise not to write about it – not until the time is right, not till I give you permission. Publicity could ruin the investigation."

Jeff did not smile, although he wanted to. This Captain Toro had just offered him the bargain he had intended to make. Captain Toro immediately fascinated him. For a town outside the capital, Chiclayo seemed to have a big time police officer, one who was as bilingual as he was. Every instinct in his body screamed that while he had initially come here on a kind of lark, Kenji had been right. There was a story here, likely a bigger story than he had originally thought. Naturally, it was only big because it involved Americans but he didn't say that to Toro. "Okay," Jeff agreed. I won't write anything till you give me the okay."

"I have to meet with Professor Henley at the hotel. There have been additional events. I'll tell you about them as we walk. In fact, there has been another murder."

Jeff stood up, glad to be leaving the office and its lingering odor of stale smoke. He towered over Toro.

"I need a hotel," he said. "Is the one we're going to okay?"

"It's not the Intercontinental. It's a clean little residential hotel."

"Guess I'll check in for a while." He did not mention that he was anxious to meet Professor Henley himself.

Captain Toro spoke quickly as they walked. Nonetheless, he drew a vivid and nauseating verbal picture of the h*uaca's* murder and of the model's dead body. Jeff felt a little surprised to learn the woman had been involved with Henley. Perhaps Corrie had good reasons for not talking much about her family.

"Here we are," Toro said, opening the front door of the hotel. Jeff followed Toro toward what he supposed was the breakfast room as the smell of coffee grew stronger.

They walked through the alcove and Jeff stopped short. There across the room he saw his vision. It was Corrie Henley and she was every bit as beautiful as he remembered her. She looked up and her mouth opened in surprise.

"Jeff?" she said, a tone of total amazement in her voice.

For a second Jeff just looked at her, then walked over to her, bent over and kissed her cheek.

"You two seem to know one another." Toro's half statement-half question was asked in a surprised and somewhat suspicious tone.

Corrie smiled. "Jeff Richards. Yes, we met the summer I was in New Mexico."

"She introduced me to the wonders of Mimbres pottery," he said looking into her eyes. For a long moment he was lost in memories, then as if he had just remembered the others he looked about. One of the two men with Corrie was older and had iron gray hair. The other was good looking, but his complexion was pasty. He seemed annoyed and the first words to cross Jeff's mind by way of description were, 'anal-retentive'. Not that he said anything.

"Dad, this is Jeff Richards. Jeff, this is my father Jonathan Henley and this is Jack Marsden, my boss."

Jeff shook hands. Boss – he hoped that was all this Jack Marsden was to her. Just seeing her made him want to relive that night in the *City of Rocks*.

"What are you doing here?" Corrie asked.

"I work for International News Service. I covered the situation at the Japanese Embassy a while back. I've been traveling around South America and just got back. When I heard about the goings-on here I flew down and rented a car."

"Just how did you hear about them?" Jonathan Henley asked, lifting his brow.

"Sorry, I can't reveal my sources. What matters is, I've promised not to write anything till I get the go ahead from Captain Toro, here."

Jeff glanced at Toro and noted that he seemed annoyed with all the socialization.

Toro pulled out a chair and sat down. "I came here to hear what happened last night."

Jeff sat down too. He deliberately took the chair next to Corrie.

"I guess I better tell you all I remember," Corrie suggested.

Officiously, Toro took out his notebook. As she spoke, he took copious notes in Spanish.

When she finished, Toro put down his pen and shook his head. "We'd better go out to your house, professor. I'll need to look around."

"Of course."

"Let's postpone going to Lambayeque until tomorrow," Jonathan suggested. "I'll have to get the maid to clean things up after the captain and I look around the house. Then he turned toward Herr Ehrlich. "I think Corrie and I had better stay here for another night."

"Ja, Ja," Herr Ehrlich said. "The more guests the better."

Jeff stood up and took Corrie's arm. "Why don't you show me around town while your dad's gone."

"I could use some exercise, besides we have some catching up to do." She stood up too and took his arm. For some reason she couldn't explain, seeing Jeff made her feel good. Maybe it was the fact that he was part of a calmer past, or at least what seemed like a calmer past. Her mother had been dead two years when she met Jeff but her father had not begun seeing other women. The women her father ultimately took up with caused tension between them. This woman who had been killed seemed all too typical. They were all so unlike her mother. She didn't understand how he could be attracted to them, it seemed insulting to her mother's memory and even when she tried to hide her feelings, she knew she did not succeed. Seeing Jeff took her back to that time when she had no issues with her father, when they were still close. He also took her back to that period in her life before she had started working for a living, to those happier carefree days of university. And she felt forced to admit, just being with him made her feel protected. Jeff was a big man and could easily have been a linebacker with his muscular physique and broad shoulders. She thought of him as a football player who got lost in the library; his intellect was more than equal to his brawn. In spite of all that, and the fact that five years had gone by, he seemed no older then when they had last met, he still had a boyish openness. Maybe, she thought it was his unruly red hair and the line of freckles across his nose. She wondered if he still had his humorous cynicism. He made her laugh, feel comfortable, and she thought, he made her feel safe. She glanced at Jack and again thought how awful he looked.

"I'll be upstairs doing some reading," Jack said abstractedly.

"Are you all right?" she asked.

He shrugged. "I'm a little nauseous. Probably something I ate."

"We'll meet back here for dinner," Jonathan suggested, as he assiduously avoided any comment on Jack's digestive system. "And tomorrow we'll go have a look at what the grave robber found."

"How far is Lambayeque?" Jack asked.

"Less than an hour's drive," Jonathan replied.

Jack nodded and thrust his hands into his pockets, "Later," he muttered as he headed off to his room.

Jack climbed the stairs to the second floor because the elevator, which was the size of a clothes closet, made him feel claustrophobic. In any case, it groaned unhealthily, as if at any moment its cable might snap sending its passengers to their death.

He unlocked the door and looked around. The maid hadn't been yet and not wanting her to come, he hung out the 'do not disturb' sign.

The furniture was far too large for the room. Between the four-poster double bed, the massive dresser, the wardrobe, and three chairs, there was hardly room to navigate.

He sank into the only comfortable chair and stared at his locked briefcase. If he examined its contents again, he would be ill. And yet he knew he would examine it again because it held a terrible fascination. He felt drawn to it, even though what was inside represented one of the most completely revolting experiences of his life. *Not now,* he thought leaning back in the chair and closing his eyes. He would look one more time, but not immediately.

This whole trip is not turning out as planned, it's turned into a nightmare. He had expected to get closer to Jonathan Henley by wooing Corrie. But Corrie didn't seem interested, and Henley didn't seem to like him much. Not that he really cared, he wasn't trying to win a popularity contest. It was more that he needed Henley and that Corrie would have been an enjoyable diversion. And who the hell was this Jeff Richards who had just turned up? He and Corrie seemed to know each other rather well and worse yet, Richards was a reporter who had ingratiated himself to the absurd little police captain. Again he looked at his briefcase. Could more things go wrong? He shook his head and turned his thoughts toward Ysabel

Ramirez. What was she doing here? That is, beside the obvious: sharing Henley's bed.

Seeing her lying dead in Dr. Mendoza's morgue had shaken him to the core, though the thought that someone would find out who she really was, shook him even more.

Surely, considering this was Peru, it would take a long time to find out that Myra Rojas was, in reality, Ysabel Ramirez. Maybe they would never find out. He couldn't even be certain that the Peruvian police would check her fingerprints and dental records against Interpol's records. But Christ! What if they did? No, it was not a chance he could take. Of course, he didn't have to worry about that now.

Jack got up and went over to the bureau where his shaving kit sat. He unzipped it and took out a bottle of Tylenol and codeine. He poured some water and took two tablets before returning to his chair. His head was pounding.

Ysabel, Ysabel, who did this? He ran his hand through his hair and again closed his eyes. This wasn't the strongest drug he took, but he wanted to be in good form. This would just make him sleep, not render him unable to concentrate. In any case, this was a prescription drug, he didn't want to risk anything illegal in Peru. Jail in a country like this wasn't just incarceration, it was hell.

He let his mind drift back ten years to when he had first met Ysabel Ramirez. She was stunning, with a cat-like grace that silently offered sexual experiences well beyond the ordinary.

A mental picture of her entangled with Jonathan Henley crossed his mind and he immediately blotted it out, fighting to maintain the image of her with him, the memory of her that never failed to arouse him. Not that she was the only woman in his life at the time.

He had been on a fellowship in Germany when he met Ysabel. She had come from Spain to study. From the moment they were introduced he had been entranced. She was a master linguist who

spoke perfect German, as well as French, English, Spanish and
Quechua. She was working on cataloguing Inca artifacts and other
pre-Columbian pieces. But Ysabel had no ambition to become an
academic. Ysabel said she wanted to work in a gallery, to become a
legitimate dealer in pre-Columbian artifacts, "And naturally, one
must know what one is doing," she confided.

That wasn't how it turned out. Ysabel became a dealer but not
one sanctioned by law. She dealt in stolen artifacts she sold to the
highest bidder.

She drew him into her circle but when she got caught, she did
not implicate him. He knew it was because she would need him
again. Ysabel didn't go to jail. She somehow escaped custody and
simply disappeared. He realized that she had now materialized as
Myra Rojas, Peruvian model. She had undoubtedly set her cap for
Henley. Obviously, he was to be her entree back into the
tremendously lucrative world of black market pre-Columbian Moche
artifacts. Doubtless Henley wouldn't play. He didn't like Henley but
he knew that Henley was as straight as an arrow.

He cursed under his breath. If his own connection to Ysabel
was discovered, it could ruin him. It could be the end of everything
toward which he had worked so hard. It wasn't just his relationship
with Ysabel, of course. There were all those girls, all those beautiful
blond girls who had mysteriously been murdered. There were six in
all and every one of them worked in the museum. He knew them all
and he knew they had all been murdered in exactly the same way
Ysabel had just been murdered. *Got to stop thinking. Got to forget
this, got to put it aside.* Jack felt a pleasant numbness overtaking
him. He sat absolutely still and let the codeine devour his
consciousness.

#

Dr. Mendoza was the only pathologist in Chiclayo. In addition, he had a busy general practice. On Tuesdays, Wednesdays and Fridays he held a clinic, assisted by four nurses. It often seemed as if he saw half the poor population on those three days. They paid with chickens, vegetables, grains, and bread as often as they paid with money. But he enjoyed his work, and until recently, his life in Chiclayo had been leisurely. The people he tended suffered mostly from cuts, minor construction injuries, snakebites, and old age. But in recent days, his skills had been tested, skills he had almost forgotten he had.

First, he had been called on to examine the putrid decapitated body of the *huaca.* Next, he had to perform an autopsy on the woman. Not that these were the only murders ever committed in Chiclayo. There were others, but they were different. The usual murder was by knife and the result of a drunken brawl. Now and again he would see a gunshot wound. These were unusual. They had been absolutely intentional and utterly brutal. They unnerved him.

Dr. Mendoza, coffee-cup in hand, headed down the hall to his cold room. Today, he would bag the body of Myra Rojas and pack it in dry ice for transport to Lima where a more sophisticated autopsy could be performed. For some reason he did not understand, Toro had ordered a complete identification check. Toro was an odd fellow, not the kind of policeman who usually worked in a place like this. He had big city credentials, and he acted as if Chiclayo were the crime capital of the world.

Mendoza opened the door of the cold room and flicked on the light. Even his years of medical experience did not prepare him for the sight he stared at uncomprehendingly.

The body of Myra Rojas was still on the table where he had examined it. But someone had broken in! The room was covered with congealed blood and her body had been horribly mutilated!

Mendoza crossed himself and warily circled the table. Her teeth had been knocked out with some tool, probably a hammer. Some

88

were on the floor and floated like pearls in the pools of dark blood. Most seemed to be missing. And her hands! They had been cut off! Stranger yet, they were nowhere to be seen.

Mendoza leaned against the wall in a semi daze. *Who did this terrible thing?* It was evil, pure evil. He thought of the decapitated *huaca* again. Perhaps there was some sort of devil cult in the area. This was all very unnatural. He staggered out of the room slamming the door behind him. Toro would not like this at all.

CHAPTER FIVE

In the distance visible waves of heat drifted like spirits above the asphalt. Jonathan Henley and Captain Raoul Toro were on their way from Chiclayo to the ancient city of Sipán, where Henley's *caseta* was located. They drove in silence, both lost in thought.

Captain Raoul Toro was thirty-five years old, of moderate height, had dark observant eyes and a swarthy complexion. He was not one of those Peruvians descended from the Castillian conquerors nor were his ancestors of European or Asian stock. His father was of mixed heritage, a Mestizo, while his mother was a pure blooded Quechua. He was, by objective standards, quite a handsome man. He was also a man of many secrets, an intuitive man, a good judge of character, a man of great loyalty, and a devout catholic. The bear facts of his life were on his official record but there were many things about Raoul Toro that did not appear on any record.

Many Peruvians who sprang from families of native heritage were dirt poor but Raoul Toro was born into a family clinging to the jagged edge of the middle class in a country that had almost no middle class. As a child, his father was orphaned by an earthquake, taken in by the church, and eventually trained as a teacher. His mother was a talented weaver. After he was born, his mother became extremely ill and as a result of her illness, she was barren. Both parents dedicated themselves to their only son and were rewarded by Raoul's intelligence and ambition.

Raoul studied hard and won a scholarship to a preparatory school and then to a training college. When he graduated, he entered seminary, but he was only there a year. His mentor counseled him to leave the seminary and suggested that he apply to the federal police force. There, he proved himself more than able. After two years, Raoul applied to be among those sent to Washington for further education and training. The Bishop of Lima, Father Hernandez, for whom Raoul had served as alter boy for many years, stepped forward and personally recommended him. Raoul Toro was among those chosen. He spent more than four years in the United States studying.

The Federal government of Peru well knew the value of the discoveries in Sipán. They foresaw trouble and they placed him in Chiclayo to provide law enforcement leadership.

If asked, at this moment, Raoul Toro would have said that things had already grown more complicated than he had ever anticipated they would be. Nothing in his training had prepared him for the strange occurrences of the past few days. Frankly, he did not know what to make of it all. He had, however, made certain judgements. He had decided that Jonathan Henley was a man caught in the middle and did not seem to know why he was at the center of the hurricane. He was also certain that Henley's daughter was innocent of any involvement, and the reporter had checked out. His passport, visa and press credentials were in order. About everyone else, Captain Raoul Toro had grave suspicions. Herr Ehrlich, the hotelkeeper, was always lurking about, as was his newly hired assistant Filipe. Dr. Mendoza was forever asking questions, and the recently arrived Jack Marsden irritated him for reasons he could not yet define. The murdered grave robber and woman obviously knew something or were thought to have something that someone else wanted.

"You're quiet," Jonathan Henley commented as the Jeep bumped over the road.

"Just thinking."

"None of this makes much sense does it?"

"It makes sense to someone. I think there is an antiquity of great value. Someone thought the grave robber had it, now that same someone thinks you have it. Can you think of what it might be? I'm stymied. Whatever it was they were looking for, it was something more valuable than what was left behind and what was left behind was a worth a small fortune."

Toro's conclusion was the same as his own, the same as Myra's. He had not told Toro about all of his conversations with Myra.

"Can you think of anything, anything at all? If we just had some idea of what the killer or killers are after it would be a big help."

"It boggles the imagination. Hard to conceive what could be more valuable than what was there. Maybe it's a map to some undiscovered find, something tremendous."

Toro didn't respond.

"Or maybe the guy who wrote *Chariots of the Gods* was right. Maybe it's something that explains the ancient mysteries," Jonathan meant his comment to be humorous. He was surprised when Toro turned toward him sharply and in his peripheral vision, he saw Toro's dark eyes flash.

"There can be no such thing."

"I was joking. That's the stuff of fiction, not of science."

"My mother's people have stories about such things. Those stories are black superstition. They're anti-Christian."

Toro's tone was flat, not angry but definitely controlled.

To Jonathan, it seemed clear that Toro had discarded the beliefs of his ancestors with a vengeance. A voice prompted by past experiences cautioned Jonathan not to pursue Toro's comment. He thought back to a truly turbulent period. During much of the 1970s he had worked in Bolivia. There, and in most of Latin America, the church had been at war with itself. Liberation Theology was championed by the Jesuits, who supported communes and land reform, while the status quo, was upheld by organizations such as the Opus Dei. Hundreds of priests and nuns were murdered, the most notable of whom was Bishop Romero of El Salvador. Even now, Jonathan could hear the Bishops voice when asked if the death threats against him had come from within the Vatican. He had replied, "There is the Vatican and then there is The Vatican." A few days later he was assassinated while performing a High Mass just as he lifted the Chalice. It was a classic religious assassination.

Bolivia, as it turned out, was a hot bed of activity. A few years later, Klaus Barbie, a German war criminal living in Bolivia, was captured and returned to France. It turned out that during his years in Bolivia he was involved with a secret, ultra conservative Catholic organization called the *Fiancées of Death*. They were the specific group blamed by many for the Bishop's murder. Barbie himself had been smuggled out of Europe by Croatian Priests and U.S. Counter Intelligence then headed by Wild Bill Donovan, who was generally thought to be a member of *Opus Dei*. The war within the church now appeared over, but paranoia remained. Toro's reaction to folklore, made Jonathan feel that Toro was no doubt a bit reactionary. Still, Toro was interesting and he decided he wanted to learn more about him.

"Is your mother Quechua?"

"Yes. My father was part European and part Aymara. That makes me a little bit of everything."

Both the Aymara and the Quechua had legends adopted by New Age types. But in his own experience Jonathan had found nothing to substantiate that such stories had any basis in fact. In his opinion, giving credit to aliens from outer space shortchanged the ingenuity of peoples like the Moche and the Incas. He agreed with Toro that the stories were stories and nothing more but his own reasons for rejecting the folklore had nothing to do with religion. He considered the stories entertaining. Clearly Toro thought them blasphemous.

Toro lifted his hat and with a red handkerchief he took from his pocket, he wiped around his forehead under the sweatband. "One thing I think we can be sure of, whatever it is we're looking for, the person or persons seeking it, knows exactly what they're looking for."

"I daresay. That puts them at a distinct advantage."

Jonathan turned onto the side road and then stopped in front of his house. "Home sweet home."

They climbed out of the Jeep and Jonathan opened the front door. "Jeez," he breathed. "What a hell of a mess!"

Toro shook his head. "A mess indeed."

"Why all the books?" Jonathan asked out loud. The upended, open books were the first things he noticed. Every single book on his shelves had been pulled out and was on the floor. Automatically, he bent over and began picking them up. His books were large and filled with colored illustrations. They were expensive archeology books and art books and it physically pained him to see them scattered about in a way which could damage their spines.

"They're certainly not looking for a book among Moche ruins. But it might be logical to suggest that whatever it is that is being sought, it is about the size of one of those books and might easily be hidden on your book shelf, or perhaps in a book," Toro observed.

"Most of the books aren't open. I'd say your first guess is right. It's as if someone checked to make sure all the books were books."

"Yes. Perhaps what we're looking for is a box that's the size of a book. Something, if placed on a shelf would not be obvious."

Toro moved away from the bookshelf and began to look around the house. "They seemed to have searched the whole house pretty thoroughly," he called from the other room.

"I guess it's safe to stay here, then."

Toro rejoined Henley. "I know it's an imposition, but for awhile, I think it might be safer if you and your daughter stayed at the hotel. After what happened last night, I'm more concerned about the trip back and forth from town than I am about your being out here."

"You're right. Sure, we'll stay in the hotel." He had no intention of exposing Corrie to more danger. He stuffed his hands in his pockets, "Just give me a few minutes to pick up some clothes and my notes."

"Take your time," Toro said sitting down. He glanced at his watch. It was nearly eleven. Not even noon and he felt tired already.

#

"It's not much of a town," Corrie said as she and Jeff sat down on a bench facing the familiar fountain in the center of the park. If she counted all the towns in Hispanic America with town squares and three tiered fountains like this one, it would take her a lifetime.

"Believe it or not, Chiclayo's an improvement over Lima."

"I've been to Lima, you don't have to convince me. Why on earth did you decide to stay there?"

"Lot's of reasons. I find the situation in Peru interesting. The country's fascinating. Lima is my jumping off place. Besides, there's a Dojo there."

"I presume that means you're still practicing Aikido."

"Yes. There's a Japanese Sensei at the Lima Dojo. I've made lots of contacts in the Japanese community."

"And what brought you up here?"

Jeff laughed gently, "A hot tip from a confidential source."

"About the murders?"

"Yes. I confess I might not have come if Jonathan Henley weren't your father. I relived our summer together in my mind. I wanted to talk to your father, find out if you were married, and find out where you were. I didn't expect you to be here. Corrie, what happened to us?" He leaned over toward her.

"Time and distance," she answered.

"That guy, that Marsden fellow, you and he aren't – well, a couple?"

"No, we are most certainly not a couple."

"Good."

She raised a quizzical brow, "Why?"

"I don't know. I didn't like him much. Of course I would dislike him more if you two were attached in some way."

She reached over and touched his hand, "Rest assured we are not. Except that he's my boss."

"Too bad. I think he's a slime ball."

"Oh, that's a definite opinion considering you just met."

"I admit it. I'm a snap judge of character."

"Keep it a secret, I agree with you."

"If you really feel that way it must be difficult working for him."

"As soon as this is over and I'm home, I'll change jobs."

"That bad?"

"Not yet, but I think it might get worse."

Jeff lifted one brow; "He's got the hots for you, hasn't he?"

"That's a colorful way to put it. But I guess it's accurate. I rather suspect he has the 'hots' for lots of women. You know, if it's possible to take advantage, I think he would."

"He tried to take advantage of you?"

"He made a pass and I rejected him. So far he hasn't made another. That's not a case for sexual harassment."

"Still, if you feel you have to quit your job, the effect is the same."

"No. I won't be quitting entirely because of Jack. It's more that just being here makes me realize how much I miss fieldwork. I've never asked my father to help with my career, but it's different now. I know I'm qualified. I imagine he can keep me busy."

Jeff reached over and covered her hand with his. She didn't pull her hand away. "We're making small talk," he said looking into the depths of her eyes. "Corrie, I know we can't take up where we left off, but I'd sure as hell like to start over."

Corrie turned her hand and squeezed his. Jeff was sometimes a little cynical – probably as a result of his profession and his experiences. But he was honest, and he was easy to be with because he was a known quantity. She wondered how on earth she had let him slip away the first time. "Not *all* over, I hope," she said in a near whisper.

Jeff leaned over and brushed her lips with his. They were sweet and soft. This was hardly the time nor place for a full embrace, but God he did want to hold her. "I'm not going away this time," he said into her ear.

"Nor I," she replied. They looked into one another's eyes for a second. She felt the electricity between them and though they had just agreed that they could not take up where they left off, it seemed they would.

#

The noonday sun beat down mercilessly. Unconsciously, Jonathan ran his tongue over his dry lips. "I'm glad to be staying in town for awhile." He turned his Jeep onto the main street. "It was lonely out there without Myra."

"I'm afraid we'll have to stop by my office so you can sign the report on the break and enter at your *caseta.*"

"Sure. It's way too late to reconsider and go to Lambayeque today." As close as he and Captain Toro seemed to be getting, there was always the required paperwork.

He pulled to a halt in front of the police station and followed Toro inside. To his surprise, Dr. Mendoza was sitting outside Toro's office. He was an unearthly pale and looked shaken.

Toro sensed it too. His first words were, "¿Que pasa?"

"Something horrible has happened," Mendoza muttered hoarsely. His gravelly voice did not mellow even when he tried to speak softly.

Toro touched Mendoza's shoulder to silence him. Then he motioned them both into the office. He closed the door. He slipped

97

behind his messy desk and looked up. His expression as much as said, 'now you can go ahead.'

"It's that woman," Mendoza said slowly. "I went into the cold room this morning and found it had been broken into. Someone – mutilated her body."

Henley felt ill. He forced himself to sit down, to push the mental pictures, which filled his mind to go away. Still, he felt ill. *Why would anyone mutilate her body?*

"Mutilated? How?"

"*Más terrible.* Someone cut off her hands and pulled out her teeth."

"*Madre de Dios,*" Toro said, crossing himself.

"Why the hell would anyone do that?" Jonathan's angry thoughts burst forth. It wasn't bad enough that she had been murdered. This was truly barbaric.

"Hands and teeth – I imagine so she could not be identified by her fingerprints or dental records."

"I've already identified her," Jonathan said.

"You told me who you thought she was. Maybe she was not the person she claimed to be, or more accurately, perhaps she did not tell you who she really was."

Jonathan slumped into the straight-backed chair and shook his head, "I suppose that's possible."

"It's the only reasonable answer," Toro concluded. Had he been alone he might have smiled. Someone was going to be very upset. He had already taken Myra Rojas' fingerprints as well as her dental impressions. The fingerprints had been faxed to Lima and to Interpol as well as to the FBI. He would now send the dental impressions on as well. It seemed clear to him that someone did not want her true identity known and that the dead woman's real name was not Myra Rojas. This mutilation, in spite of how horrible it was, came too late. It might, in fact, be the first real break in this case.

Toro looked at Henley and could see he was upset. Still, he had no intention of sharing the fact that he had already taken prints and impressions from the woman. But as soon as he was back in his office, he intended to fax both Interpol and the FBI and ask them to put a rush on his original request. No, he wouldn't tell Henley or Mendoza anything just now. He might, after all, be wrong about them. He turned to Dr. Mendoza. "Bag the body and we'll send it to Lima in the morning."

Mendoza nodded. "I'll be glad to get her out of my office."

"It's a start," Toro replied. "Come along, doctor, I think you need a drink."

#

Jason Conway sat in his study, the lights off, and the drapes opened. Outside it was snowing, and he felt as if he were trapped in one of those cheap glass paperweights.

Jason Conway contemplated his modest existence. Most men in his position would have built a mansion or even several mansions. Certainly many, who had far less money maintained homes on both coasts as well as one in a resort area like Palm Beach or Palm Springs. Bill Gates had built a modern castle filled with electronic wizardry complete with his own salmon run, outside Seattle. Forbes had a mansion too, though his real passion was politics. He poured millions into being his own most ardent supporter. No, none of that was for him. He was the only man with as much money as Bill Gates and he chose to live alone in a penthouse on the top floor of a skyscraper in Boston. His only other real estate was a three room, truly rustic cabin in Montana. The cabin was a retreat, a place few people knew about, and a place where he could go to think. He kept out of the public eye. He smiled at the thought that some newspapers compared him to Howard Hughes, proclaiming him to be a recluse. Hughes, however, eschewed public life and public   places because of strange compulsive beliefs that caused a neurotic fear of germs. I go out often, he thought. Quite safe since no one recognizes me. His most steadfast rule was never to allow himself to be photographed. He thought himself compulsive about a few minor matters, but in general he knew he was no Howard Hughes. Rather, he was a man who used his considerable resources on his most ardent interests in life. One of those interests was in protecting his privacy in a culture where celebrity gossip had reached the state of an art form, and publications dared not go more than a short time without a celebrity feature. The public's hunger for the private details of the lives of others made him sick. It was the thing he hated most about the Twentieth Century. The second thing he hated was the tendency to surround oneself with material possessions. "A grave misunderstanding," he grumbled as he sipped his scotch. "Too many people equate possessions with power."

As he saw it, if you lived in a place that satisfied your every need, you had no incentive to leave and thus, bottled yourself up. Ultimately you lost your edge as a big time player. In short, if you were satisfied with being a king, you didn't need to become emperor. If you were satisfied with being an emperor, you would have no need to be a god. The key to achieving ultimate potency was never to be satisfied. You had to focus on the fact that you were never fulfilled, that you could never really have enough power.

This was, of course, America. Every rich man was expected to give something back, to donate to charity, to leave a legacy. Carnegie left libraries, the Rockefellers left art museums, and Hearst had left the ultimate symbol of his personal power neurosis; a most magnificent, if completely tasteless, castle for tourists to wander through and gawk at.

Jason Conway did not disagree with giving, but he gave most generously to that which he hoped would help him achieve his ultimate goal. He had built the Conway Archaeological Museum from the ground up and funded its field workers in more than ten locations. The truth was, he was now only personally concerned with one location, but his apparent fascination with archeology worldwide, masked his special interest in Sipán. Toward the maintenance of this façade, he funded not only the Conway Museum but also many museums around the world. The fewer people focused on Sipán, the better. As it was, recent events in Sipán indicated that someone did suspect it held secrets well beyond its ancient artifacts. Indeed, he was certain he knew who the someone was. This troubled him, but did not surprise him. He was a man who knew his enemies.

If Jason Conway was surprised by anything, it was that Jonathan Henley had not yet begun to ask the vital questions. But then, Henley was a scientist and science often rejected the obvious. To understand, to accept the existence and meaning of the treasure, a man had to have knowledge and imagination in equal parts.

Jason Conway went to the window, closing the drapes and plunging the room into total darkness. As he did often, he pushed a button by his desk and the screen on the wall lit up. In a moment, the image of a wooden tablet covered it. He stared at the markings on it, feeling almost mesmerized by the power he knew it possessed. The tablet was covered with incised signs placed in boustrophedon script. Many linguists had studied the fragments that had been found on Easter Island but none had succeeded in translating it. He was the only one who knew the fragments, were, in actuality, copies of a small portion of this tablet. He had removed the original tablet from the Island and secretly kept it. Moreover, he knew there were other tablets and that together they formed a whole.

He turned, distracted from the image on the wall, by the sound of his fax machine. He walked over to it and in a moment tore off the message.

So, Captain Toro wants Interpol and the FBI to rush. Well, he wanted them to rush too. The sooner he knew the true identity of this Myra Rojas, the better. But clearly someone else did not want her identified. He could have employed his own people to investigate

101

her, but it seemed Toro was doing just fine. In any case, it was a simple matter to monitor Toro's fax line. Doing so kept him informed on a range of activities in the area.

He turned back toward the image on the screen. In all the years that he had been seeking the other tablets he had only made one error in judgement. He had shown his tablet to one other person, and that person almost immediately knew what it was.

A buzzer sounded and Jason clicked the image off. "Come in," he called out to his only servant, Martin.

"Sir, you have a call from that German fellow."

Jason nodded. 'That German fellow' as Martin always called him, had only one number and that was to the special phone in the bedroom. "I'll get it," he said, waving Martin away. If Katsura, his personal assistant had been about, he would have let her take this call. Katsura was quite breathtaking, and ever so much more patient than was he.

#

Jack woke up at the sound of his wristwatch alarm. He sat up and pressed the light button on his watch. It was 2 a.m. He got out of bed and switched on the light, and again looked with loathing at his briefcase. He had to rid himself of its contents now before it was too late, before it began to smell.

He hated looking at its contents again. He hated the thought of what he had to do. But there was really no alternative.

He dressed quickly choosing to wear his jeans and a sweatshirt rather than his khakis. He reasoned that the darker and more casual his clothing, the less conspicuous he would be. He looked back at his briefcase. He couldn't throw it away. Someone might find it and perhaps it could be traced to him. Worse yet, as he had the briefcase when he checked in, how could he explain loosing it? He shook his head in dismay and trying not to really look he opened it. Inside, the clear plastic bag he had found in the doctor's office, was filled with dark congealed blood through which he could see the black fingers attached to black hands. Floating about were the hard pearl-like teeth. Miraculously, the seal had not broken. He looked about frantically, then ran to the bed and pulled the pillow out of its case. He popped the plastic bag into the pillowcase together with the knife and bloody pliers he had used. He had already wiped his fingerprints off both. He looked back at the bed. How would he explain where the pillowcase had gone? He couldn't, but he could claim he only had one pillow to start with. He returned to the bed and folded the pillow, then stuffed it too into the case.

He put his keys in his pocket and opened his door quietly. He tiptoed down the dimly lit corridor, down the back staircase and away into the night. The river was not far.

#

"Did you sleep well," Jonathan asked.

"I did. It must be the air," Corrie answered.

Jonathan checked his watch. "I wonder where Jack is. I want to get an early start. Even though it's a short drive, it's damn hot on the desert by noon."

"Good idea. Jeff's coming too."

"I meant to ask you about him."

Corrie wondered if she blushed, "We're old friends. As I told you, I met him in New Mexico."

"I'm your father and I sense something else, or perhaps I should say something more."

She put down the spoon with which she had been eating her melon and looked her father in the eye. "Once upon a time there was more. We just lost track of one another. But I will tell you I think we're both glad to see each other again. That's it. End of story. We'll both just have to wait and see."

Jonathan looked away. "I didn't mean to pry. Anyway, he seems like a nice guy."

Corrie looked more seriously at her father. "He's a good man, dad. I'm glad he's here."

Jonathan looked back up into her face. There were words unspoken, questions unasked. "You didn't ask me about Myra," he hedged.

It was Corrie's turn to look away. "I didn't have to ask."

"I can't make love to a memory," he said, knowing he had said it to her before.

"I might want you to, but I don't expect you to."

He wanted her to say she understood, but she did not. He imagined she had gone as far as she could and for that he was grateful.

Jonathan finished his melon in silence. "I see your Jeff coming now. Look, I'm going upstairs and urge Jack along."

As he left the dining room, he waved at Jeff.

"Morning," Jeff bent down and kissed her lightly on the cheek.

Corrie glanced around guiltily, "Please, not in public."

"Sorry. Just grateful to catch you alone."

"It won't last long. Dad just went upstairs to fetch Jack."

"Yeah, it's a good idea to get started and cross the desert before noon."

"Just what dad said."

"You know what? I've got a hell of a desire to take you up to Cuzco. The place fascinates me and I'd sure like to be there with my own archeologist."

"I haven't been there since I was a teenager. I'll see if I can get away for a few days."

"It's well named."

"It is indeed." In Quechua 'Cuzco' meant navel, and it was indeed a navel. A long narrow valley surrounded by the world's tallest mountains. It had once been the capital of the huge Inca Empire.

"Oh, here comes dad. Let's keep this plan to ourselves for just now."

"Sure."

"Where's Jack?" Corrie asked.

"Damndest thing. I knocked and knocked. Then I got the maid to open the door. Jack wasn't there."

"Maybe he went out to breakfast elsewhere," Jeff suggested.

"No, he wouldn't have done that," Corrie said. "He could have gone for a walk."

"The hell with him," Jonathan said, under his breath but still quite audibly. "I told him to be here at nine and it's nearly ten. I'll tell Ehrlich to tell Jack we've left and that he can follow in his car. It'll be less crowded anyway."

"And piles more fun," Jeff said mischievously. He sensed Henley's dislike for Jack Marsden. "I'll just take these rolls with me, and I think we should take some extra cartons of juice."

"Already have them," Corrie said breezily.

Jeff winked at Henley, "I like a woman who thinks of everything."

In no time they were headed north on the Pan American Highway, across the arid desert. The ocean was on one side of the road while on the other side the foothills rose gently toward the Altiplano and the Andes. Remarkable irrigation systems turned the valley into a rich agricultural area where rice, sugarcane, cotton, corn and fruit grew. They talked casually comparing the area to California's Imperial Valley. They passed white washed churches and water towers that rose to meet a blue sky. Now and again they passed a wealthy walled-in hacienda surrounded by farmland. The contrast between rich and poor was palpable in this ancient land of the Moche.

"So much trouble. Conquerors, revolutions, poverty and natures most violent offerings – earthquakes, volcanoes, hurricanes – still, it's a pretty intriguing place," Jeff concluded.

"This land is washed in blood." Corrie was looking out the window, she sounded far away and he knew she was thinking about the history of the place.

#

Captain Raoul Toro hated the smell of this room. "Shit," he said loudly. Then he repeated it and stomped his booted foot on the floor.

"It's an epidemic," Dr. Mendoza concluded. "It used to be that all the murders in Chiclayo were the result of fights between drunks but this is different."

"I'll say it's different." He stared hard at the body of Jack Marsden. He'd been garroted like Myra. But that was not the most interesting aspect of his murder. In his right hand he clutched a pillowcase, which they had to pry loose because rigor mortis had already set in. Its contents were gruesome. It contained Myra's hands and teeth as well as a squished up pillow, a pair of pliers and a knife.

"He must have been the one to mutilate the woman," Mendoza concluded.

Toro shrugged. "Maybe." He hated drawing the obvious conclusion. Anyway, it didn't explain who killed Marsden.

"He wasn't murdered in the hotel," Mendoza announced with authority. "His body wasn't dragged. There's every indication he was killed right where he was found, on the bridge over the river."

"Probably trying to throw the pillow case into the water."

"He wasn't robbed either. His wallet had over $300. U.S. dollars and a lot of *nuevo sols* as well."

Toro did not say that Marsden's murder was related to the other murders, though clearly it was. Mendoza wasn't stupid. In fact, for a small town doctor he seemed rather smarter than might be expected. "It will all come together," he said feeling slightly less confident than he sounded. "I'll tell Henley when he returns," Toro added.

Mendoza abstractedly rubbed his forehead. This whole thing was giving him a headache.

#

Ramon Garcia drove rapidly South on the Pan American Highway toward Lima. It was a long drive and he knew he would be compelled to stop and spend at least one night in a hotel on his journey. It was also a long and out of the way journey back to his headquarters in Ecuador. He was, in fact, headed in the wrong direction. *Stupid Peruvians and Ecuadorians!* He might have driven directly home, but the border crossing was difficult because it was a hostile border. Ecuador had never accepted its borders with Peru. Many believed the bad blood between the two nations had begun as far back as the fifteen hundreds when the two Inca half brothers, Huascar who ruled from Quito, and Atahuallpa who ruled from Cuzco, fought over which one of them was the supreme Inca. Atahuallpa prevailed, forever making Peru the stronger of the two. Ramon sneered, like the sons of Abraham, these people too were victims of history. Still, it was a bother to have to travel so circuitous a route. Not that it was impossible to make a crossing; it was just that it involved an incredible amount of paperwork. He did not want the record of his excursion into Peru to exist. Yes, it was far better to drive back to Lima and then to take a plane to a third country, and then fly back to Ecuador.

He narrowed his eyes and concentrated on the road. He felt much better today than he had felt yesterday. Doubtless he would feel even better tomorrow. The voices had gone away; indeed it was as if they had never been there at all. All rationality had returned and thoughts of the girl, of Ysabel, and of Jack Marsden receded to the dark edges of his mind. His full concentration was now on the task at hand. He felt absolutely certain he would be successful because he was destined to rule.

CHAPTER SIX

Iron bars covered the opaque glass windows of the squat sandstone building on the main street of Lambayeque. The building was heavily guarded since it temporarily held the treasure found in the caves beneath the grave robber's house.

"Looks like a jail in a small western town," Jeff commented as they were admitted through heavy doors. The building had few windows and the architecture lacked imagination.

"Good guess. It used to be a jail," Jonathan confirmed. "The cells have been turned into vaults where precious artifacts are held until they have been sorted through and catalogued. The building next door belongs to the army, so there is no shortage of guards and security is maximum."

The corridor was narrow and they walked single file with Jonathan leading the way and Jeff bringing up the rear. He liked walking behind Corrie. She moved with an enticing swing emphasized by her khaki skirt and brown T-shirt. Her mane of blond hair was pulled up in a ponytail and tied with a multi-colored scarf. It too moved from side to side. Her walk was indicative of her whole personality; bouncy, and full of energy. He had always found her energy exceedingly attractive; it drew him like a magnet. She was enthusiastic about almost everything. When she talked, she used her hands, her facial expressions were animated and her eyes danced. Almost immediately he had decided she must take after her mother. Her father seemed a nice guy but he was calm, deliberate and apparently reserved. Not that he knew Jonathan Henley that well. A morning spent in the back seat of a Jeep was not the best way to get acquainted.

"This way," Henley said, beckoning them through double glass doors and down another long corridor at the end of which were more double doors. Henley pushed the doors open and they entered a smaller a room. An armed Peruvian guard sat behind a desk in front of a steel vault door. He put down the magazine he was reading, and then quickly scrambled to his feet.

"*Señor* Henley! *Esta es una sorpresa!*"

"I'm sorry, Luis. I should have phoned. Luis, this is my daughter, Corrie, and her friend, Jeff Richards. "We've come to examine the artifacts I had deposited." The guard stood up and whirling about began to spin the lock. When he was done, he pulled open the heavy door.

"This way," Henley gestured. Then he turned back to the guard, "Luis, we're expecting a fellow named, Jack Marsden. When he arrives direct him to us, but ask for I.D."

"Si," the guard replied.

Jonathan led them past the vault door into another corridor off which there were many small rooms. They entered one and as soon as Jonathan Henley turned on the light, Jeff whistled through his teeth. The shelves were lined with priceless artifacts, each one tagged and numbered.

"Hard to believe the murderer was looking for something even more valuable than what's here," Jeff said.

"You are one of many to make just that observation. It's the crux of the matter, and if we knew the answer we might know why Myra and the grave robber were killed," Henley said.

"It's strange that Jack isn't here yet." Corrie looked at her watch. "I sort of assumed he would be right behind us."

"Jack is not always the world's most reliable person. I suggest you look around here, and then we can go for some lunch. If Jack hasn't turned up by the time we finish, well, the hell with him. We'll go back to Sipán and he can come up here alone."

"Sounds good." Corrie turned to the far shelf. Ignoring the bejeweled gold pieces, she picked up a large pottery bowl. "It's in remarkably good condition. "What's this woman looking at?"

Jonathan came over and took the piece of pottery from Corrie. He stared at it and shook his head. "A picture, I suppose."

"But it looks as if she's reading," Corrie said slowly. "Didn't you tell me that the person who broke into your house went through all the books?"

"Yes," he answered slowly. A vision of the room filled his mind – "Do you suppose they were looking for a picture of some sort?"

"Suppose there were something that could be read? Wouldn't it be pretty valuable?" Jeff asked.

"I'll say," Corrie breathed. "We'd all have to re-think a whole period and a ton of academic research."

"It can't be," Henley shook his head and returned his eyes to the pottery bowl. "No, the lady must be examining a picture.

Probably a pictograph." Carefully, he replaced the bowl.

"This Jaguar, or whatever kind of cat this is, is really beautiful." Jeff picked up the cat and turned it slowly in his hands.

"It's eyes are made of Lapis." Corrie leaned over and touched it. "This is the sort of thing that most grave robbers are after."

"When you've finished in here, there's another room," Jonathan told them.

"Was all this in one chamber?" Jeff asked.

"Three chambers," Jonathan replied. "There's one more shipment to be sent up here."

"I'm going to look in the other room," Corrie announced.

They lapsed into silence, as they examined the treasure.

Corrie left them and stood for a moment looking at the totality of the treasure in the second room. She picked up a second piece of pottery and ran her fingers over it, even as her lips parted slightly.

The design on the oval pot depicted a man of regal bearing dressed as a giant bird sitting on a throne. At his foot lay a square something – what? A chill consumed her. The pot clearly depicted the vision she had seen on Easter Island.

Impossible. I'm being dramatic. My visions are not reality they're just the result of my over active imagination.

Corrie held the bowl, then sat it down on the bench. Fanciful thoughts warred with logic, while legends challenged facts, and finally she cast it all away. She vowed she would never tell a soul what crazy thoughts and sights had filled her mind in the few moments that she held the pot, or indeed during those few moments on Easter Island a few years ago. *Well, maybe she would tell someone. The right someone.*

Jeff paused in the doorway and watched Corrie. She was holding a piece of pottery and staring at it intently – no, not just intently, it was more complicated than that. She was utterly and completely lost. She was totally unaware of his presence just a few feet away. It was as if her mind had been transported elsewhere and her body left behind. She was quite simply in a trance. He continued to watch as her expression changed. Suddenly she was back from her mental journey. She looked up, surprised to see him.

"How long have you been there?"

"A few minutes. You were totally absorbed." He tried to sound light hearted even though he wanted to ask her what she had been thinking about.

"I was. Sorry, call it a professional hazard."

She wasn't going to explain. At least not right now and he decided not to ask.

Jonathan opened the door and looked in on them. "It's been over an hour, what about some lunch and something to drink. I think we've waited long enough for Jack."

Corrie turned her eyes toward her father. When he mentioned Jack, the tone in her father's voice revealed his irritation.

"Where do you suggest?" Jeff stuffed his notes into his backpack.

"Is that little place near the bank still there?" Corrie asked.

"It is," Jonathan replied. "By heaven, you do have a good memory. It's been a couple of years since you were last here."

"I never forget a good restaurant," Corrie joked as they headed off.

Jeff watched Corrie thoughtfully. She was open and forthright but she also had a mysterious facet to her personality. Still, he felt certain that if he asked her about the pottery she had been studying so intently, she would confide her thoughts. He decided to wait until they were alone though he wasn't entirely sure why.

The drive back revealed a spectacular landscape of the sort that would be classified as a bad painting had it been a work of art. The sun illuminated the hills and valleys of the undulating sand dunes. The wind had shaped them into mounds that cut like half moons across the treeless, barren panorama.

"It's really odd that Jack didn't turn up," Corrie said. "He was the one so anxious to see the artifacts."

"Jack's an odd duck," Jonathan observed as they approached the outskirts of Sipán. "I've always felt he has two distinct personalities. One is the surface Jack and the other is a Jack that's always hidden."

"He seems a bit robotic," Jeff put in.

"A somewhat lustful robot," Corrie added.

Jonathan scowled, "Did he make a move on you?"

"Make a move on me? I wonder how many fathers would use that terminology."

"Well did he? Robotic or not, Jack Marsden has a reputation of being a ladies man."

"I suppose it takes one to know one," Corrie retorted.

In spite of the light banter, Jeff heard the edge in Corrie's voice. It was not the first time he sensed a strain between father and daughter, now he realized it had to do with women.

"I let Jack know I wasn't interested. That was the end of it."

"Jack doesn't like, 'no.'" Jonathan ignored her 'takes one to know one,' comment.

"Well, he hasn't made a second pass. In fact, ever since we got here he's seemed abnormally distracted. Not that the murders aren't shocking, but still it's not like he knew either of the victims."

"That we know of," Jeff said from the back seat. What was going on here was hardly common, especially among those who lived in the rarified world of academe. Had he been covering a drug smuggling ring, then murder would not have been unusual but there were apparently no drugs involved here, just works of ancient art. They were valuable to be sure, but the gold and jewels of the Moche were all under lock and key. What was it the murderer or murderers wanted?

Jeff was still ruminating when Jonathan Henley pulled up in front of the hotel. They all clamored out of the jeep and headed inside. Captain Toro was waiting in the lobby.

"We were expecting Jack," Henley said, shaking hands with Toro.

Toro's expression clouded, "He's dead, murdered."

"My God," Corrie whispered. Instinctively, she leaned against Jeff.

"Corrie, I want you to go home." Jonathan Henley said, seriously.

"If someone wants to kill me they can do it here or in Boston. I am not going home and that's final."

Jonathan looked at her for a long moment. He knew his daughter too well to argue. And of course she was right. She would be just as vulnerable in Boston.

"I wish you'd reconsider," Jeff said.

"Well, I won't. I'm staying here till we find out what's happening." She turned to Captain Toro, "How was he killed?"

"He was strangled, like the woman. But there is more. Come into the dining room and sit down. I'll tell you what I've learned. In any case, I have a few questions."

They all followed and sat down. In seconds Herr Ehrlich was there to take their orders.

Jonathan ordered a double scotch, Corrie had juice and Jeff had a beer with Captain Toro.

"Why would anyone kill Jack?" Corrie asked, for everyone. "He just got here, what could he possibly have to do with any of this?"

"Perhaps quite a lot," Captain Toro offered. "Probably more than any of you imagine."

Toro took a sip of his beer, licked the foam off his thick dark moustache, and continued.

"Let me start with Myra Rojas. She's been positively identified from fingerprints and dental records as one Ysabel Ramirez. For many years she's been involved in the theft and sale of protected artifacts."

"Shit," Jonathan hissed. He looked down into his drink. He could all but hear Corrie thinking, 'I told you not to get involved with that kind of woman.'

Toro continued in something of a business-like monotone. Clearly he was proud of his sleuthing. "When Jack Marsden was in Europe, he had a relationship with this Ysabel, and though he was never actually implicated, he may well have been involved with her illegal activity."

Jonathan Henley cursed again. He could feel his face flushing. He had not thought about his relationship with Myra at all. It had never once occurred to him that she was interested in him *only* because of his work. Not that he had been blind to her acquisitive nature. He realized now he had taken her desire for things valuable too lightly. He was waiting for Toro to say something more, to ask how much he had told Myra, maybe even to accuse him of helping her smuggle artifacts out of the country. Toro, however, simply continued with his findings.

"Myra – Ysabel, dropped out of sight for a period of two years, then she surfaced as the mistress of a wealthy Arab. A man who has been linked to international art thefts, among other crimes."

"What other crimes?" Jeff asked.

"He is under suspicion for terrorist activities."

Jeff felt his elation growing. What had begun as a type B story that might have made it into the 'arts' section of the Sunday Magazine was turning into something a hell of lot bigger. His journalistic antennae shot up. "Does this wealthy Arab have a name?"

"Karim Ali Ahmed."

"Karim Ali Ahmed." Jeff repeated. It was not an entirely unfamiliar name to him. But he knew he had seen it mentioned only in passing, largely with regard to financing. Karim wasn't well known and it seemed to Jeff that Karim had dropped out of sight for a while. At least he didn't remember reading about him recently.

"What happened to this Ysabel after her affair with Karim?" Jeff asked.

"She disappeared again and resurfaced in Lima about two months before she met Professor Henley."

"She was almost certainly mutilated in order to prevent identification, Toro added. It was a clumsy job and Jack Marsden did not know that her prints as well as a wax impression of her teeth had already been forwarded to both Interpol and the FBI."

"Jack mutilated her?" Corrie asked in shock. The mental picture that suddenly darted across her mind was sickening.

"Apparently, when he was found, her hands and teeth were with him. He was probably going to throw them in the river."

Corrie drank some of her juice and wished she had ordered something stronger. "How could Jack do such a thing?" she said in a near whisper.

"Presumably he didn't want to be linked to her," Toro said with a shrug.

Jonathan was feeling grateful that no one asked him how he could have been so stupid as to get mixed up with someone like Myra. He really didn't want to admit in front of his daughter that he was thinking with something apart from his brain. "This hardly answers all the questions, he finally said. "Jack didn't kill her – he wasn't in the country at the time, and we don't know who killed Jack."

For the moment, Jeff kept his silence. All things considered, one question loomed rather large for him in particular. Kenji's smiling face kept replaying in his mind. Was it an honest tip, or had he been sent here because he knew Corrie Henley? Someone wanted something – it was worth killing for and there appeared to be complications that went way beyond simple grave robbing.

"I'm going back to Lima for a couple of days," Jeff announced.

Corrie looked at him and as if she sensed why he wanted to go. She announced, "I'm going with you."

Glad to have her out of Sipán, Jonathan smiled. "Good idea."

Then, as if to answer Toro's unasked question, she smiled. "I didn't bring much with me to Peru. I need to do some shopping." It was a lame excuse since there was probably nothing in Lima that was not available in Chiclayo. But Toro didn't look puzzled nor did he ask any questions.

"I'll have to notify the museum of Jack's death," Jonathan said tentatively, wondering if Toro would object.

"If they want me to come back, tell them I quit," Corrie said casually. "No matter what happens, I'm going to stay down here."

Toro said nothing. They all behaved as might be expected. Their curiosity could only help him. *Dance to my music,* he thought to himself.

#

Summer - dried brittle cacti shuddered in the wake of the hot desert wind like the skeletons of gardens past. Jeff's thoughts were full of another desert, another summer wind; a place that was even hotter, where grass fires sprung up spontaneously and burned till they reached the Rio Grande.

"Where do you live?" Corrie had asked.

"In an RV," he had answered. "On Motel Road. There are a couple of good parks there, one with a great indoor pool. You have to have an indoor pool because the sun is so hot you'd turn into a piece of charcoal if you sat outside."

"And it would be like swimming in soup," she laughed.

"I think more than half the population of Deming lives in trailers or mobile homes," he added. "Well, you know. It's cheap, the climate's right. An RV is small so it doesn't cost much to air-condition."

He took her to his RV and she was amused because the park was called *The Vineyard RV Park* and the vineyard was a couple of miles away, though at least there was one.

"It's a lot more elaborate than the trailers archeologists live in when they're on sight," she said admiring his Fifth Wheel.

"Hey, I like it."

He had kissed her then and she had told him she liked the trailer too. That had been a memorable night, though not the most memorable night.

"Where do you live?" Corrie asked as if echoing his memories. The cloud of dirt and dust that so often floated above Lima came into view. The airport was on the coast, Lima was slightly inland.

Her question roused him from further nostalgic mental wanderings. "Oh, I have a little apartment in the home of a Japanese couple."

"Is it private?"

"Sure. I even have my own entrance."

"Can we stay there?"

He didn't ask what her question really meant because he hoped he knew.

"Can't think why not. It's not close to the shopping area, though."

"I don't really need to shop. That's not why I came."

He grinned, "I knew that. So, you tell me, why did you come?"

"I didn't want to argue with my father about staying in Sipán. Anyway, if someone wanted me dead, they would have killed me the night I was run off the road."

"I want you to tell me about that night."

"I will. But I didn't see the person who did it."

"So, did you only come with me to avoid an argument with your father?"

"That's part of it. Mainly I came because I know you. You have some sort of idea and you wanted to come back to Lima and check it out."

"Hmm, a woman who is both perceptive and stubborn."

"What's your idea?"

"It's not so much an idea as a curious coincidence. This fellow in my Aikido class who works at the museum said he had a tip that might lead to a story. Then he told me about the murder of the grave robber in Sipán.

"If he didn't tell you so you could get a story, why do you think he told you?"

"I think I might have been told because I know you."

"How would he know that you knew me?"

"That's my first question."

"You think the mysterious murderer wanted to use you in some way because you know me?"

"I'm not sure what I think. But I don't believe in coincidences."

"I suppose talking to him might lead to something."

"We can only try." He guided his rented car down a residential street. Finally, he pulled into the driveway of a rambling old stucco house, the front of which had a Japanese style arch over the front door. Corrie followed him through a meticulously kept side garden and around the back to a side door.

"I left in a hurry," he said by way of explanation as he opened the door.

She laughed lightly, "You never were up for neatness of the year award. I remember your trailer. It was always cluttered."

"Not dirty, just cluttered. Papers, books, you know the tools of my trade."

She tossed her pack onto the sofa. "I know."

Her smile was warm, intimate. Again memories shot through him. "That makes into a bed. Of course my bed is in the other room."

She lifted her brow, "I think maybe it's too soon."

He simply nodded. It was a rejection that offered a future liaison. He glanced at his watch. "I think we should head right down to the museum. Maybe we can catch Kenji for lunch."

"Lead on," she replied.

#

"There he is now." Jeff indicated a young Japanese making his way down the museum steps.

"Kenji!" Jeff called out.

Kenji stopped dead, and for a single second looked like a trapped animal. He glanced about furtively, as if he thought he might be watched, and then he walked toward them, his smile clearly forced. "You surprise me, Jeff san."

"I'm sure I have. Kenji, this is Corrie Henley, Corrie, this is Kenji Yamamura, my fellow Akidoist."

"I am pleased to make your acquaintance Miss Henley. Naturally as I work at the museum I am familiar with your father's work. He is a very talented man. He makes the past come alive."

"Thank you," Corrie replied.

"Going out to lunch?" Jeff asked.

Kenji nodded and again glanced around uneasily.

"Come along, Kenji. We have to talk."

Kenji did not object, he simply followed Jeff's lead. In moments the three of them were out on the crowded streets. "We'll go to the park," Jeff suggested "There's a tea house there."

Kenji simply nodded.

In a few minutes, they reached the park.

"You act as if someone is following us. What's going on? How did you know about those faxes and just why did you really tell me."

"I wanted to help you find a story."

"I'd like to believe that, but I don't."

Kenji looked down, his face ever so slightly flushed.

Whatever else he was, Kenji was not a good liar.

"Jeff san, I did not want to get you into trouble."

"Who do you work for?"

"I work for the museum. I sent you to Sipán because my sister asked me to do so. She works for Mr. Conway."

"Conway!" Corrie exclaimed. "The philanthropist? The same Conway who funds the museum?"

Kenji again nodded.

"Is that *the* Conway of Conex Systems?" Jeff asked.

"Yes," Corrie replied. "He gives a ton of money to museums and of course completely funds the Conway in Boston."

"Mr. Conway said you knew Miss Henley and suggested I tell you about the murders so you would go to Sipán. He said Miss Henley would trust you and tell you what her father knows – you would become his eyes and ears in Sipán."

"My father works for Mr. Conway. Surely he can be more direct." Corrie knew she sounded sarcastic.

"I don't pretend to understand," Kenji said looking down.

"What is it Mr. Conway is looking for? Jeff asked.

"Something – I'm not sure what. It is something the Moche had, something that was hidden."

"An artifact?" Corrie asked.

"Something special. I only know there are others that have been found in other places. My sister told me that the man who possesses all of them will be the most powerful man in the world. That he will have the power of the Gods."

"Sounds like this Conway has way too much time on his hands."

"No, Jeff san. Mr. Conway is very intelligent. He is also, how do you say it? Down to earth. I don't know what it all means, but the power of the Gods might mean many things. After all, the ancients might have considered electricity the power of the Gods."

Corrie found she was fixated on the word, 'others'. Again she thought of the tablet fragments on Easter Island. "You said there were others?"

"From other places. That's really all I know."

At the very least an artifact that tied ancient peoples together in some way would shake the foundations of contemporary academic theory. Corrie couldn't dispel her image of the birdman, the depiction on the pot, or the tablet fragment – the Rongo Rongo.

"Is that why Mr. Conway funds so many museums?" Jeff asked. "Is he trying to find more of these things –whatever they are?"

"Maybe. I only know what my sister has told me."

"I think Mr. Conway has delusions of grandeur."

"Apparently they are delusions worth killing for," Corrie reminded Jeff.

Kenji again shook his head. "Mr. Conway hasn't killed anyone and he did not commit any of the crimes in Sipán. There are others looking for these things. That much I do know."

"What others?"

"I'm not sure. My sister indicated some Arab was searching for this special artifact."

"Karim Ali Ahmed?" Jeff asked.

"Yes. I'm told he's very dangerous."

"Are you telling us the absolute truth?"

"Yes. Please, we must not be seen together. Mr. Conway will be very angry."

Jeff wanted to say, 'Screw Mr. Conway' but he didn't. Kenji was obviously concerned and for some reason he believed him. Conway was known to be a secretive man.

"Mr. Conway controls much. He has power over people's lives," Kenji said.

The comment confirmed Jeff's own thought. "Too damn much power, if you ask me." Jeff's disgust was undisguised. "It's obvious he checked my background."

"Not yours," Kenji said. "Miss Henley's background. You just came up. He remembered reading your byline when you were covering the hostage story. He has what might be called a photographic memory. He asked me to find you, and I told him I knew you."

"How convenient."

"Karma," Kenji said. "Mr. Conway thought you worked for one of the other groups because you knew Miss Henley and because you were still in Peru. But he changed his mind when it turned out you had been away and only recently returned. Besides you had never even been near the dig in Sipán. He said it was a coincidence, though he didn't believe in coincidences."

"That's what I always say."

"I swear that's all I know," Kenji insisted.

"Better than nothing," Jeff replied. "Want some tea?"

"No," then smiling for the first time Kenji said, "I don't like tea. Maybe some saki, though."

123

\#

"My office," Jeff said with fanfare as he switched on the light.

"Its every bit as small and cluttered as your trailer."

"I don't think I could work in another environment."

Corrie smiled.

"Look, I'm lucky to have a place big enough to work from – besides it has good phone lines which I need for the computer. In the morning you'll see that my office looks out onto a wonderful Japanese garden lovingly tended by Mrs. Obata, my landlady. And the university is just across the road, which is why I have such a good internet connection."

"I saw the side garden coming in this morning. Given the Japanese love of beautiful delicate things, I must confess I've never understood the Japanese interest in Peru."

"I understand their interest in Peru, but not in Lima."

"Yes, but they all live in Lima."

"True," he said abstractedly. Jeff leaned over and switched on his computer. In a second the color screen lit up with icons displaying all his available programs.

"That's a really big computer for a reporter."

"Ah, but my trusty lap top docks with it, so I'm entirely portable."

He pulled out his chair and sat down. "Maybe this will help and maybe it won't. I'll e-mail the INS librarian. Let's see what the archives have on this Arab terrorist with whom Myra, or whatever her name was, was involved."

"I trust you don't expect to find him that easily."

Jeff turned to her and grinned, "Nah, I just want his news history."

"I'll bet Conway could tap into Mossad's files on this Karim person," Corrie said playfully.

"Well, I'm not that well connected. Anyway, Mossad is vastly over rated."

"Thriller writers have to have some icon," Corrie said.

Jeff nodded. Their conversation was always easy. "Let's go have a drink. It will take awhile to get some answers."

It was slightly more than two hours before Jeff got a response. The librarian's search of INS files began to yield archival references. "Do you know what a laborious job this would have been just four years ago?"

"I do."

"Hey, here's his obituary."

"He's still alive."

"Not to INS. Hey, we keep prewritten obits on about every prominent person. How do you think we can come up with an instant retrospective when some celebrity dies unexpectedly."

"You people really are amazing – if not a bit gruesome."

"Well, his obit ought to give us a thumbnail sketch of his life to date. It's a start."

Jeff turned back to his computer more seriously and opened one of the files he had been sent.

"Karim Ali Ahmed," he read. He scrolled down and a shadowy picture appeared.

Karim's face appeared to be long and thin. He had a beard and a long straight nose. His skin looked dark, his eyes almond shaped. A bernous covered his head and hair.

"He's quite handsome," Corrie said looking at the image on the screen. At least what you can see of him."

"You're just trying to make me jealous."

She laughed and touched his shoulder fondly. "Just kidding. That picture is so bad I imagine a shave and a business suit would change his appearance completely. As long as he's dressed that way he could be anyone."

"Yeah, anonymity by way of stereotype."

Jeff whistled through his teeth as scrolled down and read. "He's sure got a lot of bread. But there's not much about him personally."

Then Jeff whistled again. "Hey, look at that. This guy is thought to have been involved with breaching the computer security systems of both governments and banks. Interpol calls him the first 'computer terrorist.' He's thought to be Sudanese, but educated in Egypt."

"That's really strange, isn't it?"

Jeff turned to look into her eyes. "What? Being educated in Egypt?"

"No. The computer thing. Conway is interested in this mysterious artifact and he's a computer technology billionaire and so is this Karim."

Jeff frowned, "Maybe, but that may just be a coincidence."

"I thought you didn't believe in coincidences."

"I don't."

Again she smiled.

Jeff folded his hands behind his head and leaned back as he continued to read.

"Power. Jeff how can this artifact or artifacts have power?"

"His to know, ours to find out." Jeff began to shut down the computer. A truly bizarre idea had come into his mind, an idea so bizarre he didn't feel he could even share it with Corrie. At least not yet.

"Nightcap? I'm bushed." He turned the computer off and stood up.

She straightened up too, "Sure."

They were standing close and once again he was lost in her eyes. He wrapped her in his arms and kissed her mouth. She responded and for a long moment they tasted each other's lips hungrily and relived their memories.

"If I don't let you go now, I won't," he whispered.

She leaned into his chest. "Don't let me go. It's not too soon."

\#

The winter weather was unseasonably warm in Madrid. The sidewalk cafes were open and business was thriving even though it was still early in the evening.

Emilio de Leon sipped his favorite aperitif, Pernod. He was a meticulous man who had been reared to appreciate the finer things in life, a man of aristocratic bearing.

Emilio's dark suit was conservative, his shoes buffed, so that their brown leather looked like fine wood. His nails were recently manicured; his thin hair combed back. Had he been standing, onlookers would have noticed that he was tall and lean, they would have rightly guessed his age as being in the mid-sixties and they would have said that he had apparently cared well for himself throughout his lifetime. He was, in all ways, a distinguished looking man with piercing blue eyes that seemed to dissect others.

The man who sat across from him was his opposite. He was heavy set, bald, and his teeth were bad. He tapped his short fat fingers impatiently on the metal table in the sidewalk café. If he had not been tapping fingers, he would have been moving his foot. He was in perpetual motion, unable to sit still.

Emilio could not help noticing that his companion's fingernails were bitten to the quick and this made his hands seem even stubbier.

Emilio's distaste went far beyond his companion's appearance, however. There was something about this Anatoly that Emilio found hard to describe, something unnerving. The man had darting black eyes that made you uncomfortable, yet when he choose, he could hold you in their hypnotic grasp. Emilio supposed that Anatoly was a sort of modern day Rasputin, a person who was simultaneously compelling and revolting. *Perhaps I feel this way because I know so much about him.* He chastised himself. It really wasn't that he knew so much about Anatoly, it was *what* he knew.

Anatoly was in his late seventies, though his corpulence puffed out his wrinkles and as a result, he looked younger. After World War II, he had worked tirelessly with American Counter-Intelligence to help smuggle Nazi War Criminals from Europe to South America. He was said to have been one of the Croatian Priests who assisted Klaus Barbie, the Butcher of Lyon, to freedom in Bolivia. More spectacularly he had been intimately linked to the escape of Eichmann and for many years before his death, Anatoly had maintained close ties to Dr. Mengele. Emilio hardly considered himself a religious or political liberal, but Anatoly was, as the popular saying went, 'to the right of Attila the Hun.'

Anatoly stood up suddenly. He pushed his chair backward with such force that it nearly fell over. "I have to pee," he announced in a voice loud enough to cause others to look up from their drinks.

Emilio stared into his Pernod and motioned in the direction of the toilet.

It was a relief to have Anatoly gone for a minute. This was a difficult meeting. First, Anatoly revolted him, second they were forced to speak to one another in English since it was the only language they shared.

He leaned back and contemplated the Biblical story of the Tower of Babel. Once, when mankind was young, he and Anatoly would have spoken the same tongue, Indo-European. It was the language from which almost all European languages sprang. Indo-European was not just the root of Modern European languages either. It was the root of Sanskrit and Farsi as well. Sometime around 2500 BC, he reflected, the languages began to split apart resulting in the Babel of Biblical lore. He thought of these facts every time he had to communicate with someone whose mother tongue was not Spanish. Croatian was certainly not a language Emilio had ever felt prone to study.

Anatoly returned, and as clumsily as he had stood up, he now sat down, scrapping his chair across the tile floor. Emilio shivered. The sound was like a fingernail on a chalkboard.

"I can't understand your calm, your detachment," Anatoly muttered. "It's all falling apart."

"As far as we're concerned, it was never really together," Emilio replied with maddening calm.

"We have to find it!" Anatoly doubled his fat hand and hit the table.

"There, there, dear fellow. We will find it. It is all a matter of patience. If we're lucky, someone will find it for us."

"And so we just sit back and wait."

"More or less. Mind you, I think our man should be better informed. When it is time for him to act, he must not hesitate."

"Agreed. You should go to Chiclayo and speak with him."

"Yes, it's time to call in our markers, so to speak."

"I can count on you, can't I?"

"You can," Emilio promised as he put down his drink and stood up abruptly. "I can't stay. I'm expecting a phone call." It was an absurd excuse, but he couldn't stand another minute in the company of this brutish oaf. He turned and walked rapidly away, leaving Anatoly to pay the bill. His first instinct was to wash his hands. Anatoly always made him feel unclean.

CHAPTER SEVEN

558 AD The Valley of the Moon

A silence, so profound, that it spoke as loudly as any noise
filled the great hall of the Temple of the Sun God. Llayo stared
down at the High Priestess, Taqaya. She was dressed in a flowing
purple robe woven with silver threads and embroidered with jewels.
As was the custom, it was made from twenty-eight separate panels
of cloth sewn together. Each panel bore the symbol of one phase of
the moon. A silver headdress hid her long dark hair and her skin
shimmered with an ointment permeated with silver dust. She lay on
a large flat altar, above which was a huge sunburst with a serpent
representing each of the sun's rays. Taqaya lay beneath the sun
because the moon was subservient to the sun.

Llayo was adorned in his feathered fuchsia robe. His owl mask,
with its angry looking curved beak, covered his head and face. Llayo
was *The High Warrior Priest,* surrogate of the Sun God, supreme
ruler of the Moche. Taqaya, surrogate of the Moon Goddess was his
mate. Taqaya was dying.

Llayo stood by her side and watched her last moments with
deep sadness and grim resignation. There would be a new High
Priestess, she would be sanctified after the sacrifice when she drank
Taqaya's blood. But how could it be the same? It could not be the
same. It would never be the same again, and Llayo knew it.

The surgeon stood nearby. As soon as Taqaya died, he would
siphon off her blood and then quickly mix it with the fruit of the
Ulluchu plant to keep it from congealing. The blood would remain in
a sacred container for one cycle of the Sun. Then a murderer from
among those criminals, who were held in the cells of the doomed,
would be sacrificed. Following the sacrifice, Taqaya's blood would
be poured into the sacred shell and the candidate selected to be the
new High Priestess, the surrogate of the Moon Goddess would drink

it. What remained would be mixed with the blood of the sacrifice and poured into the Sacred Spondylus Shell. All the Priests and nobles would sip blood from this shell. It would be as it had always been. Ritual and tradition quelled the anger of the Gods, did they not?

Beneath his long black beak no one could see that Llayo bit his lower lip. He shook his head. In his heart he knew that things were not as they always had been. In spite of everything, in spite of their strict adherence to the teachings of the Gods, terrible changes had come over the land. Many of the People of the Sun God were dying in the same way that Taqaya, the surrogate of the Moon Goddess, was dying. One by one they took to their pallets and wasted away till death took them. There was no explanation. It happened to the young just as it happened to the old. Llayo wondered if, when the last of the People of the Sun were dead, others chosen by the Gods would emerge from the ground, clawing their way from the depths of the earth to give birth to a new race. It was how his own people had come to be; it was, as he understood the ancient teachings, how all peoples came to be. Indeed, he feared a new conquering race might already have emerged. There were tales of such a people in the land from which the sun seemed to rise. It was said they lived in the valleys behind the great mountains. Again he told himself that if the signs of the end were as he interpreted them, there were steps that must be taken. But how could he be certain? He prayed daily for some instruction from the Gods. The Gods were silent.

Llayo stepped closer to Taqaya. Her magnificent eyes were closed, her breathing labored. He wanted to speak, but he did not want the others to hear him. It wasn't right. He was the High Warrior Priest, surrogate of the Sun God, and the Moon Goddess had a special relationship with him. He was not supposed to feel for her what a mere man felt for a woman. And yet, though he had never spoken of it, and seldom even dared to think about it, he did love her as common men loved women, as husbands loved their wives. It was

131

expected that he and Taqaya would mate but they had found a joy in one another that should not have been. Sorrowfully, he wondered if her death was a punishment for their love.

He waited for a long moment, and then he spread his wings and leaned over. His wings completely obscured his actions from the prying eyes of the other priests.

Beneath his beak, he wet his mouth and then kissed Taqaya's colorless lips. She stirred ever so gently and he murmured words of love to her, praying she could still hear him. He remained, hovering over her for a long while, and then he lifted his great-feathered wings and stood back. Taqaya inhaled and shuddered. She breathed no more.

#

The twenty-four hour cycle of the sun and moon passed far too quickly for Llayo. As soon as Taqaya's body was taken away and the final death ceremony was complete, he had fled to his private chambers where, in privacy and seclusion, he wept for many hours. It would not do for others to see him; not even his servants could know the depths of his love for Taqaya.

When darkness covered the land, he ceased weeping and turned instead to his memories. He reflected on his years of serving as surrogate of the Sun, ruler of the Moche.

He had lived to see one hundred and ninety-six moons when he was recognized as the surrogate to the sun. One moon after his ascension, Taqaya, who had lived only one hundred and eighty moons, was sent to be his mate. They had been mates for one hundred and thirty moons. It was a long time for a mortal, especially as most men lived no more than five hundred and twenty moons before passing. He and Taqaya had grown together, they thought alike, enjoyed the same foods, and relished in walking by the shimmering water at twilight. They had often searched for shells

together. Even now, in his mind's eye, he could see the look of
wonder and delight on her face when she found a beautiful shell
deserted by its inhabitant and washed by the salt water till its inside
glistened with hues of turquoise, pearl, and deep purple. She showed
a similar joy in the beautiful stones of the mountains and in the
flowers of the temple garden. How she had loved life! How he had
adored her! He knew he loved Taqaya and she loved him. It was not
supposed to be, but it had happened. He could only pray that his
people were not suffering because of their transgressions.

Beyond the confines of the walls of the temple, the sun rose.
Llayo had not slept, and his room remained in darkness so that the
coming of the morning caught him by surprise. His servants came
and he knew it was time to dress. Today, Wantuq, the girl selected to
be the new surrogate of the Moon Goddess would come to him. It
would be difficult, the ceremony was arduous and his heart still
ached for Taqaya.

On this auspicious occasion Llayo's servants dressed him in the
golden robes that bore the same symbol of the sun as that carved into
the wall above his raised dais.

Wantuq was dressed in an iridescent silver robe that shimmered
just as did the new moon. She lay face down, prostrate at his feet on
a rich sky blue carpet. Wantuq's legs were separated and her arms
outstretched. She was a petite girl, a virgin as were all those from
among whom she was selected. She had masses of dark hair, smooth
skin, and large eyes.

She quivered ever so slightly which, under the circumstances,
was quite understandable. She had endured watching the sacrifice
and drunk the sacred blood. It was now time for her to be taken to
the royal chamber, where she would be deflowered and become his
mate.

Llayo raised his golden scepter and tapped it seven times on the
stone floor. From each of the four corners of the great chamber a
warrior stepped forward. Each was dressed in robes of jet-black

133

feathers and wore a horrific facemask with a vicious curved beak. Each took a corner of the carpet and lifted it together with Wantuq high into the air. Then, while the flutist played, they proceeded down the long corridor to the bedchamber. Llayo, scepter in hand, followed. It was as it had always been. The initiation of Wantuq was his duty.

The carpet was placed atop the bed, and immediately the warriors bound Wantuq to the bed. Bound, she was unable to struggle, were she so inclined. In all likelihood she would not struggle. She had been reared in the Temple of the Moon with twenty other possible candidates. She knew her duty and the consequences to her people should she not fulfill the rituals set forth by the Chosen, who long ago had delivered the wishes of the Gods.

In silence the guards left and the sound of the flutes followed them. The great door closed, and Llayo was left alone with Wantuq.

He walked to the side of the bed and looked down at Wantuq who now trembled uncontrollably.

"You're frightened," he said trying to calm her with a gentle tone.

She looked up at him; her great dark eyes wide open. "You will plunge your scepter into my sacred place and turn it slowly, I cannot bear it! I cannot bear the pain!"

He almost laughed but he did not. To laugh at one so frightened would have been unkind. "I shall do no such thing! Who told you such stories?"

"The other candidates." She hesitated, "Is it not true?"

"It is not true."

He studied her. He could see that while she was still apprehensive, she was no longer terrified.

He said nothing more but silently he parted her dress so that he could see her breasts. They were not soft and voluptuous as Taqaya's had been. They were hard, small, and round because she was so young and a virgin. He ran his hands over them and she

134

squirmed slightly and closed her eyes. He ran his hand down her flat stomach and between her legs. "I do not want to hurt you, but I'm afraid it will hurt a little."

She answered only with a shiver. Slowly, he began to ready her; well aware that her bodily lubrications would ease the passage of the Sacred Golden Phallus of the sun with which she would be deflowered.

He began to touch her secret place, massaging it slowly, till shortly her tremors gave way to rhythmic movements. Her hips began to undulate, her mouth opened and her skin became damp. He was careful not to fully pleasure her, but only to taunt her, to make her desirous so that she would be ready.

At last he reached for the special oils that stood ready on the nearby table. He applied them to her whole body, feeling the soft glow of her flesh. Soon she glistened and was once again squirming about with wanton cravings.

"Not today," he whispered in her ear. "The ritual must be observed. The ceremony is not yet over."

She said nothing though her skin glowed and her breath came in short wanton gasps.

He took the onyx box from the table and opened it removing the Sacred Golden Phallus. It was jewel encrusted, and each of its seven rubies and seven sapphires caught the light. It was quite magnificent, but no larger than the phallus of the average man. It would fill her, but not hurt her. Slowly, he slid it into her passage, rubbing her gently as he did so. Again she groaned with desire and this time, she cried out.

"You must wait for your pleasure, Wantuq. It will come. The Sacred Phallus must remain thus for many hours." She groaned and went limp in acquiescence. From the jug on the table, he poured her a cup of the liquid made from fermented fruit. Then, slipping his hand beneath her slender neck, he lifted her head and let her drink. "Rest Wantuq. Rest and feel the sun glowing inside you."

Llayo then left her. He departed the chamber and passing through an alcove, he entered a smaller room. There, he disrobed and lay down to wait. When one cycle of the sun had passed, he, the surrogate of the Sun God, would remove the phallus and plant his seed inside Wantuq. It would be as it had always been.

#

Wantuq lay by his side, sleeping peacefully. The ritual had been completed and she had known fulfillment. Llayo eased off the bed and pulled on his robes. A pensive expression on his face, Llayo looked down on Wantuq. She was quite lovely, but to his eyes not as lovely as had been Taqaya. Again he reminded himself that his love for Taqaya might well be the cause of the tragedies that now engulfed his people. He drew in his breath, he had confided in no one. It was better to keep thoughts such as these to oneself. Llayo ran his hand over his own smooth cheek and wondered if his eyes revealed his thoughts. When last he had looked in the reflecting pool in the garden, his expression had not reflected his worries. He hoped that was still the case. It would not do to have his people, who depended on him, know about his self-doubts and inner fears. To give confidence, he had to project confidence, even when he did not feel it.

After a time, Llayo left the bedchamber and walked down the long empty corridor of the Temple of the Sun. It was time to listen to the laments of his people, time to dispense advice. But what advice could he give to those whose loved ones were dying? How could he explain the long drought that had ended in torrential floods? What cause could he site for the horrific temperature of summer that killed the crops and caused livestock to fall down and die? What explanation was there for the disease that killed so many, the illness that had killed his beloved Taqaya?

He had just reached the door of the Great Hall when K'ek, Head of the Royal Guard stepped in front of him and bowed.

Llayo waved his hand, giving the man permission to speak.

"A stranger has come," K'ek told Llayo in a low, secretive tone.

From time to time outsiders ventured into the land of the Sun God. If they were peaceful, and if they agreed to live according to the laws of the Gods, as revealed by the Chosen, they were allowed to remain. But such matters were usually decided by the local priest. It was highly unusual for a stranger to come to The Temple of the Sun.

"The stranger is dressed in fine cloth. It is the color of the sunset and is trimmed in golden threads," K'ek revealed. "He is strong and unafraid. He speaks our language and he asks for you."

Llayo pursed his lips together. Gold and jewels were beautiful and plentiful, but cloth was what determined a man's wealth. The stranger came from wealth, Llayo was not certain what that meant but he could see that K'ek was in awe of the stranger and awe was far from K'ek's usual reaction to strangers. A sign – he had asked for a sign. Could it be that this stranger was the sign?

"I must speak to this stranger in private, I must know more of him and where he came from."

K'ek bowed from the waist, then he hurried away to bring the stranger.

Llayo watched from his throne as the stranger was ushered into the Great Hall. He immediately understood why K'ek was wonder-struck by this tall handsome man dressed in a wealth of fabric. In addition to a full tunic, the stranger also carried a rich scarlet robe trimmed with dark feathers. His hair was straight, shoulder length, and as black as the plumage of the crow. His skin was swarthy, his nose long and straight. But his most striking physical feature was his height. Compared to Llayo, who did not consider himself short, the stranger was something of a giant.

"Do you understand my words?" Llayo asked.

"I understand," the man answered.

Llayo gripped his golden scepter and wondered if there were others as tall as this stranger lurking in the hills, perhaps waiting to attack the weakened Moche.

Llayo hoped his own apprehension did not show. Certainly, if the stranger was fearful, he did not show it. Llayo thought for a minute. "How do you know our language?"

"I know many tongues."

Llayo frowned. It was not the answer he had expected. He himself was highly educated but knew only his own language, though he knew others existed and were spoken by those who lived beyond the Valley of the Sun.

"How is this so?" Llayo asked. With each moment that passed his misgivings grew. This stranger had a presence about him, an aura that was intimidating. *But I am the surrogate of the Sun God! I have power. I could have this stranger arrested.* His own inner assertions did not quell his feeling of being overpowered by this man.

"It would not do to have me arrested," the stranger said, as if he had read Llayo's mind.

Llayo shivered and fought to maintain his composure. The stranger was well spoken, clearly intelligent and educated; these aspects of his presence were mysterious but not disturbing. But the fact that he seemed to be able to read minds was most unsettling, as was his apparent ease and confidence. Perhaps, Llayo thought, among his own people he had been a warrior priest. In any case, he was no common person. Llayo looked about and gave the signal for all the others to leave. When they were gone he turned to the stranger, "Who are you?" Llayo asked, "Speak the truth."

"I will speak the truth. First of all, we will speak of the Paqarinas."

"Proceed," Llayo replied. He felt stunned, his voice was barely audible. He was beginning to feel real; a fear he hoped the stranger did not notice.

The Paqarinas of which the stranger spoke were sacred places in the ground. It was taught that the Gods had many Paqarinas, and that they existed not just here, in the Valley of the Sun, but beyond the mountains, and in lands far distant. It was told that there were Paqarinas in every place where the sun shone. It was further revealed that the stars, which were the knowing eyes of the gods, determined the location of these sacred places.

"The Chosen emerged from Paqarinas," Llayo said. "There is a Paqarina here, in the Valley of the Sun."

"There are seven most sacred Paqarinas in all. Beyond the mountains, all men believe that Paqari-tampu is the most sacred Paqarina," the stranger told him.

So he is from beyond the mountains! "I have not heard of this place," Llayo admitted. He did not believe any place to be more sacred than the Paqarina in the Valley of the Sun. It was from that Paqarina that the Chosen who gave the Moche the law had emerged. He held his tongue and decided to hear the stranger out before engaging him in argument.

"Would you know a Chosen one if you saw one?" the stranger asked. "Now it is you who must speak the truth."

Llayo was taken aback by the unexpected question. He looked into the eyes of his inquisitor, and mouthed the word, "No."

"I came from the depths of the earth through Paqari-tampu. Your people are dying. I have come to lead them forth."

Llayo was so stunned he could barely speak. The Chosen ones who selected his ancestor, the first surrogate of the Sun God, had emerged from a Paqarina many thousands of moons ago. Was this truly another of the Chosen? How could he know?

"I see you are wondering how you can be certain I speak the truth. Think with care, Llayo. The surrogate of the Sun God must have wisdom enough to test me."

Llayo thought for a long while. If this stranger were truly one of the Chosen he would know the secret that only the surrogates of the Sun God knew. It was a secret passed on from one surrogate to another. Yes, that was the only possible test but he knew he must be careful.

"Speak to me of the Chosen," Llayo requested.

"We come from the bowels of the earth. Those who came to the Valley of the Sun left two things. They left the law which was revealed in their words and they left *The Key*."

Everyone knew of the law but only the surrogate of the Sun God and Moon Goddess knew of *The Key*. It was the one secret he had never shared, not even with his closest advisors. The stranger's knowledge proved his story.

Llayo stepped from his throne and knelt before the stranger. "I am your slave. You are truly one of the Chosen."

The stranger held out his hand. "Rise up and walk with me. I have come to save your people."

Llayo nodded. "You are one of the Chosen. You must have special quarters. Where will you stay?

"I will stay here, with you."

"Shall I tell the people?"

The stranger shook his head. "You will tell no one, not even your mate the surrogate of the moon. You will allow me to remain here, in the Temple of the Sun. You will say I am an adviser come to help in a time of trouble. You will call me Shikulla.

"It shall be as you wish," Llayo promised.

#

Wantuq knelt by the Pool of Tranquility in the private garden adjacent to the Temple of the Sun. She combed out her long straight hair with a jewel-encrusted comb. The comb was hand carved from the bleached bone of an animal. Above, the full moon shone so brightly that Wantuq could see her image in the still water.

Suddenly there was a shadow that momentarily blocked the light and she turned with a start to see Shikulla, the 'advisor' that Llayo had brought to live in the temple. "You must show him great respect," Llayo had instructed her.

Wantuq had felt miffed at this instruction. She was after all the surrogate of the Moon Goddess; surely Shikulla should show her respect. Still, she did what Llayo requested. "Good evening," she said curtly.

Shikulla stared at her for a moment and his eyes made her think of the hungry desire filled eyes of the sacred Jaguar just before it was fed.

"Did I startle you?"

"Before you came only Llayo and I used this garden. It was closed to all others."

"You resent me."

Quickly she shook her head. If she replied honestly, Llayo would be angry.

Without invitation, Shikulla sat down beside her. Without a word, he reached out and touched her hair, letting it slip through his fingers. "What has Llayo told you about me?"

She turned her eyes away from Shikulla's lustful gaze, "Only that I should show you respect."

A smile crossed Shikulla's lips. "And he did not tell you why?"
She shook her head.

"Look at me!" Shikulla demanded. His tone was menacing, and she turned toward him, suddenly feeling frightened.

He lifted his finger and ran it round her lips slowly. "I am Chosen. I come from the Paqarina beyond the mountains. "You will obey me, absolutely, utterly and without question."

She shivered but dared not turn away. "Llayo did not tell me," she murmured, "How could I have known?"

"He was told not to tell you but I have decided you should know."

Wantuq continued to look down. He was a frightening man even if he was one of the Chosen.

"Lie down, Wantuq. Undo the knot on your robe so that I may see your body."

Wantuq lay down on the soft grass and did as he ordered. Inside, she felt afraid. Why did he want this? Was she to mate with one of the Chosen too?

For a long time he only looked at her. Then the craving in his eyes erupted and he fell on her, filling her as the phallus had, but moving, as it had not. Llayo had also taken her thus, but Shikulla was larger and rougher. He held her down, moving above her, rubbing against her flower and causing her to cry out not with pleasure, but with anguish.

He pushed into her one final time and she knew that the seed of the Chosen had been sent to her womb. She blinked up at him, "What shall I tell Llayo?" She asked as her eyes filled with tears.

"You will tell him nothing."

He withdrew from her, yet still loomed above her. "We must leave this place. You and I and a selection of healthy nobles and artisans will depart 14 moons hence."

"Where will we go?"

"We will travel across the Great Water."

"How?" she asked, her eyes wide.

"In special reed boats. I shall direct their building."

"What of Llayo?"

"He cannot come, the surrogate of the Moon Goddess can only have one mate."

Tears filled Wantuq's large eyes. Llayo was gentle and gave her much pleasure. Shikulla filled her, but did not care for her pleasure. Yet it was not her place to choose between them.

"You will tell him nothing of this conversation and nothing of what has passed between us. You will encourage him to help me prepare the people to leave. You will not tell him that he will remain here."

She nodded, terrified of even attempting to argue with one of the Chosen. And surely he was one of the Chosen or Llayo would not have accepted him as such. But leave Llayo? Was the surrogate of the Moon Goddess to spin away into the star-studded night, never again to be with the surrogate of the Sun God? It did not seem right, and she was filled with fear.

#

Llayo walked along the rocky shore. Now and again he stooped down to pick up a handful of pebbles in order to examine them. The Chosen who delivered the law came from the earth; the Sun and the Moon were supreme, overseeing both the surfaces of the earth, and those sacred places from which the Chosen emerged. The rocks were from the earth too; he always examined them, searching them for clues. After a time he came to a large flat rock and he climbed up on it. He stared out at the Great Water. It stretched as far as the eye could see till it met the sky. He sat for a long while lost in thought.

"Is it well with you?" Shikulla asked from behind him.

Llayo turned, "Yes," he replied, though in fact all was not well with him. His heart was troubled and his mind confused.

"You are one of the Chosen. You have said we would travel across the water. But I see no land there, only the place where the sky meets the water.

"Summon the servant. I shall want refreshment before I answer this riddle."

Llayo motioned for the hovering servant to bring them refreshment and in a moment the man returned bearing a bowl of fermented juices and some hot flat bread.

"If we are to find homes across the water, there must be land," Llayo said. "But there is nothing, only the seam where the water meets the sky like two bits of cloth sewn together."

"High in the mountains there is also a Great Water. If one stands on the shore one can also see where the sky meets the water. But, if one gets into a boat and sails for three days the line where sky and water meet changes. It disappears and there is land.

"Disappears?" Llayo said in amazement.

"Yes. Although it cannot be seen when one begins ones journey, there is land beyond, there is an opposite shore."

Llayo felt supreme shock. What magic could cause the line where the sky met the water to simply disappear? But it would not do for a surrogate of the Sun God to look surprised.

"What is this Great Water in the mountains called?"

"Titicaca."

"Titicaca," Llayo repeated.

"We will take boats across the Great Water to another land." Shikulla dipped his flat bread into the fermented juice and then took a bite of it. He chewed and swallowed; waiting for a question that did not come.

"You are a wise surrogate of the Sun God. You listen and you ask questions. You know this land is dying," Shikulla finally said.

Llayo nodded. To leave this land seemed strange indeed. His feelings of ill ease were hardly relieved by Shikulla's words.

"Only the healthy ones will be taken, many provisions will be needed."

"And the journey will take three days?"

"It will take longer than three days to cross this water. We do not know how far we must travel before the line disappears and land can be seen."

"Then we journey into the unknown," Llayo murmured.

"We will take with us what we can. Above all we must take *The Key*."

Llayo did not move. *The Key* was hidden in a place known only to him. It was locked in a box made of rare wood. Shikulla had not mentioned it since the first day of his arrival. "Yes," he replied softly. But he did not mean 'yes'. Everything inside him screamed that *The Key* should not be moved, that it belonged here, that it belonged to this place. Even if his people saved themselves by leaving, surely *The Key* should stay. He said nothing to Shikulla but he decided to think on this rather than make a rash decision.

#

The sun burned down on the land mercilessly. Llayo walked through the garden on his way to the great hall. Once filled with lush plants and blossoms of all hues of the rainbow, the plants of the garden were shriveled, brown, and beginning to droop downward. It was all he could do to keep from crying. It had once been so alive! So vibrant! He remembered the taste of the sweet melons. How succulent they had been! Now his garden was filled only with the brittle skeletons of bushes and the ground was littered only with the hard, dry, unopened buds. Llayo wept for the dying plants as he wept for his people.

He forced the garden from his mind when he reached the gate that led to the path. At the end of the path was the side entrance to the Temple of Sun. He could weep no more over the past. His decision had been made and the workmen toiled without rest on the boats that would take the healthy ones out over the water. The risks were great, but the rewards might be great as well.

Llayo had entered the temple and he now stepped through the inner archway covered only by a drape of beads and knotted ropes. He knew he was a man of routine and that today he had broken his routine for the first time in a very long while. At this hour of the day he usually received his people, but today he had sent them away and asked them to return tomorrow. Today, he wanted to think and perhaps consult with Wantuq.

Llayo did not intentionally walk like a cat but his slippers were made of soft cloth and he was not a heavy man. His steps made no noise as he approached the drape of beads that hung across the entrance to Wantuq's bedchamber. He stopped short when he heard a familiar sound. It was Wantuq. She cried out. It was a cry he knew.

He leaned forward and peered into her bedchamber. Wantuq lay naked and Shikulla leaned over her, his phallus hovering, ready to plunge into her.

For a moment Llayo closed his own eyes. He stood stark still, too mortified to run. Then he turned, and as silently as he had come, he fled. Something was wrong. Something was terribly wrong!

He reached his own bedchamber a shaken man. If Shikulla had been one of the Chosen he would not be taking Wantuq as a man takes a woman! But what could be done now?

If he revealed Shikulla as an imposter, he would have to publicly admit that the powerful stranger from beyond the mountains had successfully deceived the surrogate of the Sun God. How could he explain that he had believed Shikulla to be one of the Chosen? No one would understand.

The preparations had gone too far! Long strong reeds had been brought from the estuary of the river and for more than fourteen moons the workmen had been binding them together according to Shikulla's instructions, readying them for the voyage across the Great Water.

Worse yet, Shikulla had chosen the most powerful nobles to accompany him across the Great Water. They wanted to be saved.

They wanted to journey forth. If Shikulla told them he was one of the Chosen they would believe it. Llayo knew that everyone would turn on him. Llayo shook with anger even as he felt the sting of defeat.

The only matter that was still a mystery was the matter of *The Key*. How had Shikulla known of it? Llayo half smiled as an idea crossed his mind. His solemn duty, as well as the solution to his dilemma suddenly seemed quite simple.

#

The time had come. Everything was in readiness.

The morning was filled with tension. Never had so many boats lined the sandy shore of the Great Water. Shikulla had chosen his companions well. All those who now prepared to launch the armada of reed boats were young, healthy and enthusiastic.

Shikulla commanded the ten vessels that held the artisans, their families and their tools. To each of those boats strong ropes were attached to a supply boat. Twenty-five more boats held the families of those who had decided to set forth together with yet more supplies.

Six boats carried the nobles and many more carried the warriors and their families. At the very head of the fleet was a large dugout in which Wantuq and her servants were to travel. He was supposed to travel in that boat too, but he knew that was not the true plan. And though he was not to be among those crossing the Great Water, he was fascinated with the preparations.

Shikulla had come up with a brilliant plan. Each boat had five flags of different colors. Since they would not be able to communicate readily once they had left the land, they would use the flags to indicate their well being, or use them to signal for help in case of any emergency. Each boat was attached to five other boats.

Shikulla had provided each vessel with a map of the heavens and directed them to keep on as straight a course as possible.

"Have you brought *The Key?*" Shikulla asked.

Llayo nodded. He opened his heavy woven sack and indicated the box inside.

Shikulla peered inside. It was as Wishlay, The Memorizer, had described it. Shikulla smiled. "I shall guard it with my life."

"You must, it is *The Key,* the supreme gift of the Gods."

Shikulla half smiled. "You have guessed that you will be left behind, have you not?"

"I know. I must stay with the rest of my people."

"Yes, that's it. That is the reason why you cannot come."

"I should like to bid Wantuq farewell."

"I shall send her."

Shikulla took the sack and waded toward his boat. He made a signal and in a few minutes Wantuq came, her large eyes filled with tears.

"Do not cry, little Wantuq. I will be fine."

"I do not want to leave you, Llayo."

"You must go. It is destined." He reached out and took her hand, lifted it to his lips and kissed it. "May the Gods protect you."

She nodded silently, then turned and ran back toward her boat.

As the sun's light was seen rising over the mountains, the boats began to launch out into the foamy surf. Llayo felt a knot in his stomach as the wind carried them further and further from the land.

Llayo stood alone staring at the Great Water until the sun sank into it. He was still the surrogate of the Sun God, and though he was left with only a parched land and a dying people, he knew he had made the right decision. Had Shikulla truly been one of the Chosen he would have known where *The Key* was hidden and he would have known that what he took with him was not *The Key*. Perhaps the people were meant to go, but *The Key* was meant to stay. He knew that truth in his heart. He also now knew that there were men who pretended to be Gods, clever men who could fool even the surrogate of the Sun God for a time.

#

Wantuq had not remained in her boat for long. She considered all of the options and in the end, she decided to put her fate into the hands of the Gods, she chose the water rather than Shikulla. As soon as darkness enveloped the boats, she slipped over the side, taking only a round log on which to cling. If the winds carried her to land she would be saved. If they did not, she would die when she could no longer hold on.

But the Great Water had shown mercy. She was alive, lying in the sand, and quite able to move. *But I don't know where I am,* Wantuq thought. She had lost all track of time. She knew she had been on The Great Water for most of the night. In the early morning, the wind had come up. It had carried her to land, though to be sure, she did not know what land. She had immediately fallen asleep.

She stood up and stretched, then she looked about. Far down the sandy beach she saw the log. Was this her land, the land from which she had come? The Great Water was on one side, the mountains on the other. But she was afraid to hope, afraid even to think of The Temple of the Sun in the Valley of the Moon.

Wantuq trudged down the beach, and then just as darkness began to envelop the land, she came to the thread of Golden Water. She knelt down and drank, and then she crossed the Golden Water on the Bridge of Vines, built by her people many years ago. It was a place she knew well, and her heart soared. She was not more than a few hours away from the Temple of the Sun.

By the light of the moon, Wantuq passed by deserted fields and empty houses. It was as Llayo had said, the people were dying. Yet she saw no fresh graves or bodies left to the elements. She saw only the evidence of what had once been and was no more. The emptiness

149

amazed her; the thought of being alone forever frightened her. *But I have been saved for a reason. I must go on, I must learn my destiny.*

At last she came to the Temple of the Sun. She passed into the once magnificent gardens. She entered the Temple through the side door and called out, "Llayo! Llayo!"

"Who goes?"

Wantaq blinked in the dim shadowy light provided by a lone torch. There, on his throne Llayo sat leaning on his scepter. "It is I, Wantuq."

He stood up and ran to greet her, his arms held out. "Wantuq! How have you returned?"

He embraced her, not caring about protocol. "I never thought I would see you again."

"Nor I you, Llayo. But the Great Water carried me back just as it carried the others away. I took a log to hold on to, I jumped off my boat as soon as it was dark and Shikulla could not see me."

"You are a gift from the Gods. I should not have sent you with Shikulla."

"More important, you should not have sent *The Key*."

He smiled and laughed for the first time in many months. "I did not. I sent only the box."

Wantuq squeezed his hand, "You are sly, Llayo, but most of all you are wise. *The Key* did not belong with Shikulla. It is not his *Key*; he is not one of the Chosen. He is evil."

Llayo shook his head. "I'm so happy you have returned, though we will have little company."

"What matters if we are alone? We shall care for one another until we are summoned."

"Who will prepare our tombs?"

"We shall," Wantuq replied. "And when the time is near we shall seal ourselves inside and go to sleep with *The Key* nearby."

Llayo took Wantuq's hand. "You are truly a goddess." He kissed her cheek tenderly and thought how fortunate he was to find love twice.

Wantuq returned his kiss. *Rupay Qishyan,* she said softly, *"Rupay Qishyan dius – my Sun God."*

CHAPTER EIGHT

562 AD. Easter Island

Shikulla leaned back on his haunches, water from the clear pool dripping from his chin. He had drunk his fill from the shallow pond, and to his dry parched lips, this water seemed sweeter than any fermented fruit.

Though he admitted it to no one, Shikulla felt puzzled by this place. This other side of the Great Water was not as he had imagined it. First, no matter how far one walked adjacent to the Great Water, if the mountains were on one's right, the water was on the left. If one turned around and retraced one's steps then the mountains were on the side of the left hand and the water on the right. He believed that this land was circular like the moon and the sun and that it must float in the very middle of the Great Water just as the moon floated in the sky. He reminded himself that he might be wrong. After all, he had not yet walked far enough to know for certain if he would return to the spot where he had started. Yesterday he had dispatched Tupa, a trained runner, on a three-fold assignment. First, he was to look for others of their number, who might have been washed up along the inhospitable shore. Second, he was to investigate the shape of the land by going as far as he could within two cycles of the sun and moon, and third, he was to look for any people who might already inhabit this place.

From their current camp it appeared that the hilly land extended right to the water. Inland the ground was undulating and grassy. Closer to the water, it became rugged and rocky. There was no sandy shore. Unlike home, there were no great mountains either, only one high peak. It was as if the whole place was vomited up out of the Great Water. Yet it was clear that there was sufficient fertile land to plant the seeds they had brought. Most important, there was water without salt; clear, freshwater that could be drunk and used to irrigate the crops. In the Valley of the Moon the Moche had built elaborate irrigation channels from the tall mountains to the valley floor. These channels carried water from the lush mountains to the dry fields in the valley. It could be done here too, he was certain of it.

Shikulla took stock. The boats with the artisans had survived and so had some of the boats filled with warriors and their families. But the rest had apparently perished, a sacrifice demanded by the Great Water. He was unsure of how long they had been on the water, only that it was more than one cycle of the moon. How far they had traveled was also a mystery. The stars in the night sky that he believed to be the eyes of the Gods were no longer in the position they had been when their journey began. On some nights, the truly dark nights, which were the most frightening, the eyes of the Gods could not be seen at all because ghostly clouds fell out of the sky and surrounded the boats in a soft white mist.

Then, just when many had given up all hope, they saw the land. Most felt they had been saved. But landing had not been easy. All but two boats had been smashed in the attempt and they had all had to scramble into the water and fight to reach the shore. Most of their belongings had washed up later, carried onto land by the waves or marooned in pools when the water retreated from the shore as it did twice in every cycle of the sun and moon. Jutting black rocks beneath the water guarded this land, jagged sentinels, uneven and dangerous; inanimate warriors, partially submerged in the biting choppy water.

"Shikulla!"

Shikulla looked up. It was the warrior Tupa who ran toward him. Tupa stopped and leaned against a huge rock and caught his breath. "This land is not like a circle, it is a circle," he said breathlessly. But it is not a perfect circle such as the sun, it is bigger on one side than on the other."

153

Shikulla nodded. If this was so, it was not a circle at all, but rather some other shape. But he could not expect Tupa to understand such things. It could have been any shape, perhaps even the shape of a farmer's field. The important matter was that unlike the land they had come from, which had the Great Water on one side and the mountains on the other, this land had the Great Water on all sides. He was right. It floated like a giant flower in a less than tranquil pond.

"There are people," Tupa revealed breathlessly.

"People?" Shikulla said in a loud voice. It was the most important fact of all. But Tupa was babbling on about the shape of the land.

"Yes, they live in a village, in the same direction as that in which the sun sets." He pointed off into the distance.

"Did you encounter these people?"

Tupa shook his head. "I saw only the one village. There were crops and some animals. There were boats on the shore, not boats like ours, different kinds of boats. They're shaped oddly and appear to be heavier.

Shikulla was not, at this moment, interested in the boats. "How many people are there? What do you think?"

"Not so many." He withdrew his *quipu,* a cord to which many smaller varicolored strings were attached. It was used for calculating.

"I could not count people, so I counted huts. There were forty-eight."

Shikulla looked about. Thirty of them had survived but numbers were not always the deciding factor in these matters. Given the circumstances guile might well succeed. To his way of thinking it was always better to seduce rather than fight. In any case, dead men could not do the work that needed to be done.

"We will gather our belongings up and go to this village. We will try to make peace."

154

The stirring under the tree caused Shikulla to turn. It was Maraq, daughter of the most influential of the nobles. Her father had gladly given her to him after Wantuq disappeared. She stretched and looked at him with her large dark eyes. "Are we going somewhere?"

"Yes. A village has been found. We will go there."

She looked at him without surprise and pulled herself up. He stared at her and thought that the once beautiful Maraq now looked quite plain. Her robes were faded and the sun had darkened her pale skin, her hair was matted, and worse yet, her soft lips were dry and cracked. "Clean yourself up!" he shouted irritably. "The mate of a God should not look like a girl who tills the earth."

Tears flooded her eyes but she said nothing. In a moment, she ran away toward the stream.

"Hurry up!" Shikulla shouted.

Shikulla reached down and grasped the bag that carried *The Key*. He was unsure if he should hide it or bring it. Perhaps, he thought, he should open it and look at it. He decided to wait. His instructions had been not to open it, though Wishlay the Memorizer, who had given him the instructions, could not have foreseen the necessity to leave the Valley of the Moon, the incredible difficulty of this voyage or the existence of a group of people who might need to be pacified. Indeed, Wishlay the Memorizer had expected Shikulla to return to the shores of Titicaca with *The Key*. All Shikulla had been told was that *The Key,* which the Moche possessed was one of seven left by the Gods and which, when combined with *The Key* his own people already possessed, would lead to unimaginable wealth and power. Even the possession of one *Key* was said to give its owner great power.

But what did Wishlay's desires matter now? He had decided to keep *The Key* and not to even try to return home to the shores of Titicaca. If it had value, he would discover its uses. But perhaps it was all only a story. Perhaps it had no power. Shikulla did not know. For the moment he cared most about his own position, about remaining in charge. Of late, he had begun to feel like the God he led others to believe he was. It was a good feeling. He did not believe he needed *The Key* to achieve his ends.

A smile of self-satisfaction covered Shikulla's face. What had been done once could surely be done twice. He had relieved Llayo of his power. He could easily fool these people as well.

Shikulla adorned the feathered robes that he had taken from Llayo. He inspected his ranks, aware that while some of the warriors were expendable, the artisans were not. It was their skill that would impress the people of this place as well as build and provide for he and the others. These were men of enormous talent. They knew how to move great stones and how to construct temples and build water channels. He bent down and picked up a handful of rocks. As far away from his home as he knew this land to be, the rocks were familiar. They were the kind of rocks that abounded near mountains that spit fire from the mouths of the earth gods. This realization emboldened him. He knew that even if the people of this place did not know it, his Gods were here just as they had been on the shores of Titicaca in the place called Tiahuanaco where once he had lived. It was from Tiahuanaco that the High Priest, the Chief Memorizer of the Past, *Wishlay*, had sent him on his journey to find and bring back *The Key*. Well, he had found it and now he possessed it. But he could not take it back to *Wishlay*. *Wishlay*, who was supposed to know all, knew nothing. *Wishlay thought he selected a warrior to retrieve The Key. I am more than a warrior.* He looked down into the pool of water and saw his own image. *I am a God; only a God could have delivered these people here. I will rule them as well as those who live here. It will be my own kingdom. I shall be more powerful than Wishlay.*

#

Kamu Kaloni sat on his throne of woven palm leaves and stared out on the people of his village. Behind him, Nalee, his daughter, stood straight, her hands folded in front of her. Her father was troubled. He had been distressed for nearly a week because strangers had come ashore on the far side of the island. He had made no move against them but prudently, he had them watched.

That morning, before the sun reached the center of the sky, one of the observers had returned. He breathlessly announced, "They are coming. They carry spears and look vicious."

Nalee stared into the distance and contemplated what she already saw in her mind's eye. Long ago her people had fled the constant warfare that existed between the island peoples. Fighting was impossible. Her father had no weapons and his people would not defend themselves. She was the only weapon in her father's arsenal. She would be offered as a wife to the leader of these outsiders. Through her marriage peace would be maintained.

Nalee heard the signal of the sentries on the wind. They were coming, these intruders from the sea.

They marched boldly, confidently in a straight line through the center of the village to the grandest hut outside of which was her father's throne. When they reached the throne they stopped and the tallest of them, dressed strangely as a great bird of prey, stepped forward.

"I am Shikulla." Shikulla knew they would not understand. He spoke slowly and distinctly and pointed to himself.

"Kama Kaloni." Her father replied from his throne.

Shikulla did not bother to bow. He assumed this Kama Kaloni was their king even though he wore few clothes and his throne, which was faded and brown was woven from the broad leaves of the trees that lined the shore. It was pitiful when compared to the throne of the surrogate of the Sun God.

Shikulla came to the swift conclusion that this king had little power and ruled an inferior people. Still, his eyes were drawn to the woman who stood to one side of the one who called himself, Kama Kaloni. Her hair was as black as the rocks that were spewed from the fire mountains. Her skin was golden, and her eyes were large and ever so slightly slanted. She was a feathery woman, tall and slender, yet plump enough in the places men desired their women to be plump. Her dress was of a type he had never before seen. It was a bright color and it was draped over one shoulder, leaving the other bare. Her legs too were bare, as were her feet. She was truly exquisite and he felt immediately drawn to her without so much as a single thought for Maraq.

Kama Kaloni took his own spear and broke it. This Shikulla assumed was a symbol of peace. Shikulla stepped forward, the man on the throne, this Kama Kaloni, pushed the young woman forward, and made motions with his hand.

It seemed clear that Kama Kaloni was offering the woman. Shikulla smiled and took her hand. Then he dropped her hand and broke his own spear as a symbol of his acceptance of the bargain. Thus, without either knowing the language of the other, peace was secured.

In time, Shikulla thought, they would learn one another's language. He smiled. He would have the people make great statues and set them along the shore to honor the Great Water. They would build a huge temple, like the Temple of the Sun. He would be their leader.

He looked around for Matuq but could not see her. Well, she would turn up. He turned to the young girl he had been given and thought, *I really don't need Matuq anymore.*

Two heavy, squat men, sat cross-legged on the ground and beat instruments made from hollowed out pieces of wood with the skins of sea animals stretched tightly over one end. The sound they made when beaten echoed throughout the village and beyond. Shikulla had never heard this so-called drum before coming here. It produced a far different sound than that produced by the flute, which was the chosen instrument of his own people. The flute could be made to sing, its music floating melodically on the breeze but this instrument was deep and resonant and he imagined it to be like the heartbeat of a giant.

And yet Shikulla found this sound to his liking. He found the dancers to his liking, and he found the woman, Nalee, aroused him, as he had never been aroused before. When she danced for him her eyes flashed while her body swayed this way and that, imitating the motions made when mating. He grew so desirous that he feared just watching her dance would cause him to spill his seed on the ground. He did not care about other women, this girl Nalee was worth ten others.

She finished dancing and came to him, holding out her hands. He took them and followed her to one of the huts. It was festooned with the strange wildflowers he had seen growing in this place and they smelled sweet like her flesh. She said nothing but slowly slithered from her dress, revealing a ripe curvaceous nakedness that once again caused him to rise even as beads of sweat broke out along the top of his forehead.

She bowed down before him and to his shock; she enfolded his member in her hands and stroked it gently. Shikulla closed his eyes and looked heavenward. This was surely the way a God should be treated! Then of his amazement, she parted her lips and drew his member into her lovely mouth. She moved back and forth, flicking it with her tongue. He fell backward onto a pile of cushions but she did not let him go, she fell with him.

In his excitement, he could hold his seed no longer and it spurted forth.

Then to his surprise she slithered up the length of his body, pressing herself to him. He grasped her large breasts and then moved his hands over her till they were under her rounded buttocks. Again he felt himself rise.

Perspiration made their bodies slippery, and they both groaned with earthly pleasure in what seemed to Shikulla a white-hot heat of molten fire. Again he spilled his seed, this time into her. Then, for a long time he slept. Nalee lay by his side.

Nalee did not, however, sleep. She had not wanted to be the bride of the stranger, but it was not as bad as she imagined. And there was peace. Her father would live and her people would survive. The Gods of War had been appeased. Nalee smiled with satisfaction. She knew what pleased a man, and this man was no different than others.

#

The sunlight poured through the window of the hut. Shikulla stretched and sat up. The place beside him was empty, Nalee had already gotten up.

Shikulla rubbed his head. There had been many drinks and it occurred to him that these people drank a fermented liquid far more potent than that which he was used to consuming.

He pulled his legs over the side of the sleeping platform and looked about. His eyes fell on the bag that contained *The Key*. He had debated too long. He stood up and went to the bag, pulling its drawstring open. He brought the bag to the bed and sat down. Then he withdrew the ornate box. For a long moment he stared at it, then he opened it.

Shikulla stomped his foot and let out a loud curse. The box was filled with pebbles! Llayo had deceived him!

At the sound of his voice, Nalee came running, her eyes wide.

He turned to her mystified as she stared at the box. There was no mistaking the surprise in her eyes.

She came forward and touched the box, running her finger over it in awe, her lips parted.

He opened it to show her it was full of pebbles and she nodded, almost as if she understood. Then, in a movement that surprised him, she began pulling on him, motioning him to follow her.

Nalee was insistent and she kept repeating words in her own language as she pulled him along.

He followed only because of the look of urgency in her eyes. They walked for many miles and then she beckoned him to follow her up a narrow path. Silently, they wound their way up the mountain. Shikulla followed, pausing now and again to look down. From this height he could see the Great Water and the rocks that guarded the land. He could see the valley and the village beyond. It was an ideal spot for a village, for the nest of a Great Birdman.

He asked Nalee no questions because as yet they could not understand one another. Yet he continued to follow her.

After a time, they came to a place where the ground leveled off, though they were still far from the summit of the mountain.

Then Shikulla saw it and he stopped short. It was the entrance to a cave.

Nalee again motioned for him to follow.

Almost at once they came to a pit inside of which coals burned. An old man tended the fire, and he hardly looked up to acknowledge them.

Nalee went to the wall and took down a torch. She lit it from the coals that burned in the pit and led him on into the depths of the cave.

They entered a large chamber, off of which dark tunnels led in different directions. The inside walls of the cave glimmered in the torchlight. Shikulla touched the rock. It was black and smooth; it was the familiar rock found in the fire mountains. He wondered if these people also sharpened and fashioned it into tips for their hunting and fishing spears.

Nalee held up her torch.

At the far end of the chamber there was an altar made of the same black stone and atop it there was a box. Nalee pointed to it.

Shikulla went to it, feeling a cold chill climb his spine. The box was identical to the one he thought had contained *The Key*! He lifted it and examined it; he felt it with his fingers. He could not believe it! But how had it gotten here?

Another chill passed through him. This cave! It was not unlike the caves near Tiahuanaco! This cave must be a Paqarino! He opened the box and inside was a wooden tablet. It looked exactly the same as the tablet his own people possessed; the tablet Wishlay had shown him. It was covered with the same neat rows of mystical marks.

Shikulla sat down. What could this mean? His box was empty yet the tablet was here! It could only mean that the Gods had been here too. This was a sacred thing, a powerful thing. He decided instantly to have the artisans make copies of it.

After a time he stood up. He was alive, he was strong, and he had found a people to rule. Surely the presence of this tablet from the Gods was a sign that they smiled on him, that they had truly chosen him.

CHAPTER NINE

Jeff propped his head up with one arm and looked down at Corrie who slept beside him. Her blond hair was splayed out on the pillow, her lips ever so slightly parted.

She was wrapped in the sheet, having drawn it protectively about her in the early morning chill. She was so beautiful, he felt in awe of her. The taste of her was as sweet as honey; the memory of her writhing in his arms was nearly as arousing as the reality. "I won't let you go again," he promised her in a half whisper. She had cautioned him not to make promises when they were in the midst of lovemaking. She was right. He appreciated her good sense. They had, after all, just been reunited. Moreover, their time together in New Mexico had been short – only part of the summer. He knew that lasting relationships were built on two people really knowing one another, on mutual interests and on time spent together. His profession might take him anyplace; hers would most certainly take her to remote areas on archaeological expeditions. She seemed to know as well as he that neither of them could make a long-term commitment now. Still, he didn't want this relationship to be fleeting.

In a moment, temptation overcame him and he let his hand slip beneath the sheet to touch her. She moved a bit, then opened her eyes. Her first expression was one of surprise; her second was filled with the memory of recent pleasure.

She moaned as he continued his gentle probing. She turned about and put her arms around his neck, pressing the full length of her body against his.

"Oh, my" she whispered in his ear.

"Oh, yeah, I'm ready." His voice was husky. His hands eagerly explored her hot flesh as he kissed her again. In a moment they were tossing with each other, fondling one another, kissing and caressing.

"Morning becomes electric," he said, laughing at his appropriation of the title of the Greek drama.

"Or erotic," she whispered. Then, "Oh, don't stop – I love it when you do that."

He laughed, "I've found your weakness, my woman."

She enfolded him, "I've found your strength," she teased back.

He closed his eyes and tried to think of other things. If she kept it up – it was no use. He held both her breasts and entered her, trying hard not to come, still trying to hold himself back till he felt her on the brink, twisting beneath him, silently letting him know she was ready. Then he knew he could hold back no longer and in a twin miracle they both plunged into pleasure, their tension broken in a wild pulsating spasm of sheer joy. "I really do love you," he gasped. "It doesn't matter what we're doing or what time of day it is. I love you, Corrie Henley."

"I promise to remember under what circumstances you made that declaration."

He grinned at her and she slid away and got up. "We've got to get going or we'll miss the plane back to Chiclayo."

"Anxious to get back to your father?"

"Yes. I'm worried about him."

"At least we don't have to rent a car to get to the airport. We can take my car and leave it parked there."

"I hope Captain Toro doesn't ask what I bought."

"So, tell him the truth. Tell him we fell into bed and stayed there for two days."

"I will not! Besides, it hasn't been two days."

She put on her underwear and then her jeans and T-shirt. She shook her hair and brushed it back, off her face. It was a characteristic movement, something she did when she was trying to think of something.

Reluctantly, he rolled out of bed too. Corrie was right; they didn't have much time. But then, he reminded himself, it was not likely that the plane would leave on schedule.

#

Once again the sun was dipping into the sea. It shone through the back window of his jeep as they drove toward the Lima airport. Fortunately, that morning, before they left, Jeff had called the airport and discovered their flight was cancelled. He rescheduled on the late afternoon flight. "We've got awhile," he told her.

Suddenly there was unexpected time to kill. They had tea and toast in his landlady's Japanese garden . It was, as Jeff had promised, a refuge in the otherwise grim city.

"How long do you think you'll stay in Sipán and work with your father?"

"I'm not sure. I find the Moche fascinating."

He looked at her intently, "I've seen the expression on your face when you're examining artifacts. Tell me Corrie, what do you see?"

Her face flushed slightly, "You'll think I'm crazy. Sometimes I think I'm crazy."

"I'd never think you were crazy. Tell me, I was watching you the day we were looking at the artifacts your father found. You were transfixed."

"Do you promise not to laugh?"

"I promise."

"I see things as they were – I imagine the whole scene. It's as if it all comes alive for me. The daydream, or vision or whatever you want to call it doesn't last long. See, I just can't explain the experience without sounding like a flake."

He had taken her hands in his. "You don't have to explain, and you don't sound like a flake. Look, I'm a believer. Some people's intuitive powers are just greater than others."

"Thanks for not laughing."

"I want to laugh with you, not at you." He didn't declare his love again nor his intention not to lose her. She had just illustrated how much she trusted him and he knew that there were things he would have to tell her too. She hadn't yet asked if he had any secrets. Perhaps she hadn't asked because she trusted him to tell her all about himself. He realized now that their summer romance had been just that, a summer romance. The lovemaking was hot, the confidences few. He knew now that they were on the way to the next level, that level of loving trust. "The better someone knows you, the more they can hurt you," his mother had once said. He supposed that was true since you were apt to confess your weaknesses to those close to you.

#

Many hours later, they were back in Chiclayo, driving in from the airport.

"Mountains in front of us, the sea behind us," Corrie mused, "There's something mystical about the Andes, it's as if they're the rim of the world."

"You have a poetic streak."

"Do I?"

"Yes. And I love you," he said. "Please note, we are not in bed."

"I wonder if he'll notice," Corrie said as she let her hand drop to Jeff's knee.

"Who?"

"My father, I wonder if he'll notice that we're – you know, together."

Jeff laughed, "How would he know? Am I wearing a sign that says, 'very happy guy who got lucky?'"

"No. But he's observant. You know, when two people are intimate their space relationship changes. They touch more often and they stand closer together."

"Ah, so your father is an interpreter of non verbal communication."

"I think you could say that."

He turned the car, and the familiar main street came into view. In moments they pulled up in front of the hotel.

"I hope dad is all right. It seems like every time we go somewhere we return to find out someone else is dead."

They got out and went inside. Corrie smiled, feeling instantly relived. Jonathan Henley was waiting for them.

"Good trip?" he asked anxiously.

"Very," Jeff replied for both of them. "Not that we really found much out, it's more that we have some clues now, something to go on. We're getting an idea of who the players are even if we don't yet understand the game."

"I'm looking forward to hearing everything. Have you eaten?" Jonathan asked.

"Not since lunch. We're famished. It's not like we've just flown on a real airline, you know. They don't serve anything on the plane and there aren't any fast food restaurants out there."

"How well I know it. Hey, enjoy it while it's not here. Can cheeseburgers and Inca World be far off?"

"Inca World? Oh, really," Corrie said, a bemused look on her face.

Jonathan shrugged, "I can see it now. A huge roller coaster round the valley of the sun, Disneyland South."

Jeff liked Jonathan Henley's sense of sarcasm and distaste for the seamless cultural sameness of the developed world. His humor was quite evident in his banter with his daughter. It was an attitude he shared and once again he thought how much he liked Henley. Just as well, he told himself. In spite of all the difficulties he knew they would have to overcome, he kind of hoped that one day soon Henley would be his father-in-law.

"Just let me go wash up. I'll meet you two in the dining room," Corrie waved and hurried off.

Jeff nodded as he too headed off to his room. He would quickly change and shower, but he damn well hoped to be sleeping elsewhere tonight. Corrie's room was a floor below his and while he would keep his room for the sake of appearances, he intended being with her.

Corrie walked down the dimly lit corridor. She stopped outside her room and fumbled in her bag for the key. *A quick shower, clean clothes and I'll be a new person*, she thought.

The door swung open and Corrie flipped the light switch. Outside, it was dark and as her room faced the garden, no street lights shown through the window. "Damn!" the light did not go on, and she assumed that the bulb needed changing. She walked across the block of light provided by the open door. *Turn on the bedside lamp.* She had just reached the bed when the door slammed shut and the room was plunged into total darkness. Corrie turned about suddenly and was caught in the iron grip of large arms. A cloth was pushed over her face before she could utter a single sound. She struggled for a moment, and was only dimly aware of the odor of chloroform as the blackness of the room turned into the darkness of unconsciousness.

#

As usual, the tables in the dining room of *La Gan Vida,* were covered with crisp white linen tablecloths. In the center of each table a candle flickered. The candles were designed specifically to drip in a multitude of colors in order to create a miniature rainbow in wax on the sides of the Chianti bottles into which they had been thrust.

Jeff had come back down to the dining room almost thirty minutes ago. He tapped his foot nervously and stared at the candle. "These were real popular in the fifties. My mom had one. She said she worked on it for nearly two years and couldn't bear to throw it out because it reminded her of her youth."

Jonathan smiled, "I think every Italian restaurant in Boston had them for awhile."

"Herr Ehrlich must have bought them wholesale." Jeff looked nervously toward the door again. He glanced at his watch. "I know Corrie; she's been way too long. I'm going upstairs to make sure she's okay."

He shoved his chair back and stood up. Jonathan Henley did likewise, "I'm coming with you."

They had been making small talk. It was evident that as time dragged on both of them wondered why Corrie had been gone so long.

They crowded into the closet sized elevator and pushed four. They strode down the hall together when simultaneously they saw that the door to Corrie's room was ajar.

"Corrie!" Jeff called out as he burst into the empty room.

He flung open the bathroom door to find it as empty and as dark as the room. Jonathan Henley turned on the bedside lamp. Corrie's bag was on the floor, its contents strewn about.

Jeff could feel his heart beating wildly. Why the hell had he let her out of his sight? He sniffed, "Smell that? It's chloroform."

Jonathan Henley was holding onto the bedside table to steady himself. "I should have made her go home," he said in a hoarse voice. "Should I notify Toro? Not that I intend waiting for him to find her."

Jeff shook his head.

Jonathan Henley sank onto the bed. He looked utterly defeated and bewildered. "She's all I have," he said slowly.

She's all I want, Jeff thought.

"What did you learn in Lima?"

Jeff could hear the fear in Henley's voice. He needed something to hold on to, some explanation. "In a nutshell, we learned that at least two parties are interested in some artifact."

"What two parties?"

"Conway – the head of Conex and benefactor of the museum that funds your work, and the Arab Toro mentioned, the one who was tied up with Myra."

"What was his name?"

"Karim Ali Ahmed, he's a Sudanese of shadowy background who may be linked to a terrorist group."

It was as if Jonathan was struggling with the concept. Then after a minute he mumbled, "Conway I understand, he's an acquisitive bastard but this Karim Ali Ahmed? When did terrorists become interested in artifacts?"

"When the artifact involved is believed to have great value. Maybe it's worth more than any of us can imagine and he wants the money to fund his activities. Right now we can only guess. Anyway, I'm going after Corrie."

"What has Corrie to do with any of this? Why have they taken her? Damn, I should have made her go back to Boston."

"I don't think it would have mattered. She's a way to get to you. One or both of our two player's thinks you've found or will find what they want. Clearly they intend to trade it for Corrie."

"I can try to phone Conway right now."

"No. Besides we have no way of knowing if he's got Corrie or this Karim Ali Ahmed has got her. You stay here and wait to be contacted. I'll go to Conway."

"What about Toro? You don't think I should call him?"

"Hell no! Who knows who he works for – I mean beside the Peruvian Federal Police. Let's keep this between the two of us, at least for the moment."

Jonathan Henley nodded. "Find her," he said gripping Jeff's shoulder.

Jeff pressed his lips together. "I will. I have to."

#

La Guardia was a mess. It was filled with ill- tempered passengers, autocratic flight staff, and over zealous security staff. An ice storm in the Midwest had caused the cancellation of innumerable flights and confusion ruled supreme.

Jeff pushed past expensive stores, once again noting that airports were all turning into shopping malls. He stepped out of the terminal and inhaled. After so many hours on the plane even the air in New York smelled fresh. He wished he had been able to sleep on the plane, but his mind refused to stop working and to make matters worse, the further he flew from Peru, the further he felt he was flying away from Corrie. Part of his feeling was instinctive, the other logical. No matter who had her, they probably would not travel far. Border crossings and customs made roaming about with a hostage close to impossible.

All his instincts told him that Conway didn't have her. His reasoning was a bit muddled, but he kept asking himself why Conway would bother. Henley worked for him, Corrie worked for him. If he had wanted to use Corrie to make Jonathan help him, he could have kidnapped her in Boston before she ever left for Peru. Nevertheless, he had to see Conway. Conway was one of the few people who had the international resources to find Karim Ali Ahmed, and he was certain that it was Karim who had taken Corrie. He was just as certain that her life was in danger.

171

He looked up as the shuttle bus pulled up in front of the terminal. He had to change to a commuter flight and thus was compelled to change terminals. Another hour or so and he would be in Boston. He had wired, faxed and phoned Conway's only known number from the plane. Conway was a hard man to get hold of but Jeff was certain Conway would want to see him, especially since it was Conway who was responsible for him being involved in the first place. In fact, based on what he had read about Jason Conway, it would not have surprised him to discover that Conway knew he had left Peru and was on his way. He wanted to confront Conway, and something told him that Conway would allow him to do so, if only to find out what he knew.

#

Jason Conway crumpled up Jeff's fax and tossed it across the room into the wastebasket. He had already received the wire and the phone message. "A bit redundant, our Mr. Richards." He was talking to himself. He talked to himself often. Still, a little redundancy could be forgiven, he decided. Mr. Richards had no way of knowing if those who received the messages would pass them on. Conex was, after all, a large company and Mr. Richards had used a general address.

Jason Conway at all times maintained a 'preferential list' and though they did not know it, Henley, his daughter, and Jeff Richards were now on it. Any messages from the preferred list were immediately passed on.

As much as he hated reporters, he knew he had to see Richards. In any case, Richards wanted something, so his temporary silence could be bargained for and if necessary, his permanent silence guaranteed. "Not as if you're from big time media." He thought of Richards and imagined their meeting.

Vaguely, he wondered if Richards would be surprised when the limousine met him. He leaned back and checked his watch. It wouldn't be long now. He felt a little like a puppeteer. It was not the first time he had felt he was the master manipulator; it was a feeling he liked.

The phone on the table next to him rang and he picked it up to hear Kenji's anxious voice on the other end.

"So that's why Richards is on his way here -," he muttered. "Thanks." He hung up. Corrie Henley had been kidnapped and Richards was coming here because he needed help.

He scowled and thought about his competition. Doubtless the one to have all the tablets would have the upper hand, but they would need each other anyway. The 'goods' so to speak, required a delivery system. He had a delivery system and more important, his competitor was no stranger to him.

He let his memories flood over him in order to bring his competitor into focus. Vaguely he wondered how much the boy had changed over the years.

They had met just as he was starting out in business. Computers were massive in those days, but he was among those who saw the future. He was looking for a programmer when a young kid presented himself. The kid didn't even have a college degree but he was a mathematical genius. It took him only a week to conclude that the kid, who called himself Karim, might have benefited MIT but that MIT had little to offer the kid. He hired the kid. He was reasonably sure Karim was sixteen or seventeen when he was twenty-five. Since he was now fifty-eight, Karim would be forty-nine.

When first he obtained the Easter Island tablet, he showed it to Karim. The two of them knew what it was, they both saw it instantly. Not that they could make use of it. It was only one; they both knew there had to be more.

After a time Karim had gone on to other things. He dropped completely out of sight but now he had resurfaced, wealthy and with an unsavory reputation. Still, Conway felt confident. Karim needed him. He would need him even if he had all the other tablets. Naturally, he intended to do his best to see to it that Karim did not obtain all the tablets. On the other hand, if he himself had them, he would not need Karim. He was the one with the delivery system.

#

Jeff shouldered his pack and made his way toward the escalator in Boston's Logan Airport. Even through the tinted windows he could see that it was snowing out. He cursed under his breath. Snow would make a cab harder to get, not that he exactly knew where he was headed.

"Jeff Richards. Jeff Richards to the American Airlines Information Counter. Jeff Richards to the American Airlines Information Counter."

Jeff automatically looked up at the somewhat garbled sound of his name. He had halfway been expecting a page, so he had been listening. And he thought, if he hadn't been listening, he would have missed it. It was a marvel to him, with all of today's technology, that the speaker systems in airports were almost completely unintelligible.

He turned on his heel and headed off toward the information counter. *I ought to be falling down asleep.* The truth was, although tired, he was going on nervous energy. It was not a good thing. He was pretty sure if he flapped his arms he could take off without a plane.

"Mr. Richards?"

A uniformed driver with a swarthy complexion and dark moustache stepped to his side.

"Here," Jeff said.

"I'm here to take you to Mr. Conway."

Jeff didn't say anything, he simply followed the driver. They left the airport through a special VIP exit that Jeff had not even known existed. Directly outside, the long black sleek limousine was parked in a special VIP parking space.

"One of the privileges of having more bread than the airline, right?"

"I just drive, sir," the driver opened the door with a suitable flourish, "Make yourself at home, sir. There's a bar on the left and display screen in the center. There is a choice of short programming or a direct feed from the stock ticker of all the indices."

'All the stock indices.' Jeff did not laugh, though he wanted to laugh. If he gathered up all his money he probably couldn't pay for a hundred shares of GE. He'd gotten a cash advance on his credit card to pay for this trip.

Jeff climbed into sumptuous soft leather luxury. The windows weren't simply tinted; they were covered with actual window shades. It was a real cocoon. He did not avail himself of the bar nor did he activate the screen. Instead, he leaned back and closed his eyes. Good thing it wasn't a long ride, he acknowledged. His nervous energy was now giving way to weariness; weariness brought on by the comfort of the soft leather on which he sat and the absolute silence inside the limousine. This was not, he reminded himself, how the other half lived. This was how about one twelfth of one per cent lived, though he supposed that after the first couple of billion more billions didn't make all that much difference to one's standard of living.

He was on the edge of sleep when for some reason he began to think about the driver. How was it to drive people about all day? What kind of guy took such a job? He thought about the driver's face – was he Italian? And what kind of accent was that? His accent was slight, but it was there, nonetheless. Jeff sat up straight as adrenaline suddenly surged through him. They were allegedly on

175

their way from Logan Airport into Boston. Logan was on a spit of land that extended out into Boston harbor. The ride should not have taken long, but more important, they should have been in stop and go traffic. To his knowledge Conway lived somewhere near the Charles River. But the limousine did not seem to be starting and stopping as it would have had it joined the traffic flow on Storrow Drive that ran by the Charles River.

He lifted the shade in the limousine and peered out through the tinted glass. They were definitely not headed into the city.

He leaned back against the seat and told himself he was stupid. He had blithely gone off with a perfect stranger, now he was in a car headed God knew where. Assuming Conway would see him, then it seemed clear someone else did not want him to reach Conway. The only someone he could think of was Karim. Probably this was Conway's limousine. It seemed likely to him that something had happened to the original driver.

Carefully he slid over and tried the door handle. It was locked and he knew damn well only the driver could open it. He decided against yelling and screaming. When he reached wherever he was being taken, he might pretend to be asleep. That way, when he suddenly resisted, it would be a surprise. Of course the driver might just be taking him out in the country so he could be shot. In which case he would have to change his plans and act more quickly. He concluded it would be better to play drunk than sleepy.

Better not to struggle, he told himself again and again. On the other hand he'd better prepare to fight for his life. He turned on the video and opened the bar to look for possible weapons. There was an assortment soft plastic bottles filled with cola, ginger ale, and lime soda. There was an array of alcohol. His eyes fell on a small bottle of Tabasco sauce used to make Bloody Marys. He quickly shook its entire contents into a plastic glass and added a splash of vodka. Next he popped the shade off the rear window and tore out its wooden roller. It was at least two feet long. *A stick in the sleeve is worth two in the bush.* He started to think it all through. When the door was opened he would just stagger out and act as if he didn't know where Conway lived. He'd see how many there were and see if they were armed. If he was lucky, and if he surprised them, he might be able to take them. His Aikido training was about self-defensive strategy and maintaining spiritual calm. This was his biggest test ever and he had to admit he was failing the spiritually calm aspect. He could all but hear his heart beating, but as they drove on, he managed to achieve a degree of control.

They drove for almost an hour. Jeff clicked on the intercom to the driver and slurred "Hey, Reemind me too, ah, thank Conway for the great limo service. Nothing better than good booze. Hey will we be there soon?"

"A few more minutes."

There was no 'Sir' this time. *Stupid, stupid stupid.* He could hear the driver's Middle Eastern accent. Why had he not noticed it before.

The limo glided to a stop. The door on his left was yanked open. He felt a cold icy wind, tinged with salt air.

"Get the hell out of there," the driver said. It was a long way from the polite, subservient tone he had used earlier.

Jeff groaned, "Am I heeere!" He staggered out of the limo holding the glass in his right hand. It was cold and blustery, the wind ripped right through his light clothing. Another car pulled up. It skidded to a halt on the stones. Two men scrambled out. The driver yelled something in Arabic. One of the arrivals responded in English, "Drunk, huh." He spit on the ground.

Jeff squinted at them uncomprehendingly, trying to look mystified. As far as he could tell, only one, a big swarthy skinned guy coming toward him on his left, had a gun drawn. Jeff waited till the gunman got close enough. Then he simultaneously threw the contents of the cup directly into the eyes of the driver and letting the stick slip from his sleeve, hit the hand of the gunman with a forceful blow of the stick. The driver screamed out in pain and shouted, "I'm blinded!"

The gun dropped. Without a moment's hesitation Jeff hit the gunman in the face with stick. As he came forward to grab Jeff, Jeff dropped down across the attacker's front punching him in the ribs and throwing him head first into the side of the limousine. He crumpled to the ground. Jeff was on his knees as he quickly turned to the third man who was in the act of reaching for the gun on the ground just to Jeff's left. Jeff moved instantly toward him, grabbing his hand and twisting both his hand and the gun toward his assailant. It discharged grazing the guy's thigh. He went down screaming in pain and clutching himself. The driver had acquired some sight and came charging at Jeff who extended his arms to meet his attacker. Jeff threw him head over heels onto the rough stone. He groaned after landing but he didn't get up again. Jeff quickly went through the man's pockets. He had a huge wad of bills. Jeff stuck them in his pocket and then grabbed the gun and emptied it into the tires of his assailant's car. He decided to take it rather than leave it, so he tossed it onto the front seat of the limousine.

He wiped the sweat off his forehead. Then he rubbed his knees. He was about to climb in when he paused for a single second and then leaned over. There was noise coming from the trunk. He opened the trunk from the front seat, and then went back. The driver was curled up in the trunk, stripped to his underwear, bound and gagged with duct tape. Jeff ripped off the duct tape.

"I'm freezing," the driver managed.

"Bet you are. Come on, there's a blanket in the car."

"He has my uniform," pointing to the groaning guy on the ground.

"We really don't have time. I don't want that one to come to and I certainly don't want anyone to stumble on this little scene. Hurry up. Get in."

The driver did as he was told. Jeff threw him the blanket. "I'll drive, you tell me where."

In moments they were lost in traffic on the interstate. Jeff drove fast, but not fast enough to attract the police. After all, it wouldn't look good that he had a recently discharged gun, had a wad of money, and smelled of alcohol.

The limousine driver handed him a key card for the underground garage. "We're a sight," Jeff said as they headed through the dark garage toward the elevator.

"Doesn't matter. No one will see us. It's a private elevator. You'll need the key-card again."

The condo building was way above average and the elevator that ascended to the twenty-fourth floor penthouse suite was leather lined with a thick carpet. It came to a smooth stop, the doors opened, and they emerged into a stark white marble foyer that held several statues and two busts on marble columns. A somber butler greeted them and muttered something under his breath before rushing off.

He returned minutes later and sent the driver in one direction and led him off in another.

The butler ushered him past a formal living room filled with more artwork and into a small, more warmly furnished study.

"Mr. Conway will join you presently," the manservant told him.

Jeff sank into a leather sofa and tried to conjure up an image of Jason Conway. For as often as Conway's name was in the papers, Conway's picture had never appeared, at least to his knowledge. Just why Conway was so secretive was of no concern to him. In any case, considering Conway's fame, the desire for absolute privacy didn't seem all that unusual.

He took stock of the room he was in. It would have been cozy had there been a fireplace instead of a huge screen that took up almost the entire opposite wall. It was like a great glass eye and it made him uncomfortable. It occurred to him that it might be one

179

way glass, but he discarded the idea. Conway was a computer man extraordinary, a master of the networks. In all likelihood the screen was one giant monitor.

The door opened and Jeff looked up, or more accurately, down. "Ah, the persistent Mr. Richards."

Jeff's own mental picture of Conway had been of someone like Bill Gates, a kind of smiling boyish person with thick glasses and disorganized hair. That image was a long way from the reality of Jason Conway.

First, Jeff had to mask his surprise. Jason Conway was a very short man, though not a midget. Conway stood just slightly higher than his own waist. He had receding hair and bright dark eyes. He was overweight, and his voice had a distinct raspy quality.

"You look like hell."

Jeff scowled at him. "Thanks for your concern."

Conway shrugged. "What happened?"

"Your driver was waylaid and stuffed into the trunk of your limousine. I was picked up and driven half way to Maine before I was dragged out of the car by two guys who wanted to kill me."

"I thought there had been trouble. Even when the traffic's bad it doesn't take that long to get here from the airport." He laughed, clearly thinking he had made a joke.

"I was almost killed," Jeff snapped.

"Well you have all that training – I'm sure it proved useful." Jeff just stared at him.

"Now, now, relax. You've been in transit a long while. I've arranged for supper later. In about an hour. Is that all right?"

"Yes."

In addition to being raspy, he spoke in bursts and he spoke quickly, rather as if his sentences were shot from a gun.

"Will you have a drink?"

"Yes, but first I'd like to give you this. It needs to be gotten rid of." He dangled the gun by its trigger and Conway gingerly took it.

He didn't mention the cash. He decided since it was doubtless Karim's money, he would use it to pay for the trip.

"And I'd like to wash up. Where's the bathroom?"

"Sure, fourth door on the left. Come back here and we'll discuss the rules."

Jeff didn't ask what rules. He just left to clean up. As he sat on the toilet, he withdrew the money. He counted it once and then again. There was over twelve thousand – eight one thousand dollar bills and forty hundred dollar bills plus a couple of twenties. Big bills were hard to get rid of – but he packed it into his billfold anyway.

In a few minutes he returned to the den. Jason Conway handed him a drink and they both sat down.

"I like the way you just up and took off, decided to brave the lion in his own lair," Conway said as he hopped up into his chair.

"Are you a lion?"

"When it suits me. First the rules. Then we'll talk."

"Rules?"

"Yes. You are to write nothing about me that is not in the printed material you'll receive when you leave. Under no circumstances is my photo to be taken and you are to sign a confidentiality contract forbidding you to write a description of me. Is that clear?"

"I don't have a camera and I didn't come here to interview you," Jeff answered with weary irritation.

"Your facial expression gives your feelings away. It's a bad habit, especially if you're playing poker."

"I'm not playing poker or any other game," Jeff snapped.

"Be that as it may, I still require that you follow the rules."

"And if I don't?"

Conway walked to his bar and poured himself a second hefty shot of straight scotch. "Then I'll have you killed."

He said it so casually, Jeff almost laughed. But he didn't. Conway probably wasn't kidding. "Okay. I'll follow the rules."

"Good. Now, why are you here?"

"Corrie Henley has been kidnapped."

Conway's expression did not change. "I know that. I'm not the one who kidnapped her."

"I didn't think you were but I think you may have the resources to find her."

"Umm, possibly. Why would I want to find her?"

"Because then her father might find what you want."

It was a bold move forward and he was not at all sure how to follow it up. Maybe he was playing poker. The trouble was, he was playing with faceless, numberless cards.

"I don't think her father knows what I want."

Jeff drew in his breath. "That *will* make it harder to find. Why don't we stop playing this silly game? Why don't you tell me what it is you and Karim Ali Ahmed are looking for?"

"Ah, so you know about my friend Karim."

"Oh, yeah. I kind of think he may have been responsible for my reception at the airport. I'm also reasonably sure he has Corrie.

Conway ignored him. "I suppose finding the girl would be in my interest. If Ahmed Allah has her he will hold her for ransom."

Jeff felt slightly relieved. At least Conway saw a reason for helping him. "First things first. What the hell is this all about?"

"I have no intention of telling you everything. It would be far too dangerous. But a little enlightenment is necessary. Let me draw your attention to the screen."

He pointed to the wall screen and pressed a button on a remote control he took from his pocket. Immediately a picture filled the screen. It appeared to be a tablet about the size of an art book. Conway pushed the button again and the picture was enlarged. Jeff could see the tablet was covered with symbols.

"This is the Easter Island tablet. There are copied fragments on Easter Island for all to see but I have the original, the only whole tablet of all the pieces on Easter Island."

"I really don't understand."

"There are others like it. Seven to be exact."

"Do you have them?"

"No, but I know where they are."

"What's so damn valuable about these tablets?"

"Our mutual business does not necessitate going into that, Richards. Let's just say one is no good without all of them and if I have the one I know was buried by the Moche, then I can avail myself of the others."

Jeff continued to stare at the screen. The same bizarre idea he had when he and Corrie had been looking up Karim's biography on his computer crossed his mind now. He didn't say anything to Conway. The less Conway thought he grasped the better. He took one last look at the tablet. The value clearly was in what it revealed, or rather what all seven revealed. Then too, maybe the value was in what some people *thought* it revealed. He tried to concentrate on the markings that covered it. The markings were in continuous rows, with no spaces in between. Some long buried fact jabbed at the edge of his mind but he couldn't bring it into focus. He was too worried about Corrie, about getting her back alive.

"Okay, so now I know what you're looking for. But what about Corrie?

"You will send Henley a message which I will have delivered by someone trustworthy. You will describe what he is to search for and tell him that if he finds it, it is to be kept secret and given only to me. In return for his help I will assist you in locating his daughter."

"Is something wrong with e-mail?"

"Hardly secure."

Jeff didn't argue and he assumed the same was true of phone calls. "If I may ask, why didn't you tell Henley what you were looking for in the first place?"

"It wasn't necessary. If he found a tablet such as the one I have shown you, he would have known what a sensational discovery he had made and would have notified the museum immediately. Thus I would have been informed right away and been able to take steps to protect it."

Jeff did not say what he was thinking; that an academic discovery was one thing but that it seemed obvious the tablets had value far beyond that. *And therein lies the real mystery, seven wooden tablets that were worth killing for – wanted by a wealthy eccentric computer billionaire, an Arab with shadowy financial dealings, and only God knew who else.*

#

Ramon Garcia inhaled the rarified Andean air. Some would have been made dizzy by it, but he was now used to the lack of oxygen in spite of having spent so much time at sea level. Not that Quito was at a very great altitude. It was in one of Ecuador's many intermontane valleys and was around nine thousand feet.

He retrieved his car from the garage where it had been left for safekeeping and began the long drive home. The best that could be said for the journey was that it was down hill most of the way and all but the last fifty kilometers were on the Pan American Highway.

It was seven o'clock Sunday morning. Church bells tolled constantly, but the streets were nearly deserted.

Quito was an old and quite lovely city by any standards. For many years after its founding by one of Pizarro's Conquistadors, it had been a center for artists and craftsmen from all over Hispanic America. Beautiful old houses with wrought iron balconies were common, and many homes were veritable museums filled with intricate carvings. But there was also an aura of decay in Quito; he thought the aura suitable for a city built in a valley surrounded by volcanoes.

He thought for a moment about the girl. Shortly after he arrived home, he would have her brought from the place where she had been taken initially. Not that she would remember much. He had instructed his men to keep her drugged.

He quickly turned his mind to other thoughts; dwelling on the girl might cause him to become overwrought just when he had regained control. What was at stake was his destiny, the destiny of the world. It was far more important than the fate of one girl.

Next he thought about the old man, the one the English nurses had called, "dotty," by which they meant foolish or obsessed. He was, of course both. He was obsessed with the tablets and foolish because he had never figured them out. He was born too soon; he had obtained the tablets at the wrong moment in history. He didn't know what they were and he could not even make capital on them in academic circles because by the time he tried to float his theory, he was already thought peculiar and his ravings were shrugged off as more evidence of his deteriorating mental state. Ah! If only carbon dating had existed!

"I shall have no such difficulty," he said aloud. He knew exactly what the tablets were and exactly what had to be done with them.

CHAPTER TEN

750 AD. Bombay, India

The fortress on Gharapuri Island faced the Arabian Sea. It was a solid wall of stone, windowless except for small slits around an enclosed catwalk at its top. From these slits, the sea could be watched and the movements and intent of vessels entering Bombay's inner channel could be monitored. Inside its thick walls, the fortress was dark and dank. Rope ladders led up to platforms on nine levels, off the platforms there were rows of tiny cells. The tenth level led to the catwalk. Once the fortress had held prisoners, now it was deserted and only the skeletons of the incarcerated remained within the crumbling cells. The fortress was a lonely place, some said haunted by those who had died imprisoned and forgotten.

Rajiv, one of seven Brahman Priests who called themselves the *Sons of Kali,* paced. His anger was evident in his body movements, in his facial expression and in the tone in which he spoke.

"We must find it," he shouted. He spit out his words.

Sadish who sat on a stone bench against the wall followed Rajiv's every movement with darting feral eyes. "We've searched their entire compound, torn out the walls, and destroyed everything. The sacred box is gone, and with it the treasure."

"Tell me something I don't already know." Rajiv recalled every detail of the night they had attacked the Guardians. Not one of the twelve had been left alive. Their throats had been slit; rivulets of blood had run across the floor of their compound, their deaths were a glorious sacrifice to *Kali.*

He looked up at the giant statue of the Goddess that stood on one side of the room. She rose from the floor to the third platform. *Kali* was a fierce terrifying aspect of *Devi,* the Supreme Goddess, the consort of *Shiva.* Her face was hideous, black, and smeared with blood. Her teeth were bared like those of a mad dog, her tongue protruded from a twisted mouth. She had four arms that held a shield, a sword, the severed head of a giant, and a noose. *Kali* was naked, adorned only in a garland of skulls and a girdle of severed hands. *Kali* was said to have grown fond of blood when she killed the demon, *Raktavija.* It was told that the demon could reproduce itself a thousand fold with each drop of his blood that hit the ground. *Kali* slew him with her sword and lifted him high, drinking his blood before it could reach the ground and he could multiply.

There were those who did not understand the different faces of Devi as Rajiv and his compatriots did. The ancients had taught all about the faces of good and evil, about the need for both. One could simply not exist without the other.

Rajiv knew that all believers had Gods to good and evil. He knew these things because Bombay had long been a seaport and it had been visited by Greeks, Egyptians and Persians. He had learned of religions that revered the day and feared the night. Light and darkness, black and white - *Kali* meant black in Sanskrit and he knew full well that no *faith* was without a God or Goddess of Darkness, be it Osiris, the Egyptian Prince of Darkness, Lucifer the fallen Angel, or Ahriman, the Persian God of evil. And had not the ancient Greeks had the concept of chaos – a world before the Gods appeared and slew the evil monsters?

In fact, *The Sons of Kali* were probably older than their name. They were a secret society of twelve members, though five had recently perished. New initiates would soon join their ranks so that their number could remain constant.

There were stories; tales passed on from father to son. Few Brahmans knew these tales, but he had been privileged to hear them because he sprang from a special family, because he was the hereditary leader of *The Sons of Kali.* That was why the treasure had to be found. It was the destiny of he and his compatriots to find the treasure that for many centuries had been in the hands of *The Twelve Guardians* and restore it to *Kali* its rightful owner.

187

It was said that once, long ago, those who were today called Brahmans, had seen to the spiritual needs of all the earth's people. Then there had been no Hindi, Urdu, Marathi, Egyptian, Greek, or Farsi language. There had been one language spoken by all, one Priesthood who served all. The Priesthood was hereditary, as was the priesthood of the Brahmans who descended from it. The priests had come from the sacred caves, here and elsewhere. The Gods had given them the treasure. He did not know when the privileged who knew the tales became separated from the others, or when two distinct groups who claimed stewardship over the treasure came into being. He only knew *The Sons of Kali* had to retrieve the treasure from *the Guardians* and that in spite of overtaking them and killing them, the treasure was still not in his hands. It was lost; he feared it might be lost forever.

"What are we to do? Sadish asked.

"We are to keep looking. We are to ask questions. They had it, and now it is gone. Someone took it. We must not cease looking. You and the others are to go forth and ask questions. I want to know where the families of the deceased live. I want to know if they had friends, I want to know all there is to know of these men. If others must die, then so be it. We will find the treasure. As he spoke, he turned toward *Kali.* "We serve you," he whispered.

Sadish bowed and backed away from Rajiv. There was no question that more blood would be spilled. Rajiv was not just the leader of their band, he was possessed by *Kali.* Rajiv terrified Sadish, even though Sadish was a man who had seen much evil.

#

Candra was the richest man within a radius of one hundred miles. His fertile land reached to the Ghat Mountains on one side and to the river on the other. Over two hundred tenants worked for him, and he had built a school and a beautiful temple. He lived in a fine hilltop house with forty rooms and seven terraces. Those terraces located at the rear of his house faced the mountain cliffs that rose to meet the sky.

Everyone agreed that Candra was a man of great accomplishment and considerable generosity. At the age of forty he had increased his inheritance ten-fold. He had greatly improved his own house and the houses of those who worked for him. He had built a school for the children, encouraged the arts and paid musicians to provide fine music at religious festivals. His personal quarters were filled with sculptures and at least twice a week he reclined against satin pillows and listened to Samudya, the Master of Music, play the lyre. Candra possessed nearly every luxury a man could own and yet he yearned for that which was beyond the material world. He desired knowledge and understanding. In his early years all he had thought of was consolidating his power, but there came a time in a man's life when power was not enough, there came a time when a man asked, 'why?'.

"Uncreated, eternal, infinite, transcendent – it is being and non being – it is the sole reality, the ultimate source and goal of existence," Maheesh, the Brahman Priest said.

"Brahman," Candra concluded.

Maheesh, nodded. "It is the *All.* Brahman causes the universe and all beings to emanate from itself, transforms itself into the universe, or assumes its appearance. Brahman is all things, and is the self of all living beings. Brahman is the creator, preserver, transformer, and reabsorber of everything. Ours is the search for the ultimate reality."

"And when I pass?" Candra asked. "What will happen to me?"

"If you follow the *Way of the Ancestors, you will travel* through dark nights for half a year during the southern course of the sun, and failing to reach a full year, your soul will return to earth, enclosed in a raindrop. If you fall on a plant eaten by man, and that man impregnates his wife, your soul will be reborn."

Candra did not ask Maheesh what would happen if he followed the *Way of the Gods* instead of *the Way of the Ancestors*. He knew he could not follow the *Way of the Gods* because he was not sufficiently holy to be ready for Brahman. Each life was a new opportunity to take yet another step toward Brahman.

"It is so complicated," Candra complained.

"Some concepts cannot be explained. The secret of understanding is to let your mind embrace an idea the way a woman's womb embraces the embryo."

"I try to understand."

"You do better than most. But then, you might do better if you were not so distracted."

Candra smiled. He enjoyed Maheesh on two distinct levels. On one level he enjoyed him as a religious instructor and guide. On another level he enjoyed him as a mentor, a man of wisdom who helped him to see and solve everyday problems.

In actual fact, their relationship was something of a marvel. Candra had not known Maheesh long. Indeed, the Brahman Priest had come to him only a few months ago.

It was as if fate had ordained their meeting. Candra was alone by the river, watching as it flowed from the mountains to irrigate his land. He was in his special place, a place of great tranquility, and a spot he visited often. He was not certain how many years he had been coming to that place where the river turned, but he was certain he had first been here with his mother when he was only a babe in arms. In any case, it was a place to which he came to contemplate and he had reached that stage in life when contemplation seemed to take him over, when finding the answers to life's riddles seemed a most important task.

He was lost in thought when he saw Maheesh. He knew instantly from his bearing and the manner of his dress that Maheesh was a Brahman Priest. He wore long flowing white robes trimmed with gold thread. He was about Candra's own age, and yet he had a regal bearing and a special kind of peace about him.

Candra had approached the stranger. "You are a Brahman Priest, are you not?"

"I am, Lord Candra."

"You know my name?" Candra was surprised.

"I make it a policy to know the names of the men who own the land I cross."

"You're welcome here. Will you take supper with me?"

"I would be most grateful."

If asked now, Candra could not explain why he had invited the stranger to supper, or even why he welcomed him. He was convinced their meeting was Karma. Perhaps their souls had spoken to one another for he was instantly drawn to the Brahman. In the months that followed they became close friends, Maheesh stayed and became his personal spiritual advisor.

"You are lost in thought. I know something troubles you."

"It's my forthcoming marriage," he confessed.

Maheesh's bright eyes danced with interest but he did not smile. "You are a man with many wives now, how can one more make you nervous?"

Candra squirmed slightly with discomfort and his face flushed with embarrassment. "My bride to be is the most beautiful woman in the district, perhaps in all of India. And she is young, much younger than I."

Maheesh still did not smile. "I think this is not what you mean to say."

Candra cleared his throat. "You're right. I mean to say that I would rid myself of all my other wives simply to make this one happy. I love her."

"Ah, and does she love you?"

"How could she. She has never even seen me."

191

"I can instruct you on how to make her happy. Indeed, she will want no other. But you must have confidence, not just in yourself, but in her. Happiness and physical fulfillment are the forerunners of love, so I believe she will come to love you."

Candra felt nothing but awe. Was there nothing these Brahman Priests did not know? He had never dreamed that this was a matter with which Maheesh could help.

"If you can teach me secrets that will enchant her I will do anything you wish."

"I wish nothing for myself, but everything for Lord Shiva."

"I do not understand," Candra said, a frown covering his face. When he said he did not understand, he meant that he did not understand specifically what Maheesh desired. It seemed to him that whenever he spoke with Maheesh he used that phrase, 'Nothing for myself, but everything for Lord Shiva.' But surely that was the way of a Holy Man; all Holy Men eschewed material possessions and chose instead the way of inner enlightenment. Still, it seemed clear to him that Maheesh did want something specific, something tangible.

"Please, tell me exactly what you desire."

"I will, and I can only hope it is not too much to ask."

"If you can bring me Indira's love, there is no limit to my gift."

"Very well, not far from here, in the mountains, and carved from the stone cliffs there are Holy Caves. Do you know of them?"

"I have heard of them but I have not visited them."

"You must go one day and seek the light. Those who emerged from the caves brought knowledge. They must be honored; among the most honored must be Lord Shiva."

"How would you have me honor him?"

"I would have you hire artisans to carve a temple to honor Lord Shiva in one of these caves."

Candra's face knit into a frown. "Like the nearby Buddhist Caves of which I have heard?"

"The same, yet different," Maheesh replied. "I will instruct the artisans, though I expect to pass long before the undertaking is complete."

"If it pleases you and if you can make Indira love me, I shall be more than happy to do as you wish."

"It pleases me, Maheesh said. "When is your wedding?"

"In seven days time."

"In seven days you shall learn how to make a woman love you, but you must, as promised, have only this wife. You must forsake all the others."

Candra felt completely elated. It was a bargain he relished.

#

Indira sat curled up on a round ruby red satin cushion. Her hair, thick and black, fell almost to her knees when it was loose, as it was today. Her face was small; her features like a fine sculpture. She had huge dark eyes and thick lashes. Her body was delicate yet her breasts were full. When Indira moved, the tiny bells that fell from her ears, that circled her neck, and that she wore on her wrists, fingers, and anklets, tinkled sweetly announcing her approach.

"This is fine cloth, more than elegant enough for your wedding," Shana, the tradeswoman told her. She unfolded it from the bolt with a great flourish.

Indira looked at it and then beckoned the woman closer. She felt the cloth with her fingers. This was rich sari cloth indeed! It was red and was woven with gold and silver threads. It had a gold border so that when it was properly draped, the border would be on the bottom, in the front, and over one shoulder.

"I approve," Indira's mother said from her corner of the room.

"It pleases me," Indira replied.

"You only get married once. You must look your best."

Indira smiled. *Married, was she really to be married? In my whole life I have seen no men save my father and brothers.* She shivered slightly with anticipation. She had been trained, of course, to assume the responsibilities of a wife. As well, she had heard stories from other women. She was unclear about some things, but on the whole she looked forward to marriage.

"Are you frightened my daughter?"

"In a way, but father says Candra has other wives, so I will have much company."

"That was before he knew he would marry you. Candra has now pledged to give up all his other wives."

Indira suddenly felt filled with panic. "I shall be alone! I shall have to run the house myself! I alone shall have to satisfy my husband!"

Her mother smiled, "No, no. Candra has many servants. My daughter, for a man of Candra's wealth to give up his other wives is a great compliment. He has honored you."

"I suppose he has but it will be strange. I'll miss everyone so much."

"You can come and visit. Perhaps some of your cousins can come and stay with you."

It was an odd feeling. She had been raised in her father's compound and her father had twelve wives and forty children. Thus she had thirty-nine cousins and eleven aunts. There was almost no work to do as all the wives, their servants, and their many children shared the labor. But once married she would have only servants. And what of her husband? Could she alone fill his needs? It seemed like far too much of a burden for one of no experience.

"Is he handsome?" she suddenly asked.

Her mother shrugged, "He is not unpleasant to look upon. And he is said to be a kind man. You cannot ask for more. Love only comes in time; it does not travel on the wind like the scent of sweet flowers.

"I want to be a good wife," Indira said softly. But in her heart she was afraid. It was all unknown; it was like walking from the light into darkness.

#

Maheesh trudged along the steep path that led to the caves. It was a hard journey, yet he relished in it. It seemed to him that the higher one climbed, the more peaceful it became. He adored the utter silence, the feeling that if one listened very carefully, one could hear words of wisdom on the wind and taste knowledge in the clean aroma of the trees. There was a peace here he had never known when he lived in Bombay with the other *Guardians.* There, where the land met the Arabian Sea, the streets were always teeming with people, and as he had learned, danger lurked in unexpected places.

Not that here, in the Sahyadri Hills, he was safe. He kept his eyes open and took care. But what more could he do? He had changed his name, traveled far from Bombay, and now planned to take the sacred box to a resting-place. It was safe now, and if he took great care, he could fulfill his obligation to the *Guardians.* Let the *Lord Shiva* protect the sacred box and its contents. He did not know what else to do. There was no one to consult, no one to whom he could tell his tale. Again, he reminded himself that these hills belonged to the Gods, it was their treasure, and he was merely its earthly keeper. He tried to calm himself. In only a few days the artisans would begin work on the carvings within the cave which Candra would dedicate to Lord Shiva. Then he would take the sacred box to hallowed earth, and it would once again be safe in the guardianship of those to whom it belonged.

He approached the first of the caves. They were hidden from the eye by dense brush. The Chalukays, who were even wealthier than Candra, had commissioned the carving of many of these caves. The Chalukays were devout Buddhists and Buddhist monks labored

195

in the caves they had turned into places of worship. To his way of thinking the Buddhist caves were surrounded by an aura of grace and serenity. Two caves, recently finished, housed images of both Hinduism and Buddhism under one roof. One was dedicated to Vishvakarma, the patron saint of craftsmen, and the other to Chaity and Vihara, with a seated Buddha placed in the stupa. This cave was two stories high and had startling artwork depicting a most colorful pageant of dancing dwarfs.

He had in mind having Candra's workers construct something more elaborate for *Lord Shiva*. He fancied a temple built from one stone, a great monolith. This would be a mountain abode for Lord Shiva who would guard the sacred box, though only he, Maheesh, knew of it. He intended slipping it behind a great stone, in a space that would provide a natural vault. It was all he could think of, and heaven knew he had thought on this matter night and day. His father's father had not been specific as to what should be done with the treasure, but after much meditation, he decided it should rest in the care of Lord Shiva in the earth from whence the Chosen had come. Who better than Lord Shiva to guard it through the centuries now that the others were gone?

He reached the cave he had selected and he walked through it, touching its walls, trying to imagine how it would look when it was completed. A feeling of serenity filled him. In his heart he knew he had made the right decision.

#

Candra sat cross-legged on the grass with the book spread open before him. "Vatsyayana is a man of great genius. This book is most detailed."

"*Was* a man of genius. He has long since passed and doubtless his soul has already returned."

196

"I have never dreamed of such things as are in the Kama Sutra, yet I'm quite certain a woman will find these exercises of restraint quite pleasurable."

Maheesh smiled, "If Indira is half as beautiful as you say, it is you who will have to exercise the restraint."

Candra lowered his eyes, "I shall succeed because you have taught me to rise above carnal thoughts."

"You will be with her and not be with her."

"Yes. That is it. That is how it must be."

"Tomorrow you will wed and tomorrow night you will know if I have advised you well."

"I am certain that you have. In any case, the artisans have begun their work. It shall be as you wish, a monolith."

"I visited the caves and will go again just after your wedding. I will remain there; it is a place of meditation."

"I shall miss you."

Maheesh laughed lightly, "You will have other matters to occupy you."

#

Candra had been wed now for six days and nights. For many days he had thought about this night, of what would transpire and of how he wanted his bedchamber to look. Not that appearance was all. He wanted the room to engulf them, to surround them with sensuality.

He had his servants begin early in the morning. The room was thoroughly cleaned. The bed was covered with new white satin cloth and piled high with multicolored satin cushions. The room was then illuminated by more than fifty candles impregnated with the scent of sandalwood. The gown he selected for Indira was made up of seven layers of diaphanous iridescent cloth, it was truly magnificent.

197

Candra recalled the past six nights and what had transpired on each of them. He followed the instructions in the *Kama Sutra* slavishly, each night preparing himself with hours of meditation before meeting with his bride.

On the first night she had appeared in a virginal white gown, her magnificent black hair splayed out over her slim shoulders. He could see the apprehension in her dark eyes, and yet she came and sat by him with the resolution of a girl who had been well instructed to fulfill her duties. She trembled slightly, causing the bells she wore to tinkle. She kept her eyes lowered and her small hands folded so they would not shake. He wore only his robe and he could see she wondered at what he looked like. Still, this was not the night for revelations.

He began talking to her in a low soft voice. He told her not to be afraid; he told her he would not take her on this night.

"I displease you," she said, still not lifting her eyes.

"No, no. You please me greatly. But I want you to love me, so I must let you know me." Even though it was extremely difficult to keep from touching her soft skin, he only talked with her, reassuring her, making her comfortable. He was rewarded by her soft voice, even by the sound of sweet laughter when he told her a funny story.

On the second night, they listened to music, he gently kissed her, and he applied scented lotions to her arms, her ears, and her long graceful neck. As he moved his fingers seductively on her ears, he saw that she had a little chill and that she moved closer to him, so close he could hear her breathing.

On the third night he repeated his actions of the second night but then he removed the top of her gown and gazed on her perfectly little breasts. He had her lie down so he could slowly apply heated oils to her swelling nipples. He moved his hands slowly, tauntingly over her flesh, touching her in intimate places, watching as she glowed and moved about with excitement. When he finished, she held her arms out to him and he knew she desired more. But he only kissed her gently and told her the time had not yet come.

On the fourth night, he removed all her clothes, and again applied the oils and perfumes to her body. On this night, he massaged her whole body, beginning with her toes and ending with his hands in her wealth of hair. He lingered on her breasts till her brown nipples were tight like small hard nuts. Again she begged him to stay, again he left her.

On the fifth night, he massaged her whole body again and kissed her breasts while softly touching her place of ultimate pleasure. She cried out and clung to him, then she heaved her hips upward and fell into the most delightful pleasure, begging him for more and clinging to him as none of his other wives had ever done. But once again, he kissed her lips and whispered into her ear that this was not the night of total fulfillment.

On the sixth night he did all the things he had done on the previous five nights. He taunted her till she wept for him, and he promised her tonight it would be different, that tonight they would truly come to know one another. Now all was in readiness.

#

Sadish hardly looked like a Brahman. Most Brahmans had aristocratic bearing, refined features and an attitude of superiority. But Sadish was short and stout. His fingers were stubby and when he spoke he lacked the graceful movements that so often attracted attention and made people listen. He was, in fact, quite the opposite of Rajiv, whose facial features were nearly perfect even though the expression on his face was often frozen in utter coldness.

On this occasion, Sadish was virtually jumping up and down on the stone floor of the Gharapuri Fortress. He was excited, even though it was a distressed excitement.

"We have found the answer to the riddle!" he announced in a high pitched voice.

Rajiv stared at him coldly. "Simply tell me without your meaningless embellishments."

"There were more than twelve *Guardians*," he said, still breathless with his news.

A scowl covered Rajiv's face. "How can this be? There were twelve; there have always been twelve. It is the sacred number. There cannot have been more than twelve."

"Yes, but one of the Guardians was gravely ill and his brother was being trained to replace him when he passed. That brother knew everything. He knew of their secret mission and of their vows."

"Did he have the treasure in his possession?"

"We believe he may have had it for safe keeping. Since he was soon to be among the sacred number, we think he was being tested."

Rajiv's hands doubled tightly into fists as he attempted to control his anger. He felt outsmarted, out maneuvered. It was not a feeling he liked.

"Do we know where this brother is?"

We believe he has changed his name to Maheesh. It is said he headed inland, perhaps to take refuge in the sacred mountains.

Rajiv made a face. "Find him."

Sadish nodded. "We are looking now. I am certain we will be successful."

"And when you find him, you know what must be done. He must not die till he has revealed the whereabouts of the treasure."

Sadish backed away, "I understand."

"Let *Kali* be your guide." Rajiv turned to face the statue of *Kali*. Her hideous countenance seemed to be smiling down on him.

#

Candra looked up when the door to the bedchamber opened and Indira stepped into the room. To his eyes, she seemed more stunningly beautiful than she had appeared on any of last six nights.

She came to his side, her bells tinkling as she moved.

For a long moment he could only look at her. Then, he whispered, "Tonight, my bride."

He removed the first layer of her gown, and kissed her ears, then her slightly parted mouth. He fed her a sweet and they shared a glass of wine. Then he removed the second layer of her gown.

He sat her down and brushed her hair with a silver brush, then he lifted it and kissed her neck, her ears, and her throat. He removed the third layer of her gown and ran his warm hands over her. She shivered in his arms and clung to him, "Another layer," she begged.

The forth, fifth and sixth layers of her gown were slipped off amid hugs and anxious kisses. He looked at her now, he could see her naked through the final layer. She was ready for him, anxious for him to once again arouse her.

He had her lay down and then he parted the final layer, pushing it aside and covering her with kisses. Her nipples hardened and as he began to apply the scented oils, she moaned with delight as he lifted her hips. She was once again ready to feel supreme pleasure. But he did not immediately allow her that pleasure.

Next he applied warm oils, and then he again massaged her entire body even as she begged him to return to her secret flower. At last he removed his own robe and lay down beside her, taunting her lovingly till he felt her body filled with wanton tension, desirous of him.

He slipped inside her and she clung to him as he moved against her. They were lost in their own passion and in a moment the tension snapped and he felt her beneath him, trembling, tingling from head to toe even as he knew his own long awaited fulfillment. The night was young. There was time for more pleasure. He leaned back and smelled the wonderful scents that filled the room. All his senses were satisfied. He saw beauty, smelled delightful aromas, tasted the intoxicating forbidden fruit and felt tender velvet flesh. With no other woman had he known such satisfaction. Candra was a happy man.

#

It was a nearly perfect day. The sun shone brightly and the trees rustled with the soft wind. Candra climbed the last few feet on the path and stopped only briefly at the entrance to the cave before going inside.

Candra looked on the work in progress with pride. It would most certainly be an awe-inspiring tribute to Lord Shiva.

"I'm surprised to see you," Maheesh said as he appeared from a small alcove. He motioned Candra to sit down with him and share in his noonday meal of bread, cheese, and mango.

"I had to come and tell you how happy I am. I did everything the book suggested. Indira declared her love to me many times and said again and again that she wants no other."I felt certain it would be so."

"I shall double the money I intended to spend on this project. You are my guide in all things."

Maheesh smiled. "You're a generous man. I am grateful. It will, even so, take many years to complete."

"Then my sons shall carry on for me," Candra promised. "This cave temple shall be built and it will be the most magnificent of all the Elora Caves."

"Candra, I must warn you that when next you come, I will not be here. But even so, you must continue. Will you promise?"

"Of course, but where will you go?"

"I have a destiny to fulfill. My present reality is one of great danger. I feel this danger as sometimes I have felt joy.

202

"Danger? What kind of danger? I could assign soldiers to guard you."

"They would not help."

"But what is it?"

"I cannot share this with you, Candra. I must ask only that you finish the temple.

"I shall. I promise, I give you my solemn word."

"Now let us eat. After today, you will see me no more."

Candra felt mystified. But the ways of the Brahmans were often strange, so he did not ask further questions.

#

Maheesh moved the stone with care. He had worked with the artisans for days, helping to carve and learning to use their tools. When they left at night, he moved to a secluded part of the cave and worked alone on his little project. He had begun with a ledge and gradually he had made it wider and deeper. At last it was the right size and he removed the treasure from its bag. Then he slid the treasure into the space and slid a stone in after it. It was virtually invisible. He filled all the cracks around it with small stones and soon this part of the cave's wall looked as the rest of it did. The artisans would not work here; it was too low, and in a dark corner. No, no one would find it here; it was safe for eternity, buried within the walls of a cave that would become a temple. It was stoned in without a trace.

Maheesh turned and walked rapidly away. Lord Shiva would guard the treasure now; there would be no more *Guardians*. If *The Sons of Kali* found him, they would torture him till he told them where he had hidden the treasure. He had no intention of allowing that to happen. He quickly gathered his belongings and went out into the cold, clear night.

He climbed down the mountainside toward the river that wound its way around the base of the mountains. He had sensed grave danger for the past few days. Fear was gripping, it crept up in the darkness of the night, and it consumed many of his other thoughts. Maheesh did not fear death; he feared having his body betray his sacred promise. That was a fate more horrible than death. No, they would not take him alive. They would never learn where the treasure was hidden.

Maheesh reached the waters edge. The river moved swiftly, in the hills it was raining, and the rain swelled the river. He reached into his robe and withdrew the vile of clear liquid. He drank it and almost immediately his body began to grow numb. He waded out into the water till only his head could be seen. He took a last breath of the clear night air, took one last look at the moon and the stars. "Farewell to this reality," he gasped. His body was totally numb and he offered no resistance as the rushing black water sucked him under. Maheesh was no more. His secret died with him. No one would ever know, but Maheesh's lips had formed one last smile. The *Sons of Kali* were defeated.

CHAPTER ELEVEN

1532

Francisco Pizarro leaned over the rail of his galleon. In spite of the early hour, the morning was already hot and humid. In the distance the coast of an apparently barren land stretched as far as he could see with the naked eye. Miles of sand plains were punctuated only with sweeping curved dunes shaped by the winds. It appeared to be a completely inhospitable land, a land without plants or animals, a land deserted by the angels. *There is more. Beyond the dunes there are mountains and lush valleys – you can't see it all. But I know there is more.*

In Spain it was fall and cool breezes would be blowing off the Mediterranean. Here, in this southern clime, September was the beginning of summer. Beyond the sand dunes and low hills that characterized the coastal regions he knew there were mountains. The mountains here were not like the Pyrenees; the mountains here reached the sky, their peaks obscured in clouds. It was said that at high altitudes the air was rarified. Until a man got used to it, it caused lightheadedness and sometimes stomach upset.

Pizarro returned his eyes to the sea. The Pacific Ocean was a different color than the Mediterranean just as the Mediterranean was different from the Atlantic, which was, in turn, different from the sea that surrounded the islands of the West Indies. Long had he wondered why the oceans were so distinct? Their color was obviously determined partly by the sky but that did not account for the fact that even when the sky was blue, the oceans had different hues. The sea of the West Indies was turquoise, the Atlantic blue, the Pacific a greenish blue. He did not believe the differences were attributable to depth and had decided it might have something to do with salt. He had noted that this ocean appeared to be slightly less salty than the Atlantic. He shrugged; these were all questions to be answered in time by those who studied such things. His mind already danced with all that had been learned in his lifetime. He felt as if he were living on the cusp, as if the whole world were changing. That which had been thought to be true for hundreds of years was now questioned.

Not that one spoke of these things openly. The Church frowned on scientific discoveries that challenged the faith – those who served the church were interested only in the kind of discoveries that yielded wealth. Their definitions were narrow; they failed to understand that even the discovery of new land and great wealth contributed to change. Men who traveled saw things – things that challenged their beliefs. He was excited by all discoveries – scientific as well as geographical. In his heart he knew he was destined to be a part of sweeping changes. He was brave enough to venture forth, to risk his very life but he was not brave enough to confess his inner thoughts – those verged on heresy and heresy could result in torture and death.

He considered the fact that he had been born less than twenty-five years after the invention of the printing press. That wonder had already changed everything. Once rare hand copied books on navigation were now available in print.

When he was only fifteen, Ptolemy's *Almagest* was translated and published as, *The Epitome*. Its wide spread availability affected how many viewed astronomy, and thus navigation. When he was seventeen, Columbus sailed across the sea in search of a passage to India, but found instead a whole new landmass. The extent of that landmass was just becoming known, this barren shore which he now faced was part of it. When he himself was forty-two, Hernán Cortés had discovered and conquered Mexico. He had brought untold wealth home to Spain, virtual rooms of gold, silver and precious stones. His own calling was closely akin to that of Cortés. As he stared at the land beyond the breakers, he knew his destiny was there, a short distance across the water, beyond the coastal deserts.

He felt his destiny more strongly than he could explain. For most, the idea of finding wealth such as he imagined was a dream, but for him it was a certainty. He knew it was there, not just because he had heard tales of it from every Indian he had encountered but also because he felt it in his bones. To believe in fortune, to accept the will of the stars, and to believe in destiny as he did, would no doubt be defined as a heresy. But he confided his heresy to no one. He prayed with his priests but in his heart he accepted favors from the devil.

Francisco Gonzalo Pizarro, Governor of New Castile and Viceroy of this land, I am a man of destiny. I have come a long way from poor little Francisco, illegitimate son of a handsome Captain with a roving eye and a humble farm girl who yielded to a stranger.

He thought often of his maternal grandparents with whom he had lived for much of his childhood. He had worked as a swineherd on their farm. It was a series of local wars that had led him to a military career. After several years, he went to fight in Italy and after that, he went to *Hispaniola* with the new Spanish Governor. But he knew in his heart that he was not meant to be a mere civil servant.

He grew restless and he joined other expeditions. He sailed the Pacific coastal waters, laying anchor and traveling inland for as far as he dared venture without adequate supplies.

It was on one such foray that he encountered a caravan of Indians. They were well dressed, had many llamas, and carried both gold and jewels. Among their number, traveling alone without her parents was a sixteen-year-old girl.

The girl was bright-eyed and had a regal bearing. He strongly suspected she was someone of importance. He forbade any of his men to harm her, though naturally he confiscated the wealth carried by the group with whom she traveled. He sent the others to work crews, but the girl remained with him in order to study English with Father de Luque. She learned very quickly and she accepted Catholicism willingly. At her Baptism she was given the Christian name of Francisca. Over the past four years, with the exception of his time in Spain, he had spent much time with Francisca. From her he had learned about this land and its inhabitants.

In spite of the fantastic tales he heard, the Governor of Panama would not fund further expeditions. The men who followed him urged that he return to Spain, which he did. Again, fate smiled on him because when he reached Madrid, he discovered that he had arrived at the same time as Hernán Cortés. Cortés liked him, and helped convince Charles V of the possibilities that existed along the Western Coast, South of Panama. So it was that he, Francisco Pizarro, once a swineherd, returned to Panama with a coat of arms, a title, and a mission to conquer New Castile, or Peru, as the Indians called it. *Peru*, he liked that name far better than New Castile, which surely lacked originality. Francisca had told him that Peru was a Quechua word and, as he understood it, it meant 'abundance.' What he could see from here did not look in the least abundant but he knew there was more.

While he was in Spain, Francisca remained with Father de Luque who not only taught her English but learned Quechua himself. Now with Francisca and Father de Luque at his side, he had once again set forth. Daily, Francisca proved more useful than he could ever have imagined. He never doubted her loyalty but he could not help wondering how she felt about her own people. Did she feel disloyal to them? He did not ask.

He left Panama in January with one ship, one hundred- eighty men, and thirty-seven horses. Later, he was joined by two more vessels. They plied the waters further south, laying anchor and rowing ashore in various spots.

This was a remarkable place. All along the coast there were offshore islands. Not tranquil islands with coves and peaceful inlets such as those in the West Indies or the Mediterranean, but islands that jutted skyward, islands without plants, rocky desert islands without beaches or harbors. They were like the mountains that rose from the high plains a few miles inland from the shore beyond the desert.

"You've sought a lonely spot to contemplate our future."

Pizarro turned away from the rail to face Father de Luque who had come up behind him. In the evenings the two of them, together with Francisca, talked with local Indians they took aboard their ship after trading sessions.

They heard stories of the Inca Empire that confirmed those Francisca had told them. All the Indians spoke of its vast wealth. It was all just as Francisca had said. They learned there was a civil war fought between two brothers, Huascar and Atahuallpa. Huascar was declared Inca and ruled Cuzco. His half brother Atahuallpa, who ruled Quito, refused to pay homage. Huascar sent a huge army against Atahuallpa and it was defeated. As Atahuallpa swept south to Cuzco, it was said that thousands were killed. Atahuallpa, the usurper, took Cuzco. "Unthinkable," one old survivor confided. "The Son of the Sun was tumbled from his golden litter. He was dressed as a woman and made to eat excrement in Cuzco's streets. Later he was made to watch the execution of his family and nobles."

About the matter of the civil war, two different stories were given for its cause. The first was that Atahuallpa and Huascar were twins and that their birth, had, for the first time in the history of Inca, caused a dispute over who would be the absolute Inca, the supreme ruler. The second story had it that Atahuallpa and Huascar were half brothers, one ruling from Quito, the other from Cuzco. The position of Inca was hereditary, and their father had left no clear heir. None of this mattered to him. The important fact was that there *was* a war and that the Inca Kingdom was divided.

"Shall I leave you alone, or distract you?" Father de Luque asked.

"Distract me; I spend too much time planning in my head."

"A military man can not over plan anymore than a priest can over-pray."

209

"Tonight we'll weigh anchor. In the morning, we'll take small boats ashore and head inland."

De Luque crossed himself. "May God be with us."

Pizarro said nothing. He was not, himself, a deeply religious man. Still, he had a duty to perform for the Church and for Spain. Conversion of the population and treasure for the King were part of his bargain. For himself, for his brothers, and for his close supporters, there would be wealth, glory, and position if they prevailed. He often considered the odds. They would be outnumbered but he felt he could count heavily on the discontent of those who had been subjugated by the Inca. Then too, he could take full advantage of the dispute that existed between the two brothers. It was as if destiny had paved his way. He felt elated, if only because the time for action was at hand.

#

"*Madre de Dios,*" Father de Luque said in a near whisper as he crossed himself and mumbled a silent prayer. The valley was filled with death. The ruins of dwellings smoldered, smoke mixed with the low-lying morning mist. Bodies swung from trees where once leaves had shuddered in the wind. It was not possible to count the number of dead, but every man knew the horrific scene meant they were getting closer to this Atahuallpa and his army.

"They're peeing in their pants," Pizarro said to Father de Luque. He laughed loudly to show his men he was not afraid of their unseen foe. "Cortés did it and so will we!" he shouted. One or two shouted back, a few were made sick to their stomachs by the putrid odor of rotting flesh that rose to meet the morning breeze.

Francisca, paler than he had ever seen her, rode with her scarf around her face, protecting herself from the stench. Her hands gripped the reins tightly.

Pizarro gave the signal and they continued upward, away from this valley of death, this valley where Atahuallpa had slain his enemies.

They marched forward until it was almost dark. They descended into the fourth valley. As the shadows of twilight fell on the mountains, Pizarro made his second decision.

"*Aqui!*" Pizarro called out as he raised his hand bringing the two columns of men and horses to a halt.

It seemed a pleasant spot. There had been no killing here. They had spent part of the day in the dry arid desert, before beginning their climb. Here, there were rocks that gave shelter, trees that would yield wood for buildings and for heat. There was a winding river that could provide water for drinking and bathing.

"What shall we call this place?" Father De Luque asked.

"San Miguel," Pizarro shouted. "San Miguel is the Saint who has brought be the most good fortune. We'll build a headquarters here, and of course, a church. Let's get started."

Pizarro dismounted, sliding from his stead with ease. He stretched and began walking about the site he had chosen. His men were well trained. The cooks were already setting up and others had gone off to cut some of the trees along the river in order to begin building shelters. Explorers lived in a world of improvisation, making the most of what was at hand. Soon enough those who knew how would begin making adobe blocks. These would be used for permanent shelters and ultimately they would be used to construct the church.

"Is this a good spot, Francisca?"

Francisca drew her heavy blanket around her thin shoulders. "It is a good place. If we wait, they will come to us."

#

Many months passed and San Miguel grew. Indians came and went on trading missions. They took away tales of the strangers just as they delivered terrible tales of Atahuallpa's conquests.

Atahuallpa and his conquering army were six hundred miles from Cuzco where his forward army, composed of his best troops, was already pillaging.

"Should we not go on?" one of the nobles asked, a touch of anxiety in his tone.

"No. I am anxious to see the strangers of whom the messengers speak."

The noble looked down at the ground. "It is told that they have strange beasts and staves that command lightening."

"The Inca is not afraid. I am the Son of the Sun, I have nothing to fear."

The noble lifted his eyes. "You are all powerful," he said firmly. It was never good to show hesitation, cowardice or fear in the presence of Atahuallpa. Like sloth, such characteristics were punishable by death.

"I have decided to stop here in the Valley of the Hot Springs and enjoy the baths. My army will occupy the hillsides; the town will be evacuated so the strangers can camp there. Now is the time to confront these strangers. I have consulted the oracles and am told that I am invincible. Send forth a party and invite the strangers here. I will receive them, listen to them and decide their fate."

The noble bowed from the waist and backed away from Atahuallpa. He hoped nothing in his mannerism betrayed his own apprehension.

#

Even before the guard alerted them, Pizarro looked up and noted that a parade of strangers approached. As was always the case, they were on foot, though they used their llamas as beasts of burden. To the guard's eyes these llamas were weird looking creatures. It was as if an odd mating had produced a creature that had the coat of the sheep and the temperament of the camel. The creature was slender with long legs, a regal neck, a short tail, small head, and huge ears.

The guard shouted and all Pizarro's men stopped work and looked up. Not that the approaching parade of strangers was an unusual sight. They were often approached by the local inhabitants.

Pizarro quickly summoned the good father and Francisca. They mounted their horses and prepared to greet the strangers.

Father de Luque rode to his side. Francisca rode slightly behind the priest. She had told him that her Quecha name meant 'quiet' and as Pizarro looked on her, he thought it had been well chosen. He gave a signal and a group of his men who also mounted their horses fell in behind them.

Pizarro's other men took advantageous positions should any fighting break out. The strangers had no knowledge of firearms, but word of the magic weapons spread rapidly. Most who approached them came to trade or simply to greet them. They came in peace because they feared fighting.

As the group drew closer, Pizarro could see they were no ordinary group of traders. They were dressed richly and there were many llamas. Jewels and gold seemed to mean little here where a man's wealth was judged by the richness and quantity of the cloth her wore.

Pizarro held up his hand to draw his column to a halt. He studied the strangers thinking them handsome with their dark eyes, angular faces and high cheekbones. All of them seemed well dressed. These, he was certain, were the nobles who served the Inca.

A great feeling of excitement filled him. His long wait was coming to an end!

The one who led them stepped forward. He did not look at Pizarro but rather at Father de Luque and Francisca. He spoke quickly, or at least it sounded quick. Pizarro had learned a few words but for the most part this language was as strange to him as Spanish was to the Indians.

Their leader paused and Francisca turned to him. "These men bear gifts. They are emissaries of The Inca, Atahuallpa. He invites you to meet with him at the place of the hot water baths."

Pizarro forced a stern expression. Their language may have been unknown but their air of superiority was unmistakable. He hid his elation. "How far is this place?"

"It is three days walk."

Pizarro thought for a moment, and then nodded.

Francisca translated and the leader agreed. He then spoke again to Francisca.

"They will remain here until you are ready to go."

"We shall be ready tomorrow morning," Pizarro announced. There was hardly any time to waste. He immediately decided to leave sixty men at San Miguel. The rest, sixty-two cavalrymen and one hundred-six foot soldiers armed with Toledo blades, guns and crossbows, he would take with him.

Hernán de Soto came to Pizarro's side. "They are many and we are few."

Pizarro wore a sly smile. "Strategy my friend. Guile is our secret weapon."

#

All was as planned. Atahuallpa's army camped on the hillside; the strangers had come into town. Surrounded by his nobles and protected by his personal guard, Atahuallpa was to meet with them on the temple steps.

Atahuallpa filled his broad barrel shaped chest with air. This was a place of great beauty, a chosen place where the earth often spoke to those who lingered. Sometimes it would rumble sending fear through mortal men. But he knew no fear from the rumblings of the Gods. He was their equal, especially here. This was a sacred place where a stream filled by the overflowing hot baths wound through the green valley. From this stream a dense vapor arose giving the whole place a mystical appearance. He wondered if his guests would be impressed by this wonderful gift of hot water from the Mountain God, Viracocha. Somehow he doubted it. They did not look as if they bathed often.

Atahuallpa stood on the steps of the temple, fully regaled in his bright red robes and multi-colored feathers. He stared at the group of strangers with disdain. These beings in tin helmets that sat astride their so-called horses were clearly not Gods. He looked down his long aristocratic nose and decided that, not only were they not Gods, but they were no doubt inferior men.

He, *the Inca* had just defeated his half brother in battle and had come to the valley of the steaming waters with thirty thousand troops to enjoy the hot springs. These interlopers had less than two hundred men and at this moment only fifteen stood before him. Why should he be afraid?

Hernán de Soto dismounted and with the priest on his right and Francisca on his left, he approached Atahuallpa.

"I am instructed to invite your Royal Highness to a feast at our camp on the far side of town."

Francisca spoke softly. Never had she thought she would actually be speaking to *the Inca.* Though they were related, he did not know her, nor had any of his entourage met her. She fought for control. *How I hate him!*

Atahuallpa looked at de Soto and tried to take the man's measure. But it was no use. This stranger was an enigma and even though he himself felt no fear in the face of so small a contingent of men, his spies had warned him that the strangers could be dangerous.

"I am a God," Atahuallpa replied. "Is there a God among you? I can only dine with equals."

Francisca translated, though not quite accurately. She fully understood the Christian religion to which she had been converted. She also understood her leader, Francisco Pizarro. He would not let Atahuallpa live. Nor, she decided, would Father de Luque notice her slight mistranslation. It would make no difference. She turned to de Soto. "*The Inca* is a God. He wants to know if there is a man *of* God among your followers."

"Tell him there are two. Father de Luque and Father de Valverde, the Senior Priest." De Soto felt it entirely proper that the two priests should speak with the Inca.

Francisca turned again to *The Inca*, "There are two Gods among these men. They will dine with you."

"Then I accept," Atahuallpa replied. "Tell the strangers they may occupy the Plaza." Then Atahuallpa offered de Soto and his men the ceremonial *chicha*.

These arrangements made, de Soto mounted his stallion and galloped up to the place where Atahuallpa sat. He urged his horse to rear and the nobles, who surrounded *the Inca*, ran for cover. But Atahuallpa sat stiffly on the royal stool. He did not even blink.

De Soto then turned, and with his small contingent of men rode away. Tomorrow Atahuallpa would come to them. He would also bring his army down from the hillsides. De Soto knew that Pizarro intended to have an ambush waiting. The experiences of Cortés in Mexico had shown these people to be vulnerable. They would not give up and convert to Catholicism nor would they accept the sovereignty of Charles V. Thus, their leaders had to die. It was a simple truth.

Pizarro congratulated de Soto and then he went about designing the trap for the Inca. In the triangular plaza, with an entrance at its uppermost point, he laid his ambush. He would hide his forces inside buildings that had doorways sufficiently high for horses and riders to pass through. All the entranceways faced inward toward the walled plaza.

Pizarro then summoned Francisca. He sent her with quill and parchment to a safe place of observation where she could record what she saw.

He himself wrote, *November 16, 1532* across the top of the parchment.

It was nearly dark when, at five o'clock, Francisca heard the sound of hundreds of sweepers who swept the path where *The Inca* walked. She left her tower and went to the doorway below in order to see more clearly.

Francisca closed her eyes and for a time, she simply listened. She felt she was poised between two worlds. A step one way would sweep her back into the world from which she had come, a step the other way would carry her into the unknown world of these strangers who had come from the sea and who spoke of wondrous things of which she could hardly imagine. But perhaps it did not matter which way she stepped. *I feel like a stone rolling down the mountainside. Change was at hand and even if I stand still, it will overtake me. I embrace the future.* She looked upward – her Gods, their God - whatever would happen was ordained. As never before, she gave herself entirely over to fate.

She listened to the sounds in the distance. She had heard sweepers before. They sang as they worked, producing a low humming sound, the sound of a million honeybees. Ah, how clever Atahuallpa thought he was! He had waited till dark because he

217

believed horses were useless after dark. This foolishness alone proved him to be quite mortal in her eyes. *I hate him. I have reason to hate, reason to seek revenge.*

The Inca entered the plaza on his golden litter attended by his richly dressed nobles and thousands of menials. Then, beneath a torch, Father de Luque came forward and read from his prayer book.

The Inca listened. When Father de Luque finished, Atahuallpa took the book and studied it for a moment. But it did not speak for him, so he threw it to the ground.

Hardly had the prayer book hit the hard earth then the sound of bugles burst forth, guns echoed off the walls, horses reared and the same Spanish war cry once raised against the Moors, filled the plaza. *¡Santiago! ¡Santiago!*

The hoofed monsters trampled Indians, swords dripped blood, and those who had attended Atahuallpa fled in panic. The great golden litter turned sideways and Atahuallpa tumbled to the ground.

Francisca stared at him. The end was at hand. It was the second time in a year that a *Son of the Sun* had fallen from his golden litter to the dusty earth.

Then she saw that Pizarro himself had seized *the Inca* from the midst of the fighting, plucking him like a dead fish from putrid water. Thousands lay dead and dying, and she no longer doubted the power of these people with whom she had cast her lot. The few had vanquished the many.

Suddenly, Pizarro was at her side. "Conquistadore! I shall go down in the pages of history. I shall be greater than even Hernán Cortés," he whispered in her ear.

"You are already, greater," she whispered. "You have plucked the sun from the heavens."

#

Francisca crouched in a corner of the temple. She had slept in this corner, her head against the hard stone, her blanket pulled up tightly around her. But morning brought little comfort. Tears ran down her face, tears she did not bother to brush away when Pizarro entered.

Francisca shivered with the memories that filled her. Christian or not, in her heart she was of these people. Even though she had known it would happen, the sheer brutality of it rocked her entire being. Her family was closely related to Huascar and supported him in the fight against Atahuallpa. Atahuallpa had killed her entire family with great brutality; it was only an accident of fate that she had been away. Not that Pizarro knew she was a princess. He only knew she had been quick to learn his language and that she was useful to him.

Yesterday, Atahuallpa had been taken. Father Valverde and Father de Luque had urged him to become a Christian and to accept the sovereignty of Charles the V. He refused. Now he was held prisoner.

Pizarro sat down on a stone bench and for a long moment seemed to be studying her. "You are not just any young Indian girl, are you?"

She looked up and shook her head slowly. "No, I am an Inca Princess. A cousin of Huascar." There was no point in trying to keep her secret any longer or in lying to him.

"Do you feel avenged? He killed Huascar; he has killed many of your people."

"It pains me to see anyone die. But yes, he killed my whole family as well as many of our people.

"You're intelligent and sensitive. I did not expect you to be joyful. Make no mistake, Atahuallpa's fate and mine are bound together. History may say we deserved each other. Did you record it all?"

"Yes. I believe what you say is true." She stood up and walked to his side, handing him the parchments.

"Is Atahuallpa still alive?"

"Yes, I will ask for a ransom. When it is paid he will have another chance to accept our terms. If he still refuses he will be burned at the stake."

She shuddered and yet she understood. The sacred book said that he who lived by the sword would die by the sword. Athaullpa had certainly lived by the sword. So did Pizarro. That is probably what he meant when he said that their fate was bound together.

"I've come to you because I need to know what to ask for, I'm sure you can tell me."

"What do you want?" she asked boldly.

Pizarro liked Francisca; she was highly intelligent and not unattractive. Still, he had never touched her. He wanted to marry her off to a rich knight and landowner, a man who was already in Panama and would soon come here, to Peru. Such a union would offer Francisca security and it would bind Peru to the Spanish throne. But he said nothing of his long-range plans. He still needed her; indeed he needed her more than ever now.

"I want wealth."

"By that you mean jewels, silver and gold."

"Yes."

"Then ask that a room be filled from floor to ceiling with these riches. And ask for *The Key*. Pizarro stared at her. "I do not understand, what is this key?"

She shrugged, "I have only heard stories. I think it is the key to untold riches and powers. Atahuallpa will know what you mean. But I caution you, tell none of the others about *The Key,* it may, after all, be nothing but a tale told by grandmothers."

Pizarro felt a bit mystified. Still, he instructed her to go to Atahuallpa and ask for him to order his intermediaries to prepare these things. In the meantime, he decided to change the name of this place to Cajamarca and make it his headquarters. He deemed one of the stately buildings adjacent to the hot springs entirely suitable for his occupancy. In any case, if he were to order a room filled with gold, silver and jewels, it had might as well be a large room.

Weeks went by. Atahuallpa languished in captivity. He steadfastly refused to accept Catholicism or the rule of Charles V.

Caravans and caravans of wealth arrived. Pizarro watched with supreme pleasure as the large chamber was filled. Not even Cortés had found this much wealth! But when he asked for *The Key* he was steadfastly told there was no such thing.

Time and again he returned to Francisca. Time and again she repeated her tale of *The Key*. Finally she shrugged. "It must only be a story," she admitted sadly.

At last the great chamber was filled.

Father Valverde, Father de Luque, Pizarro, Francisca and four soldiers went to Atahuallpa.

"Receive Christ and bow down to Charles the V and you shall go free."

Atahuallpa looked at his captors. "No," he replied.

"Then you shall burn alive!" Father Valverde declared.

Atahuallpa stared at him, his lip quivered. It was a horrible way to die.

"*The Key,*" Pizarro demanded.

"It is here," Atahuallpa replied.

"I have not seen it. Is it here Francisca?"

"No, it is not."

"Take him away!" Pizarro shouted.

Father Valverde turned again to Atahuallpa. "If you receive Christ I can offer you strangulation rather than burning." Father Valverde hated loosing a soul.

Atahuallpa dropped to his knees. "I will accept your God."

The Priest immediately began the questioning. When he was finished, he blessed the quivering *Inca.* Then, Atahuallpa, his eyes closed, was taken to a wooden stake. A rope was placed around his neck and two soldiers tightened it while Atahuallpa gasped for air, till he could gasp no more. *The Inca slumped forward.*

Francisca closed her eyes tightly till she felt Pizarro touch her gently on the shoulder. She could not even look on the crumpled form of Atahuallpa. *My family is avenged. I must find the Key.*

#

Francisca walked slowly toward the room that was filled with treasure. Pizarro had summoned her and she assumed it was because he had found something he did not understand, or perhaps a visitor had come, someone for whom she would have to translate.

When the guard admitted her, Francisca was surprised to find Pizarro sitting alone. He motioned her to sit down near him. For a few minutes he did not speak, then he leaned toward her.

"You have been loyal and a great help, Francisca. I want to reward you. Choose something from this room for yourself, something you would like to keep. Her heart leapt inside her chest. She had hoped against hope for this moment.

She looked about and after many minutes bent down and lifted a box. "I shall take this with your permission."

Pizarro took the box and opened it. Inside there was naught but a wooden tablet with odd markings. It was a puzzling thing. But perhaps it was like the strings they counted on, perhaps it was some calculation. "I'm sure this is quite worthless."

No words could have meant more to Francisca. "It is meaningful to my people, but I suppose worth little in Spain."

"Then take it if it pleases you."

"Thank you," she replied.

Later, in her private quarters, Francisca ran her hand over the tablet and thought of Francisco Pizarro. It was one thing to be greedy, it was quite another not to know the worth of things. Ah, the great Francisco Pizarro! Francisca was proud of herself. She had tricked this acquisitive conqueror. She had *The Key,* Pizarro had naught but the Inca's gold.

#

The sun shone brightly off the snow-capped peaks of the Andes even though it was warm in the valley. Francisca made her way across the courtyard to where Pizarro waited by a small pond.

"You asked for me."

Pizarro motioned her to sit down on the bench.

"You have been of great service to me." He spoke in a somewhat somber tone.

"I have learned much in your service."

"Tell me, Francisca, what do you think of Sebastian Garcilaso de la Vega?"

De Vega had only recently arrived in Cuzco from the coast. She had been told he was a very wealthy man, a man close to the King. He had been given much land and she understood he had land in Spain as well.

"He seems most charming. We have met only a few times."

"He tells me you were most helpful in negotiations with those who will oversee his property when he returns to Spain next year."

"I did my best."

"His admiration for your intellect is one thing, but I must tell you he also finds you a most attractive woman."

Francisca did not know how to answer. She did not even know how a Spanish woman would react to such a comment. Language was one matter, but there were many aspects of these people who played at being gods that she did not understand. For one thing, they

223

divided the land giving this one five hundred acres and that one a thousand. As if the land was theirs to give! But she was exceedingly careful of what she said and how she acted. She was mindful of how fast one of her kind could go from being free to being a slave.

"I am honored," she replied carefully.

El Duque de Vega wants to marry you Francisca. He says that such a marriage would bind our two peoples together.

"Has he no wife in Spain?"

"She died long ago. He is a lonely man. It is true that he intends to return to Spain, but he would leave you here to manage his estates."

Sebastian Garcilaso de la Vega was tall and slender. His neatly trimmed goatee gray, his eyes almond shaped, and his skin tanned from the sun. Francisca thought him quite handsome, and true enough, when they were together he had shown her every consideration.

"Before you answer, let me say that this marriage would give you status. You would have security."

Francisca looked into Pizarro's eyes. He wanted this and she decided it would be for the best. "I will be honored to become his wife," she said softly.

#

De Vega did not return to Spain. To Francisca's great surprise, he confessed his love for her and for his new country. When she became pregnant he rejoiced, and when the child she bore was a boy, he wrote his new son into his will and officially adopted him under Spanish law.

The years went by and young Garcilaso grew up on his father's estate. He became fluent in Spanish, Latin, Greek, and his mother's tongue, Quechua. He was, to his mother's way of thinking, like a sponge. He absorbed both traditions; he was a link between the old world and the new world. His father put great faith in his son and young Garcilaso governed his father's estates in Peru.

But more important, Garcilaso possessed his mother's greatest gift, *The Key* and with it, a history of its origins as they had been passed on by The Memorizer, an ancient Priest of a people who came before the Inca and who lived on the shores of Lake Titicaca.

In the fall of 1560, after his father died, Garcilaso went to Spain where he came under the protection of his father's brother. He served in the Spanish Army and became a captain, then he entered the priesthood and began to write. Never, did he break his promise to his mother. He told no one of *The Key*, of his mother's notes about it, nor did he ever give it up. Yet, he was a writer and so he secretly copied and translated his mother's notes concerning *The Key*. He kept *The Key* and the notes in his vault since he feared that what was written might be considered heretical. His mother had written that there were *Seven Keys* and that they would one-day change the world by changing the beliefs of all men.

CHAPTER TWELVE

Delphi Greece, 1896

The scene was mystical and it seemed to Ritter Gruhn as if all the spirits of history gathered in this special place. The valley beneath the mountain was filled with mist just as the distant higher mountain peaks were lost from view. The whole panorama had a ghostly appearance, as if the higher mountain peaks were hanging from the clouds.

Professor Gruhn looked down the rugged hillside. It was steep and rocky, with low scrub bush occupying the ground between the more substantial trees. He was mid-way up the mountainside, having followed a narrow path to the place where he had camped. The path, he decided, had been made by wild goats or roe deer rather than by people.

Above the floating mist the sky was a cloudless blue, below him, as if it were in the bottom of a teacup, the Temple of Delphi was being carefully unearthed by his compatriots.

He thought how odd it was to be standing in a place that had been inhabited for so many thousands of years, even though it appeared as a barren wilderness.

Professor Gruhn looked east where the sun was rising and immediately he thought of Apollo, God of the Sun and patron of truth, archery, music, medicine, and above all, prophecy. Mythology had it that it was Apollo who established the Oracle at Delphi to give advice to Greece. Over time, the Oracle had given both good and bad advice, though most of her pronouncements were as clouded in misty language as the valleys and peaks were clouded by fog.

Above where he stood, the mountains of the Pindus chain rose, eventually reaching skyward over eight thousand feet. He was on the slopes leading to Mount Parnassus where legends gave birth to still more legends.

It was said that the God Zeus released two eagles, telling one to fly east and the other west. They met in the valley below, in *omphalos*, the 'navel' of the world, where the temple was now being restored.

Again he looked down. Through all his years of studying the classics, the oracle had fascinated him. Now he was here, he was part of the excavation team.

"This is the navel of the world," he announced in a loud voice. A chill swept over him, not because he was cold, but because the spirit of this place embraced him in her arms. It was the vision of antiquity, the *élan vital* – the vital force of the powerful earth goddess, Gaea that held him fast. For a long moment he could not move because he was so filled with being here, of standing in this spot where mythic gods had struggled.

After a time, Professor Gruhn began to gather up his belongings. He was slacking off and felt a bit guilty. Last night he had decided to take his tent and camp out on the side of the mountain alone rather than stay in camp with the others. He had a selfish desire to be alone with the past he so adored, to let what had once been here flow over him in the stillness of the night. Perhaps, he had thought as he dozed off to sleep the night before, he would be possessed of the incubus and be given dreams such as those the oracle sometimes gave those who consulted her. He smiled to himself. He lived far too much in his imagination, his books and in his work. He well knew that the oracle had been a middle-aged woman whose own dreams had come from chewing Laurel leaves that gave her hallucinations. Alas, he was only a lonely middle aged man, steeped in history and archeology whose few hallucinations came only after he had drunk too much Scotch. Damn those Scotsmen with whom he had worked in Egypt! They had introduced him to their liquor and now he found importing it a great expense!

Still, his flight of fancy included more than the cost of imported Scotch. Thoughts of his days in Egypt immediately made him think of Rosalind. How he missed her when she wasn't with him! He knew he had aged, but she seemed ever young, as if somewhere in her travels she had found and taken a magic potion guaranteeing eternal youth. Her long thick red hair still flew when she danced, her eyes still flashed with passion, her body was still firm. Yes, his Rosalind was a Celtic gypsy, a wild free soul whose fascination with the past was no less than his own. He smiled; they would be together in only two more months. He could hardly wait. But for now the Temple of Delphi called. It was a siren call, a call he could not resist even though it had meant leaving Rosalind behind in England.

He finished folding his tent and re-stuffing his belongings into his backpack. It was less than two miles back to the main camp, where he assumed, the others would have already eaten breakfast. He hoped they had left some tea for him.

He followed the same animal trail down the mountainside that he had followed up. When he got a little closer he would hear the others. It was quite impossible for him to get lost as long as he was going down hill.

Professor Gruhn had gone only a few steps when he felt the earth tremor. Not that tremors were unusual in Greece. Indeed, there were often heavy and quite devastating earthquakes. Instinctively, he stepped closer to the side of the slope in case any large rocks had been loosened above. He stood still for a moment waiting to see if there would be more tremors. But as no rocks fell and the earth did not again shake, he turned to continue his journey down the mountainside. As he did so, his eyes caught the glint of something shiny behind the bushes close to the side of the mountain. He bent to investigate and saw a coin, which he picked up. Finding ancient coins in Greece was an even more common occurrence than a slight earth tremor. Both Greece and Turkey had an abundance of ancient Greek and Roman coins. Still, this was a remote spot and he was walking on an animal trail, not a path used by people.

He moved some of the earth with the side of his shoe and as he bent over once again, he saw that behind the bush was a ledge, and behind the ledge, a narrow opening.

Filled with curiosity, he set down his pack and fumbled about looking for one of his small tools. When he retrieved it, he began digging at the opening. Then, quite suddenly, the earth around the opening fell away, doubtless the result of the earlier tremor. The entrance to a cave was revealed.

It was hardly safe to go rummaging about caves, especially after an earth tremor, so for a time he simply peered into the darkness, his imagination filled with thoughts of an undiscovered treasure trove of ancient artifacts.

His inner voice told him to return to camp for the proper equipment and some help. But his desire to make some profound discovery on his own held him there. Finally, he got out his lantern and lit it. Then, on his stomach, he forced himself halfway through the opening, shoving the lantern in before him.

The walls of the cave had no drawings and there were no obvious antiquities of any kind to be seen. There was not so much as a broken piece of pottery.

He lay for a few minutes half in and half out of the cave, his lantern flickering in the blackness, casting odd shadows on the limestone walls. Hidden in the darkness beyond the light of his lantern there might be tunnels leading to various chambers. He moved the lantern to illuminate more of the cavern and then he saw a strange object. It looked like a wooden box. He stared at it and finally pulled himself on his elbows further into the cave. He crawled on his stomach like a snake till at last he could reach the box. He pulled it toward him and grasping it firmly, crawled backward out of the cave. He sat on the sparse grass and stared at the wooden box for a long while. It was not an ornate box and it was quite impossible to tell its age.

Finally, he opened it and as he stared at its contents. The thrill of discovery engulfed him. It was far stronger than the wild feeling he so often had in the presence of history, it was akin to a sudden drunkenness.

Inside the box was a wooden tablet covered with markings. He did not understand the markings, but he had seen such a tablet before! How could this be? His question shook his own academic foundations, and right then and there he decided to do something most unethical. He decided he would tell no one of his discovery, at least not until he had investigated the tablet's twin. He would have to leave immediately for Spain, and quickly he began thinking of reasons he could give his colleagues for his sudden departure. He decided to feign illness. He smiled to himself. If he told them why he was leaving, or what was in his mind, they would think him insane in any case.

#

Carlos Edmundo Molino was a small nervous man whose compulsive habits made him the ideal curator for a small family museum. He never tired of dusting, polishing, and arranging the artifacts in his care. Few people came to his little museum, but he did not care. In his heart, he knew he was performing a task for future generations.

The museum was located in one of the out buildings of an old stone castle the tower of which overlooked acres of farmland and a meandering river. It was summer when even fewer people came so he was doubly excited when Dr. Gruhn arrived.

"I cannot tell you what an immense honor it is to have the famous archeologist, Professor Ritter Gruhn with me, here, in my humble little museum. I do the best I can; still this is a lowly place. I assure you, I could do more if I had more modern display cases. Yes,

yes, I am so glad to have you. So few people take the time to visit here."

Gruhn did not add, 'especially in the heat of summer when only a mad man would come here.' But he thought it. Still, as he looked at the tablet he knew it was worth the trip. The trick was not to let this little man know how very valuable this bit of wood might be. "I've been here before, you know."

"Have you?"

"Yes, five years ago."

"Oh, oh – I do remember, now. You came in the spring. But why did you not identify yourself then? If only I had known who you were!"

Gruhn said nothing. He turned his full attention to the wooden tablet.

"It's so intriguing." Gruhn ran his finger over the markings on the tablet. It was identical to the Delphi tablet, the markings were clearly in the same script, yet they were not in the same order, indicating they were part of a series of two or more. He did not mention the Delphi tablet to Señor Molino.

"And it has a rather fanciful story as recorded by *The Inca.*"

"*The Inca?*" Gruhn questioned.

"Ah, si, Señor Garcilaso de la Vega was often called *The Inca.* He was quite famous; he is even in the encyclopedia."

"Ah, yes. I remember now. When I was here some years ago, I saw this tablet but I do not remember reading any thing about it."

"What is written is not on display. Most people are not impressed by this tablet. It has no precious jewels nor is it made of gold."

"Still, it is interesting. What do you know of it?"

"Only what *The Inca* wrote. It is sort of a, how do you say, *leyenda.*"

"Legend," Professor Gruhn confirmed.

231

"Señor de Vega wrote the tale from notes left by his mother. She was an Inca Princess."

"Do you have this legend?"

"Oh, yes. Do you read Spanish?"

"Yes. But first tell me more about this de Vega."

Carlos grinned as he warmed to his task. Hardly anyone cared about the reason for this museum. This Professor Gruhn was an important man, his interest was wonderful!

"Garcilaso de la Vega was the son of Señor Sebastian Garcilaso de la Vega, a wealthy landowner and knight."

Gruhn sat down on a stool next to where the wooden tablet lay on a table.

"Young Garcilaso grew up in Peru where he managed his father's estates. It is said he grew up seeped in two traditions – the lore and culture of his mother, the Inca Princess, and the refined traditions of the Spanish nobility. He had a private tutor so he learned both Latin and Spanish. When his father died, he came to Spain where he was taken in by his uncle. Young Garcilaso was a most learned man. He wrote a history of Pizarro's conquest of Peru, he wrote wonderful poetry, and he translated the Italian Neoplantonic dialogue, *Dialoghi di amore* by Leon Hebreo. He became a priest. He was most devout."

"Did he publish the legend of this tablet?"

Molino shook his head. "Oh, no, no. Let me explain. Garcilaso died in 1616. Naturally the family kept his manuscripts and artifacts. The last in the direct line ordained that a family museum should be erected and thus many of Garcilaso's belongings are here. The manuscripts that deal with his mother's people, the Incas, are in the vault. They are very fragile, but I would allow you to look at them if you promise to be careful."

Professor Gruhn felt as if he were on the verge of stepping over the edge of an intellectual precipice into a canyon of forbidden knowledge, or at the very least forgotten knowledge. He ran his hand through his thinning hair as he always did when he was nervous. This tablet came from South America! His came from Delphi! What could it mean?

"I will take the greatest care with the papers," he reassured Molino, trying as best he could to control his enthusiasm.

"I will fetch them for you. Come, come, there is a small room with a comfortable chair. You can sit there and read."

"You're very kind."

"Just wait, I'll be right back."

How many hours had he been here? Gruhn was not at all certain. He only knew that for many hours he had been pouring over de Vegas' writings and the time flew! His heart raced with what he had learned, with his imaginings, with what all of this might mean.

De Vega spoke of places called, *Paqarinos*, sacred caves from which intermediaries appeared. The legend went that these caves existed in various places in the world, and that there were seven in all. It was also written that the Gods who appointed the intermediaries, who were to carry on for them, had left the seven tablets. But for what? This was not entirely explained, though it seemed people believed that the tablets were to be used in some way to summon the Gods back to earth.

Delphi – Cuzco, both were sacred cities to ancient people. Both had a sun God! Could it be? His mind wandered to the work of an obscure German academic. The academic, Werner Hauptmannn, believed that once, thousands of years before the birth of Christ, there was not just a common Indo-European language but a world wide Priesthood. Could these priests have been the intermediaries? Hauptmannn had hypothesized that the Druids who spiritually led the Celts, and the Brahmans, the aristocratic Priesthood of India, were the only remnants of this worldwide priesthood still in existence, though their origins were long lost, even to them. If this were so, there would be other tablets – certainly in England and in India.

He leaned back in the comfortable chair and closed his eyes. A plan began to form in his mind.

Professor Ritter Gruhn drew in his breath. It was not ethical to keep the knowledge of the tablets to himself as he had, nor was what he was about to do even legal. Indeed, it was a crime, the most serious crime. But what was he to do? Knowledge, he admitted for the first time, could be extremely dangerous. It could, in fact, be worth killing for.

#

The morning was hideously hot and humid. By eleven a.m. it seemed as if even the stone walls of the police station were sweating in the unwavering heat.

Armando Gomez, the Prefect of the Cordoba police, looked about disdainfully while Señora Molino fretted, wringing her handkerchief over and over.

"Has anything been taken?" he asked, wondering why anyone would want yellowed manuscripts, bits of pottery, tattered uniforms, or old rusted armaments. It wasn't as if the museum held jewels or gold. There wasn't even any silver.

"Not that I can tell. My husband was the curator; I did not know the collection well."

"Well, do you know if anyone came to see him?"

"No. We live some distance away. I don't know who comes and goes from there."

Señora Molino was a little woman whose thin dark hair was held prisoner in tight emaciated braids that were wound about her almost perfectly round head. Her skin was slightly sallow and it occurred to Gomez that Molino might have done away with himself rather than face another night with his wife. Still, jumping from a tower window and landing draped over a stone wall was so messy. Molino was known to be a neat man, and Gomez felt strongly that if Molino had killed himself, he would have been more methodical, and very much more orderly.

"Who would do this?" Señora Molino wailed once again. "My husband was beloved by all!"

"Perhaps not by all." Gomez muttered. "Tell me, who supports this museum?"

"The Duke. There isn't really much to support, he only paid my husband a small salary. But it was enough. My husband always said that history was important. He loved his work, and we had the cows, chickens and a small bit of land."

"Yes, yes," Gomez replied even while wondering why Señora Molino had to make so very many comments. It was as if she suffered from some sort of talking illness. Each time he asked her a question she answered it with many, many more sentences than were necessary.

"I shall have to assume there has been foul play, even though we have no idea who might have committed such a dastardly act," Gomez concluded.

"Oh, what shall I do?" Señora Molino shrieked in a high pitch. She turned toward him and buried her face in his chest. He stood limply, finding this whole affair unsettling and indeed, most annoying.

"Please, Señora, you must control yourself."

"I'm sorry."

He snapped his fingers and one of his underlings appeared. "See that this woman gets home safely."

His two underlings escorted her away. She began chattering to them immediately and disappeared from view even as she poured out her sorrow.

#

Professor Ritter Gruhn leaned against the plush seat in his private compartment. How glad he was to have left Spain! The trains were atrocious. Soon he would be on his way to England, not that he looked forward to the channel crossing, nor indeed to the austerity of England. Each time he returned to England, he marveled how a place separated from the continent by a mere twenty-six miles could be so utterly different.

He thought with irritation that it had been ninety-eight years since a consortium had been organized to see about connecting England and France by a tunnel that would run under the channel. The most necessary project was on again, off again. As far as he knew, at the moment, it was on again. He was, nonetheless certain he would never live to see England joined to the continent. The idea had more resistance than support. England, he thought was still safe. It would remain 'different' in the extreme.

He smiled to himself. Things were not all dismal. He would arrive and immediately be reunited with Rosalind. He could only hope she would be glad to see him, heaven knew he would be glad to see her.

Rosalind was English but well traveled and cosmopolitan in every way. When he married her she was the widow of Klaus Von Foch, a well-known German archeologist. As a result of having been married to Von Foch for so many years, she was fully versed in the art of German cookery. Hence, their home in Hampstead was one of the few places in England he felt assured of having decent food. The absence of good food, he admitted, was his main reason for disliking England. The British were completely lacking an edible national cuisine.

"Rosalind, Rosalind," he said aloud. In addition to serving good food, Rosalind was beautiful, charming, cultured, and educated. He had been in love with her for years, even when she was married to Von Foch. He had never told her of his love during her married years, and he seriously doubted he would have the courage now to confess to her just how long he had adored her. Rosalind was completely faithful to Von Foch while he was alive, though in Gruhn's imagination she had committed adultery many times.

Rosalind had spent years in Egypt and India with Von Foch. He wondered if Von Foch had ever heard of a tablet like the ones now in his possession. *I know there are others. I must find them,* he vowed once again.

#

Rosalind virtually floated out of her boudoir. Her red hair was wild and loose; her pale green dressing gown diaphanous. It billowed in her wake.

He rushed to her and took both her hands in his, "You are a vision, my darling. I've thought of you each and every day since I left."

"I just finished a long letter to you! This is so, so unexpected! It's wonderful! I was dying of boredom!"

"Well, I'm home to entertain you. Let me assure you, you won't be bored for long."

"And what have you brought to entertain me?"

Her eyes sparkled and she wound a strand of her magnificent hair around her index finger as she often did when she was excited. "An enigma, a puzzle of the first order. But first, we must leave immediately and go to the travel agent. We must book a trip to India."

"India? I don't understand."

"There is something there, something we must begin looking for at once."

"I do love India! I love the little train that goes into the mountains. I love the food. I love almost everything there is to love. But what are we to search for, tell me."

"Come Rosalind. I have something to show you."

He gripped his bag in one hand and took her hand in the other. "Come into the study. I will show you now."

He carefully removed the two tablets from the box in which he had packed them. "There," he said proudly.

She looked at them, ran her finger over them, and then looked at him. Her expression was strange, as if there was something she was struggling to understand. "Where did they come from?"

"They are two of seven. One is from Cuzco and the other from Delphi."

He knew that for a moment her breath was taken away. She was a woman of great imagination and considerable knowledge.

"Good Lord," she whispered. "They are just like the one from Ellora."

And now it was his turn. He felt the color drain from his face, felt his hand began to tremble. "Ellora?"

"The caves, the holy caves."

"Do you know where this tablet from Ellora is?"

"Oh, yes. It's in the trunk with Klaus' things."

"I never dreamed-"

The expression on her face changed slightly, "Does this mean we are not going to India?"

He suddenly laughed and embraced her, "We are going! I must see where it was found! You must show me, you must tell me everything."

Rosalind threw her arms about him and began kissing him. He embraced her, running his hands over her. At once he felt younger; at once the desire of youth filled his loins as he began to undo her robe. "We shall find the answers together," he whispered. "It will be our discovery."

Janet Rosenstock and Dennis Adair

239

CHAPTER THIRTEEN

Wiltshire, England, 1937

The morning was warm and sunny, the atmosphere clear. The pilot enthused about the weather. "A perfect day to experience the thrill of flight, Dr. Buckley. You won't be sorry! It's an incredible adventure!"

Blanford felt grateful for the weather though he was surprised by the deafening noise of the engines.

"Just down from Cambridge are you?" The pilot, a somewhat grizzled character shouted. Blanford turned to read his lips.

"Yes, just graduated," he shouted back.

"So, what are you? An historian?"

"Archeologist," Blanford replied.

"Oh, one of them blokes what digs up bits of this and that."

"You could say that," Blanford replied. The engine seemed even louder, and the ride frighteningly bumpy.

As if he knew what he was thinking the pilot grinned. "Wind drafts! They're always bad here. But these Gypsy Moths are fine planes. Fine indeed."

Blanford nodded. The constant shouting was hurting his throat.

"Never flown before, have you?"

"No. Never."

"It's spectacular from the air, it is. But I suppose you'll walk around it too."

"That's my intention."

"Oh, there we are! Just look at that, will you? It's a wonder anyone thought it was anything from the ground. I mean, just consider how much more obvious it is from up here."

Blanford looked down on the immense circle that composed the famous Neolithic Monument of Avebury. It was far larger than Stonehenge. He was normally a stoic man, but unable to control his

enthusiasm his expression changed and he smiled. Everyone had
said that seeing it from the air was a far more exciting experience
than seeing it from the ground but until this moment he had not been
able to imagine it. How right they were! He could see the great circle
built into the chalk uplands and the huge monoliths that so interested
scholars. Inside the great circle were two smaller circles, known only
as the North Circle and the South Circle. The ancient embankment
was clear, even if some of the village had unwittingly sprawled into
the great circle.

"Can we fly round one more time?" he shouted.

"Your shillings, your choice!" the pilot shouted back.

Again they circled and again Blanford stared at the pattern. It
was amazing, truly amazing.

"I don't see how they built it, those stones weigh tons!" The
pilot said loudly, shaking his head.

"Well, that's the mystery, isn't it? It's the largest open air
temple in Britain." There was much more he could have told the
pilot, but speaking over the noise of the engines was nearly
impossible.

The stones of prehistoric Avebury were enclosed by a huge
earthwork, a ditch with a bank outside it. The area inside the ditch
was fully 10 hectares. Within the circle the original stones numbered
about one hundred. From the south and west, avenues of standing
stones had once extended for over one and a half miles. It was
thought that once the earthwork contained as many as one hundred
and eighty giant stones and that more than four hundred lined the
avenues outside. But these had been torn down and buried over the
last thousand years. Yes, he could have delivered a proper lecture on
Avebury to the pilot but he didn't.

Slowly, the plane turned again and then straightened out and
headed back to the little airfield. It was not, he reminded himself, a
proper airfield. It was a farmer's field which had been cleared to
accommodate the Gypsy Moth.

"Where are you staying?" the pilot asked.

"In Avebury, at the Red Lion Inn."

"I live in the village myself."

For lack of anything better to say, Blanford muttered, "A charming little place."

"Tell you what; I have something I'd like to show you, what with your being an archeologist and all."

Blanford squirmed slightly. He immediately wished he hadn't admitted to staying in Avebury. Still, the man had not charged too much and he supposed that a few minutes spent in the evening when he had nothing to do would be all right. "What sort of something?" he asked.

"Something my brother found when he was a child. It's been with me for a long while but I haven't a clue what it is."

Perhaps it was some artifact unearthed while planting the garden. That was fairly common. In London they were always finding something or other. Construction of the tube had yielded a mother lode of historic artifacts from ancient Britain.

Maybe you could drop by my house. It's a quarter mile down the road from the inn, number thirty-three."

"What time?"

"After tea. Say about five."

"Very well."

"Hold on," the pilot shouted. "We're going down to land."

Blanford felt slightly ill and decided he didn't like this part of flying. It was as if the ground were coming up to meet him. He closed his eyes and only let out his breath when he felt the wheels hit the rutted ground.

After high tea, Blanford went to his room to change. To his way of thinking, the rooms in the inn appeared to be about the same age as the Neolithic monument. The floors creaked, the walls slanted precariously, and water damage smudged the ghastly flowered wallpaper. It was a place to sleep and nothing more. In fact, he decided, any more time spent within its confines could only result in claustrophobia.

He left his room behind and walked down the streets of the village. It wasn't a large place and he supposed it might not be here at all if it weren't for the monument. There would be farms, and perhaps a vicarage but probably not the village itself.

He found the pilot's cottage and knocked loudly on the door.

"Oh, you came. I wasn't sure you would."

"Curiosity," Blanford said, though in fact he felt not one iota of curiosity.

"By the way, I don't think I told you my name. I'm John Peters."

"Blanford Buckley," he replied, shaking Peters' hand limply.

"I'll go and get it."

Peters disappeared into another room and soon returned with a square package wrapped in newspapers. He set it on the table and carefully opened it.

Blanford peered at the object. It was not at all what he had expected but he cautioned himself to take care not to express either surprise or delight in the odd wooden tablet that was covered with strange markings in boustrophedon script. But how could have it been found here? This was surely an artifact from some other place.

"Where did you say it was found?" he asked trying to sound nonplused.

"Not far from the monument. It was under a big stone in a kind of earthen vault."

Blanford picked it up and turned it over slowly. Perhaps this was some sort of hoax. It was just the sort of thing his classmates might try to pull on a young Cambridge Don. It wouldn't be the first time that a 'manufactured' artifact had fooled an academic.

"When exactly was it found?"

"Oh, let's see. My brother was eight or nine and I was five. My brother's dead now and I'm fifty so I guess it was around 1892."

"I see." Blanford strained to sound non-committal. Damned if he would give his classmates the satisfaction of pulling one on him.

"I doubt it's worth much," he said slowly. Of course he would be expected to offer some huge amount for it.

Peters shrugged. "I just want to get rid of it. I'm tossing everything and moving on. Do you want it?"

This was not the way Blanford's imagined script went. "I could take it back to Cambridge and examine it."

Again the man shrugged. "Take it back and throw it in the Cam River for all I care. I just want to get this place cleaned out. I'm going off to London to open a flying school."

"Oh," Blanford said softly. If this was a trick it was a very odd one. "Well, I will take it, thank you."

The man re-wrapped it and handed it to him. Blanford took it. The first question that popped into his head was, could it be real? The second question was, how did it get here? After those two questions there were many more.

#

Blanford shook out his umbrella and stepped into his semi darkened flat. Then he slipped out of his coat and hung it on the coat rack near the door.

He immediately put on his knit woolly and poured himself a dry sherry. Then he went into his front room, turned on the lamp and sank into the chair.

As he so often did, he stared at the wooden tablet on his mantle. He had possessed it now for nearly three years and he still did not know what it was or even if it was real. He had long ago discarded the theory that it had fallen into his hands as a prank, but that made the mystery of the thing even deeper. The symbols on it resembled nothing ever found in the area – or any other area that he knew about. The characters were neither runic nor cuneiform. It was written in boustrophedon script but then many ancient people had used such script.

Having kept it for so long, he could not now take it to other experts. Still, he supposed his procrastination had accomplished something. He had become an expert himself, one who was sought out and consulted. He had produced two books on ancient script that had been reviewed well by his peers. Now, the government had contacted him concerning an important position in MI-5's codification and encryption section. "Good enough to break German codes, but not good enough to figure you out," he said, speaking to the tablet. In a strange way, it had become a kind of companion, a mystery that just could not be solved.

In a few minutes he got up and went back into the foyer. His mail was on the little table by the door where the charwoman had left it. He flipped through the bills and stopped when he came to a violet envelope. He opened it as he returned to his parlor.

Inside, he found a note written in a shaky hand. Likely its author had suffered a stroke.

16.8.1940

My Dear Professor Buckley,

I am the widow of Professor Ritter Gruhn. I have recently read your book and would very much like to meet with you concerning a matter that was close to my late husband's heart.

I would be able to receive you on Wednesday next. If you could come around five we can have high tea if it pleases you. Please call if you can accommodate my request. My number is Hampstead 5824.

Sincerely, Rosalind Gruhn.

Blanford folded the letter and leaned over toward the phone. Whatever it was she wanted would certainly provide more entertainment than staying home alone.

#

Rosalind Gruhn sat by the dying fire, rubbing her bony hands together and staring at the large brown liver spots that covered their backsides. Like Elizabeth I, as she aged, she had banished all mirrors so that now she could only imagine what she looked like.

She knew her hair was snow white because strands of it fell on her dark sweater. Her skin felt like brittle crinkly tissue paper to her touch, and her blue eyes were cloudy with cataracts. Once she had been a beauty, had turned men's heads, and was known far and wide for her flamboyance. Her memories were vivid and unusual for she had done things few others had even dreamt of doing.

At that thought, her eyes were drawn to the picture on the mantle. It was in a wooden frame, behind glass to protect and preserve it.

Although the photograph was in black and white – brown and white actually, it revealed a beautiful young woman with thick curly hair. The heavy boned corsets demanded in the late 1800s rigidly sculptured her fine figure. She was thirty-seven when the photo was taken; today she was eighty-five. In 1892, when the picture had been taken, she had given birth to no children, and as a result, she retained the youthful appearance that many women her age had lost.

What a marriage it had been! Klaus Von Foch had swept her away from stodgy old England and into undreamed of adventure. He was in his forties when they wed, at the height of a brilliant career as an Egyptologist. They took a luxurious ocean liner to the Middle East, and after a month of sightseeing they landed in Cairo where Klaus was to continue his explorations.

They lived in a huge tent near the sight of the dig. They had wonderful meals prepared by a special cook and served by a bevy of servants. They consumed champagne every night. Klaus was a man of many faces. One was the face of the disciplined academic; another was a lover of fine food, drink, conversation, and even dancing. He was, she recalled with a warm feeling, a good lover too. Name and heritage aside, he was anything but a German stereotype. Except perhaps in his work. In his work Klaus was organized, and deeply engrossed. He kept copious notes.

But what had given her the most pleasure was the fact that she was always at his side. He made her a part of his work, he allowed her to take notes for him. He taught her. What she cherished most was the fact that he had always treated her as an intellectual equal.

It was late one afternoon at the height of the desert heat that they broke through into the tomb of the pharaoh. It was a rich find, a tomb full of incredible artifacts, valuable objects made of gold and encrusted with jewels for the great king to take into eternity.

That evening they ate in the main chamber of the tomb, they drank imported French champagne, and while some of the diggers sang and clapped, she had danced on the crypt that held the mummy, her tangled wealth of red hair flying with the rhythm of the clapping.

A faint smile covered her face as she wondered if she was the only woman ever to have danced on a Pharaoh's tomb. She regarded her marriage to Klaus as her first incarnation and deeply regretted the fact that Klaus had died only six years after their wedding.

She and Von Foch lived in Germany, and for several years they traveled and worked in India before Klaus became ill. After he died in 1896, she returned to England.

Dr. Ritter Gruhn, her second husband, was also an archeologist. They returned to India together and she took him to the Ellora Caves where Klaus had found the mysterious tablet. Ritter believed it had been hidden there long ago - perhaps by a Brahman priest.

They continued to search for others, believing as the notes compiled by de Vega stated, that there were seven in all. At the same time, Ritter tried in vain to make sense of the markings on the three tablets in their possession. But it was all in vain. Ritter died, she had the tablets, but she had no idea what to do with them.

Still, in her heart she knew they were precious tablets from distantly separated places. The first was from Delphi, the second from the New World via Spain, and the third from India. But where were the rest?

"I shall never know," she said aloud. On the stone hearth she had laid out the three tablets, each with similar markings, each an ancient artifact. "Each a puzzle," she murmured.

For months now she had contemplated what to do with the tablets now that she was approaching death. Then, while perusing the Sunday London Times, she saw an article on Sir Blanford Buckley, England's leading expert on the ancient Druids. The article mentioned that Buckley believed in the theories of Werner Hauptmannn. Klaus believed in Hauptmannn's theories too. It came to her in a flash! Blanford Buckley was the one to contact. She had the tablets, perhaps he would know more about them, and perhaps he had seen something like them.

It was then that she heard the doorbell ring. "I shall be right there," she called out. She stood up and quickly covered the tablets on the hearth with her shawl. Then she walked to the front door.

"Madam Gruhn?"

Rosalind peered at the young man. He seemed to be thirtyish, and she thought that wasn't really so young but only seemed so to her. "Professor Buckley?"

"Yes, one in the same. I must say I am most intrigued by your note."

"Please come in," she crooked her finger and opened the door. He followed her down the corridor and into the sitting room.

"You have many beautiful things," he commented.

"And they're all real, Professor Buckley. As I wrote to you, I'm twice widowed and both of my husbands were well known archeologists."

"I'm familiar with their work."

Rosalind tilted her head ever so slightly, almost flirtatiously, "I've been reading about you, about your interest in the Druids and in various ancient scripts."

"More than an interest. It's an obsession, I would say. Of course the Druids had no script."

"I know, nor did the Incas. But I will come back to that. Have you heard of the theories of Hauptmannn?"

Buckley was suddenly in his element, "Indeed. He theorized that long before the dawn of Christianity, in pre-history, a single, powerful, priesthood ruled the earth. He believed the only remnants of this priesthood to survive in recorded history were the Druids and the Brahmans." He looked at her, "I'm afraid Hauptmann has been somewhat discredited, however."

"We trace many of today's languages to Indo-European, and world religions have commonalties just as languages do. My husband thought Hauptmann's theories to be completely sensible."

"I would like to think he was right."

"My late second husband possessed solid reasons for his beliefs." Rosalind peered at Buckley like a cat peers at a mouse. She tried to judge his reaction.

"You're most intriguing. May I ask what these solid reasons were?"

"I have made inquiries about your academic credentials and about your character. I have found nothing to indicate I can't trust you. But I must have your word that what I am about to show you will remain confidential."

"I give you my word."

"Lift that shawl, Mr. Buckley."

He leaned over and pulled the shawl away, revealing the three tablets.

"By heaven," he breathed. For a very long moment he could not seem to get his breath or organize his thoughts, then he blurted out, "They are like my tablet!"

A chill shot through Rosalind and she could feel her heart beating faster, "You have such a tablet?"

"Yes! Unearthed near Avebury."

"Ah, more to add to my own puzzle. These are from Cuzco, sacred city of the Incas, from Delphi, above the oracles cave, and from the sacred cave carved to honor Lord Shiva in Ellora, India."

He touched the tablets reverently. "Madam, this is a staggering discovery."

"My husband believed it would lead us to a great treasure."

He nodded, "A great treasure known only to the ancient priesthood."

"What are we to do with this discovery?"

"I must think on this. Madam, I am sure it is rude of me to ask, but do you have any brandy?"

Again, Rosalind smiled. "I do. I thought you might ask. It is in a decanter in that side table together with glasses. Will you pour me one as well?"

"My pleasure, Madam."

It was at that moment that the sirens began screaming.

"Oh, dear heaven, not another raid. I feel ill every time it starts," Rosalind sighed.

Buckley nodded. "Let me help you," he said standing. Together they turned out the lights and hurriedly put on their coats. It was early September, but nonetheless cold. It was the sixth straight night of German air raids over London.

"We can't take the tablets," he said uneasily. "They're too bulky, not to mention conspicuous."

"One of my concerns since this all began," she fretted. "I usually don't even go to the shelter. I stay here with them."

"Come along. They've survived for centuries. We'll come back as soon as the raid is over. But tomorrow we must take steps to protect them permanently. Who knows how long this war will last."

"How can we protect them?" she asked as they hurried down the darkened high street.

"Bury them, dear lady. We must carefully write down all we know about them and then take them out into the country and bury them where no harm will come to them."

Rosalind smiled up at him. He seemed a competent take-charge sort of man, not unlike her husbands. Yes, burying the tablets seemed a good idea. It would not do to let them fall into the wrong hands or be destroyed by German bombs.

#

The wind blew across the English countryside moving low clouds, obscuring and then revealing the sun through a high mist. The light was incredible. It was that surreal light that so marked the paintings of John Constable, that soft dreamlike light that preceded an afternoon shower.

It was intriguing scenery. The hills were evergreen, gentle inclines with sudden outcrops of rock. Then the car turned and the great stones of Avebury came in view. One could only guess *why* the ancients had erected them here; it was harder to imagine *how* they had succeeded.

"Is this where you found your tablet," Rosalind asked.

"Yes, and this is a good resting place for all of them. At least for the time being." He lied of course. He had not found the tablet; it had been given to him. Still, he knew where it had been found.

"It's a sacred place," Rosalind breathed. Somehow it pleased her that the tablets would be hidden in such a place.

"We'll drive away from the village. I know a place that is secluded and safe, a place where they can't be reached by German bombs."

They drove on and Rosalind wondered what the children who played by the side of the road thought when they passed by.

251

Doubtless they were taken for grandmother and grandson, though she did not like to think of herself as being so old, especially as this young Professor Buckley made her feel young.

They turned down a shrub-lined lane. Buckley stopped the MG and they got out and walked down a path to a cairn of rocks. It was a lonely place. There were no houses nearby, no prying eyes.

Dr. Buckley bent over and with considerable effort, moved a slab of rock. Beneath was a square hole. It was where the pilot who had given it to him said his brother had unearthed the tablet. Gently he put all four tablets inside together with the notes written by de Vega. He painstakingly covered them up. "They'll be safe here," he said in order to reassure Rosalind.

Rosalind held her tongue. In her heart she knew this was all a façade and that he had no intention of leaving them here for more than a few days. He would take her home and return to retrieve them. But she said nothing. She was old now and her trusteeship of the tablets was over. Buckley would know what to do with them; it was another's turn to guard their secret until all of them could be found.

"Are you satisfied?" he asked as they turned about and drove back toward London.

"I am satisfied that they will be safe with you."

"But three of them are yours."

"I have no heirs, I will soon die."

"You shouldn't talk that way."

Rosalind shook her head. "The idea of death and passing is always troubling for those in the prime of life. But I know it is almost over for me, and I accept it. I have lived well."

"You *are* a remarkable woman," Buckley said.

"I give you my three tablets young man, so you shall not feel guilty when you come back to retrieve them."

His face turned a deep pink and he opened his mouth to protest, but Rosalind put her hand on his arm. "No, no. Don't lie to me. Be honest."

He waited a long moment before answering her. Then, he simply whispered, "Thank you."

"How long will you leave them buried?"

"Till I have thought of a truly safe place for them."

"Good. Will you come and see me sometime; will you tell me how your quest for the others is proceeding?"

"I should be happy to do so."

"One day the world will know of this treasure. I think it will be a very great surprise indeed."

#

Blanford Buckley stared at the article in the London Times and then back at his precious tablets. He had waited ever so long. He had waited too long. Rosalind was long dead, the war was over, and though rationing continued, life was beginning to return to normal.

He had written his well researched paper and mentioned Hauptmann and his theories. He had arranged for a display and examination of the tablets and he had invited all the "right" scholars to come and view them.

But Rosalind was not there to corroborate his story. When asked about the tablet, which had originally belonged to de Vega, he told them all about the small museum where it had been found. He even told them about the murder of the museum's head, the circumstances of which Rosalind had confided in the greatest confidence. He soon learned that all the records pertaining to the murder had been destroyed in the Spanish Civil War and that no members of the family survived to tell the tale. The end result of it all was that the entire community of his peers were laughing at him and proclaiming him to be the victim of an elaborate hoax. The

Times article called him "a well intentioned, if sadly vulnerable academic, who wanted to believe too much."

But it was true! Tears filled his eyes. His reputation was ruined by a truth no one would believe. He pressed his lips together and decided to return the tablets to their hiding place. The time was simply just not right.

CHAPTER FOURTEEN

Corrie opened her eyes for a moment, then closed them. At first she was only aware of her pounding headache, then sheopened her eyes again and gradually became aware that she was lying in the middle of a large four poster bed in a semi-darkened room. She lifted her hand to her temple and rubbed it. *I've got a whacking headache.* It was not the kind of headache you have when you're hit in the head or fall against something. It was the kind you have when you drink too much or are drugged. She remembered having felt this way when she came out from under the anaesthetic after her appendectomy. *That's it, I was drugged.* She closed her eyes again. *God, what have they given me? How much have they given me?*

She lay still for a long while until by degrees, she began to remember. The third time she opened her eyes, the room and its furnishings came into focus slowly, painfully. She fought to bring back the details of how she got here. She remembered the struggle in her hotel room and the smell of the chloroform cloth as it was held over her face. She remembered regaining partial consciousness once and being given an injection. It seemed as if she recalled vibrations – as if she were on a plane – just as the injection was given. But she knew she had never been fully conscious and that there were only moments between the chloroform wearing off and the effect of the injection. Those few minutes had been only a distortion of reality.

I ought to be frightened. The fact was, she was apprehensive and deeply mystified but felt strongly that if whoever was responsible for her kidnapping wanted her dead, she would already be dead.

After a time, she pulled herself up in bed and tried to assess her surroundings more accurately. She was in a large room with drawn drapes along one side. There were two doors, one on each side of the room. She could make out a massive chest, a dresser, and a wardrobe in the Spanish style. In an alcove, beneath what seemed to

255

be a lamp, several chairs surrounded a table. No doubt one of the doors led to a bathroom making this a reasonably large self-contained bed-sitting room. It appeared to be a pleasant prison, but it was a prison nonetheless.

Slowly, she pulled herself from the bed and grasping the side of the bedpost and then a dresser for balance, she made her way slowly toward the drapes. Her head began to clear and mercifully stopped pounding. She reached the drapes and very carefully pulled one corner back slightly. She looked out into a walled courtyard. The only light came from other rooms in the house and from the light of the full moon. Then she saw him! A man, dressed in fatigues and carrying an automatic weapon leaned against the wall. She quickly closed the corner of the drape, wondering if he had seen her.

She looked down and saw that she was still dressed as she had been, still very much in need of a shower. She walked to the alcove and flipped the switch, flooding the room with light. Beneath the lamp, on the table, was a note neatly printed in English. It read, "When you wake, please ring the bell." For a moment, she contemplated the *please*. Her kidnappers seemed quite polite.

She hesitated for only a moment, before she rang the brass bell.

After a short time, a woman entered the room. She was a small woman wearing a long black robe and sandals. A black scarf worn in the Moslem manner covered her hair and she carried a pile of towels and clothing.

"Where am I?" Corrie demanded. "I want to know why I've been brought here?"

The woman looked aghast and quickly lifted her finger to her lips in a gesture of silence.

"Please," she whispered. Corrie could hear the pleading in the woman's tone. "Please just do as I ask. You are to go into that room and bathe." She pointed to a door on the far side of the room. "Here are clean clothes for you. I have also brought a scarf. You are to wear it at *all* times when you are away from your room. It is our custom. If you do not wear it, you will be severely punished."

The woman's English was good, though she spoke in simple sentences and something in her demeanor seemed almost childlike. "When can I eat? I'm hungry." She wasn't really hungry, but she wanted to hear the answer to the question.

"My husband will speak with you as soon as you are clean and dressed modestly. Then we will take some food. You must obey our customs, I beg you to do as you are told. He has promised me you will be treated with respect if you just cover your hair and do as you are told."

Corrie could see the look of concern in the woman's dark eyes, as well as hear the fear in her voice. Perhaps if she did not do as she was told the woman would be held responsible. She had traveled in the Middle East and well knew the customs of the region. Covering her hair was a little bothersome but what difference did it make? If it meant getting on better with her captors and making the woman like her, it would be worth it. Something in the woman's behavior seemed to indicate she disapproved of Corrie being held captive. Perhaps, the woman might be able to help her escape. She nodded her agreement and took the bundle of towels and clothes. She vowed silently to pursue a relationship with the woman. Her common sense told her that her captor must be Karim Ali Ahmed. He was a Moslem and by all accounts a Moslem zealot.

"What is your husband's name?" Corrie asked, seeking to confirm her own suspicions.

"Karim," the woman answered, bowing her head.

Corrie did not respond. He might be planning to kill her but not at the moment. She felt certain that she was here to be held for ransom so that her father would cooperate. Her situation was hardly comforting but she felt she had a little time to get the lay of the land and make an escape plan. Perhaps she would find out what this was all about. At the moment, she hadn't a clue just exactly where it was she was going to escape from because she didn't know where she was. She had no idea how long she had been kept drugged or how far they might have traveled. She could be in the suburbs of Lima, the desert north of Chiclayo, or in the Sudan for that matter. As if that were not troubling enough, she had no money, no credit cards and no identification. And, she reminded herself, the house was guarded. The man outside her window looked far from friendly.

"When you're ready ring the bell and I'll return."

Again Corrie nodded. Was the woman as subservient as she appeared? She hoped not. "Wait," she called out suddenly. "I forgot to ask your name."

The woman turned quickly, her hand on the doorknob, "Fatima," she replied before slipping through the door and closing it.

#

Jonathan Henley opened the door of his *caseta* and turned on the light. The maid had cleaned since the break-in and his small comfortable front room had been restored to its former tranquil state.

He sat down and wiped his brow. Unfortunately, his surroundings did not help turn off his thoughts. Myra had disappeared and turned up dead. Now Corrie had disappeared. So far everyone who disappeared turned up dead. He pushed that thought from his mind. It had been three days now and there had been no body found. Perhaps she was alive. Perhaps Jeff was right. *Let him find her,* Henley silently prayed. He continued to rationalize that no news was somehow good news.

He had just begun to relax when he heard the car pull up outside. *Shit. I thought I'd be alone here. Damn! I need to be alone.*

Wearily, he went to the door and opened it just as the young man who stood on the threshold had lifted his hand to knock.

Henley peered at him curiously. He was Japanese.

"Mr. Jonathan Henley?"

258

He nodded, and as he did, he realized his caller was vaguely familiar. That was it, the fellow worked in the museum in Lima. He assembled displays.

"I'm Kenji. I work for Mr. Conway. I am also an acquaintance of Jeff Richards. I have met your daughter as well."

Henley ushered him in. "You're the one they went to see in Lima." Jeff hadn't mentioned this Kenji's name. It was a guess.

"Yes. I am the one."

"May I ask what brings you here?"

"I was waiting for the right moment to see you. The hotel is full of people. My mission is confidential so I followed you here. I have a most important message for you. It is from Mr. Conway and Jeff."

Henley felt a surge of elation. Jeff had succeeded in getting in to see Conway.

Kenji handed Henley an envelope. "This is the message. I was told simply to deliver it."

Henley took the large envelope. "Can I offer you something, tea?"

Kenji shook his head. "I must return to Chiclayo. My plane leaves in an hour."

Henley didn't answer. He watched from the doorway as Kenji hurried away, toward the small car he had parked across the road.

Henley took the envelope into the living room, sat down at his desk and opened it.

A longish letter from Conway fell out together with a short note from Jeff. The third piece in the envelope was a close-up photo of a tablet. He frowned; the tablet resembled some fragments that had been found on Easter Island. Corrie had visited Easter Island three years earlier, seen the fragments and been fascinated by them. Could there be a whole tablet?

He read both communications slowly. They confirmed his observations by stating that the tablet in the photo had been found on Easter Island. He was asked to search for another like it among the

Moche artifacts and in the chambers beneath the grave robber's shack. Even more unlikely, Conway made reference to other tablets found in different locations all over the world.

Were they all mad? Was he truly expected to find a tablet like the one in the photo in the graves of the Moche? Though it might never have been successfully translated, the people responsible for the tablet in the photo most certainly had a written language or at least hieroglyphics like the Egyptians. He pondered the whole matter. It *was* conceivable that the Moche and the inhabitants of Easter Island had some connection. It was long accepted that two distinctly different peoples had inhabited Easter Island. Doubtless one group was there before the other. One was Polynesian in origin the other appeared to be from the mainland. And then there was the mystery of the great monoliths. It was widely accepted that the natives of Peru, the Moche as well as the Incas, had the technology to have moved the stone monoliths from the quarry where they were made to where they now stood. Yes, many academics believed it was entirely possible that a tribe or tribes from South America had settled on Easter Island along side the Polynesian inhabitants.

He decided he could intellectually accept the idea that there might be a connection between the Moche and the Easter Islanders. But Conway's insistence that there were seven tablets altogether and that they had been found in distant parts of the world supported another theory altogether. It was a theory that had floated about for years but which remained unsubstantiated and in some circles, laughable. The theory had it that there was once an ancient priesthood that ruled the world. If the alleged tablets could prove that theory was true, it was an earthshaking discovery. It would connect peoples who were never before connected in the minds of scholars. Conway also seemed to believe that when all of the tablets were together that they would lead to some treasure of vast proportions. He supposed that explained why someone was willing to kill for them.

He leaned back and closed his eyes; glad he had checked out of the hotel where both Ehrlich and Toro were always about. At least he wouldn't have to answer questions about Kenji's visit. As it was, Toro had asked more than once about the whereabouts of Corrie and Jeff. He had lied, telling him they had decided to remain in Lima for a time.

Again he looked at the picture of the Easter Island tablet. Well, now he knew what he was looking for. He simply had no idea where to look, although he knew he would start back in the chambers beneath the grave robber's shack. There was certainly nothing like it among the artifacts already found.

#

Corrie glanced in the mirror over the ornately carved dresser. The garment she had been given to wear was not unlike the one worn by Karim's wife. It consisted of a long dark skirt, a kind of loose shirt, an over-blouse, and a vest. It was very definitely the layered look without any fashion component. As for the scarf, she put it on as instructed. It came over her forehead and was folded at the sides so that not a single wisp of her blond hair was visible. She was only too well aware of how devout Moslems felt about female hair and its supposed libidinous quality. There was no need to irritate this Karim Ali Ahmed who by all accounts was a ruthless man in the midst of his own Holy War.

She drew in her breath and lifted the bell, ringing it as she had done before.

#

Jeff had woken up three times during the night. When at last it was morning, he was still tired but once again filled with nervous energy.

261

He made his way toward the dinette where Conway's silent manservant brought him coffee, the Boston Globe, and asked what he wanted for breakfast. He asked for toast, knowing he should eat more, but feeling no hunger.

He was half way through the paper when Conway joined him.

"I believe we're making some progress," Conway said, more or less jumping into his chair and allowing his short legs to dangle over the edge.

"What progress?"

"I have two possible locations where Karim might have taken the girl."

Jeff did not ask how Conway had come up with the locales. He supposed that using a main frame and his own secret network resources, he had somehow been able to trace messages sent by Karim Ali Ahmed from the locations in question. Few people would be able to do such a thing, but Conway was the master of the new computer networks and devout zealot or not, Karim was one fully computerized Moslem.

"What two locations?"

"One in Germany, but I think that's only a point through which he forwards messages. The other is in Ecuador. I think the Ecuadorian location is most likely. It's not far from the Peruvian border."

"Tell me the exact place. I'll go at once."

"Like some knight in shinning armor? Forget it. It's probably highly guarded. You'll either end up dead, or you'll scare him off and we'll never find him or your lady love."

"Time is important to Corrie."

"He won't kill her till he has the other tablet. Henley hasn't even found it."

"So what do you suggest?" Jeff asked irritably.

"I suggest I monitor this location for at least thirty-six hours to confirm the fact that Karim is there. If he is, we'll go in – together and with some force."

Jeff stared at Conway and wondered if he could trust him. It was a futile question. At the moment there was no choice. He didn't bother to ask about the "force". For all he knew, Conway had his own private army.

#

Karim Ali Ahmed had finished his evening prayers. He went from his prayer room to the common room, and there sat down on the floor, his legs crossed, to enjoy his evening water pipe and relax to the sweet sound of the santur, an eastern dulcimer. It was by far his favorite instrument and he always traveled with both CDs and tapes.

He was deep in thought when he looked up and saw his wife standing silently in the doorway. She had no doubt been there for several minutes.

Their eyes locked. That was her signal to speak.

"The woman is ready," she said.

"Bring her in."

Corrie followed Karim's wife and sat down on the cushions to which she was directed. She hoped his wife would stay, but she did not. In fact she disappeared so quickly it added to Corrie's nervousness.

"Ah, Miss Henley, I am delighted to welcome you to my humble dwelling."

He spoke to her, but did not make any kind of eye contact. It was rather as if he were talking to the far wall. "I should like to say I am delighted to be here, but I cannot since I was abducted by force."

"I quite understand."

263

He continued to avoid looking directly at her. Perhaps he did so for some cultural reason so she too avoided seeking eye contact and concentrated on his voice. His English was very good, very smooth but he had an odd accent. It was not entirely a Middle Eastern accent; there was something else, something altogether weird. Was it the faintest trace of a Brooklyn accent? It occurred to her that he might have practiced a Middle Eastern accent in order to cover some other accent. She wanted to ask but she did not. Something told her that Karim would not welcome any personal questions.

"How long do you intend keeping me here?"

"I am afraid I cannot answer that question, Miss Henley. Even after your father locates what I am seeking, I shall require certain assurances before I can afford to allow either of you to go free."

Corrie forgot herself and looked at him directly, vowing not to show fear even though she now felt it. "It's nice of you to be so candid."

"I have no reason to lie."

His eyes locked on hers for the first time. Corrie fought off a violent shiver. His eyes were very dark, almost as if they were all pupils. She sensed more than just evil. His eyes conveyed an animal wildness, a lack of control. Still, his voice and tone were completely controlled. She looked away, deeply disturbed by what she felt. After a moment, she managed to regain her own self-control.

"At least tell me what this is all about. I'd like to understand why I'm here and what it is that my father is supposed to have."

He ignored her question. "Let me offer you some refreshment."

"Thank you, I am hungry." She was lying. Her stomach was churning. *But I should eat. I need to eat to help neutralize the drugs.*

He clapped his hands imperiously and his wife appeared almost instantly bearing a tray of steaming rice and some curried meat as well as flat bread. To her surprise, she was also given a goblet of red wine.

As if he knew what she were thinking, he said, "It's true, I don't drink. But I think it is quite all right for my guests to partake."

Corrie said nothing.

He again avoided looking at her when he spoke. His tone was cold and unemotional.

She swallowed her thoughts, forcing herself to concentrate only on rescue or escape. "Will you at least tell me where I am?"

"You are still in Latin America. That is as much as I shall tell you."

Under normal circumstances she would have persisted. But this was not a man with whom a woman argued. As controlled as he sounded, she knew he was far from controlled. Moreover, his wife's subservience spoke volumes. Middle Eastern women who were subservient in public were not usually so in their own homes. Karim's wife was totally subservient. She seemed to quiver at his every word.

"More wine?" At that moment Karim lifted his head once again and she was again drawn to his dark eyes. They were frightening. She nodded even though she didn't really want the wine.

To her surprise, he stood up and walked over to her, stopping to pick up the carafe of wine. Silently, he filled her glass himself.

Corrie watched, afraid to lift the glass off the table for fear her hand would shake.

He reached out and touched her shoulder with long, strong bony fingers. "You are such a fortunate young woman. You are to have the experience of a lifetime, you will see and hear things of which others have only dreamed…" his voice drifted off. Then as if summoned by some silent command, he turned suddenly and left the room.

Corrie drew in her breath and shivered, thinking that Karim was more than a computer terrorist. She wondered if he was even truly a Moslem, or whether his seeming observance of Islam was simply a cover-up. *The feel of his hand, the tone of his voice, his strange accent; he's less concerned with worshipping God than being one.*

#

Emlio de Leon looked out the plane window. Its nose was pointed eastward as it lifted off the ground, leaving Barajos, Madrid's International Airport behind.

It had been a difficult trip. First he had met with Anatoly and then he had been subjected to the opposite extreme, in the person of Archbishop Reinecke. Reinecke was a skeletal man with sunken eyes and pale narrow lips. He did not look like the head of one of the largest organizations within the church, but he was the head of 'The Path,' and he wore his authority heavily, as if it were steel plated armor. The membership of *The Path* was predominantly made up of lay persons. It was a secret society that lobbied for the return of the Latin Mass and the rituals that had existed before Vatican II. In addition, its members supported a number of smaller groups who claimed to have seen the Virgin – groups that had been rejected by the Vatican.

But *The Path* existed for reasons other than the restoration of rituals, more important reasons.

Even within the church there was a special need to monitor the faith, to make certain it was not diluted in any way. In Latin America their job had been especially arduous. There, the Jesuits, once the strictest of all orders, had become inexorably entangled with politics, with humanism and with something the Jesuit revolutionaries chose to call, 'Liberation Theology'.

Ridding the church in Central and South America of Liberation theology had called for drastic measures. More than three hundred priests and nuns had to be eliminated, and there had been one very public execution of an archbishop as he said mass.

The threat of Liberation Theology had kept the members of *The Path* very busy during the seventies and early eighties. Between 1985 and the present, not much had occurred that called for the organization's special talents. Nonetheless, members of *The Path* remained ready should a need arise.

Such a need had only recently made itself known. It was hardly the kind of thing he had expected to arise. In fact, it was entirely out of his realm of experience. But then he absolutely knew he was not alone. This had to stop now. It could not be allowed to go further.

He checked his watch. It was a long flight to Los Angeles, and from there he had another reasonably long flight to Lima where he would catch a local flight to Chiclayo.

As soon as he got there he would check in with his contact. If there were new developments, his contact would have heard of them. Not that it mattered. The tablet and all those connected with it had to be destroyed as soon as it was found. Thinking that no one would ever believe the truth about the tablets, the church had ignored them. They had even allowed Blanford Buckley to display them, realizing that he would be ridiculed and discredited. But if the seventh tablet were discovered, if all the tablets fell into the hands of one person, if their use were discovered, they could ruin everything. Put simply, they would destroy the faith.

#

Jonathan Henley opened the door to find Captain Toro on his doorstep. "I was just on my way out," he said.

"I must speak with you," Toro announced. His expression was grim and Jonathan immediately felt a sinking sensation.

He ushered Toro inside, "More bodies?" he asked, trying not to sound as concerned as he was.

"No, that's not why I'm here."

Jonathan was sure his relief was palpable.

"You lied to me," Toro said. His voice was cold. "I trusted you, and you lied to me."

Jonathan pointed him toward a chair. "Not because I wanted to – she's my daughter."

Toro didn't look up. It was as if he were thinking, trying to decide if this were an important lie. Finally, he did look up, "You told me they were still in Lima but I know they got off a plane from Lima at the Chiclayo airport when they were supposed to. Then they both disappeared. Tell me the truth now."

"Corrie and Jeff did come back from Lima as scheduled. We met at the hotel. She went up to her room to shower and change. She didn't come back. When Jeff and I went up there we found her purse on the floor with its contents on the rug. Nothing stolen. We could smell chloroform. We're sure she's been kidnapped."

"And Mr. Jeff Richards! Where is he?"

Hardly a surprising question, Jonathan thought. If only the answer wasn't so vague. "He went to find her." He leaned back wondering how much to tell Toro, wondering if it mattered.

"How does he know where to look?"

"He went to Jason Conway."

"You believe Jason Conway kidnapped her?"

"No. But he has vast resources. Jeff hopes he will help find her."

Toro lit one of his infernal cigarillos. He drew on it and expelled the foul smoke into the air. "You're not telling me everything."

"Conway is after this thing, whatever the hell it is. Apparently others are after it too."

"I think you know what it is they are looking for."

Jonathan nodded. "I do, but in and for itself it has no value. I don't know why everyone wants it."

"Please tell me."

"It's a wooden tablet with some kind of writing on it."

"You haven't found it, have you?"

"No."

"It's time for you to return to your search."

"If I am to get Corrie back alive, I can't have you leaning over my shoulder."

Toro grinned, "My name may be Toro but I shall become El Gato for the time being."

Toro meant bull, gato meant cat. "Thanks," Jonathan replied. He intended returning to the chambers beneath the grave robber's shack immediately. Maybe there was something he had overlooked.

#

Jeff looked out the window on a frozen Boston. Overnight there had been an ice storm and the barren trees in the park along the Charles River had been turned to glass. In the bright sunlight, under the blue sky, the whole landscape looked as if it had been sprinkled with diamonds.

Far below the window, in the park, skaters were already on the ice in the pond. He was aware of moisture in his eyes. He wanted to be down there skating with Corrie; he wanted to be holding her right now.

"Jeff Richards?"

He turned suddenly at the sound of the familiar female voice.

"Katsura?" He felt as if he had come full circle. She had initiated one mystery and now appeared in another.

"What the hell are you doing here?" He blurted out his question.

"I'm Kenji's sister. I work for Mr. Conway."

He knew damn well he was the victim of duplicity but why had they bothered? "Strange you didn't mention that before."

"There was no need for you to know then."

He felt somehow set up. But to what end?

269

"Do you live here?" He decided to hold his questions about the Japanese Embassy.

Her expression was flirtatious, "I have my own private quarters. This penthouse takes up the entire top floor. But you are really asking if I am Mr. Conway's companion, aren't you?

"Just curious."

"My relationship with Mr. Conway is whatever is called for at the moment."

"That's some leading answer. But frankly this isn't about you even though I have a lot I would like to discuss with you."

"I imagine you have." She walked toward the window. "Have you eaten?"

"I just finished." To his surprise, she put her hand on the nap of his neck and began massaging it with just the right amount of pressure. He closed his eyes, giving into the sensation of her practiced moving fingers.

"Take a short time to digest your food, Jeff-san. "You have been too long traveling and too long tense. You need to work out the kinks. There's a practice room here. Let's go and do some Aikido, and after that we can relax in the hot tub."

He was well aware of the fact that his whole body felt like a rubber band that had been stretched for way too long. Practice and a steaming hot bath might be just the thing. "Sounds good." Vaguely he wondered why Conway had a practice room. He certainly did not look as if he had been working out.

"What is your rank, Jeff-san?" she asked as she led him down the hall.

"I'm San Dan."

She laughed, "I'm a Yon Dan. I wouldn't want to be too hard on you."

One rank higher, this could be a rigorous experience. But then, yesterday was a warning to keep in shape. Maybe she'll open up after practice. Maybe she'll explain the whole Japanese Embassy thing.

Katsura glanced at her watch. "I'll meet you in the foyer in half an hour."

He picked up the paper again and sat down. He wasn't really reading. He was turning the pages and looking at the pictures. He couldn't think about much of anything save finding Corrie.

In half an hour he went to the foyer and found Katsura waiting. She motioned him to follow her down a hall on the opposite side of the foyer from which he had come.

They passed several closed doors and finally she stopped and opened a door on the left. To his surprise he saw a large airy room with good mats on the floor. There were tropical plants along one wall, and a picture of O'Sensei with flowers to one side. "That's the men's change room." She said pointing off to one of two doors.

She didn't have to tell him where the hot tub was. It was on the enclosed balcony, he could see the steam rising from it.

"I think you'll find a gi and hakama in there that fits," she called out casually.

"All the comforts of home," he replied. He felt somehow as if he had been expected.

In a few minutes they were together on the mat. They knelt and bowed to O'Sensei and then did their warm up stretches. After twenty minutes, Katsura stood up and he knew it was a signal that they should get started. They bowed to one another and immediately she attacked him with an attempted blow to the center of his head but he quickly shuffled to her side, avoiding the blow. He grabbed her shoulder, putting her off balance and then he threw her. She rolled back, stood up and came at him again with a blow to the side of his head. Jeff blended with the blow and threw her again. With each of her attacks he was able to evade, deflect, and harmonize.

Katsura was like a rolling ball as she took the falls. She was immediately up and right back at him. He was about to do another hip throw when she countered his movement and threw him. He also took falls and rolled back into a standing position. They were flowing ying and yang in their white gis and black hakamas.

Jeff could feel Katsura's precise movements. His size didn't matter as she was able to cause him to be off balance. She was a very good Aikidoist. He was growing tired but felt an opening when she tried to perform a submission wrist-lock. He was able to come into her center just ahead of her attempt and counter with his own. Her face went red and she tapped her side as he applied the move then released it in a throw. She quickly got up smiling, ready to attack, but Jeff put up his hand and bowed. His counter move had re-energized her it seemed. They'd been going for thirty minutes non-stop.

"You're very good Katsura. You've worn me out."

"Ah, Jeff you are likewise very good. That last counter move was well done."

"I'm ready for the hot tub anytime."

With the slightest of waves, she turned toward the change room.

To your corners, he thought as he went off to shower and change.

When he returned from the changing room in swimming trunks, Katsura was already in the hot tub. He could see she was wearing the briefest of string bikinis. He slipped into the water, well aware of the fact that she was staring at him.

"It's too bad you are in love with someone else, Jeff-san. I suspect we would have been most compatible."

He felt his mouth go dry. Her look was penetrating, her tone suggestive. He decided to be direct, though he was sure she would not be.

"Why didn't we practice when you came to the dojo in Lima?"

"I had other matters on my mind."

"Were you on some sort of assignment for Conway?

"Yes."

"Is that the reason why you didn't tell me you were Kenji's sister?"

"Yes."

He kept hoping she would elaborate but she did not. "And were there really paintings in the embassy that you wanted to show me?"

"Prints, not paintings, valuable block prints as I told you. Actually, I wanted to see them myself. Jason was going to try to buy them."

"And the terrorist attack?"

"I learned it was to take place just before it happened."

He recalled now that shortly after their arrival she had said she had to make a phone call. He supposed that she had checked in with Conway who had somehow learned of the impending attack. "From Conway?" he asked evenly.

"Yes."

"How nice of both of you not to tell anyone else." He felt bitterly sarcastic. He could hardly forget the months of captivity the hostages had endured nor could he readily forget the deaths.

"Mr. Conway has unique methods of monitoring certain groups. To expose those methods would render them useless in the future. After all, you are not asking how he has located your Corrie Henley, are you?"

She sounded as sarcastic as he knew he had sounded. She was right. He hadn't asked and until he found Corrie, he wouldn't ask.

#

Jason Conway sat in his computer room tapping the desk with his short stubby fingers.

"And your assessment?" he asked Katsura.

"I think he is only interested in the girl."

"You can't get him interested in you?"

"I could no doubt get him into bed. But it wouldn't mean anything. He wants her."

"What about power? What about the tablets?

"I don't think he cares. I think he just wants the girl."

"And his fighting ability?"

"He's good. Better than he should be. Of course I have no idea how he will react in a real situation. He's great on the mat but faced with Karim's men, I'm not certain."

"He did all right the other night."

"Yes, that's a good indication."

"You think he's worth taking with us."

"Yes."

Conway looked at her hard. This was unlike Katsura. She was highly competitive but she seemed unwilling to go after this Jeff Richards even though she appeared to like him. Perhaps that was for the best; Richards did not seem the kind who would be willing to share Katsura.

He shrugged. "I'll let you know when the plan is ready."

CHAPTER FIFTEEN

1967, New York City

Mir'yam Rabinowitz paused to catch her breath and wipe her brow. She was soaking wet, though not pleasantly so. It was mid-August, the temperature was at least ninety-eight and she was quite certain the humidity was even higher. Without air conditioning, New York in August was a nightmare. It was worse if you were working.

She took a deep breath and went back to scrubbing the kitchen floor.

She always got down on her hands and knees with a brush and a rag. This was the only way since mops seemed to do nothing more than move the dirt around. She scrubbed almost frantically; the floor just couldn't be too clean.

"Mir'yam! Are you home?"

"In here, Bella, I'm just finishing the floor. Sit down, I'll be right in."

"Look at you," Bella said, holding out her hands. She had not sat down; she had come directly to the kitchen door where she paused in front of the gleaming wet floor. "You shouldn't be down on your hands and knees."

Mir'yam looked up. "And why not? It's the only way to get the floor clean."

"As if your floor was ever dirty! Mir'yam, you should be celebrating."

"Have I something to celebrate?"

"As if you didn't know."

"I don't know." Mir'yam stood up and wiped her hands on her flowered apron. "Come on, come in the living room and sit down. When the floor's dry I'll make some tea."

"To celebrate?"

"To celebrate what? Tell me."

"The SATs, you know the test for college. Didn't Sheldon tell you?"

Mir'yam sat down and looked up at her neighbor. "Sheldon went to the movies. It's air conditioned, he said it was too hot to stay home."

"He may be the smartest boy but he's not the most thoughtful."

"Smart? Oh, I know he's smart all right but what about these SATS?

"My Myron says Sheldon got the highest grade in all of New York, not just the city but the whole state. Maybe the highest in the whole country! Mir'yam, he can go to any school he wants. You probably won't even have to pay."

Mir'yam stared at her friend. Myron was Bella's son and while he and Sheldon were in the same class, they could not really be called friends. "Is it true?" Mir'yam asked in disbelief. "Why didn't he tell me himself?"

"Maybe he's modest."

"Modest, yes, my Sheldon is modest." Sheldon was extremely withdrawn and often appeared to be shy but she didn't say that. Sheldon was always reading and studying. The truth was she had long ago lost track of what he studied. She had trouble balancing her checkbook but Sheldon had begun talking about calculus and quantum physics before he was out of elementary school. He was always studying some language or other and she could not recall having ever asked him a question he could not answer. But Sheldon did not show himself to others readily. For years in school he had hidden the extent of his knowledge from teachers and classmates. He always got the best grades, but he insisted that it was better not to excel so much that he would be singled out. His test score surprised her and she silently wondered if Sheldon had now decided to reveal himself.

"So lucky," Bella said rocking in her chair. "You're so lucky to have such a son!"

"It hasn't been easy but it's been worth it. He's a good boy." He was a good boy, though she acknowledged there were aspects of his personality that troubled her.

"I don't know how you've managed alone. You should get a medal for having such a son."

Mir'yam closed her eyes. Yes, she was proud, but inside she worried. She did not really understand her son. Sheldon kept to himself, he had secrets and on more than one occasion she had seen him talking to himself – not just muttering as many people do, but speaking in another voice and with a frightening intensity.

#

The trees in the park offered shade from the sun but there was no relief from the penetrating humidity.

Sheldon Rabinowitz sat on a bench and watched the pigeons as they circled around. Every now and again, he reached into a brown paper bag that sat by his side. From it he withdrew bread crumbs which he threw at the birds. They fought one another for each tiny morsel.

He was not here to feed the birds, however. He was waiting for Rachel Cohen. She was a beautiful girl, the most beautiful in his class at school. She had blue eyes and long blond tresses. Her parents were from Stockholm and he thought her exotic and quite different from all the other girls he knew. She was different not only in appearance, but in attitude.

His parents were Jewish refugees. His mother had borne him when she was forty and his fifty year old father had died the year after he was born. Even today, twenty years after coming to America, his mother bore the psychological scars caused by her horrific memories of the Holocaust. The world had betrayed the Jews but Jews also knew betrayal on the most personal level. His

277

mother had vivid memories of hitherto friendly neighbors turning on her parents and of their children taunting her.

The result was his mother's lifelong mistrust of Gentiles. He was well aware that she had few friends and that she was suspicious of strangers. She lived in an entirely Jewish world, a ghetto that was both physical and mental. But Rachel's family was different. Rachel was different. "My father says that when the Germans came they ordered all Jews to wear the yellow armband with the Star of David. But everyone – the whole population - wore it in protest, even the King of Denmark. We were protected; the others did not betray us."

As Rachel had grown up in a home where anti-Semitism did not linger as a primordial fear, she was not like his mother or most of his classmates. Rachel was free; she was to his way of thinking, entirely unique.

Sheldon Rabinowitz knew he was unique too. He determined that as a result, he and Rachel clearly belonged together. His teachers all said he was a mathematical and linguistic genius and they did not even know how much he really knew. At sixteen he could speak five languages with fluency – five languages not counting Hebrew which he had learned as part of his after-school religious studies. Now he had gotten the highest possible marks on the SATS and his teachers all said he could go to any university he chose and study whatever he wished. Even the Rabbi praised him. "You'll do us proud, Sheldon."

His voices made other promises; they offered more interesting possibilities, more exciting experiences. They told him he was very important. They told him he was the long awaited Savior, but they warned him to say nothing until all was revealed.

Sheldon looked up and saw Rachel. She always came here on Sunday afternoon. She came to walk her little dog. He took a deep breath, and for a moment felt absolutely paralyzed. She was wearing a blue cotton dress with a full skirt that billowed in the warm breeze.

Her dress was sleeveless and her arms were snow white like her bare legs. Her hair was flying free.

He steeled himself and then walked toward her. He felt like a robot. Every step was forced in spite of the fact that he had rehearsed this moment a thousand and one times. He had worshipped Rachel from afar for over a year, in his dreams he knew her intimately, in his imagination he had created a lover and a companion.

"Rachel," he said when he was a few feet from her.

She looked up, surprised. "Hello Sheldon. What are you doing here?"

"It's hot," he said awkwardly.

"Yes."

She did not smile, but rather turned slightly away. He cleared his throat, "Rachel, I was wondering – well, would you like to go to the movies with me this afternoon?"

Her facial expression changed ever so slightly. "I'm sorry, I can't."

He felt the sting of her tone. "You can't or won't," he asked, aware of his own sudden mood change.

"Can't and won't." She turned and pulled her ugly little poodle along with her. *Go to the movies with Sheldon?* Sheldon was tall and altogether too skinny. He had masses of dark hair, swarthy skin, and deep dark set eyes that she did not trust. He wasn't ugly, but he did not appeal to her in the slightest. He *was* smart, but she thought him odd, even weird. Once she had seen him talking to himself and there were disconcerting stories about him, about his temper and his solitary existence.

Sheldon felt stung by her look as well as her rejection. He pressed his lips together and shouted after her, "You'll be sorry! I got the highest SAT marks in all of New York!"

In his world, in his mother's world, his accomplishment meant something. But it meant nothing to Rachel Cohen.

"You're a jerk," she said turning to look back at him. "You're a real spaz."

Sheldon turned and ran. Spaz was an ugly word! Her tone was ugly. He hated her! How could he have worshipped her for so long? He turned and ran blindly.

His mind was crowded with conflicting voices, he felt vaguely as if he would explode when he finally found himself in front of the theater. He bought a ticket and hurried inside. He found a seat in the crowded but mercifully cool movie house. He wiped the sweat off his brow and sunk down in his seat. The lights dimmed, the film called, **Khartoum**, was just beginning.

Thousands upon thousands of riders galloped across the dry desert, their robes billowing in the wind. When they dismounted, they bowed down, faces in the hot sand. When they stood up there was awe in their eyes. They bowed down to the Mahdi whose dark eyes held the secrets of the ages, whose mysticism could not be denied.

Mahdi! Mahdi! Mahdi! Their cry rang in Sheldon's head. He could not take his eyes off the screen and when the film was over, he waited and sat through it again. When it was over the second time, he ran from the theater. He ran all the way to the library to read about the Mahdi. As he read, he trembled. This was it! This was his long awaited revelation. His hatred of Rachel retreated to the edges of his mind where it would linger and slowly fester till it matured and demanded revenge.

It was uncanny! Muhammad Ahmad ibn'Abd Allah, the Mahdi, was the son of a boat builder. Had not his own father worked at the Brooklyn Navy Yard as a ship builder? Was not his own mother called Mir'yam, like the mother of Jesus? That was it! He was to be the Savior who would reunite the Semitic peoples. For now, however, he was to live as a Moslem, he was to live exactly as the Mahdi had lived.

The Mahdi was a mystic. Sheldon regarded himself as a mystic. He carefully read and wrote down how and where the Mahdi had been educated. He vowed he would follow the same path until he understood Islam as well as he understood Judaism. When he left the library, Sheldon felt inflamed. He vowed to go to see **Khartoum** again tomorrow. He had to think, he had to find a way to follow his voices and fulfill the prophecy.

Wearily and quite drained, Sheldon headed home.

"Sheldon, is that you?"

"Yes, Mama." He sank into the easy chair in the corner. It was ill, its stuffing was coming out and gobs of grayish cotton material trickled from a well worn wound on its left arm.

"You didn't tell me about your college tests. I'm so proud. If your Papa was still alive he would be proud too."

Sheldon stared at his mother. It was going to be difficult to make her understand that he wasn't hers anymore, that he had divine parents, that in fact that he was not really even Jewish – at least not in the way she understood Judaism.

"I have to go away," he said slowly.

"To school? Yes, I know you will want to go away to school. Bella says maybe you should go to MIT. That's in Boston. I have some money saved, we could move to Boston."

"No, Mama."

"I understand. You haven't made up your mind yet."

He didn't answer. It was better if he just let things develop. "I'm going to bed now."

He stood up and walked over to her. Awkwardly, he kissed her cheek, and then he left her there on the sofa, not understanding anything.

#

281

It was Friday night and Bellevue was humming. Dr. Myron Buchman headed for the desk.

"How many Messiahs have we tonight?" he asked the duty nurse with a wink.

"At last count, five Messiahs, two Beatles and one Bob Dylan. Why?"

"I just left one of them. Some kid named Sheldon Rabinowitz. He goes most of them one better, he thinks he's a Moslem-Jewish Savior. He has "Jerusalem Syndrome" with a twist.

The nurse nodded. "Jerusalem Syndrome," was not uncommon among young Jewish schizophrenics. She had worked in Israel for nearly a year and they treated about a hundred patients a year for this particular form of schizophrenia.

Dr. Buchman shook his head, "This one is sad. Dr. Rosen saw him earlier. Do you know his I.Q. is right off the scale? Are his parents here yet?"

"His mother is in the waiting room. Apparently she's a widow."

"That's even sadder, guess I'll talk to her now. God, I hate this."

"Will we be keeping him?"

"Not this time. I'll send him home with some lithium and we'll see how long it is before he ends up back here."

"The only ones who don't come back are the ones who end up in other hospitals," the nurse said seriously.

Dr. Buchman waved at her and headed off to the waiting room. She was right. Bellevue had a revolving door. Into emergency, given drugs, back on the street, don't take the drugs, and back to emergency. Sheldon had a condition for which there was no cure. A few patients got better on regular medication; most of the time they got worse. They had re-occurring psychotic episodes that often intensified and grew more frequent. They lived in a world of terrifying and painful illusions as they followed the instructions of their internal voices. More often than not, the voices led them to a state of megalomania and they adopted the belief that they were a great religious leader or an icon of popular culture. Sometimes schizophrenics tried to harm themselves, sometimes they harmed others. Most just suffered alone in a personal hell. The problem for he and other doctors was an inability to know which ones might become violent and which would not. One simply had to wait for the condition to develop. One might easily become a killer; most would merely spend the rest of their lives preaching in the park.

"I don't understand," Mir'yam Rabinowitz said as she leaned against her friend, Bella's shoulder. "He's a good boy; he always did well in school. He studied hard and got the highest score in all of New York State on his SATs"

"Mental Illness has nothing to do with intelligence," Buchman told her.

"I tried. I tried so hard. His father's dead, it's true I had to raise him alone." Tears tumbled down her cheeks.

"Mrs. Rabinowitz, your son's condition has nothing to do with anything you did or did not do. I'm sure you did the best you could."

"She's a good mother," Bella confirmed, "I've watched her."

"I still don't understand," Mir'yam said softly. "What did he do again?"

"He was found in the subway wearing a loin cloth and preaching. He was ranting about Jews and Arabs being the same and about being a savior. Some ruffians beat him up and he was arrested and brought here."

"Why would my Sheldon be doing that? Why would he say those things?"

"Mrs. Rabinowitz, your son apparently suffers from schizophrenia. We need to do more tests and he has to be on medication."

"And then?"

"With proper treatment, his episodes can be controlled. This is a condition that is under intense study. We learn more about it every day."

"He can go to university?"

"Yes, if he stays on his medication. Our preliminary tests show your son to be extremely intelligent."

Mir'yam felt as if she were in a trance. It was true that Sheldon had always been different. Once he had even told her about voices in his head. But she had not understood, she did not understand now.

"He can go home tonight. We'll see him on an outpatient basis starting next week."

Mir'yam pulled herself up and dabbed at her eyes. "Can I take him now?"

"You can pick him up downstairs as soon as he's dressed. Just be sure he takes these as directed."

The doctor pressed a vial of white pills into her hand.

"I'll get a cab to take us home, Mir'yam." Bella's voice was strong and Mir'yam let herself be led away. The corridors of Bellevue were crowded, yet they seemed empty to her. It was hotter today than it had been yesterday, yet she felt cold. It didn't matter what the doctor had said. In her heart Mir'yam Rabinowitz knew that Sheldon was going to leave her forever and she felt strongly that after he was gone she was never going to see her brilliant son again.

#

Sheldon lay in his narrow bed and stared at the ceiling. He was turning into someone else. He could feel it, he could feel himself drawn to the desert, feel himself turn toward the call to prayer from the minaret, feel himself meditating and delving into the heart of eastern mysticism. He saw himself in long robes, he envisioned women in veils. He envisioned himself as their master.

The whole episode in the subway was a mistake. People weren't ready. I'm not ready. I can't stay here. I must make my plan to leave.

He lay in his bed for hours until he knew it was nearly three in the morning. Then he got up and dressed. He listened at the door and when he heard no one, he crept out of the door and into the hallway. His mother had given him his pills hours ago, probably enough pills to render him unconscious till morning. But he had not taken them; he had spit them out as soon as she turned her back.

His mother had always been a sound sleeper. He went back inside his room and gathered up what he needed, stuffing it messily into a duffel bag. He took his secret savings from underneath his mattress, and then he composed a note to his mother.

Dear Mama,

Tomorrow you will find me gone. Please tell everyone you sent me to stay with a relative in California for a long rest. Please do not try to find me. They will lock me up again and they will tell you I am insane. Mama, they don't understand. No one understands. I promise you, Mama, I will be all right. Don't worry.

Love, Sheldon.

He put the note on the kitchen table. He stared at the signature. It would be the last time he ever used it. His name was now Karim. Sheldon Rabinowitz was dead.

#

For some time after he left Sheldon to die, Karim worked for a man called Jason Conway; a pioneer in computer technology. The huge UNIVAC computers had wet the appetite of the visionaries. "Miniaturization is the future," Conway believed. Sheldon agreed it would not be his future but it would make his future possible. Conway paid him well and Conway had shown him something extraordinary. It was a wooden tablet found on Easter Island but they both knew it was far more. Deep in the recesses of his mind, he

285

carried a mental image of the tablet and often he wondered if he would ever link it to his own destiny. Then the Gods had directed him. He had gone to Cambodia and fate led him to the second tablet. His search began.

#

Karim put his diary aside and turned to the window to look down on London's teeming streets. Here, and when he was in New York, he always had the feeling of being at the heart of the beast, yet he admitted he liked both cities and recognized them as being unique and exciting as well as depraved. In truth, he liked London more. New York made him uncomfortable. It caused a hundred hidden memories to surface and not only did he hear past voices but familiar faces danced through his thoughts. They were faces from another life, the life lead by poor pathetic Sheldon Rabinowitz.

He had been searching for other tablets now for slightly over a year. There was no doubt in his mind that they had all been found, even that one or more might be in the hands of a single person. He felt a certain urgency because he knew that Jason Conway was searching too.

His search was methodical. He placed ads expressing an interest in artifacts that had examples of various types of script. He tirelessly explained his 'study', thus receiving invitations to museums that had holdings that appeared to fit the description of that which he was studying. He had his employees accept all invitations and appear to photograph the artifacts that he had been invited to see. Using an identity he had created, one Dr. Hayallah, a graduate of the university in Khartoum, he quickly established a reputation in the academic world. He had built up a tremendous catalogue of relics that all had ancient script and symbols – none were what he sought but he had not given up. At the same time, he made the appropriate contacts in the world of illegal artifact trading.

He had met Ysabel and for a time she had assisted him in searching for the tablets.

He quickly put his diary in his top desk drawer, when his assistant, Ghazi, knocked on the door. He told him to come in.

"I have found someone whose story might interest you," Ghazi said, before he had even completed his bow.

"Someone?"

"Yes. I have been seeing a woman, a Moslem woman from Egypt. She works as a nurse in an old age home in London."

Karim nodded. Ghazi was the slow methodical type. He was the master of verbal plodding.

"One of those in her care is an elderly Englishman who says he is a Druid priest. He claims he has tablets that prove the Druids were once a world-wide priesthood. Naturally, I wouldn't bother you with this tale from a senile old man had not tablets been mentioned."

"What hospital?" Karim snapped. Whatever else Ghazi had to say was no doubt superfluous.

"He is probably insane," Ghazi hedged, shaking his head.

"I did not ask for an assessment of his condition. I asked the name of the hospital."

"Belfield Acres."

Karim turned immediately and picking up the phone, ordered a car. "How much did you tell this woman?" he asked when he had hung up.

Ghazi shrugged, "Only that you were studying ancient writing. She recalled her patient. She says he babbles incessantly about it."

Karim again nodded. If and when he found the tablets, and when he had deciphered them, he would have to eliminate those close to him who knew of his quest. The new Mahdi could afford no naysayers.

"You may go now," he told Ghazi. Then added, "Phone your friend, tell her I'm coming. If this comes to something you will both be rewarded."

Ghazi turned to leave.

"What's her name? Karim demanded.

"Setara. I'll tell her you are on your way."

Belfield Acres might once have had acres, but no more. Now it consisted entirely of a rambling stone edifice completely surrounded by the dismally identical brick cubicles that were Council Housing. Inside, the hospital was more cheerful than one might have guessed. Even though the walls were stark white they were decorated with multi colored pictures donated by the students in a nearby kindergarten.

Karim was met at the door by Setara, Ghazi's lady friend. She wore a traditional head covering and a longer dress than the other nurses. Karim was pleased that Ghazi had not succumbed to the wiles of English women and had, instead, chosen a devout Moslem woman. He hoped they loved one another since they might well spend eternity together.

"Dr. Buckley's room is on the third floor," she told him, her eyes respectfully cast down.

"It is a private room?"

"Yes."

"How does he afford this?" Does the National Health Service pay for it?"

"No. He told me he inherited much money from a woman called Rosalind. He speaks of her a great deal. It seems she was married to two archeologists. I believe that Dr. Buckley became her – I believe the word is gigolo."

Karim said nothing. It was all beginning to sound quite promising.

Setara opened the door. It was a small but comfortable looking room. A large chair sat by the window and sitting in it, Karim saw an old man.

"Dr. Buckley?"

The man turned slightly, motioning Karim to his side.

Karim attempted to conceal his surprise. The man's stringy white hair reached his waist and he was dressed in a long white gown that was tied in the front with a knotted rope.

Seeing the expression on his face, Setara whispered, "He won't allow us to cut his hair and he insists on wearing that gown. He says he is a Druid Priest."

"I'm not deaf," Buckley said, staring hard at Setara.

"Leave us," Karim ordered.

"Stupid girl," Buckley muttered. "I cannot cut my hair. I'm a Druid priest. We do not cut our hair. And this is not a gown, it is my sacred robe. I shouldn't be here. I should be outside. I have no powers here, the air is terrible, there are no trees. I must go to the ancient grove. I must go there to die."

"Tell me about the ancient priesthood."

"Once we ruled the earth," Buckley said dreamily.

"You have the sacred tablets?" Karim asked, feigning total acceptance of the old man's meanderings. Frankly, it did not much matter what the old man thought.

"I am truly a Druid priest. I have the tablets – if only I could find the rest."

Karim's hopes surged. "How many do you have?"

The old man crooked his finger, motioning Karim to lean closer. "I have the one I found at Avebury and I have de Vega's tablet from Cuzco. I have one from Delphi, and another from India."

It was a huge discovery! Karim could hardly control himself. This doddering old fool had probably been telling this story for years and no one believed him. *I believe you,* Karim thought even as he suppressed a rare smile.

"I want to see your tablets," Karim said.

The old man's expression was foolish, "Lean close, I will tell you where to find them."

Karim leaned over and listened. The old man had not always been foolish. He had found an ideal place to hide the tablets.

"Thank you, Karim said bowing as he backed away. You shall be rewarded."

"There are seven. You must find them all."

Karim did not answer. The old man had hidden four and he had one, yet another, the one found on Easter Island was in Conway's possession. Only one remained to be found. Of course that one was the key to all the others.

"I will go now and return with your reward."

Buckley's head wobbled up and down, "I took good care of them. It is you who shall be rewarded when you find the treasure. At last someone believes me. They might have believed me, but the pilot died so I had no proof."

The old man was babbling on. Karim stayed for a short time, then he promised to return.

#

Karim wasted no time. He went directly to the small stone church near Avebury. He counted from the floor up as he had been instructed by Dr. Buckley. The fifth stone slid out like a drawer, revealing a vault in which the tablets were stored. In a short time he had retrieved all four tablets as well as the precious notes as translated and set down by de Vega, the son of the Inca Princess and a Spanish Noble.

Karim went home and read late into the night. But of course! The seventh tablet was buried with the Moche! When he had learned of the great find in Peru he had wondered about it. Buckley never understood that part of de Vega's notes because the Moche discovery had not been made until 1987. According to the notes, long ago, a priest called the Memorizer had sent a warrior to retrieve a tablet given to an unknown group. Most certainly, that group was the Moche who were dying out just as the Inca were coming to power. But the notes were clear, the warrior had never returned.

Now he knew everything! He decided that when he returned he would dispatch one of his men to kill old Dr. Buckley, the nurse and his ambitious assistant, Ghazi.

He closed his eyes and rocked back and forth, his arms folded across his chest. *With the power of the tablets, with the treasure, I shall be Mahdi and Savior. No one will dare question me. I will summon the Gods. I will be the undisputed leader of the world! I will change history!*

CHAPTER SIXTEEN

The morning sun glared through the window, falling squarely on Jonathan's head. He tossed, tried covering his head with the pillow, and then angrily threw it to the floor. For hours he had tossed, unable to sleep as he mentally searched the chambers beneath the grave robbers shack. He searched to no avail. It tormented him. Clearly, the chambers were meant to be a tomb, but for some reason those who had prepared the tomb had not been buried there. Again and again he visualized the chambers, aware of both their regularity and the placement of the articles within them. Each chamber was oblong; each was smaller than the one before it. As was the custom, the articles in the first chamber were the kinds of things found in most family dwellings – pottery, dried spices, and small statues. The second chamber held more intricate pottery, a few pieces of clothing and some jewelry. The third chamber had more jewelry and a few more intimate garments. It was all very odd. Over and over he asked himself what he had missed.

At the same time, his attempt to concentrate on finding the tablet was constantly interrupted by thoughts of Corrie. Was she all right? Would this Karim harm her? Images, all of them unpleasant crept into his thoughts during his waking hours, while his nights were an endless hell. The portion of the night through which he had fitfully slept was far too short. He calculated that he had finally fallen asleep around three in the morning, which meant he had slept four hours at the most. But he was sure he had awakened several times between three and dawn, quite sure that his total sleep amounted to no more than an hour and a half. Even during that hour and a half he had not been deeply asleep.

He climbed out of bed and went into the kitchen. He rummaged around the cupboards and went through the motions of making coffee. He actually stared at it while it dripped into the pot, certain it was taking longer than it had ever taken before. At last the infernal machine turned itself off and he quickly poured a cup, and forgoing milk or sugar, he gulped it down.

He drank two cups and then quickly showered and dressed. He was starting to feel more alive in spite of a certain fuzzy headedness.

He looked out the front window. There were no other cars about. Toro did not appear to be watching him. Toro was a wily fellow though, untrusting and determined. Maybe he was watching from afar. It was not Toro who really troubled him. It was who might be watching Toro.

He gathered up his necessities and checked the batteries in his flashlights. He kept forcing the image of the Easter Island tablet into his mind. He had to keep it front and center, he had to find its twin, or he might never see his daughter again.

He opened the front door and his eyes were drawn to an unmarked brown envelope on the stoop. He bent over and picked it up, turning it curiously in his hands. There were no stamps on it, though there was no mail delivery out here in any case. There was no indication of how it was delivered or by whom. *If someone had brought it in a car, I should have heard something. It's not as if I was asleep.* He shook his head again to clear it, and opened the envelope carefully. Inside there was a scrap of paper and written neatly on it the message, "At midnight, be on the side of the road with your headlights off, in the same place you found your daughter off the road."

He wondered if he should tell Toro, or if it might have been sent by Toro to test him. Jonathan could all but hear the intensity in Toro's voice as he lectured, "You didn't tell me – you should have kept me informed." But it did not seem to Jonathan Henley as if the person who had sent this message wanted Toro informed. Indeed, unless Toro himself sent it, the sender wanted to make certain Toro knew nothing. He was quite certain the message must be from Karim and must concern Corrie. If it were a test by Toro, he would just have to fail it. He had to do all he could to protect Corrie.

293

He crumpled the paper into a ball and stuffed it in his pocket. He was off on his primary mission.

The grave robber's shack was still cordoned off and ten heavily armed police officers guarded it. Toro seemed convinced that whatever had not been found, would compel the killer to return. After their last conversation, Toro was certainly aware that he was now in the killer's control, that he was to find the tablet and deliver it to Karim, or whomever, in exchange for his daughter. Toro had no doubt instructed his men to keep a close eye on him, to report if he left the area with anything. Thus, he now had two problems. The first was finding the tablet, the second was spiriting it out of the chambers beneath the shack without Toro knowing.

He climbed out of his jeep, and hands in his pockets, his bag on his back, he ambled toward the shack as he had many times before. The guards waved him through. He wasted no time in the shack, but immediately descended the stairs into the underground chamber. He lit the lantern and took out his hand-made diagram of the three chambers. On each he had marked where the artifacts had been. He shook his head. He turned the map slightly sideways. What the hell was he missing? There had to be something.

#

"Helga," Karim repeated the girl's name, again and again. It was a mantra that evoked the past – her name helped him to retrieve memories that were seared into the dark recesses of his mind, yet hidden from his daily thoughts and activities. She had been his first. He sucked in on his water pipe and expelled the heavy smoke into the still air of his private meditation room. For an instant it floated like a thin white fog over water, like the mist the morning he had taken Helga. She was an evil girl. She had flaunted her body; she had openly attempted to seduce him. She created in him a desire he

294

could not control. He hated that feeling, not even his voices could make it go away. They tried of course, and he was torn between the desire he felt, and the chorus in his head – torn till he exploded.

He met Helga while attending graduate classes in computer science in Germany. She had waist length white blond tresses, thick, vulgar hair which she wore loose. It fell to her waist and when she walked, it called out to him as clearly as if it whispered on the wind.

She was without hair in other places. Her legs were long, bare and white. Her arms were the same and even in her light summer dresses, he could not detect so much as a tuft of hair beneath her arms.

Her oval face bore an expression of brazenness and her full lips were painted a bright pink color. Had she not worked in the museum, had he simply passed her on the street, he would have taken her for a prostitute. He hated the fact that most western women, at least younger western women, looked like prostitutes. The ones with good figures all revealed yards of white bare leg, and allowed their vulgar, suggestive hair to blow loose, to caress their often uncovered shoulders.

Each time she looked at him, it had seemed like an invitation. For months he had managed to control himself, then just before summer holidays, he could stand it no more. He planned his move carefully, he took care he provided himself with an alibi, and then he lured her to a meeting in a secluded place.

She thought him handsome and said so. She walked with him to the water's edge, where the mist floated just above the water like the ghosts of the dead. She allowed him to unbutton her tiny little blouse and fondle her milk white breasts till her nipples grew hard. She allowed him to touch her intimately and she shivered in his arms. They lay on the grass, and he buried himself in her white blond hair. It slipped through his fingers like white hot metal, burning his mind. All the time he tried to mutter prayers, tried to remember, tried to make the voices go away. But he could not. The voices directed his every action. He turned her over in the soft grass and she giggled. Before she could resist he slipped the garrote around her neck and tightened it till all her fruitless struggles ceased. Then, in utter shame, he spilled his seed into her lifeless body and fled. He had done as the voices bid him, he had carefully planned it, but God help him, he had enjoyed it! She was an evil woman. He told himself that she was evil over and over. Briefly, ever so briefly, he thought of Sheldon Rabinowitz. Girls had never thought him handsome. The little blond girl, Rachel, had spurned him. Sheldon should have killed her. But Sheldon could not kill. Sheldon had no guts.

Perspiration was running down his face, and he saw that he was ready. He grasped himself and rocked back and forth. But it was not Helga he thought about. It was this new girl, this young archeologist whose hair was also white blond, whose legs were long and white, whose figure was rounded and ripe. He spilled his seed. He shook all over and then again began to rock back and forth methodically. "Be quiet!" he muttered. "I can't do it yet. I need her. Be quiet."

After a time, he stopped, wiped his brow and sat up. He reminded himself that this new girl did not expose her hair. She followed the customs. She seemed a moral girl. He had not decided what to do. His many voices gave him conflicting orders.

There were so many immoral girls. He thought for a second of Ysabel. She too had been a temptress. He had not killed her when he left Germany, but when he met her in Chiclayo, he had strangled her just as he had strangled Helga, but it was not the same. Ysabel had to die. He had no choice.

He rocked harder, and his voices again became a chorus. In his mind he saw fire, cleansing fire. He would be a strict Mahdi, a strong leader. The women would not be immoral; they would all cover their hair and lower their eyes. Those who did not obey would die. Surely a God should demand no less.

He sat for a long while. He sat still until there was quiet in his head, till his perspiration had evaporated, till his heart had ceased pounding. Soon he would have the last tablet. Soon he would have all the power that the Gods of the Universe had to bestow.

#

Jonathan Henley pulled up in front of his *caseta*. His once clean clothes were filthy with the dust from the ancient chambers. *Nothing, all day and I've found nothing.* And yet, he couldn't shake the fact that there was something obvious which he had overlooked.

He glanced at his watch. It was nine o'clock, three hours before he was to go to the rendezvous. Was someone going to meet him there? He was still torn; there was still time to phone Toro. Again, he decided against it. No, he would go alone. It was the safest thing for Corrie.

He went into the kitchen and prepared a sandwich for himself. Then he sat down at the table, and again took out the diagram of the three chambers. He stared at it. Then out of curiosity, turned it slightly. It was then that he saw it. The excitement of what he saw filled him, chasing away his weariness and filling his body with adrenaline.

There were three chambers, each one smaller than the one before it. It was all on one level, like a bungalow. But what if the chambers were above ground and were built one a top the other? They would form a pyramid!

The more he looked at his own diagram of the three chambers with his mental picture of the pyramid of the sun on its side and superimposed on top of it, he was reasonably certain of just where to look. In fact, he became convinced that behind the wall of the third chamber he would find a secret entrance to a fourth. Unlike the other three, it would have no obvious door because those who had built it had doubtless walled themselves inside. It was naturally much smaller than a real pyramid but it was, nonetheless the same shape and had it been vertical, it would all have been obvious.

297

He was tempted to return to the site immediately, but he restrained himself. He had an appointment to keep; moreover, such unusual activity would be reported to Toro immediately.

He drove his Jeep along the pitch-black road that led over the hill. When he came to the place he had found Corrie, he pulled off the road. He switched off his headlights and glanced again at his watch. It was just minutes before midnight.

At one minute to midnight, he climbed out of his Jeep and walked around. There wasn't a soul in sight. Then he heard the distinct sound of whirling blades. He stood by the side of the Jeep as the sound grew louder.

For a moment he was transported back in time. He was in a Vietnamese jungle and his nostrils were filled with the odor of cordite. The helicopter fought through the smoke and moved crazily over his head. It dropped a lifeline and he took it, buckling himself to it quickly, holding on for dear life. He was flying over treetops while simultaneously being lifted inside the steel bird. His fleeting vision of Vietnam faded.

This helicopter had not come to rescue him. He watched fascinated as it circled the area from above and then shone a searchlight down on him. It came no closer, but a bright flare was dropped from the helicopter, and almost before it hit the ground the helicopter had moved off into the night.

Jonathan ran to where the flare lay. He waited till the flare was extinguished and then picked it up. Attached to the burned out flare was a medium sized metal tube. He unfastened it and hurried back to the car. Whatever was inside was better examined at home.

Inside the house, he took the papers from the tube. One was a letter, the other a map. He read the letter first.

My dear Doctor Henley,

Enclosed you will find a map to a deserted mine in Southern Ecuador. It is quite near the border with Peru. I am afraid you will have follow these directions exactly in order to avoid the official

298

border crossing. When you have found the tablet that matches the Easter Island tablet, you will bring it to this site. At that time I will return your daughter in exchange for the tablet. Notify me of your time of arrival by sending an e-mail to the following address: tomorrowthedream@ola.com. Simply write, 'the time is now.'

"tomorrowthedream@ola.com? Tomorrow what? He shook his head; it was only an e-mail address.

#

Corrie was up and dressed when Fatima appeared with a tray bearing her breakfast.

"I thought you would still be sleeping," Fatima said.

"I feel very rested; after all, I've done nothing to make me tired."

"You're bored."

Corrie was not sure if it was a statement or a question since Fatima's English lacked inflection.

"Yes. What can I do all day? Are there household chores I could help you with?"

"There are servants."

"What do you do all day?"

"Many things. I'm weaving just now."

"Could I watch you? Perhaps you could teach me. I've always wanted to learn weaving."

Fatima looked doubtful. "I can arrange for a television and some movie tapes."

All of her instincts told her she had to get closer to Fatima. "I'd rather weave," Corrie answered. "I like to work with my hands. Besides, we would be together, we could talk."

Fatima looked puzzled. "My husband said Western women do not like such work."

She wanted to say, 'your husband doesn't know everything.'
But Corrie reminded herself to be tactful. "Well, I like such work,"

"Come with me." Fatima stood up and then silently paused to
check Corrie's scarf, making certain that it covered all her hair.
When she was finished, she beckoned her to follow.

Corrie walked behind her down a long corridor and finally into
a large airy room. The room was furnished simply with a single bed
and a chest of drawers. At the far end of the room there was a huge
loom. On it, half completed, was a brightly colored blanket with an
intricate pattern.

"It's beautiful," Corrie exclaimed with genuine admiration.

For the first time, Fatima smiled. "Thank you. The colors cheer
me."

"They cheer me too," Corrie replied.

"You can prepare some spindles for me. Then I'll show you
what I do."

Fatima brought her some large balls of yarn and some spindles.
She quickly took the orange yarn and illustrated what must be done.

Corrie took it from her, and began while Fatima sat down at her
loom.

More than once, Corrie stole a look at her surroundings.
Fatima's room had a window that did not look out on the enclosed
patio. Rather, it faced a rugged landscape with moderate vegetation.
She could see the hills and beyond, the distant mountains. It wasn't
desert nor was it jungle. She was quite sure this *casa* was located in
the Altiplano of either Peru or Ecuador. She tried to visualize the
map of this area. Surely there were rivers that ran from the Altiplano
to the sea – if she could reach one she might be able to travel
downstream to one of the coastal cites. But her chances of escape
seemed slim.

She returned to analyzing the room itself. It offered little in the
way of clues to Fatima's personality but she did not miss the fact

that there was only a single bed. Though perhaps it was not really Fatima's room.

After a long while, she asked, "Is this your room?"

Fatima looked up startled. She looked as if she were actually considering the wisdom of answering the question, then finally she replied, "Yes, I sleep here."

"Have you children?" Corrie ventured.

Fatima shook her head and looked away. Corrie could see the pain on her face. She asked no follow-up question, but she could tell that Fatima wanted children and for some reason had none. Perhaps Karim did not want them.

"Are you Karim's only wife?" she asked boldly. Not that it was such an unusual question; he might well have had more than one.

"Yes. He has taken no other." She looked down and away, her eyes suddenly filling with tears, "even though he will give me no children," she said in a whisper.

Corrie felt horrible. She was asking questions with her own selfish motives in mind. She was inviting confidences and friendship with a view toward escape. This woman was obviously a prisoner too, albeit, a willing prisoner, or so it seemed.

#

Jeff paced the floor, stopping now and again to look out the window. The ice that had bejeweled the trees had melted. Last night it had snowed again and now the scene below the window was one of pristine whiteness everywhere. Soon enough it would turn into gray slush.

In a few minutes, Katsura would appear. She would want to practice Aikido, or perhaps she would want to go skating. He felt somehow as if he were being disloyal to Corrie, as if moment by moment she was slipping away from him. To make matters worse, Katsura was always making her desire for him obvious. She stood

301

close to him, she talked softly, and she dressed seductively. Beneath her dark lashes, her eyes always seemed to be asking, "Don't you want me." He didn't want her, and he didn't trust her.

"Good morning," Katsura greeted him with what seemed like forced cheer. She was dressed in a black skintight spandex jump suit that zipped up the front. It left next to nothing to the imagination; its large gleaming metal zipper was a screaming invitation. He could hardly help but notice the fact that her legs were unusually long for a Japanese woman. Her breasts were full and high, her buttocks round, hard, perfect. Her long dark hair was pulled back, though a fringe of bangs caressed her face.

"You look like the star of a James Bond film."

"Do I? Well you know what he does with his women, don't you?"

He cursed himself. He had walked right into that one. His face was red, he could feel it. He was struggling to recover when Jason Conway came into the living room. His short round body was wrapped in a red satin robe and he was smoking a cigarette with a long holder. Conway looked absurd, like a caricature of himself. Jeff felt as if he were center stage in a pornographic cartoon.

Conway looked at Katsura and leered. Not for the first time it crossed his mind that she might have something less than a Platonic relationship with Conway.

"It's definitely Ecuador. I think we should leave immediately."

Jeff felt like leaping into the air. He didn't have to play Katsura's games anymore. He was going to find Corrie.

"Prepare what we'll need, Kat." Conway wobbled his finger toward Jeff, "See that he's outfitted properly. I'll take care of the transportation details."

He felt like a third hand, but it didn't matter. Waiting in this luxurious Boston 'prison' was over. He didn't even ask Conway how he was certain that Karim was in Ecuador. He assumed that somehow, Conway had managed to intercept Karim's communications.

"We better go shopping," Katsura purred. "You do need clothes."

He didn't disagree. Whatever he had to do to get going was what he would do.

#

They did not, as Jeff expected, travel by commercial airliner. Instead, he found himself in a luxuriously appointed, private Leer Jet. It had two private sleeping cabins, a central living room-office arrangement, a well stocked bar, and apparently a professional chef in the galley.

Conway sat in one of the leather chairs. The one he chose looked as if it were made just for him since it was shorter than the others and allowed him to sit comfortably without his legs dangling above the floor.

"Come, sit over here, Kat." Conway picked up a plush cushion and put it on the floor in front of his chair for her. Katsura went instantly and sat down.

Jeff watched, fascinated as Conway fondled her hair abstractedly, while at the same time talking to him. It was as if she weren't even there, or more to the point, as if he weren't. Maybe Conway had noticed Katsura's flirting and decided to make a point of the fact that she belonged to him. He made the point rather forcefully by slipping his hand inside her jump suit. She had her eyes closed and her mouth ever so slightly open. Jeff drew in his breath; he would have to be dead not to find this erotic. At the same time, he asked himself what the hell kind of man would treat a woman this way? What kind of woman would allow it? Conway was quite simply, a son-of-a-bitch and Katsura was clearly his property.

303

Erotic it might be but he wished he were not witness to the reality of their relationship.

"We can't go charging in, what do you propose?" Jeff asked. Maybe if he ignored Conway's actions the man would stop.

"I purpose we set up nearby and wait for the right moment."

"And that would be?"

"After Henley finds the tablet. When he comes to deliver it he'll notify us, and we'll be there."

It sounded like a lot less than a plan. It sounded as if it were a rendezvous that had all the potential to turn into an amateur version of the *Gunfight at the Okay Corral* in some isolated, God-forsaken spot in Ecuador.

Conway leaned over and whispered loudly in Katsura's ear, "Go get ready for bed and wait for me."

Jeff wanted to swear. Instead, he looked at Conway steadily even as Katsura stood up and pattered off to Conway's private quarters.

"I doubt we'll have the element of surprise. I hardly think Karim is going to allow us to crash his little party."

Conway glared at him. "Let me work out the details," he answered coldly. He then stood up ambled off to join Katsura.

Jeff shook his head and went to the bar. He fixed himself a drink, then he sat down. Maybe later he could sleep, but not right now. Too many images fought for his attention. The most vivid was of Corrie being held captive by Karim. Waves of fear alternated with waves of anger. He fantasized about what he would do to Karim if he hurt her. Then, unable to bear the thought of her being hurt, he tried again to rationalize that Karim needed her in order to get the tablet. He felt as if he would never sleep again.

#

Jonathan stood in the center of the smallest of the three underground chambers. If he were right, if there was another chamber, a hidden chamber, it would be beyond the wall that was directly in front of him. It would also be the smallest of the chambers but the one filled with the most intimate personal objects. This would be a chamber the grave robber had not yet found. If he were right, he would be the first to lay eyes on its interior in more than fourteen hundred years.

He took out a long piece of metal that was pointed on one end. He began to hammer it into the wall. At first it was hard, then he felt less resistance, and suddenly it broke through. He was right! There was another chamber and this wall was unlike the others, it was not completely made of stone slabs, part of it was earthen.

He used the piece of metal with which he had penetrated the wall to make the hole larger. He worked for hours, prying out larger chunks of solidified dirt, pushing the softer soil aside. He had been right; the chamber had been sealed off from the inside. Those who died here had buried themselves.

At last, the wall gave way. He lit his lantern and crawled into the chamber. It was musty and the dust of the ages filled his nostrils. He stood up and held the lantern high. It was then that for the first time, he encountered the two fourteen hundred year old Moche.

They were lying together on one slab of stone in the center of the chamber; two skeletons, holding hands, their hollow eye sockets looking upward. One was dressed in a bright fuchsia robe. By his side, there was a large gold sunburst. The other was dressed in a silver robe. "The Sun God and the Moon Goddess," he murmured. For a moment the tablet was forgotten as was his reason for being here. This was an incredible find! The chamber was small but it was filled with artifacts. It was clear that these two had buried themselves, after carefully constructing their own temple. They were not mummified. There had been no one to carry out that procedure. He saw the vial nearby and felt certain they had killed themselves, drifting off into eternal sleep rather than waiting to die slowly from lack of oxygen. He shook his head and was slightly aware of moisture in his eyes. There was something incredibly touching about these two. Perhaps it was their position, perhaps because they were probably quite young, or perhaps it was because they had been robbed of their tradition. No one had bound them or buried them as their beliefs demanded. Still, amid some horrible tragedy, they had seen to it themselves. Not for the first time, he wondered what had killed the Moche. Many believed it was some radical climatic change; he had a theory that it was a blood disease – perhaps something like AIDS. After all, they drank the blood of their sacrifices, who were usually criminals and were, therefore more vulnerable to disease. It had been established that The God King, whose tomb had been found in 1987, was only thirty when he died, these two were likely younger.

He held his lantern high and began to examine the contents of the room. He walked to what looked like a kind of altar along the far wall. It was built of slabs of stone. He began to feel each of them, attempting to move them. Then he touched the one that moved, indeed it was entirely loose. He pulled it out as if it were a drawer. By the flickering light of the lantern, he saw the tablet and the strange print on it.

For several moments he was consumed by his discovery. He had not really believed it, but he was now presented with incontrovertible evidence that there was indeed another tablet like the one found on Easter Island.

He sat the tablet down and for a moment slumped to the ground. Now he had to get this past the guards and get it home. He checked his watch. In another hour it would be dark. He would go then. If he was lucky, they would be eating and perhaps not paying much attention. He would have to tie it around his chest, under his jacket. That way, his backpack would be empty. Fortunately, the tablet was not as heavy as it looked.

#

Corrie put down the shuttle and looked at her handiwork. This was the first time in two days that Fatima had allowed her to actually weave.

"It is good," Fatima said. "You are good at this. You are not at all like my husband said you would be."

Corrie resisted the temptation to ask Fatima just what Karim had said. Instead she just commented, "I don't imagine your husband thinks much of any Westerner."

"My husband is a special man, descended from a long line of special men."

Special – yes, he was special. Probably for Fatima's benefit – for public consumption - Karim tried to trace his ancestry to the Prophet. "You mean Muhammad?"

"Blessed be his name," Fatima quickly whispered. Then she shook her head. My husband believes he is related to the Mahdi, he believes the Gods will anoint him the new Mahdi. Voices speak to him."

Fatima's voice trailed off and suddenly a silence filled the room. "I know only of the Mahdi who defeated Chinese Gordon in Khartoum," Corrie ventured.

"Yes. That is the one. My husband has taken his name. My husband will be an even greater Mahdi. He says all Moslems will fall down and worship him when he reveals himself at the Haj next year. They will follow him to Jihad if that is what he desires."

Corrie said nothing but rather just tried to digest Fatima's words. To declare himself, to be accepted as Mahdi he would have to perform miracles. She thought of his dark eyes, of how he looked at her and she felt utterly chilled. He was more than just a religious fanatic. He was self-obsessed; he heard voices and followed them.

307

Karim was a very dangerous man. He could no doubt justify doing anything.

She looked again at Fatima. "Do you want a Holy War?"

Fatima looked stricken and she shook her head and whispered, "No, no. But I cannot stop it."

CHAPTER SEVENTEEN

Never had Karim experienced such surges of energy, it was as if bolts of inspirational lightening were bombarding his body and lifting him to new, rare emotional and insightful heights.

The tomorrow of the entire world was about to begin, the future was at hand, and he personally would orchestrate all of it. When he had the seven pieces he would have The Key left by the Gods, he would be able to summon them. When they arrived the Gods would grant him anything he asked for, they would understand the chaos that had ruled since their departure, they would recognize him as *the super genius* who would lead the masses from that chaos into the eternal light.

He pictured the Haj, the greatest gathering of the Islamic faithful! They would all be there, all the leaders and enough commoners to spread the word. It would be the hordes of the ordinary who would carry the message, they were always believed because unlike leaders they had no reason to lie.

In his mind's eye he could see the walled city of Mecca, he could picture the people waiting, praying.

Naturally his appearance at the Haj would be his first appearance, but he would also appear as the Jewish savior. Those Christians who did not accept him would die. He would unite them all, after the great revelation he alone would lead, and all religious wars would cease.

How would he do it? How would he strike fear into all of them? Would he command the heavens open? Would he have the winds carry his name? Would he step forward from a circle of heavenly light? Whatever he chose, they would all fall to their knees! They would forget Mohammad and Moses – even Jesus, and they would realize that he, the true God-King had come. They would follow him, praise him, and worship him.

Even now, trembling with his own vision, he could feel the light, the warmth, the adoration of the people.

Perspiration was running down his forehead, his mouth was dry. He fought for control of his fingers, then he typed back his confirmation and gave Henley a time for their rendezvous. In just a few days all would be his, he would force Conway to give up the Easter Island tablet and he would send the message over Conway's radio telescopes into space. The Gods would come, the world would be his.

He clicked his mouse and sent the message, then he turned off his computer and looked up. Fatima was in the doorway, her head bowed.

"I told you never to come to this room!" He shouted angrily and she stepped back over the threshold, trembling.

"What do you want?"

"The girl, she has been weaving with me. I would like the other small loom brought."

"You would like! Who are you to like anything! We'll be going soon, there's no time for weaving."

Fatima shrunk back and stared at the floor. "What will you do with her?"

"Whatever I want! Go to your room!"

Fatima turned and fled. Karim was often ill tempered but he seemed more so tonight. And what was wrong with him? His skin was moist, though it wasn't hot. His eyes blazed. She could not think about it, he terrified her. And yet she did not fear for herself but rather for the girl. Why had he brought her here? In her heart she was afraid, more afraid than at any time since her marriage to Karim. *I must watch. I must watch. I must do what I can.*

#

Captain Raoul Toro lived in a small apartment located in a low rise complex adjacent to Chiclayo's business district. His neighbors were businessmen, civil servants, and working couples. Unlike the United States, Latin American cities lacked sprawling upper class suburbs. Instead, the outlying areas were filled with shantytowns. The well-off population gathered in the inner city, though usually they had large apartments or impressive homes. His apartment consisted only of a small living dining area, a bathroom, and a bedroom with a balcony overlooking the park. His furnishings were modern and strictly utilitarian. Nothing adorned the walls save a picture of the Virgin over the ornamental fireplace. Usually he felt his apartment entirely adequate, but tonight he felt embarrassed by his surroundings.

Toro looked into the eyes of Emilio de Leon. "It is a great honor to have you come to my home, Father."

Emlio lifted his hand and made the sign of the cross.

"You must be very tired indeed. It is a long flight. You really should have let me know you were coming. I would have made preparations. Are you certain you want to stay here? There are fine hotels."

De Leon motioned Toro with his hand, "Don't be so nervous. I shall be quite comfortable here. In any case, my visit necessitates privacy. Please, my son, sit down."

"May I at least offer you some wine?"

"But of course. I would be most grateful. I'm sure if we share a bottle of wine we will both sleep better."

Toro went to get the wine. He returned with a bottle and two glasses. He quickly filled them both, feeling the need for wine tonight. It was an unusual feeling since he seldom drank, and when he did it was usually beer. "To your safe journey," he said, lifting his glass toward Father de Leon.

"To my successful journey," the old priest added. "And to yours."

311

"Am I going on a journey?"

"Yes. Do you remember your special vows?"

"Of course, father. I belong not only to the church, but I follow the way of *The Path*.

"I must pledge you to the utmost secrecy." De Leon held up a gold crucifix.

Toro took it, kissed it, and held it tightly as he swore, "I pledge myself to reveal nothing you tell me in secret. I vow to do your will, To follow *The Path*."

"I knew I could count on you, my son. We have never needed you before, but we need you now."

"Has this something to do with the strange crimes which have been committed here?"

"It has everything to do with them. Listen carefully, my son. I must tell you a story. It is a shocking story, but I know you have strength."

Toro sipped his wine. De Leon began talking in a calm voice. "My story begins with a priest, historian and poet named de Vega."

"The Inca?"

"Yes, he was known by that name in Spain after he wrote a history of his mother's people. Of course he also wrote of Pizarro and the conquest."

"I am familiar with his work."

De Leon was silent for several seconds, "Not all of it, of that I am certain. I am going to tell you about his secret work now. It is shocking and I beg you to hold onto your faith, my son. Tonight you will be tested."

De Leon's story was long and complicated and when he was finished Toro felt drained.

"Are you committed to saving the faith?" de Leon asked.

"Of course."

"Then I shall give you instructions. We have intercepted certain messages. I promise, you will have help."

"I shall do whatever is necessary."

"Faith will guide you," de Leon said. "You must cling to the knowledge that those whom the ancients called Gods were not, it was simply that they possessed more knowledge. There is only one God, one true faith. But you must also realize that the return of those the ancients called Gods, by the means I have described to you, would destroy us all."

"I understand."

"Good. Now listen carefully. I will tell you of our plan."

#

They were all gathered in the sitting room of their hotel 'suite' in Loja. Just before landing, Jason Conway had decided on Loja as a base of operations.

Above, a ceiling fan droned round and round, producing nothing more than the movement of hot, humid air.

Jeff wiped his brow with the back of his hand. The city of Loja was less polluted than Lima but its climate was just as terrible.

"I've been in better hotels."

Conway looked up at him disparagingly, "You think I haven't?"

Conway had rented the entire top floor of the hotel. And Jeff thought charitably, he had done so sight unseen. In any case, the town was not much better than the hotel.

Katsura came into the room and sat down. At least she had changed her clothes and was now dressed in a plain, reasonably modest sundress and sandals. Under the circumstances she looked remarkably cool.

313

"Aren't we kind of obvious parading into town and renting the whole floor of a hotel? I mean if we're trying to keep a low profile and surprise Karim, I think he might hear about us."

"Karim is some distance from Loja. He won't hear about us. Kat, get my computer set up now."

Katsura nodded. She was a computer whiz in addition to her other endowments.

"I doubt this dump has fiber optic cable," Jeff said, looking around. "If it did, I'll bet the cockroaches would eat it."

"We are on the top floor for a reason, my dear boy. Katsura will climb up to the roof and assemble our portable satellite feed. Then I can assure you that our communications will be as good as they would have been in Boston."

"Some people think of everything."

"You weren't so sarcastic when you wanted my help."

"You're helping yourself."

"True."

"Has it occurred to you that Karim may have a standing army out there?"

"Everything occurs to me."

Jeff shrugged. The last thing he wanted was to be trapped with Conway and Katsura on the top floor of an ancient hotel in one of Ecuador's less important cities – not that Ecuador had any important cities – at least none that had been important in the last fifteen hundred years. He'd been trapped in Boston with them and now he felt trapped here. He wanted to get on with it, get out of here, get hold of Karim; above all he wanted to find Corrie. If they had not succeeded in disgusting him before, the actions of Katsura and Conway on the flight down had sealed his opinion of them both.

"Go unpack," Conway suggested. "By the time you calm down we'll be set up. I hate being out of contact. We've been out of contact now for more than four hours."

Jeff turned away. Unpack? He hardly had anything with him. Instead, he fixed a drink and went out on the balcony to look at the city.

He'd been staring into space for nearly half an hour when he heard Conway bellow his name.

"Got a message from Henley!" he announced eagerly. "He's got the tablet and the meet is on!" Conway was bouncing around as if someone had wound him up.

"Are we going to notify the authorities?"

Conway scowled at him. "Are you out of your mind?"

"Just because we know where he is, Karim is not going to hand over Corrie, and you're not going to get the tablet just like that."

Conway glowered at him, "Let me worry about that."

#

Corrie sat on the edge of her bed. The day had passed quickly and much to her surprise, it was almost time for dinner.

She looked up at the sound of a faint knock on the door.

"It is Fatima."

"Come in. The door isn't locked."

Fatima opened the door and slipped inside. Uncharacteristically, she closed it behind her and padded across the room. "My husband summons you," she whispered.

"It's early for dinner."

"He wishes to speak with you."

Corrie nodded and started to move. Fatima put forward a restraining hand, "You must cover your hair," she reminded her.

Corrie reached for the scarf and quickly put it on.

"You must be very careful," Fatima warned in a voice that was hardly audible. "Karim is in some terrible mood."

Corrie felt herself tense. "What's going on?"

315

Fatima shrugged helplessly. "I know little more than you. I do know he has sent his men away."

"There are no guards?" Corrie's heart leapt. Perhaps she might be able to escape; perhaps the moment was at hand.

"I think he sent them ahead. I think he will take you and meet them."

"Meet them where?" As far as she could tell this hacienda was in the middle of nowhere.

"Please. You had better go and speak with him. It is not good to keep him waiting when he is angry."

Corrie stood up and pressed Fatima's hand in hers. "Don't be afraid," she told Fatima. *Such bravery when you're too scared to move.*

Corrie forced herself to walk calmly across the room, open the door and pass through it. She walked down the long hall and then into the room where Karim waited. He was, as usual, reclining and smoking his water pipe.

"You sent for me?" she asked, pausing in the doorway.

"Yes, come in. Sit down."

Corrie did as she was asked.

"We'll be leaving here tonight. We'll be meeting your father who has found the tablet I have been seeking."

Corrie only looked at him. She could not allow herself to hope that it would all be so easy. "If that is the case, what harm could it do if you told me what is going on?"

Karim's twisted smile was evil. It was the smile of the devil. "No harm at all. I would imagine you have heard of the fragments of wooden tablets found on Easter Island."

"Yes. I've seen them."

"There is one that is whole. Conway has it. The fragments are copies of a portion of his tablet."

"I still don't understand."

"There are others, seven in all."

"What makes them so valuable?"

Karim's voice took on a far-away quality, as if suddenly he had assumed the position of teacher. She watched with amazement as he slid into this new persona.

"There are seven tablets of ancient origin. Each one of them was found in a different part of the world. I have five. Conway has one; your father is bringing the seventh. I knew the seventh was buried somewhere in Sipán. When they are put together they form a whole.

She was silent for a minute. "Did you kill the grave robber?"

"Not personally. The grave robber found chambers filled with artifacts. He tried to sell them on the underground market and I sent my men to investigate. The robber was killed. Regrettably, my men were interrupted by the Peruvian Federal Police. The police came to investigate rumors that someone had found a grave filled with artifacts. They placed a heavy guard around the shack, only your father was allowed in. I believed strongly that what I was seeking was there, hidden somewhere in those chambers beneath the grave robber's shack."

"So you kidnapped me so that my father would continue your search?"

"Yes. I sent a message to your father telling him I will return you when I have the seventh tablet."

"But you won't, will you."

Karim stared hard at her. She was a beautiful woman. Her skin was like ivory. He remembered how her hair looked. It was blond, fine and with the texture of silk. He flexed his fingers and tried to control the thoughts that now began to fill his mind.

Corrie ignored the fact that he did not answer her. She decided to ask the vital question. "Are these tablets the key to some treasure?"

He looked at her again, aware of the little beads of perspiration that now covered his brow, aware of the voices. "They are the treasure. They are the key to open heaven's gates."

"I thought Mohammad held those gifts." As soon as she said it, she wondered why she was having a discussion like this with a man who was so obviously a dangerous lunatic.

"Ah, Mohammad, Blessed be his Name, was one of the chosen. When I have all seven tablets I will be more powerful than just one of the chosen. I will be *the* chosen. I will summon the Gods to the Haj and I will have the heavens open! I will be proclaimed Mahdi. All Moslems will follow me! All Jews will follow me. Those who refuse to follow me will die. I will re-unite the Semitic peoples. I will lead the world."

She was unprepared for his revelations, his madness, and the pure evil she saw in his eyes. His eyes were glazed over and she found herself drawn into his vision, at least sufficiently drawn in to want to know more. In spite of everything, she still did not understand. "What power will you have?"

"Ah, my dear girl, the Gods are superior beings who've visited the earth many times before. They instructed the Egyptians on how to build the pyramids; they gave the ancients many gifts of knowledge. They left the seven tablets to us knowing that when we were advanced enough, the most intelligent among us would know how to summon them to return."

"Summon them to return?" What was he talking about? Extraterrestrials or Gods? She couldn't ask.

"Come, let me show you."

He pushed a button near his divan and the drapes along the back wall moved, revealing five tablets side by side.

"May I go closer?" Her curiosity warred with her common sense. Was it possible that these tablets did have some power?

"By all means, examine them. I don't expect you to understand, you're not a mathematician."

Corrie walked across the room and stared at the tablets. Each was the same size and each was covered with symbols. These were the kind of symbols on the fragments she had seen on Easter Island, but apart from that one example, she had never seen such symbols before. These tablets were identical in every way except for the order of the symbols.

"The first one was found in Cuzco, the second one in Ellora, India, the third in Avebury, England, the fourth in Delphi, and the fifth I found near Angkor Wat in Cambodia. Conway found the sixth on Easter Island. As I said before, your father brings me the seventh."

Corrie pressed her lips together. Tonight, she would find the answer.

"How exactly are they used to summon the Gods?"

"As I said, I would not expect you to see it. Do you know anything of the history of early computer languages?"

"No, I confess I don't." As insane as she knew him to be, he was making some kind of sense.

"Here, let me show you another artifact of interest. It is over there, in the display case."

He directed her attention to a large stone tablet. It was quite unlike the others, though it too was covered with symbols. In this case she recognized it as being written in cuneiform.

"This isn't the same script as what is written on the wooden tablets. This is cuneiform."

"Yes. This is Babylonian and it dates to around 1800 BC. It is a method for figuring compound interest. The algorithm is detailed, it explains how many years and months it will take to double a certain quantity of grain to an annual interest rate of 20 per cent. If this were translated in a computer language called BASIC, the machine would calculate the answer in exactly the same way the ancients did."

She knew she looked puzzled.

319

"I cannot make you understand this, I can only say that we had computer language long before we had the machines on which to use it – higher mathematics predates our other advancements by thousands and thousands of years. Ask yourself why?"

He paused, "APL was an early computer language based on symbols. In fact the initials simply mean 'A Program Language'. What is on these stones is a computer language. When I have all seven, I believe I can easily learn its secrets – there will be patterns, in a sense, it is like any other code. Others knew these tablets were important, but it was too soon. We did not have computers when the first tablets were discovered."

Karim was most certainly a megalomaniac but what he was saying sounded entirely believable. This explanation also explained Conway's involvement. He wanted the tablets too. He had the Easter Island tablet. Did he see what Karim Ali Ahmed saw in these tablets? He must have, he was a computer genius, just as this man was reported to be. Could it be true? Were these tablets a computer program left by people who had visited the earth long ago?

"You're silent now. Do you understand?"

"I'm struggling with it."

"Once long ago – before Christ, before Mohammad, Blessed be his Name, before any of the prophets there was a special priesthood. They ruled the earth with the knowledge left them by the visitors whom they believed to be Gods. They became Druids, Brahmans, and Incas. The leaders emerged from caves where they had received instruction. Then the visitors left and the priesthood continued to rule. The origins of our knowledge were lost in the dense fog of time."

Karim's face had taken on a dreamy countenance. He was rocking back and forth, his eyes closed. He was obviously brilliant, and had knowledge well beyond that of the average person.

Karim started to move and Corrie thought it wise to buy as much time as she could. He clearly enjoyed the role of teacher. "Tell me, how did you come to have five of these tablets?"

He opened his eyes and continued, as if for a very long time he had wanted to tell someone.

Karim suddenly clapped his hands together and in a few moments his wife appeared with the evening meal. "We will eat first." He turned away and pressed a button. The now familiar sound of Arab music filled the room.

Corrie finished eating and for a long while there was only the sound of the Arab music. *Time, I need time, she thought.* But in her heart Corrie knew she was running out of time, and that whatever else Karim was, he was a murderer and he no doubt intended killing her.

As if he knew her thoughts he suddenly got up and clapped for Fatima. "Tie her hands!" Karim ordered. He had withdrawn bindings from a desk drawer.

Fatima looked shamed, but she did not protest. She began wrapping Corrie's hands together with the cloth bindings.

"I am not such an ogre. See, I tie your hands in front of you so you'll be more comfortable. I must drive and I cannot have you thrashing about or causing me any trouble. The road is bad enough."

Corrie was still dressed in the long skirt Fatima had provided. She still wore the scarf as instructed. The only thing different was that she had been given hiking boots to wear so she presumed that wherever they were going, the terrain once they got out of the vehicle would be rough.

Karim opened the front door and prodded her forward, then he turned to Fatima and ordered harshly, "Stay here until I return."

The moon was bright even though it was waning. They walked toward a medium sized truck. A long sleek black Lexus was parked by the side of the house, adjacent to the wall.

Karim opened the truck door and none too gently lifted her in. Once she was in, he fastened her seat belt. He went round to the other side, climbed in, and started the truck. It was a noisy vehicle. She noted it had four wheel drive.

"Is it far?"

"Far enough, but we'll stop for a little rest."

His tone, his expression and his words were icy. This was not the tone he had used when explaining the tablets. He had slipped into yet another persona. This man was capable of rationalizing any act. He believed in a force outside of any known religion or ethical system. He certainly intended killing her, but she felt certain he would not do it until she and her father were together, until he had the seventh tablet. She had to seize any opportunity to escape. "I'm chilly," she complained.

It was damp and she could only hope her complaint was not too far-fetched.

Karim reached behind his seat with one hand and grabbing a jacket tossed it over her lap. Corrie mumbled a thank-you and eased her tied hands beneath the folds of the jacket. Now out of his sight, she began to work her hands in the bonds. Fatima had not tied her as tightly as she might have, and Corrie wondered if that was on purpose. She was convinced that if she kept at it, she could eventually slip free. Karim was consumed with driving down the dark road. She wasn't exactly sure what she was going to do when she got her hands free, but she knew she had to try to do something.

It seemed to Corrie as if they had been driving for hours when Karim pulled off the road. He drove a little further and came to a dead stop in front of a dark house.

He climbed out of the car and pulled her out the other side. She was almost free, but she dared not let him know. She needed some weapon, something to hit him with, and most of all she needed the element of surprise.

"Why are we stopping here?"

"To spend the rest of the night," he said, half under his breath. His hands were still around her waist as he pushed her toward the house.

Corrie drew in her breath. She knew exactly what he had in mind, she could sense it in the way he touched her now. It was almost as if there was electricity in the ends of his fingers.

He opened the front door and shoved her into the darkness. In a moment he had lit a lamp and the place was all light and shadows. It was a stucco house, perhaps belonging to some departed workman. It was simply furnished. He pushed her down onto a wooden chair.

"Are you a virgin?" he asked suddenly.

"Would it matter if I were," she tried to look at him, tried to make some kind of human contact. But again his eyes seemed to dominate his face. They were pools of darkness.

"I will see your hair now," he muttered.

Corrie saw his hand quiver, saw the perspiration on his forehead, saw his inability to control himself as he pulled off her scarf.

He gritted his teeth like an animal when he saw it was tightly braided. Then he tugged at the braids and quickly undid them, muttering incoherently as he did so.

"Like silk, like silk. Your hair is like gold, Helga."

Why was he calling her Helga? Corrie shrank from him, and suddenly found that one hand had slipped her bonds. What could she use to fight him, what?

He seemed to see nothing of her but her hair. He pushed his own robe aside and in one swift movement pulled her over blouse away. He stared at her, then he tore aside her under blouse, partially exposing her breasts.

Corrie saw his dagger hanging from his belt. She let him push her backward without resistance, and as she went, she seized his dagger with her free hand. There wasn't even a moment of thought as she plunged it into his side as hard as she could.

He jumped backward with a horrible shriek. She staggered to her knees, shaking the bonds off her other hand.

He was gushing blood, but seemed very much alive as he lunged toward her with an animal-like cry. His strength was incredible. He pushed her to the floor and clawed at her clothing even as he forced her legs apart.

"No!" she shrieked, but he did not stop, he seemed stronger and more determined even though he was bleeding.

She screamed again and a shot rang out. Karim half rolled off of her as he groaned loudly. She pushed him away even as tears flooded her eyes and ran down her cheeks. "Oh, dear heaven," she whispered as she looked up.

CHAPTER EIGHTEEN

The light of the half moon and the stars filtered through the trees, making it possible to see the road. Fortunately, this part of Ecuador, unlike much of the rest of the country, was neither truly jungle nor was it mountainous. The dense jungle lay in the Amazon basin, the high mountains rose in the east. They had begun their drive near the junction of the Malacatoo and Zamora Rivers where it was lush and humid. Now they were climbing the coastal mountains, the foothills of the Andes.

Jeff sat in the backseat. Katsura drove and Conway sat next to her, giving directions from a hand drawn map.

Was Corrie at the end of this trek? It was all he cared about. He was a writer, not a commando. He was unarmed and the three of them were headed into the night, knowing that Karim was a killer, knowing he had the resources to hire his own little army. Could Jason Conway be this stupid? Or was he simply not revealing his plans?

"Now what?" Katsura asked as they approached a fork in the road.

"Left," Conway instructed. "There should be a trail on our right about two kilometers down this road. Looks like we walk from there on."

"A stroll through the wilderness. Just what one needs in the middle of the night."

"Stop complaining."

Katsura's tone was sharp. She had ceased being a temptress and moved into her more natural role as a shrew.

They reached the trail and Conway had her drive the truck into the bush. It occurred to him that they might have trouble getting it out, but it was practically invisible and he assumed that was what was desired. In any case, there was no point trying to tell these two much of anything. He really wanted to tell Conway that if he was counting on his and Katsura's ability in Aikido, it wasn't really going to count for much against automatic weapons. In fact it was a bad joke. How many throws equal one burst from an Uzi?

They gathered up their gear and trudged down the trail.

They walked for nearly an hour following the trail uphill. At last they came to a wooden structure that led into the side of the hill. It was obviously an abandoned mine. It was marked on Conway's map. "Here," he announced. "I think we should wait inside."

"Wait for Henley?"

"And Karim, the man who would be God."

"Then we'll just take the tablet and leave?"

"No. Then we'll negotiate. And if negotiations fail, we'll take action. We didn't really come alone. I know you'll be glad to hear that. I had Kenji round up a small but well trained force."

It was what he wanted to hear. Still, he wasn't sure what Conway meant. "I don't see anyone else."

"You're not supposed to. Make yourself comfortable. It's eleven-thirty; it's going to be a long night."

Jeff sat down. It was damp and it seemed even damper because Chiclayo had been so dry. He wished for Henley to come soon, and for Karim to bring Corrie. He did not look forward to sitting for hours inside a mine watching Conway ogle Katsura. To make matters worse, Conway and Katsura acted as if this were all a simulated computer game. Well, if it was, he knew damn well that it was a hell of a dangerous game.

#

Corrie struggled to her feet. She could feel Karim's blood soaking through her blouse. Fatima was standing in the doorway, the gun in her hand. Tears streamed down her cheeks, and she was visibly shaking. She let the gun slip to the floor as she sank to her knees and covered her face with her hands. "I've committed a terrible crime," she said hoarsely. "But he wasn't a Moslem, he wasn't a true believer. He used the faith, he used me. He was evil." Her voice trailed off.

Corrie didn't even look at Karim. She hurried to Fatima's side and put her arms around her. "You saved my life," she whispered. "Fatima, we have to get out of here, we have to hurry."

Fatima was rocking back and forth on her knees. "I know. I know. You would have been like the others. He would have raped you and then strangled you."

"There were others?"

She nodded. "Seven that I know of."

"You didn't commit a crime."

"I did. I killed my husband."

"Fatima, he was a murderer."

"Even so, I killed him. But I couldn't let him kill you; I couldn't let him go on with his evil plan. People would have believed him. They would have followed him. I followed him for too long, I did not see through him soon enough."

Fatima rambled on as Corrie pulled her away. She picked up the gun and slipped it in her pocket.

"His men are still out there somewhere. Karim was taking me to meet my father."

"I know."

"Do you know where he was to meet my father?"

"Yes. I know everything. He thought I knew nothing, but I know everything. I know about the tablets, about what they are supposed to be. But it cannot be so, can it? There is no God but Allah."

Corrie was not sure how to answer. She enfolded Fatima in her arms, "I'm sure you're right," she said comfortingly. "Please come."

Then it occurred to her, "Fatima, how did you get here?"

"In the car, he did not know I could drive. But I can. I followed you here."

"Can you take me to the rendezvous?"

Then as if she understood for the first time she nodded, "Yes. We must go there. His men are there; your father might be killed by the men when Karim does not come."

Corrie hugged Fatima again. "Come on," she urged again. It's after midnight."

#

The roar of the helicopter's engines was made louder by the silence of the night.

"It's there," the pilot said, nudging Captain Toro in the ribs.

He looked down on the hacienda, now illuminated by the helicopter's directional beam. It was obviously deserted. No vehicles were parked outside and the entire compound was in darkness.

"Land," Toro directed.

The shrubbery around the house blew wildly in the whipping wind caused by the whirling blades as the pilot set the helicopter down.

"Ready?" Toro asked his companion, who was dressed entirely in black.

"Yup," the American replied.

Toro said nothing else. De Leon had sent these men and they seemed to know what they were doing. He and the American climbed from the helicopter and headed for the hacienda.

Toro broke open the door with a crowbar and glass flew in all directions. They stepped over it and strode into the main room. Toro turned on the light and looked around. There was no one about.

Toro scanned the room, and his eyes focused on the tablets which had been left on display. He had not expected to find them so easily, but there they were in clear view. He drew in his breath. "Lay the charges," he said to his companion. "This must all be destroyed."

The American grunted. Toro watched as the 'expert' readied the plastic explosives. It was the second time this night he had stood by and watched. Two hours earlier explosives had been planted near the entrance to the mine where the rendezvous was to be. As soon as this job was completed, they would fly back to the mine and finish Conway, Karim, and all the others off. There could be no witnesses.

In less than half an hour they were airborne once again, and as they headed away, an explosion lit the night sky.

#

Jonathan Henley paused to catch his breath. In an hour or so the sun would rise in the eastern sky but the mountains would obscure the full light of day till nearly seven. "Damn tablet," he muttered. It wasn't heavy, but it was awkward in spite of the fact that he had secured it in his backpack in order to leave his hands free. It didn't really fit; one of its corners kept poking into him.

He took the map out his pocket as well as his small pencil flashlight. He held it up, took his bearings and trudged on. The moon was bright, but not bright enough to read a map. He was sure that the entrance to the mine could not be much further. It was four-thirty in the morning.

The trail turned slightly and Jonathan stopped short. In the moonlight it took a second for him to realize that it was Captain Toro who barred his path. He stood, legs slightly apart, pointing his pistol at him.

"Shit!" Henley swore, "You scared the hell out of me."

"I'm glad you're happy to see me," Toro said through his teeth. "We'll go on together from here."

"We can't. If the man who wants this tablet sees you, he'll kill my daughter."

"I assume you mean Karim Ahmad ibn'Abd Allah. Given his history, she's very likely already dead."

329

Jonathan felt like an ice statue. Was she already dead? He summoned himself, clinging to his feeling that Corrie was still alive. "I don't think he'd harm her till he gets the tablet."

"Maybe."

"Shut up!" Henley shouted. His anger was so great he felt like strangling Toro. "And get out of my way."

"It is I who have the gun. We'll be going on together."

"Go wherever the hell you please, I'm going to find my daughter."

Toro stepped aside and Henley brushed by him aware that Toro now walked behind him, with his gun still drawn.

I could kill him now, Toro thought. But he had been ordered to kill them all. It would be better if they were all in one place. Yes, they would all be nicely sealed in a mine no one knew existed, there would be no questions.

"There," Henley said after a minute. "There's the entrance."

He headed inside with Toro right behind him. They followed the beam of light from one of the several branches of the cavern.

Conway looked up as they entered the chamber. "Henley?"

"Yes."

"Who the hell is that?" Conway asked, pointing to Toro.

"Captain Toro, meet Jason Conway."

"Let me see it," Conway said pointing to Henley's backpack.

"Yes, let's all see it," Katsura said.

"Put that gun away," Conway ordered, looking at Toro. "My men have this place surrounded."

Jeff let out his breath ever so slightly.

"I'll hang onto the gun," Toro hissed. "Your men can't get here in time to prevent me from using it."

Jonathan slipped the backpack off his shoulders. "Karim is coming. He has Corrie."

He opened his backpack and laid the tablet down on top of a flat rock.

Jeff reached out and touched it. He ran his fingers over the symbols. He looked at Conway, "You and Karim think this is a computer program, don't you?"

"It is a computer program," Conway snapped. "They came to earth, they left knowledge, and they left these."

"Destroy it, Katsura!" Toro ordered.

Jeff moved back. Toro knew Katsura?

Katsura had withdrawn a bottle from her pack and before anyone could stop her, she poured liquid over the tablet.

"No!" Conway shrieked like a pig, but Toro restrained him.

Katsura quickly lit a match and threw it on the tablet. It exploded into flame.

Conway made a gurgling sound because he was too stunned to speak. Katsura turned on him, kicking him hard under the chin so that his eyes bulged out and he resembled nothing so much as a squashed frog.

Jeff started to move, but Toro fired his gun. The bullet whistled past his head and he stood frozen to the spot just as Jonathan Henley did.

"Now no one will have this tablet," Toro muttered. "Come on Katsura. It's time to bury our archeologist and his friends."

"She works for you?" Conway blustered, even as blood was gushing from his nose.

"She follows *The Path*!"

"You've destroyed the future!" Conway screamed and he lunged toward Toro who fired point blank. Conway's hands flew to his stomach; he made a sound like a punctured balloon. He fell forward on his face.

"Little bastard!" Katsura cursed as she kicked his lifeless form.

Toro grabbed Katsura's hand and pulled her toward the entrance. "I'll shoot if you follow," he warned them.

Outside, Moustafa, head of Karim's guard watched the entrance of the mine. He saw the two emerging, "Kill them!" he shouted. Karim was not yet here, but his orders were to kill anyone who left the mine.

As Moustafa's men fired, Conway's men emerged from the rocks and more bursts gunfire filled the air. For an instant Katsura who led the three stood still, then she was hit in the chest and she spun around like a ballet dancer before falling. Toro was hit in the leg as well as the stomach. He crossed himself. "No one must ever know," those were the last words that Father de Leon had spoken to him and they were his last orders. He staggered toward the detonator that would explode the charges, which had been laid so much earlier. As a second and third bullet hit him, he fell on it. Stones were sent flying, the entrance to the mine was buried in the explosion and dust filled the air.

Inside the mine the force of the explosion extinguished the lantern. Jeff heard Henley groan, and he shouted into the blackness, "Are you all right?"

After a long moment, Jonathan replied. "I'm pinned under some rubble; I can't feel my left leg." He bit his lower lip hard enough to taste his own blood. Damn, he couldn't move, he couldn't see. "We're buried alive!

"Damn lantern. Have you got matches?"

There was a long silence, "I've got a flashlight in my pocket."

"I'm coming toward you," Jeff said. "Keep talking so I can find you." It was pitch black, blacker than he had ever imagined any place could be.

In a moment he felt Henley's arm. He knelt by him and fumbled through his pockets till he found the pencil flashlight. He pressed the switch, and even though the light was tiny, it was heavenly. "I see the lantern," he said peering through the settling dust. "I think I can re-light it."

In a moment he had the lantern lit. He stood up and surveyed the damage. "I think I can get you out from under there," he told Henley.

"I doubt I can walk."

"There's no place to walk to."

"There might be," Henley gasped. "There seems to be oxygen, if there weren't the lantern wouldn't be burning."

Jeff didn't say anything. Being buried alive was probably everyone's greatest fear. He wasn't immune to that fear but he felt hopeful. Jonathan was right. The lamp was staying lit, there had to be oxygen.

#

"Hurry!" Corrie urged as she glanced back at Fatima. "That explosion sounded close."

"It was there, it was at that place, I know it," Fatima gasped.

They followed the trail as it curved around. The sun was up now, and Corrie felt relieved to be walking in daylight. They rounded the final bend and Corrie pointed ahead. Dust from the explosion still floated near what had been the entrance to the mine.

"That was it," Fatima said in distress. "It is closed now."

Corrie heard the man's groan before she saw him. It was Kenji and he was lying face down on the gravelly rock. She headed toward him when Fatima shrieked, "Karim's guards are all dead!"

Corrie bent over Kenji who blinked up at her. He was badly wounded and she knew he was going to die. "Kenji," she whispered.

"My sister's dead. Conway's inside with your father and Jeff-san. We used explosives, we sealed the cave."

"Who?" She asked, holding onto him. She couldn't make much sense of what he was saying. "Who sealed the cave?"

"Toro, he's dead too." He grabbed her hand. "Help me."

Corrie took some water from the canteen Fatima had given her, and using her scarf, wet it and brushed his face with cool water.

Fatima was walking about, counting the dead, murmuring prayers and shaking her head in shock and disbelief.

Kenji groaned and Corrie felt him heave as he gasped for his last breath of air. He slumped backward, his head falling to one side.

Corrie stood up.

"They're all dead," Fatima said. "All Karim's men and others I don't know. There's a man over there and a woman."

Corrie went over and stared at Captain Raoul Toro. Nearby she saw the detonator. Kenji said it was Toro who had set off the explosion. Did he work for Karim, Conway or someone else? It was a confused jumble. "I think my father and my friend Jeff may still be in the mine, maybe with Jason Conway."

"I do not know any of these people," Fatima said in bewilderment.

"We have to try to get them out."

Corrie went to where the entrance to the mine had been. She climbed across the old timbers and the rocks. She called out her father's name as well as Jeff's. She could hear nothing and even a cursory examination of the site convinced her that she could certainly not dig them out alone, even if she had a shovel.

Fatima sunk to her knees and turning toward Mecca began to say prayers.

Corrie leaned down again, "Jeff! Father!"

"Corrie!"

She heard Jeff's faint cry. "Yes, I'm out here! I'll have to get help!"

Jeff crawled over the rubble and reached the spot where her voice was clearest. "Corrie, are you all right?"

"Yes – where's my father."

"He's okay but pinned under some rock."

A gunshot echoed in the morning air and Corrie turned quickly. Fatima, still on her knees had fallen forward onto the ground. Behind her, like an apparition, dressed in bloody robes, Karim swayed in the sunlight, the gun in his hand.

"You killed her!" Corrie screamed.

"She ruined everything."

Corrie stared at him. She had stabbed him and Fatima had shot him. All she could think of was that she should have checked to see if he was dead. Obviously, he hadn't been, unless of course he really was a God, and she hardly believed that.

"Where's the tablet! He shrieked.

"I suppose it's in the cave," she replied, trying to feel calm.

"Then we shall have to get it out," Karim replied, narrowing his dark eyes.

Jeff swore silently. He had been clawing at the rubble and had succeeded in finding a small opening. He could hear Karim speaking. Corrie was out there alone with a very dangerous man.

"We've got to get out of here," he said crawling back to Henley.

"See if Conway had a gun. We might need it," Henley suggested.

Jeff crawled over to where Conway lay sprawled on the ground. He supposed they might need a gun, if they could get out.

"Hello," he suddenly said. "One gun and would you believe two hand grenades?"

"Great," he heard Henley say. "If you place them right, pull the pins, and get the hell out of the way in time, you might be able to blow the rocks aside."

Henley only sounded calm because he hadn't heard the shot outside; he didn't know that Corrie was out there with Karim.

"It's worth a try."

335

He scrambled back to where the entrance of the cave had been. He cursed his lack of knowledge. If he put them in the wrong place, it might cause them to become more deeply buried. It seemed right to him that he should point them outward and on a slight angle. He did so and then looked at them. Once he pulled the pins he had very little time to get out of the way.

He gritted his teeth and pulled both pins then he tumbled backward in his best Aikido roll and just kept going. He had just reached Henely's side when the deafening explosion tore open a huge hole.

Karim turned, and Corrie who had been in front of him held at gunpoint swung about and hit him in the neck with all her strength. He dropped his gun but turned back toward her and struck her hard. He was amazingly strong considering his wounds and the amount of blood he had lost.

She staggered to her feet and as she did so, kicked him in the shins. He reached out, seizing her throat. His hands were strong and she struggled for air even as she kicked and scratched.

Suddenly Karim let her go and she saw that Jeff was there and had grabbed Karim from behind.

Karim broke away from Jeff and lunged for the gun.

Karim whirled around and fired but Jeff sensing what was about to happen did a flying leap toward Karim, just out of the line of fire. The shot missed and Jeff landed on his feet beside Karim. Jeff punched Karim in the face and grabbed his gun hand, pushing it up towards the sky away from him. Another shot exploded heavenward.

Corrie watched, ready to move, but unable to do anything. The two of them were a blur in motion. Jeff let Karim bring his gun hand down so that he and Karim were facing the same direction. Jeff's left hand was on top of Karim's gun hand. Jeff brought his right hand onto the back of the gun and twisted the gun toward Karim's chest.

Jeff put all his hip power into the twist. The gun fired into Karim's chest as he flipped through the air. Blood gushed from Karim's chest as he landed with a thud.

For an instant Jeff stood over him, then he ripped the gun from Karim's hand ready to finish him off if he moved.

Karim's lifeless eyes stared blankly back at him.

Corrie bent over, her eyes almost closed she was so scared. "Is he really dead?" she asked in a half whisper.

"He's dead," Jeff answered.

"I stabbed him before and Fatima shot him."

"Yeah," Jeff answered. "God, he was strong. He had the strength of a lunatic."

"Where's my father?

"Inside, come on, let's go get him."

"Is he hurt badly?"

"I think his leg is broken."

Corrie hurried to her father's side while Jeff began moving the rocks that were on top of him.

Jonathan Henley looked into his daughter's eyes, "We'll be coming out of the Paquarino, but not quite like Gods," he joked.

Corrie bent over and kissed his cheek. "What about the tablet?"

"Destroyed."

"What are we going to do about all this?" Henley asked.

"Leave," Jeff said emphatically. "Look, the Ecuadorians are going to be mad as hell to discover Peruvian Federal Police who were apparently in pursuit of some gang or other. They'll think this is all over drugs. We'll go back to Loja and then get the hell out of here."

"He's right," Corrie said, pressing her father's arm.

"No argument," Henley answered.

#

Corrie sat on the huge rock wrapped in a warm poncho. Jeff sat next to her, his arm around her shoulders.

"Did you settle things with your dad?"

"Yes. I never realized that he tried to find women who were the opposite of my mother. I've been too hard on him."

"Did you talk to him more about your mother?"

"Not yet, but we will talk.

"Look, here comes the sun," he said, looking East.

"It's even more impressive than Cuzco," she breathed. Below them the ancient fortress of Machu Picchu was a study in light and shadow beneath mountains that seemed to hang from the sky. Below the dense jungle that had hidden the Inca Fortress for nearly four centuries stretched out like an undulating carpet of green.

The great city of Machu Picchu was more than two thousand feet above the Amazon's tributary, the Urubamba River.

"I think it's the most impressive of the Inca finds," Corrie said. "Beneath the veil of jungle there are scores of granite shrines, fountains, lodgings, and of course the steep stairways that lead here."

"Think of the knowledge it took to build this." Jeff couldn't take his eyes off of it.

"It's like the *other* places, the monoliths on Easter Island – all those places that couldn't be, but are –"

"Conway said, 'they came, they gave knowledge, they left the tablets and they departed."

"You believe in them, don't you?" she asked.

"Yes. I think they were here. I've seen those crop fields – the ones that aren't hoaxes. I believe they're out there. I think they're watching."

"I believe some of them stayed, or maybe mated with some of us.

"It goes a long way toward explaining all those people who seem to have a sixth sense."

"Do you think they won't come back because the tablets have been destroyed?"

"I think they might have left other means by which we can summon them." He nudged her slightly and pointed up to the stars, which in spite of the slowly rising sun were still visible in the Western sky. He wrapped her in his arms and kissed her.

"Stay with me always," she whispered. "Help me look."

"I will."

There was no need for them to say more. He loved her. There would be more encounters with the collective memory of the past; there would be a lifetime of adventure together.

#

About The Authors

Janet and Dennis have been writing together for more than thirty years. They have written and had published twenty-nine novels, two works of nonfiction, acted as re-write editors, and worked in advertising and for assorted periodicals. Their business is incorporated as, Free Lance Writing Associates Inc. and their books can be found under their own names, and their pen names, Joyce Carlow, and Emma Leigh. These include their current thriller, The Key and a variety of historic fiction, romances, time travels, and erotica. For further information go to: www.joycecarlow.com .

Other Books

The Story of Canada Series
Vol. 1. Kanata
Vol. 2. Bitter Shield
Vol. 3. Thundergate
Vol.4. Wildfires
Vol.5. Victoria

China Nights and Worlds Apart
By
Janet Rosenstock